3 1833 03089 6986

HEARTS ENTWINED

Brielle raised her head to look at Reynaud in the dimness. "I'm *alone*," she whispered. "Don't you see? I have no one now . . ."

He held her eyes with his, suddenly wanting to tell her he would always be there. "You're not alone," he managed, holding back a flood of assurances.

A tear tripped down her cheek. "I was never more alone than now."

He caught the lone tear with a trembling fingertip, brought it to his own mouth to taste the salt of her sorrow. She raised tear-filled eyes to his questioningly, and so all-consuming a flood of tenderness crashed over him that the last scraps of his self-control threatened to scatter like wind-blown ashes.

"Love me," came her unexpected words, a whispered plea on the night air. And reason shattered like the finest glass.

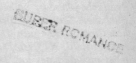

ROMANCE FROM ROSANNE BITTNER

CARESS   (0-8217-3791-0, $5.99)

FULL CIRCLE   (0-8217-4711-8, $5.99)

SHAMELESS   (0-8217-4056-3, $5.99)

SIOUX SPLENDOR   (0-8217-5157-3, $4.99)

UNFORGETTABLE   (0-8217-4423-2, $5.50)

TEXAS EMBRACE   (0-8217-5625-7, $5.99)

UNTIL TOMORROW   (0-8217-5064-X, $5.99)

Available wherever paperbacks are sold, or order direct from the Publisher. Send cover price plus 50¢ per copy for mailing and handling to Penguin USA, P.O. Box 999, c/o Dept. 17109, Bergenfield, NJ 07621. Residents of New York and Tennessee must include sales tax. DO NOT SEND CASH.

TENDER CRUSADER

Linda Lang Bartell

Zebra Books
Kensington Publishing Corp.
http://www.zebrabooks.com

ZEBRA BOOKS are published by

Kensington Publishing Corp.
850 Third Avenue
New York, NY 10022

Copyright © 1997 by Linda Lang Bartell

All rights reserved. No part of this book may be reproduced
in any form or by any means without the prior written consent
of the Publisher, excepting brief quotes used in reviews.

If you purchased this book without a cover, you should be
aware that this book is stolen property. It was reported as "un-
sold and destroyed" to the Publisher and neither the Author
nor the Publisher has received any payment for this "stripped
book."

Zebra and the Z logo Reg. U.S. Pat. & TM Off.

First Printing: September, 1997
10 9 8 7 6 5 4 3 2 1

Printed in the United States of America

Prologue

Holy Land—1191 A.D.

The sun was a bright ball of light scintillating above the earth. From within the vault of the Syrian sky, it blazed down with a vengeance on the small party of men trapped beneath its punishing heat.

One of them, the leader, dismounted his ink-black steed, despite protests from the other five men.

"Don't be a fool, St. Rémy," growled one.

"Oui, Reynaud. Just put him out of his misery," added a second man.

"Infidel dog!" muttered a third. " 'Tis more than likely one of their tricks—to feign retreat and then attack again."

Reynaud hunkered down beside the single man who showed signs of life and placed one finger on the side of his neck. As he felt for the soft, steady pulse that signaled the heart was still beating, he briefly lifted his face to the last man who spoke, squinting against the blinding brightness. Of the seven men, three were recruits, the fourth, a seasoned Templar knight known as Humphrey of Toulouse, and the last, his ever-faithful companion Taillefer and the Arab, Rashid.

"I doubt this man was left as bait. Even the Saracens are not so unfeeling—they're men, not dogs."

"My thanks, master," the Arab said, looking cool and unruffled beneath the desert heat, in the middle of a party of Christian knights.

"And 'tis just for comments like that, *mon ami*," muttered Taillefer under his breath as he joined Reynaud beside the downed man, "that you are being sent back to France."

Reynaud ignored his words as he caught a faint, erratic heartbeat. He looked down at the wounded man. "Besides," he told the other three knights, " 'tis the perfect opportunity to test your skills. Our safety lies in your hands now." He took out a skin water bottle and threw the recruits a look that emphasized his command: "Watch for the enemy."

"Water . . ." whispered the wounded man in Arabic, which Reynaud understood fairly well. He was dressed in the light mail of a Turkish horseman, his conical helmet lying beside him. Drying blood dulled the edge of the gleaming headgear, and as Reynaud unstoppered and raised the water skin to the man's lips, he tried to assess the damage to his head. Blood oozed from a laceration near one temple and had begun to clot in a meandering crimson thread across his forehead.

Reynaud scanned the Turk's body for other wounds. There appeared to be none, only powdery grit clinging to his sweat-damp skin, dusting his mail.

"Skull's probably cleaved in two," remarked Gregoire, the young knight who had advised Reynaud to put the Arab out of his misery.

"See you his brains spilling out?" Taillefer snapped in annoyance at the recruit.

"Saracens, Turks, Arabs . . . none of the infidels have any brains," said Arnaut de Bouchard, the man who had warned Reynaud not to be a fool.

Reynaud ignored him as he poured some of the precious water over the man's hairline and studied the wound. He felt rather than saw the look that Rashid threw him, but the little man said nothing at Bouchard's insult.

"And I know many Christians who haven't a brain to speak of," Taillefer said softly.

"A laceration to the scalp," Reynaud observed. Rashid had picked up the helmet and was examining it. Reynaud glanced over at him. "Turkish mace?" he asked.

The Arab nodded, for the weapon was favored among the crusaders.

"I wager he and his men were attacked by a Christian party, then left for dead. He must have taken a blow to the head after he lost his helmet."

"Then finish him off, I say!" snarled Bouchard. "He looks dead to me, anyway!"

Reynaud slowly straightened and faced the hostile knight. His golden eyes met the other man's in warning. "Were you half so skilled at watching for the enemy as you are at telling others what to do, Bouchard, you might have saved our necks." He motioned with his chin toward the distant hills where, like a horde of disturbed and angry ants emerging from their nest, at least two dozen Turkish cavalry were galloping toward them.

"Sweet Jesu!" muttered Gregoire. "They come for their vengeance."

"We can take them!" declared a young recruit passionately.

"Don't be absurd . . . we're surely outnumbered ten to one," Reynaud told him as he strode to his pack horse. He pulled a tunic from its saddle. "Head north," he commanded Bouchard and the others. "I'll catch up with you." He knelt beside the Arab and pillowed his bloodied head upon his own fresh tunic, then raised the water skin once more, this time to the man's lips. "Ride hard, now! And don't look back."

It took only a moment's hesitation for the others to obey, for they were vastly outnumbered by the approaching enemy. "Unless we wish to pay for another patrol's actions . . ."

Bouchard said, and without a backward glance led the others north at full speed.

"You, too," Reynaud said to his two remaining companions. "Go quickly and I'll follow." As he anticipated, however, neither of them budged. Rashid fussed with the balled tunic beneath his Arab brother's head, his eyes refusing to meet Reynaud's, and Taillefer brought up the horses.

With the others gone, he knew his secret was safe. That is, if it worked again. Taillefer knew about his "gift," and Rashid had directly benefitted from it long ago. Not his "gift," he mused, but rather his curse. And a source of his troubles.

Much of his energy had been channeled into striking a balance between using it for the greatest benefit and trying to keep it secret.

With a sigh, Reynaud glanced down at the man whose shoulders he supported. He wondered who the Saracen was . . . if he were anyone of significance in the tangled skein of Eastern politics, or just one of countless soldiers laying down their lives for Jihad—the Holy War.

The wounded man's thick black lashes fluttered, then raised. His eyes were cloudy with confusion, but distinguishable to Reynaud as amber in color. Golden—like his own.

Their eyes met—fused—as the Arab's expression cleared. "Christian pig!" he rasped with a heavy accent. "Templar!"

"Indeed, my friend, I am a Christian and a Templar. Tell your brothers"—he jerked his chin over one shoulder—"that we didn't attack you."

As for one fleeting yet endless moment their gazes held, Reynaud caught something intangibly familiar about the man's features. Especially the gem-gold eyes.

"Hurry, Reynaud," Taillefer urged, already mounted.

"Indeed, master," echoed Rashid, who was ready to do the same. "If they believe us responsible for this carnage, they'll kill us first and ask questions later."

Reynaud finally obliged and carefully pulled his arm from beneath the victim's shoulders. He straightened, glancing once more at the approaching horsemen, then, despite thirty-odd pounds of chain mail, vaulted easily onto his midnight mount's back and wheeled the stallion about to follow the others.

The wounded Saracen closed his eyes and blew out a shallow breath, a sigh born of pain and irony. But the pain was fading as a strange benevolence moved through him. He struggled to his elbows, feeling suddenly, miraculously, better. "St. Rémy!" he muttered in heavily accented French. "St. Rémy . . ."

2 1822 03089 6986

One

France—1191 A.D.

The faint rumble of fast-moving horses came to her in the quiet.

Brielle d'Avignon raised her bowed head and listened a moment, automatically casting an ear toward the single window high in one wall of her somber cell. The sound continued, steadily increasing in volume, and totally disrupting her prayers.

They were coming.

In an incongruously irreverent movement, she bolted from her knees with the unconscious ease of youth and health, her heart leaping to the base of her throat before it settled into a cadence of excitement as rigorous as the approaching hoofbeats. All thought, save freedom after five long years of virtual imprisonment, fled as Brielle dragged a small stool beneath the window.

It had to be them! Surely they were coming for her . . . why else would a mounted party come to St. Bernadette's immediately after matins?

For any number of reasons, whispered common sense. The convent had seen its share of pilgrims on their way to the Holy Land, and those who lived to return. *And how can you know if the abbess even mentioned you in her communications with the bishop?*

She ignored the bothersome voice and had barely straightened to her full height on the stool when a voice admonished from behind her, *"Brielle, que fais-tu?"*

Her attention diverted from her original purpose, Brielle reacted swiftly, twisting so abruptly that the three-legged prop tipped and slid out from under her, wrenching her ankle as she tried to compensate and land on her feet in a desperate grab at dignity. She bit down against a wince as the traitorous stool came to a clattering halt against her bed, before facing the abbess with excitement in her eyes and hectic color blooming in her cheeks.

"Oh, Reverend Mother!" she said in as normal a voice as she could manage, "I—I but wished to see who was approaching the—"

Abbess Marguerite's lips quivered slightly as she took in Brielle's telltale flush. "If naught else," she interrupted, her expression softening beneath her snug-fitting wimple, "you surely wouldn't want to injure your ankle or knee the very day Bishop Abelard arrives . . ." she paused meaningfully, and Brielle felt her heart flip-flop beneath her ribs, ". . . on important business."

To take you from our midst, beloved child.

The unspoken words hung in the air between them, and Brielle evinced a flash of guilt.

"They're coming for me?" she blurted, not quite able to acknowledge this newest and disturbing emotion that threatened her, with the sound of hooves ringing in her ears, and Abbess Marguerite just having all but confirmed what she had only dared dream about until this moment.

The dream that could turn into your worst nightmare.

The warning tiptoed through her mind, but Brielle ignored it, concentrating instead on the woman who now stood in the doorway and regarded her with affection and concern in her dark eyes.

" 'Tisn't that I wish to leave St. Bernadette's, Reverend

Mother," she hastened to assure the older woman, "but John the Gaunt told me . . ."

Then the realization of what Abbess Marguerite had done for her hit Brielle like a boulder.

Marguerite glanced down at the floor for a moment, her lowered lids hiding the emotion in her eyes. Brielle knew the woman was fighting an inner battle—between her affection for Brielle and the actions that could lead to Brielle's leave-taking—possibly her death.

The abbess raised her head and gave Brielle a half-smile. "I know, *mon enfant*. Duty calls. *Et je le comprends bien* . . . I understand." She drew in a deep breath and straightened her shoulders. "But now the bishop calls, and I must go and greet him properly." She moved to depart, then hesitated. "Do come down to the yard if you like, Brielle, but remember you'll have time to meet Bishop Abelard and his party when I invite them to break the fast with us."

Brielle nodded, realizing that the good woman was giving her a chance to prepare herself for the meeting that could change her life. She unconsciously lifted her hands to her hair, but her thoughts weren't on her appearance as much as pleading her cause to Bishop Abelard.

"Y-yes, Reverend Mother," she answered, her mind racing ahead to what, exactly, she would say to the bishop. And his . . . his party? Who exactly would be accompanying him? she wondered.

As if reading her thoughts, Abbess Marguerite said, "Surely you didn't think His Excellency would travel alone?"

As the abbess swung away, the bell at the front gate clanged loudly, and Brielle realized she hadn't thought much about anything beyond winning the bishop's permission and finding Geoffrey d'Avignon—ever since her father's former sergeant at arms, John the Gaunt, had arrived at St. Bernadette's from the Holy Land and told her that no trace of

Geoffrey d'Avignon had ever been found on the battlefield at the Horns of Hattin near Tiberius.

The sheer volume of many horses approaching sounded like an army, even over the noise of the bell; and it suddenly occurred to Brielle that she would assuredly be the only female in the company of a group of men—on a perilous journey to a faraway and utterly foreign land.

Sweet Mary! she thought. She hadn't considered much of anything beyond winning the bishop's permission to search for her father.

With a shake of her head, Brielle moved to right the stool and return it to its usual place. She wouldn't think about that now. She wanted to see the bishop in person—even if it was only a peek from a hiding place in the yard—so she could take his measure and therefore further prepare herself to be her most sincere and persuasive. . . .

Brielle peeked from the partially open door, her heart in her mouth.

The yard was filled with huge horses, the morning air thick with the smell of animals, leather, and oiled mail; motes of dust rose and danced before the early sun's muted light. An impressive group of horsemen, those immediately surrounding the bishop dressed in purest white, were dismounting as the rising sun shot its benevolent rays across the yard, bathing the entire scene in a mystical-like illumination. It touched their helmets and shields, turning them to pale gold, and the flowing length of the horses' manes to liquid silk. Four of the riders wore crimson crosses emblazoned across the front of their tunics, and the sun's rays tinted them blood-red against the garments' pristine backgrounds.

It was as if they had descended from the heavens above, the tableau in the yard like a mural on one of the convent walls—knights of Christ, soldiers of God. Or so it seemed to Brielle. And surely they were Christ's own knights, she acknowledged with awe, for they appeared to be Templars . . . members of the military order that escorted pilgrims to and from the Holy Land and fought infidels with rigid discipline and undiluted courage. Sieur Geoffrey had told her all about them years ago, and the picture he'd painted—the notion of the honor and even sanctity of their purpose—had made a deep and lasting impression upon the fertile imagination of a twelve-year-old girl.

Your mouth is agape, warned a voice, and Brielle immediately snapped her jaws together. A spurt of guilt hit her out of the blue as she wondered if equating the famous Templars with deities descended from heaven was blasphemous. It was short-lived, however, for there was too much of interest happening in the yard before her to give her imagined sin any further thought.

The bishop himself (there was no mistaking his red and white raiment) was being helped from his snow-white mount by two knights, although Brielle thought he appeared perfectly capable of dismounting unaided. He was a tall and slender man, with an unmistakable aura of energy and purpose behind his movements and expression. His face was unexpectedly youthful, with regular features and expressive dark eyes, the latter quickly taking in his surroundings. Brielle watched a ghost of a smile float past his lips as Abbess Marguerite went down on her knees before him. He raised her with an offered hand quickly, as though impatient with the formal ritual, or else out of consideration for the nun.

Brielle unexpectedly felt herself warming toward the prelate. Surely such a man couldn't refuse her humble request?

One of the knights closest to Bishop Abelard appeared to take charge of the rest of the group immediately upon dismounting. His stallion was raven-black, one of the few dark chargers among the gray and white mounts milling in the convent yard, and the animal's magnificent umber form presented a stark backdrop for his master's pale tunic.

As the abbess straightened and spoke to the bishop, the lead Templar removed his helmet and began to give orders in a low, authoritative voice. Horses were led to the water trough near the small stable, and several nuns who had dutifully stepped forth to extend St. Bernadette's hospitality were shooed away by the lead knight. Brielle caught snatches of his low voice—"no need to trouble yourselves, *mes soeurs . . .*" and she watched in some amusement as the sisters scurried back to the shelter of the convent like a scattering flock of rooks, obviously all too glad to leave the fierce horses to the men who rode them.

Brielle thought how incongruous was the sight of intimidating males in the yard of St. Bernadette, domain of shy and unassuming nuns. "Unusual" wouldn't have described it, for the convent sat near one of the main roads that wound through Provence, and visitors were common. Nonetheless, rarely were they females, and the striking contrast never failed to light Brielle's eyes with merriment. Many of the women of St. Bernadette had known no other life—had never known men, nor their rough and tumble ways.

Then there were maidens like Anabette, the girl in the cell next to Brielle's. Every male visitor who wasn't clergy was a target for her wiles—a possible escape from the somber and repetitive routine of convent life, and from the upcoming marriage her sire had arranged for her. "I'll wed the first willing and eligible man to come along," she had told Brielle many times, "rather than that ancient relic my father has chosen for me!"

She was, indeed, desperate, for like a sheep fleeing the wolf, she'd sought sanctuary in the chapel at St. Bernadette's when her father had decreed she wed the aging and unappealing Lord Odo. So far, however, her father had let her be, no doubt, Brielle suspected, to allow his young and strong-minded daughter to get a good taste of the austere and uneventful life of the inhabitants of a religious house; to teach her obedience and humility.

As if conjured up by Brielle's thoughts, Anabette appeared beside her, her bright gold hair eye-catching by any standard. She quickly took in the scene outside, and after Bishop Abelard was escorted into the building, she whispered to Brielle, "Why can't we show our visitors proper hospitality?" Before Brielle could blink, Anabette hurled herself right into the thick of things in the convent yard.

Brielle's stomach clenched in reaction as her headstrong friend made directly for the lead Templar's stallion. "Not all of us at St. Bernadette are so lacking in manners!" Anabette declared, in a voice loud enough to carry back to Brielle. She reached for the midnight courser's reins.

No one noticed the young woman until she managed to startle the stallion, whose master's back was turned momentarily as he spoke to another knight. Loosing an equine shriek, the great horse rose up on his hind legs, an ominous silhouette against the golden morning sky. Unthinkingly, Brielle left the shadows beside the door and dashed toward Anabette, intending to shove her out of the way of the horse's slashing hooves.

At the same instant, however, the Templar swung around, took in the impending disaster, and snaked a white-clad arm toward the reckless Anabette. He called out a command to the horse as he pulled the girl out of harm's way, but Brielle was already within range of the animal's platter-sized hooves. Too late. Out of the corner of his eye he saw her struck by a descending hoof and crumple to the ground.

"Dieu au ciel!" he muttered under his breath, and released the first girl to go to the aid of the second. A squire grabbed Khamsin's reins as Reynaud de St. Rémy knelt beside the fallen young woman. He reached to brush back her hair and examine her head, which was bleeding profusely from the temple.

Anabette screamed from behind him, which threatened to further spook Khamsin, and Reynaud snarled a command at both horse and maiden: *"Assez!* Enough!"

The man beside Reynaud's steed tightened his grip on the reins and murmured low, soothing words into the animal's ear before he looked at Anabette and said calmly, "Get back inside, *demoiselle,* before Khamsin here eats you alive."

She obediently backed away, one hand over her mouth, horror-widened eyes going from the fair-haired man to her fallen friend.

"Do as he says!" Reynaud snapped as he noticed her hesitation. He moved to unbuckle his sword belt, then strip off his tunic. The blond man handed Khamsin's reins to another knight.

"Need you help with her, Reynaud?" Taillefer asked as he bent over Brielle's still form. "A brave one, she," he added.

"Foolish is more like it," Reynaud said, attempting to stanch the blood with his tunic sleeve. "But she'll live to perform other heroic deeds," he said, as he lifted her into his arms then and stood, his exposed chain mail winking in the sunlight. "See to my weapons," he ordered Taillefer, and turned toward the convent entrance, where the porteress had retreated and still hovered, clearly agitated.

"Fetch the Reverend Mother," he bade her as he strode through the doorway.

"B-but . . . I'm not hurt. *Pas vraiement!* Not really!" Brielle sputtered as her vision cleared and, to her mortification, she realized they were headed for the infirmary.

Was that her voice, she wondered, sounding far-off and faint? Evidently so, came the realization, for her protest went unheeded and her "rescuer" continued to carry her like a babe in his arms.

Deciding she might better maintain her dignity by compliance, Brielle slid an upward glance toward the chin and cheek of the tall, stern-looking Templar above her. She could tell nothing, however, except that his jaw was strong and cleanly cut. His steel-muscled arms pinned her securely against his chest, and the rings of his mail ground into her tender cheek with his movements as he strode down the corridor. Yet his grip, one part of her mind noted, was not ungentle.

Anabette would be positively green with envy, came the unexpected thought. *Enjoy the attention!* she would have said. And for the few remaining moments that Brielle d'Avignon was in Reynaud de St. Rémy's impersonal embrace, she allowed herself the transgression of savoring a man's touch.

As they passed through the infirmary door, the clean scent of the outdoors and horses came to her. And male. It had been so long since her father had held her! And her brother had never—

The sight of Sister Françoise's concerned face, however, brought reason rushing back. Her face warmed, and Brielle suddenly wished mightily that she could simply disappear. The bishop had just arrived at St. Bernadette's, and here she was (after having already caused a commotion in the yard!) being coddled by one of his knights when she should have been helping the nuns see to their guests.

The knight set her down on the cot and straightened. Brielle would never forget her first sight of him close up. Golden-brown eyes studied her face critically, but she could read no emotion on his beautifully-drawn features. It was a cool, detached examination of her face, as if he were a physician and did it every day, countless times.

There was certainly no evident interest in her as a female. *Templars shun women, ma petite.* Sieur Geoffrey's words came back to her without warning. Of course. . . . No wonder he made no attempt to touch her face. . . .

Reynaud looked up at the apple-cheeked Sister Françoise, who was hovering nearby, obviously itching to get this male out of her domain and tend to her charge. "The *demoiselle* was fortunate Khamsin's hoof hit her exactly where it did.

A heartbeat to one side and she would have bled to death."
He reached down and slid back the tunic that he'd used as
a compress, exposing the wound. As Brielle realized how
the garment must have been wrapped about her head, she
thought surely she must have reminded him of the very infidels he battled in the Holy Land.

Her color heightened a shade, and she struggled to push
herself to her elbows. The world wavered, then settled. The
ache in her temple intensified, and a soft gasp erupted from
Sister Françoise. Suddenly the Templar's hand was on her
shoulder. "Lie still, *demoiselle,*" he cautioned, his mouth remaining in an unyielding line.

"Ecoute bien le chevalier, Brielle," Sister Françoise
scolded her gently. "Listen to the knight."

"My name is Reynaud," he told Sister Françoise. "I think
a stitch or two will take care of the—" He stopped in mid-
sentence and looked back at Brielle, a subtle shift in his
expression indicating heightened awareness of her. Sudden
interest lit his golden eyes. "Brielle d'Avignon?" he asked.

"Oui."

"Don't talk, child," Sister Françoise admonished, giving
Reynaud a warning look that had set many an unsuspecting
nun back on her heels. "Just rest and let me tend to you."

It unexpectedly galled Brielle to be called "child" before
this somber, high-handed Templar. She pushed herself to a
seat, the expression in her eyes warning anyone against stopping her. Even Reynaud de St. Rémy.

If he knew her name, he surely knew of her request to
Bishop Abelard, and she didn't dare jeopardize her chances
of leaving with the bishop's party. "I'm hale enough," she
said to both Reynaud and the nun. "I thank you for your
tunic." She tugged the tunic from her head, causing herself
added pain. The discomfort was overpowered, however, by
the scent of Reynaud de St. Rémy on the garment that slid
most unceremoniously down her face. "And thank you for
your gallantry as well, Sieur Reynaud. But I find myself

suddenly ravenous . . ." (she noted Sister Françoise's distinct
moue of disapproval and the Templar drawing in a breath as
if he would interrupt her and rushed on), "and wouldn't wish
to be the cause of either you or Sister Françoise missing
breaking the fast."

"You need your cut stitched," Reynaud said with finality.
"A tray can be brought to you afterward. I wouldn't advise
leaving this bed for a day or so." He glanced at Sister
Françoise, whose hands were on her hips now as she frowned
in open disapproval at Brielle's declaration.

It was two against one, Brielle thought in frustration.

"But I must——"

"I'll take my leave now," Reynaud cut across her words
as he addressed Sister Françoise, "knowing *la demoiselle* is
in capable hands." With that, he turned on his heel and nearly
collided with Anabette. With barely a nod at her, he left the
room.

The obvious concern for her friend instantly transformed
into a dreamy-eyed look, as Anabette watched the empty
doorway through which Reynaud de St. Rémy had exited.
With an obvious effort, Anabette turned toward Brielle and
the nun. She raised her fair eyebrows expectantly at Sister
Françoise.

"From what I've heard, Anabette, you've done quite
enough for one day," the nun told her. She shook her snugly-
wimpled head. "Bolting into the yard like a runaway mule
and causing an uproar when there was no need. . . ."

Brielle hid a smile behind the sleeve of the Templar's tunic
at the unflattering reference. But everyone knew that Anabette often needed a red flag to distract her from her outrageous thoughts and impetuous actions, and the good nun
moved to set a basin of clean water on the table beside the
pallet.

Anabette's eyes narrowed as she moved closer to watch
Sister Françoise cleanse the wound. "And I say also there is
no need for any unmarried maiden—even one living at St.

Bernadette's—to call the attention of a yard full of eligible men. Rather 'tis an *obligation!* 'Twould be one less mouth to feed here," she added, as Sister Françoise dipped the bloodied cloth into the water, tingeing it pink. "Ohhh!" she moaned and turned her head aside. She missed the nun's reproving look.

And one less pair of hands to help, and a reduction in income for the convent, Brielle thought, for she suspected Anabette's wealthy family was now paying the convent to keep her, and paying well.

"Indeed!" said Sister Françoise with a narrow-eyed look at the squeamish Anabette. "You cannot even face the consequences of your rash behavior. Go you to the refectory and fetch Brielle here a tray. And tell Reverend Mother the child will be fine in a day or two and that I will join the others after you've returned."

"Nay!" Brielle straightened so abruptly that the normally unflappable nun stepped back in surprise. "You cannot tell Reverend Mother that!" she objected, distress darkening her eyes. "I'll not be allowed to plead my cause to Bishop Abelard then . . . and even if I could, His Excellence would never delay his journey for me! For a mere scratch!"

Anabette was the first to react. She put a hand on Brielle's leg and said, *"Calme-toi, Brielle."* She surreptitiously squeezed and sent Brielle a silent message with her dark eyes. "Listen to Sister Françoise and let me bring you a tray. You can speak to the bishop another time." She squeezed Brielle's leg again, then made an airy gesture of dismissal, smiling blithely at her before she left.

When she returned with a tray, Anabette told them that she'd assured Reverend Mother that Brielle was well, and that there was no need to neglect her guests for even a few moments by seeking her out in the infirmary. "And I'm quite certain, *chère,*" she added with a quirk of her mouth, "that the handsome Templar will reassure Abbess Marguerite too, *oui?*"

Brielle threw dark looks at the chattering Anabette, who,

as soon as Sister Françoise had finished neatly stitching the wound, seated herself at the bedside and began sharing the tasty tidbits that had been prepared in the bishop's honor. "Do go and break the fast with our guests, Soeur Françoise," Anabette encouraged sweetly, and Brielle didn't miss the suspicion in the nun's eyes as they came to rest upon her friend. "I'll keep Brielle company while you're gone."

Sister Françoise stood in indecision a moment, then retrieved the basin of blood-tinged water and moved toward the chamber pot to dump it. "Very well," she said over her plump shoulder. "But no tricks while I'm gone, do you understand?" She gave both young women her sternest look, but they'd lived at St. Bernadette's long enough to know she was a sweet and compassionate woman inside, despite her bluster.

The moment Sister Françoise was out the door, Brielle narrowed her eyes at her friend. "Now what? You know I must have an audience with His Excellence, and if that grim-faced Templar tells him my injury demands I stay in bed for another day or two, of a certainty they'll leave without me! Why, I'll never even get a chance to speak to him!"

Anabette's expression softened again. "That beautiful man! What maiden in her right mind wouldn't be willing to follow him all the way to Hell?"

Even Brielle was taken aback by her friend's bold declaration. "Anabette, have you gone mad?" she whispered, throwing a look at the door.

"Why he's as handsome as a fallen angel," Anabette declared, then shrugged and popped a temptingly plump mushroom into her mouth. "You'll get to see the bishop, Brielle, and in the refectory this very morn, of that you can be sure. But first you must listen to my proposition . . ."

They cleaned every crumb on Brielle's tray of food, set it aside, then conspired to scrub Reynaud de St. Rémy's tunic sleeve until it was spotless once again.

"Quel homme!" Anabette sighed for at least the fourth time, as they spread the Templar's borrowed garment before the small fire to dry as much as possible.

Brielle had to agree, albeit silently. Something about handling one of the knight's personal articles was strangely titillating, a sensation she tried to shrug off.

Silly girl, mocked an imp. *You've been in the company of females far too long.*

Anabette helped Brielle arrange her hair as suited a modest maiden, artfully half-hiding Sister Françoise's snow-white plaster in the process.

"How do you feel, *chère?*" Anabette asked Brielle when once, as the latter was bending over the shirt, a faint light-headedness assaulted her. She'd stilled, then straightened slowly. "You're pale as ashes," Anabette added, obviously concerned.

"I just can't move too quickly," Brielle told her. "Otherwise, I'm fine. 'Tisn't every day that a steed tries to behead me," she added in an attempt to make light of the accident, then realized she'd made a mistake as Anabette's expression turned troubled. "Never mind," Brielle said softly, putting one hand on her friend's arm. "If you help me get into the refectory, you'll more than make up for any harm you might have accidentally caused."

Anabette straightened the simple bed as Brielle sat nearby, trying to collect her wits and rid her head of the annoying flashes of dizziness that came and went.

"And if I help you," Anabette asked with sudden slyness, her eyes going to her friend from beneath her lashes, "will you agree to my . . . proposition?"

Genuine distress appeared on Brielle's fine features. "I could never take part in such a scheme!" she protested. "We'd both be ruined."

Anabette turned toward her, hands on her hips, her brown eyes flashing. "What is there to ruin, with both of us sealed inside this convent? And besides, you don't have to do a thing but feign ignorance. I'll take the blame should our—*my*—plot be discovered."

Before Brielle could answer, Anabette was folding the Templar's damp tunic and handing it to her. *"Je vous emprie, ma chère amie . . .* I beg you!"

Two

Brielle moved along the cloister that enclosed St. Bernadette's courtyard. The drift of morning air through the covered walkway was chill against her skin, although it felt good on her cheeks, for they were warming with every step she took toward the refectory.

She passed the small chapel and toyed with the idea of running across the open courtyard to her left, where the rising sun was chasing away the shadows. But what dignity she still possessed would go to the winds once her sandaled feet touched the dew-soaked grass. If the cloister hadn't been so deserted, she would have guessed the breaking of the fast to have ended. But only the sweet song of the birds and the whisper of her sandals came to her in the still spring morn.

Anabette was nowhere to be seen—not even a whispered warning came to Brielle. She mentally sighed with relief, for the other girl had obviously done as promised by making certain no one was about to question Brielle's leaving the infirmary. But where was Anabette now? she wondered, and a hint of unease threatened her relief.

She forced her thoughts away from the impulsive Anabette. Surely, she mused, the meal would take longer with Bishop Abelard and his men as guests. Abbess Marguerite, Mother Superior of the small convent of St. Bernadette, was a whimsical and musical soul, typical of those born and raised in and around Provence. Brielle suspected she enjoyed entertaining guests more than most in her position, and a corner of her mouth curved upward at the thought. The good Reverend Mother was even known to strum a tune now and then on her "wicked and worldly" lute.

Out of nowhere came the thought of Reynaud de St. Rémy. Of his stern mien, and deep but unemotional voice uttering strictures to Soeur Françoise and herself. In spite of his name (for there was a town called St. Rémy in Provence), surely he'd been born in northern climes, she mused as she headed inexorably toward the dining hall, and he would no doubt be shocked to hear Reverend Mother's voice raised in song—her hands caressing a musical instrument with the dexterity of a seasoned minstrel.

"Brielle!"

Anabette's voice startled her out of her thoughts, causing Brielle to clutch to her heart the carefully folded tunic she held—and had tried to ignore. She half turned and put a finger to her lips, and Anabette swung into step alongside her. "Hear you the music?" the latter asked in a barely contained whisper.

Brielle canted her head for a moment, wondering how she could have missed the soft notes drifting toward them from the direction of the refectory. Was Reverend Mother playing her lute? For the *bishop?*

They paused before the refectory door. A male voice began to rise in song. *"Dieu au ciel!"* exclaimed Anabette. "Abbess Marguerite doesn't sound like that!"

Reynaud de St. Rémy listened with a mixture of contentment and perplexity. He loved the music of southern France, even if it was coming from the strings of an abbess's lute. And in accompaniment to a male minstrel.

Well, Abelard had warned him of the Abbess Marguerite's love of music. . . . But Reynaud would never understand these Provençals and their whimsical ways.

He folded his arms across his chest and allowed the perplexity to fade away before the more soothing contentment. God knew, he'd had enough turmoil in his life recently; he didn't need to concern himself with understanding the Provençals and their southern brothers. More and more, live and let live was becoming his belief—which was exactly at the root of his problems. And he certainly was well-accustomed to Taillefer's practiced playing. Wasn't that half the reason he now took the *troubadour* with him wherever he went?

A movement in the doorway caught his attention. The two *demoiselles* from the infirmary. There was no mistaking the bold little blonde—and that enchanting child, Brielle. They were standing still as statues, obviously transfixed by the sight of Taillefer joined in music with their Mother Superior. The blonde nudged Brielle d'Avignon in the ribs beneath her bent arms. Reynaud's eyes narrowed. What was she carrying cradled against her heart as if it were something precious?

Dieu, but he didn't need those two mischief-makers causing any more uproar while in Bishop Abelard's presence! He'd thought them safely tucked away in the infirmary under the care of the formidable Soeur Françoise. . . .

His gaze moved to the nun herself, two tables over. Her arms were folded stiffly as she regarded her charges with open disapproval.

So much for that, he thought in rising irritation.

Why are you annoyed, St. Rémy? queried a voice. *They're not your responsibility.*

He ignored the voice as he watched Anabette slip into the room, her gaze suddenly on him. As surprising as was her bold regard, Reynaud found his own returning to Brielle d'Avignon. She was canting her head, her eyes widening with obvious pleasure as she stood cradling her bundle and listening to Taillefer's voice raised in a well-known *chanson d'amour.*

Reynaud glanced at Abbess Marguerite once more. Her

eyes were closed as she strummed along with the fair-haired minstrel from Marseilles, appearing totally immersed in and at ease with a love song being sung in her convent dining hall.

Suddenly he found Brielle watching him as intently as Anabette (who was still sidling along the nearest wall, apparently toward him), only her eyes held his with a shy gentleness—certainly not the brazenness of her friend—and a fragile uncertainty, whose poignancy threatened his steady composure.

The company of women is a dangerous thing, and the Devil has turned many men from the path to paradise by providing female company. The words of part of the Templar Rule swirled through his brain.

No! he thought with a jerk of his chin, and stood abruptly, pinning the hapless Anabette to the whitewashed wall behind her with his fiercest frown. He strode toward her and she halted in her steps, her mouth dropping open in surprise. Reynaud, however, barely noted her reaction; for in an increasingly automatic response to irreconcilable feelings, he felt himself begin to retreat to a calmer place in one secret corner of his mind. . . .

Brielle suddenly realized she was staring at Reynaud de St. Rémy as shamelessly as Anabette and, in turn, more than a few of the nuns were staring at *her.* Even the knights at the bishop's table were staring.

She quickly looked away, gathered her wits, and moved along the wall toward Anabette—that silly girl! she thought with an inner grimace. What in the world was she about? Ravishment of the Templar right in the refectory? Normally, her sense of humor would have moved her to laughter at such an absurd thought, but Brielle was genuinely concerned now. The thought may have been absurd, but Anabette's behavior was only slightly less so, and Brielle was determined to save her friend from embarrassing herself before the entire dining hall.

And because of a handsome, taciturn male who didn't even know how to smile.

Then, as in an unpredictable dream, Brielle saw that some-how Anabette had seated herself at one of the tables, and Brielle found herself approaching the tall and forbidding Reynaud de St. Rémy with his newly-laundered tunic clutched in her arms like the holy grail itself.

Instantly she knew she'd made a mistake in coming to him in the middle of the refectory . . . had surely set herself up for one of the Templar's unsmiling admonitions before eve-ryone present.

But the music continued uninterrupted, both minstrel and abbess obviously immersed in their performance. Only a few pairs of eyes strayed to the knight and the maiden.

Reynaud's longer strides brought him to Brielle before she could move more than a step or two away from the wall. He stopped before her, his expression unreadable, his topaz gaze cold and distant. But he said nothing, plainly waiting for her to speak first.

"Do you accost all maidens in such a manner, my lord Templar?" she began, refusing, in spite of her increasing trepidation before this man, to appear the lamb awaiting the slaughter.

He didn't bat an eyelash, but stared at her. No, *through* her, she thought. When he opened his mouth, it was as if another were speaking. "And do you treat all guests with so direct and pointed a query?"

It suddenly occurred to Brielle that this man might have great influence with the bishop, and if he took a dislike to her, the prelate might not grant her permission to accompany his party.

With a slightly quivering chin, Brielle met his eyes levelly. "Nay, my lord. Pray forgive me. . . ." She held out the folded tunic, commanding her stuttering heartbeat to still. "I but wished to thank you for the loan of your garment. We laundered the sleeve."

Reynaud had the grace to take the tunic from her. "There was no need," he said, looking down at the article as if it were something foreign. "I have someone who sees to my clothing."

There was nothing more to say. He'd doused the meager conversation as surely as if he'd thrown a pail of water on the remnants of a fire.

An awkward silence fell between them. The magic notes of the lutes and the smooth, rich sound of Taillefer's voice faded into the background as their eyes met—his cool, hers uncertain. Brielle's lashes lowered as she dropped her gaze first with maidenly modesty.

"Forgive *me*," he said stiffly, but his fingers were gentle as they lifted her chin and then tilted her head slightly to study her brow.

His touch was soothing as cool water in the desert of their stilled dialogue, and Brielle wondered if he were some kind of sorcerer rather than a Templar knight. There had to be some remnant of chivalry within him, for it was part and parcel of a knight's code of honor.

This man, however, seemed to be chivalrous only in his touch.

Strangely disappointed, Brielle tried to nudge her chin from his loose grip. "You cannot see aught, Sieur Reynaud, for the plaster covering it."

His fingers tightened slightly, and his eyes moved from the bandage back to her face. Brielle was certain he'd taken offense at her tart reply. "And the good *soeur* was most adept at applying the plaster without shaving your hair . . . although"—he gently tugged free one strand of hair that had been tucked beneath the bandage—"she seems to have caught something here."

He watched her wince, but refused to allow himself to feel compassion, focusing instead on the way the tendril twined its way around his finger. A gossamer filament the shade of pale honey. . . .

"Sieur Reynaud?" Brielle whispered, not wishing to jerk her chin from his grip like a defiant child, yet feeling the need to get away—at least to the haven of her accustomed place at one of the trestle tables.

He dropped his hand and straightened as the music behind them began to fade away. "You are welcome, *demoiselle,* for the use of my tunic." His expression grew more distant. "May I escort you to your place?"

A hint of gallantry, she thought, albeit reluctant. The gesture caught her between amusement and bemusement, for although her beloved father would have found humor in Reynaud de St. Rémy's seeming ambivalence, Brielle was perplexed.

As she allowed him to guide her to her place beside Anabette, the thought of Geoffrey d'Avignon renewed her determination to obtain Bishop Abelard's permission to accompany him to the Holy Land. And if that included winning over this enigmatic Templar, then win him over she would.

As she seated herself, Brielle drew in a fortifying breath, looked up at Reynaud de St. Rémy over her shoulder, and gave him her most brilliant smile. The others at the board leaned toward her to express their concern over her mishap, but for a suspended moment, the message in her eyes was for Reynaud and Reynaud alone.

Although not unexpected, Reynaud de St. Rémy's presence during her audience with the bishop was unnerving. After the introductions were made by Abbess Marguerite in her small study, Bishop Abelard bade both her and Brielle be seated. The Templar, however, remained standing to one side of the bishop, in the shadows and silent as one—at first.

Bishop Abelard immediately inspired trust in Brielle,

partly because of what she had observed of him briefly in the outer courtyard and the refectory, and partly because of what the abbess, whom she loved and respected, had told her on an earlier occasion about the prelate.

"And how is your head, child?" he asked, the concern in his dark eyes obviously sincere.

Brielle felt her face warm at the thought of the unfortunate mishap in the yard. " 'Tis well enough, Your Excellency," she answered softly. " 'Tis harder than it appears." A dimple hinted at its presence, but there was a reason for that half-smile: She didn't want the bishop to think her some soft, pampered child unequal to an arduous journey.

He smiled back, then quickly sobered. "Abbess Marguerite tells me you wish to travel to the Holy Land?"

"Aye, my lord. To search for my father, Geoffrey d'Avignon." Her heart lodged in her throat as she awaited his reaction. But it wasn't that simple. . . .

Abelard glanced at the silent knight, then looked down at the table beside him, a thoughtful frown dominating his expression. Brielle got the distinct impression that he was struggling with some inner conflict, for he didn't seem the type of man who vacillated between positions. Clearly, however, if he'd made a decision regarding her, he was entertaining doubts about it.

As if on cue, St. Rémy said, "The Holy Land is no place for a Christian woman."

Brielle was taken aback at the sudden, vehement declaration. She looked over at the Templar, annoyed that he'd say such a thing. "Why, Queen Elinor and her ladies once traveled to that very place."

"Queen Elinor was obstinate and accustomed to getting her own way," Reynaud said bluntly. "She had the king wound about her finger."

"But women have just as much right to go to the Holy Land and help wrest it from the infidels," she countered, feeling her temper rise at the arrogance of this surly north-

erner. The sensation of Reverend Mother's gaze upon her
gave her pause, however, before she could say any more. It
wouldn't do at all to have the bishop believe her a potential
nuisance.

"What Sieur Reynaud means, Brielle," the bishop said in
a placating tone, "is that married women may accompany
their spouses to Outremer rather than be separated for years.
Women are safer at home. They're not meant to fight the
physical battles of men."

"But my father is missing!" she insisted, trying not to
sound like a shrew. "He is all I have in this world, and his
sergeant at arms was here at St. Bernadette's not six months
ago. He told me they never found my father's body—nor any
of his weapons. Not even his horse. Wouldn't that mean he
might have escaped the great battle of Hattin with his life?"

Her eyes locked with the bishop's as she fought to sway
him to her side by sheer willpower.

"Brielle is right, Your Excellence," the abbess told him.
"Surely—"

"Forgive my cynicism, Reverend Mother," Reynaud cut
her off, "but if Sieur Geoffrey were alive, 'tis logical that he
would have notified someone back here in France."

" 'Tis true, Abbess Marguerite," Bishop Abelard said,
pushing away from the table and slowly walking across the
room. His robes softly flared about his leather-shod feet as
he moved with a natural grace, one arm bent across his waist,
the other elbow resting upon it so his fingers could stroke
his chin. "And we cannot have you risking your life on so
slender a thread of hope." He swung toward Brielle. "I'm
sorry, child, 'tisn't that I seek to diminish the importance of
your father's life, but rather the reliability of your information."

Brielle bit down on her lip, trying to swallow back the
torrent of words that sprang to her tongue; and in an attempt
to come to the young woman's aid, Abbess Marguerite in-
terceded, "But, my lord bishop, how can you put so little

importance on the opinion of a valued man-at-arms? Surely John the Gaunt wouldn't have sought to raise false hopes in his liege lord's daughter?" Her voice was gentle, but Brielle recognized the rock-hard will behind it.

An impatient sigh came from Reynaud de St. Rémy, and Brielle instinctively knew the Templar would never agree to back her, no matter how clean his tunic sleeve, how bright her smile.

"I cannot debate the two of you without help," Bishop Abelard said, his eyes turning troubled for a moment. He glanced at St. Rémy and then back to Brielle as he said, "Sieur Reynaud has been in the Holy Land since before Hattin. He's high-ranking and close to the Master Templar himself. He can tell you better than I, exactly how unlikely it is that your father survived."

Indeed, Brielle thought, the knight must be held in high esteem by the prelate that he would allow St. Rémy to speak for him.

The Templar remained in the shadows, but there was no mistaking the cold implacability in his voice. *"Demoiselle,* often there is no sign of a soldier's body or his effects after a battle. The corpse—or what's left of it—may be unrecognizable, the garments stripped away. Sieur Geoffrey's horse, surely a valuable steed, was no doubt stolen by the enemy or perhaps it bolted. Need I go into more graphic detail?"

Brielle fought the urge to weep in frustration before these men and their prejudicial ways where women were concerned. Who were they to tell her there was no hope? If her father were dead, she would have known it, *felt* it. "Were it your father, my lord knight, or yours, Your Excellency, you'd leave no stone unturned in an attempt to discover his fate, would you?"

Bishop Abelard didn't answer the question, but looked at St. Rémy. "Could he not be a prisoner—held for ransom by the Saracens?"

"If so, may God have mercy on him, for he would be better off dead."

If Brielle thought Reynaud de St. Rémy's tone expressionless before, now it was a grim semblance of sound. The tone alone raised the hackles on her neck, to say nothing of his brutal words.

"And 'tis nearly four years since Hattin. No one survives that long in an Arab prison."

Ignoring the sledge hammer effect of his pronouncement and refusing to be moved from her faith and purpose, Brielle entreated Bishop Abelard, "My lord bishop, I pray you allow me to go with you. There is no one else to discover his fate, and I give you my word I'll be no trouble to you . . . or the Templar." She couldn't bring herself to even speak his name after what he'd said.

Abelard moved to Brielle, placed the palm of his hand to one side of her face and looked directly into her eyes. "Have you no brothers who can undertake this journey for you, *cher enfant?*"

Brielle thought briefly of Reginald and his selfish wife, Isabeau. She hadn't heard a word from them in the years since she'd arrived at St. Bernadette. Even her father had thought her safer in a convent in his absence. "I know naught of my brother or his wife. If Reginald still lives, I haven't heard. Upon my father's death, he stood to gain everything. Why would he care?"

The bitterness in her voice obviously answered any questions the bishop might have had. But not so the Templar. "Any son worth his salt would go in his sister's place rather than expose her to such peril."

Brielle looked at him, her eyes narrowing to make out his features. "My brother was never worth anything so precious as salt." Her jaw tightened and Brielle found herself staring at the silver candlestick upon the table.

"Then by papal injunction, you cannot travel to the Holy Land without accompanying male relatives," St. Rémy told her. "Or will you earn your way as a washerwoman . . . or a flea-picker? Or even a—"

"May I add, Your Excellence," Abbess Marguerite interrupted, "that theoretically, Brielle is your daughter. And I can vouch for her maturity. She's a steady young woman, trustworthy, and not given to foolish impulse."

Brielle waited for Reynaud de St. Rémy to either finish what the Mother Superior had interrupted, or even make some remark about impulse and the cut on her forehead. His words, however, surprised her. "I'll grant *la demoiselle* courage for her actions in the convent yard. Rather, 'twas her friend who was foolish. But Outremer is a far cry from a convent in southern France."

The bishop's hand fell away from Brielle's hair, and his eyes turned suddenly unseeing, focused on some invisible point. "Would you speak so bluntly—of flea-pickers and whores—to your own sister, Reynaud?"

"I have no sister, Excellence, but had I one, I would of a certainty forbid her ever to travel to the Holy Land, contingent of male relatives or nay. And in any language that would convey the message."

Brielle stood in agitation and approached Abbess Marguerite. "I—I have a small inheritance, my lord bishop, a small estate from my lady mother, and perhaps Reverend Mother would grant me a loan against it so I could pay my expenses . . . and hire several men to—"

"You would tie up valuable men to watch over you when every man is needed to defend what we have and reconquer what we've lost?" St. Rémy asked.

But Abelard said, "And where will you stay, child?"

"Jerusalem," she said off the top of her head. "At an inn from which I can make inquiries."

"Jerusalem is in Muslim hands now."

"Tyre is not," countered the bishop, with a sidelong glance at Reynaud, as if His Excellence were taking Brielle's side. "I briefly met Geoffrey d'Avignon—he and his party stayed at the monastery overnight some years ago, while on crusade. He was a fine Christian knight, a model of chivalry, and I can see why his daughter is so eager to discover his fate in the absence of concern on her brother's part." He smiled at Brielle, his eyes warm. "I can also see much of her father in her."

"She is still a woman, not a warrior," St. Rémy began, but the bishop raised his hand to silence him.

"I think mayhap we can allow the Lady Brielle to accompany us to Tyre. I plan to remain there for a while, as I have been asked to temporarily take the Archbishop of Tyre's place while he is abroad recruiting men for this newest crusade. She can hire someone to make inquiries, if she promises to remain no longer than eight weeks. . . ."

But eight weeks was so little time! Brielle thought as she packed her few belongings for their departure the next morn.

One obstacle at a time, warned a voice. *You've been granted permission for now.*

Rising excitement skittered through her as she envisioned several months of hard travel and peril-fraught situations in the midst of the bishop's contingent . . . and the uncertainty of what she would discover concerning Geoffrey d'Avignon once she'd begun to make inquiries. And the return trip home, perhaps with her father!

She tried to focus her thoughts elsewhere for fear her heart would ram right through her chest from anticipation and the fear of what she might or might not find. . . .

Where was Anabette? she wondered. She hadn't told her friend yet.

On impulse, Brielle dropped what she was doing and went to search for the other girl. She had to share her news. She also had to thank Reverend Mother in private, although she would regret never seeing the nun or anyone from St. Bernadette's again.

Brielle moved along the cloister, her eyes slitted against the light in the sun-drenched inner courtyard. Birds sang from the small trees growing within it, from the early-budding bushes. The smell of spring perfumed the air, and Brielle felt giddy. She wanted to dance in her bare feet in the lush grass of the courtyard, embrace anyone who walked by, sing out to the heavens that for the first time in five years she was taking positive action in her life.

Her attention was unexpectedly attracted by the open door of the chapel—nothing unusual in the warmer weather. Mayhap it was the smell of candle wax or incense, she wasn't sure. Propelled by some unseen force, Brielle slipped inside its shadowed interior and remained close to one wall while her eyes adjusted back to dimness.

Her heart still racing with excitement, she decided it would be an appropriate time to thank God for her success and pray for His guidance.

A kneeling figure at the railing before the altar came into focus suddenly, and propriety told Brielle to leave this person in privacy. She should just slip back out before she was noticed, and continue on her way.

But her heart jumped to the base of her throat when she realized the figure kneeling before the altar was the Templar. Her knees suddenly threatened to buckle from anger and awe and something else as she stared steadily at him. His head wasn't bowed in the typical attitude of one in prayer but, rather, raised, giving her the blurred but nonetheless splendid lines of his profile in the soft glow of candlelight radiating from brackets along the sides of the walls.

He hardly looks supplicating, came her first thought when the surprise began to abate, *but rather like an angry child of God confronting his Father.* His body was tense—she could feel it in the quiet serenity of the chapel, see it in his bloodless fingers clutched about the rail as if in desperation or fury. Or both.

Unhappiness—aye, and even misery—literally emanated from Reynaud de St. Rémy. And anger.

Brielle's every instinct told her to leave, for she was witnessing something very private and personal. But as his chin dropped to his chest in a gesture of utter defeat, she found she couldn't move her seemingly weighted feet. As if a great hand were pressing her down, she felt pinned to the tiled floor, helpless to do anything but watch Reynaud de St. Rémy's spiritual struggle.

His shoulders sagged, he dropped to a sitting position on his heels, and rested his forehead against the simple oak rail, like a doused flame.

Guilt finally broke through her fascination, and she found the strength to begin to back out the way she'd come. Surely she had no right spying upon this man—or any other—even though he'd attempted to thwart her plans earlier.

Footsteps sounded in the cloister, and the very thought of someone else interrupting the knight's anguished meditation prompted her legs to carry her out of the chapel and her hands to quietly close the door behind her.

Three

When the door closed, one of the shadows at the back of the chapel moved, emerging into the flickering glow of a wall sconce. It was a man of small stature who moved on light feet toward the Templar. He hated to see his master this way, but he knew—thought he understood to a certain extent—what this great Christian knight was suffering. This man among men who had found Rashid beside the road to Damascus where he'd lain like a piece of refuse, and nursed the Arab back to health, despite the disapproval of his superiors, and the unspoken threat of repercussions later.

Rashid paused near the altar rail, not wishing to take one misstep toward the Christian altar, but feeling the need to be close to the man he served unquestioningly. Like Reynaud de St. Rémy, he felt comfortable in any place of worship, closer to Allah, whom he believed was the same God the Christians worshipped, although few of them would ever concede such a thing.

"Master?" he said softly.

For a few moments, Rashid feared Reynaud hadn't heard him. Then, just as he was about to repeat the word, the Templar slowly lifted his head and turned to regard the little man. His striking features were ravaged, anyone would have been able to tell. But of late he had been wearing the expression too frequently, and oftentimes either Taillefer or Rashid would feel obliged to rescue St. Rémy from himself—from his guilt and self-flagellation, which both the minstrel and the Arab felt were ill-deserved, and from the "gift" he felt was an unfair burden.

"The minstrel is up to mayhem, master," he said softly, his heart going out to this man whom he secretly revered.

Slowly, Reynaud stood and turned toward the Arab. His eyes cleared and a corner of his mouth quirked. "Mayhem, you say? Now what could Taillefer possibly find to—" He paused, the quirk disappearing. "Of course, what else in a place full of women?" His eyes closed briefly. "And if they discover *you* here, my faithful friend, and in the chapel. . . ."

"They won't. And if they do, I could have no better champion than yourself." Rashid couldn't bring himself to reveal that a woman had been observing Reynaud at his meditations only moments ago. Allah be praised that she had not noticed *him* as well, for the Arab had blended in with the shadows.

Reynaud glanced once again at the golden crucifix hanging above the altar. "Your confidence is too easily placed, Rashid."

"And your preoccupation worries me, master," Rashid said quietly.

"Indeed. Enough to risk being discovered in a Christian chapel. You could cause more than a little mayhem yourself." He turned to leave with the Arab.

"My concern for you is greater than for myself."

Reynaud waved one hand in dismissal. "You mustn't be concerned with a man praying to his god. Now, tell me, Rashid, what mischief is the minstrel up to this time? Nay, let me guess. . . ."

When they reached the orchard just west of the convent buildings, however, it wasn't mayhem so much as the potential for it in a cloistered community where women did not mingle with outsiders: specifically, men. Where a saucy spit of a girl and a romantic minstrel were like tinder and spark. . . .

The sweet fragrance of apple blossoms on the benign breeze was only added fodder.

"He has every right to find the woman of his dreams and wed her, you know," Reynaud said under his breath to Rashid, as they watched from several rows of apple trees away. "He's a minstrel, not a Templar."

He felt Rashid's glance askance. Had his friend caught the unintentional note of bitterness in his words?

"But the girl is to become a part of the order, is she not?" the Arab asked. " 'Tis forbidden for one of their calling to know a man. In the physical sense, that is."

"She is only boarding here, no doubt until her father finds her a suitable husband," Reynaud said wryly. "But Taillefer is a born lover, and I doubt he'll allow the fact that she's an unspoiled maiden of means and he a lowly *troubadour* to dampen his pursuit. Especially if she gives him the least bit of encouragement." But Reynaud knew Taillefer was a *troubadour* because he had elected to be, not because he had been born of common parents.

Rashid's dark brows drew together in a frown as they watched Taillefer (sitting up against a tree trunk, strumming his lute) smile at Anabette like the spider to the fly. "A man is not to be judged by his material wealth, master. The minstrel can perhaps offer his lute to her father as proof of his love and—"

Reynaud grunted and gave the Arab an arch look. "Taillefer would never be parted from his lute—not even for love. And he would be absolutely ruined as an entertainer if he were wed."

Rashid sighed. "Perhaps his music would improve were he kept happy in his tent at night."

Reynaud narrowed his eyes thoughtfully at the Arab. "Are you homesick, *mon ami?*"

"Not yet," the Arab answered honestly. "I like this land of green meadows and gentle rains."

"Eh bien, stay here while I approach them. We don't wish to frighten the young woman."

Their eyes met. "If Khamsin didn't frighten her, master, I doubt that I would, seeing that, like you, I stand upright on two legs."

"Forgive me," Reynaud said with rue. "But the sight of an Arab to an unwordly girl living in the shelter of a convent could be her undoing."

"Surely not this one," Reynaud heard Rashid comment under his breath as the Templar walked toward Taillefer and Anabette. "And as for the one with hair like tarnished gold—"

Reynaud didn't catch the last words, and he refused to try and complete his friend's thought. Better this Anabette should have remained fixated upon *him,* for he would never—*could* never—take advantage of her.

To his surprise, however, just as he was approaching the twosome and Taillefer's song ended, Reynaud heard a feminine voice from the other side of the trees call out, "Anabette, *c'est toi?* Is that you?"

A chaperon, he thought, and rightly so . . . until Brielle d'Avignon came into view. The warm spring sun shone upon her drawn-back hair, burnishing it to a honey-blond, a muted shade of old gold, just as Rashid had observed, that made Anabette's hair look a gaudy yellow in comparison.

Something within his chest tightened, then was gone. She was only a girl—like any other girl. *And you've made a most unkind comparison,* admonished a voice.

"I wondered where you were," Brielle said, one eyebrow raised at Anabette. "My lord," she murmured more shyly in greeting to Taillefer.

"I am no lord," said the minstrel as he set aside his lute and stood. "Thank God for that! They call me Taillefer le Doux." He smiled charmingly at Brielle, then noticed Reynaud moving into their midst. His smile turned even brighter, revealing even white teeth, which indicated to Brielle that he wasn't much over twenty and in good health.

At least Anabette had good taste, she thought wryly.

"Oh, Brielle," Anabette began breathlessly, "Taillefer makes such wonderful music and—"

Brielle looked at her askance, but then *he* was there, appearing seemingly out of nowhere. Only this time his features were softened by a half-smile.

Sweet Mary, he's smiling! she thought, and grudgingly accorded him a dollop more of respect for the evident ability to do so.

Upon meeting her surprised gaze, however, Reynaud allowed his smile to disappear as if it had never been, and vague disappointment drifted through Brielle. Hard on its heels came annoyance. Annoyance at this Templar who seemed to frown every time he saw her. Heavens! Was she so unappealing? her piqued pride made her wonder.

Becoming color stained her cheeks at the very idea, and a sudden warmth in her face roused her from her brief musings. "Sieur Reynaud," she acknowledged him, trying to sound properly humble.

He nodded. *"Demoiselle."* His gaze returned briefly to Taillefer and the strangely silent Anabette nearby.

"I—I was looking for Anabette to tell her—" she trailed off, deciding that she owed this man no explanation.

"Of your impending departure, no doubt." His words splintered through hers, heavy with disapproval.

Well, she didn't need his approval now, for Bishop Abelard's was the only one that counted. *"Mais oui, chevalier,"* she answered levelly, then looked at Anabette, whose eyes were aglow—as much, Brielle was certain, from the minstrel's company as from her own interrupted revelation. That meant that Anabette might have gained an ally in her scheme and, even more distressing to Brielle, an even stronger reason—no matter how misguided—to attempt to carry out her plan.

It was Taillefer who spoke then. "Reynaud . . . *demoiselle,"* he began with all the charm of a prince, "the lady

Anabette and I have been celebrating this fine day with a little music and song," he explained, indicating the verdant grass, the blossoming apple trees and the cloud-strewn sky with a wave of one arm. "A harmless and relaxing pursuit, is it not?"

By any standard he was a charmer, a ladies' man, with his fair good looks and warm, gracious manner. There was also much to be said for his music. Brielle was certain he was capable of turning the head of any woman—no matter how experienced, or how old; certain that he'd charmed his way into many a woman's heart and bed, no matter her station. And by the look on Anabette's face, she would soon be included among their numbers.

Taillefer, however, had just met his match in Anabette, Brielle would have wagered anything, and could almost feel sorry for him. Almost.

Therefore all the more reason to dissuade the rash Anabette from her disastrous course. . . . If only Reynaud de St. Rémy weren't there, eclipsing them all with his dark and awesome presence.

"Anabette," Brielle said, "will you not come back with me? Reverend Mother wishes to speak to you."

"Indeed," murmured the Templar, and Brielle received the distinct impression that he didn't believe her. But she didn't care what he believed, nor was it any of his concern.

Anabette was unmoved. "Oh, tell her you cannot find me, *chère Brielle,*" she pleaded, then glanced at Reynaud and hesitated. " 'Tisn't truly a lie," she hurried to add, "for you *couldn't* find me at first." She gave Brielle a bright smile. "Just wait a bit before you go to her, and I'll meet you at the entrance in half an hour."

"*Oui, demoiselle,*" the minstrel added, with another of his seraphic smiles. "We had only begun our . . . lesson."

Brielle opened her mouth to protest.

"If 'twill ease your mind, I'll remain as chaperon," St. Rémy offered.

Brielle relented, for although they were both men, one was a knight of God, a Templar, the epitome of chivalry—or at least that was the ideal for a Knight of the Poor Temple of Solomon, whatever the minstrel might be. *"Eh bien,* half an hour."

She swung away, eager to leave the Templar's presence, when she heard his voice—rich in register, smooth as satin— say, "Allow me to take you back to the convent, *demoiselle."*

More quickly than was courteous, Brielle found herself saying sweetly, "Then you cannot act as chaperon, *chevalier,* can you?" Before he could reply, she turned and walked away, conscious only of his eyes burning a hole in her back.

As much as Brielle loved Anabette and wished for her happiness, she couldn't help but feel acutely suspicious. And troubled. She was not one to retreat to the background and, in spite of Abbess Marguerite's assurance otherwise to the bishop, was occasionally given to impulse; but Anabette's bold ways often distressed her as much as they amused her, and Brielle had, on more than one occasion, found herself thinking that Anabette's family had been wise to allow the young woman to remain safely at St. Bernadette's until her marriage.

Now, as the younger girl pinned Brielle with an expectant stare, she intuitively knew the outcome of her friend's plotting might be both their undoing. Or at least *her* undoing should Anabette's machinations cause the bishop to revoke his permission.

"Did you lie to me about Reverend Mother?" the girl asked.

Brielle faced her friend's anger with a wriggling conscience. "Would you rather have faced her fresh from your interlude with the minstrel? Why, your eyes are a-sparkle, your cheeks pink with excitement . . . I haven't seen you so animated since you tied Soeur Geneviève's rosary to the altar rail."

A sudden smile curved the girl's mouth before her expression sobered once again. "But Brielle, I've an ally now. At least I *think* I have an ally. And surely more reason than ever to carry out my plan."

"Why?" Brielle pressed, thinking to shame Anabette into aborting her scheme. "Think you that you'd like being a concubine to this man? For of a certainty he'll not marry you!"

It worked. At least partially, for color seeped into Anabette's cheeks. "I would never be any man's concubine! I can travel as your lady-in-waiting and—"

"And what of Lord Odo? He will not be happy to discover his betrothed has run off with a minstrel . . . nor will your father."

Anabette folded her arms and stared up at the small window. "My father considers me only as an asset—a lure to bring more wealth into the family by wedding me to a rich but balding old man with rotting teeth." She pulled a grimace. "Why, Odo's breath alone would clear Jerusalem of infidels!"

If the situation hadn't been so serious, Brielle would have laughed aloud. "You haven't even met him. How would you know except from gossip?"

"I have ways. I had spies among the servants . . . and I *did* see him when I was very young. I was hiding in the very hall where he signed the betrothal papers!"

Brielle sat upon her pallet, one hand smoothing the blanket. She stared unseeingly at her fingers, thinking how best to phrase her next question, even though she felt she was butting her head against a wall. "What if you—"

Anabette sat beside her and halted her midsentence. "Oh, *chère Brielle,* you must agree! Would you consign me to this dreary convent or to be wife to a skinny-shanked dotard like Odo?"

Brielle found it hard to resist Anabette when she pleaded

and cajoled like this—when she implied that Brielle was to blame for her present situation. And her future. Her mouth tightened in mutiny. Nay, she wouldn't let her friend lay the blame on her head.

She steeled herself and met Anabette's velvet brown eyes. "And have you considered the possibility of your plan jeopardizing *my* chances of going with Bishop Abelard? Or of the added risk to the entire party because of one more unwanted female? One more woman to feed and protect?"

Distress crossed Anabette's features, then was gone, replaced by determination. "These men are experienced knights, have already fought in the Holy Land. Two insignificant women are no true burden." She grabbed Brielle's arm and pinned the latter's hand against the blanket. Her voice lowered with fervency, "And I told you earlier, you have my word I'll never tell that you knew of my intentions. When I am discovered, I'll swear upon my Christian soul that you were not involved!"

Brielle shook her head. "But *I* cannot lie to the bishop! Don't you see?"

Obviously Anabette didn't see. "Not even for me? I don't know what more I can do to persuade you, Brielle. And you already agreed, did you not, earlier this morn?"

"I didn't agree."

"But you accepted my help getting to the dining hall. That in itself was an unspoken consent."

It was no such thing, but Brielle knew that whether she agreed to or not, Anabette would find a way to go. Or die trying.

In the past, she had often laughed at Anabette's stubborn streak, her outrageous antics. But this was different. "Then come if you will," she told her friend, hardening her heart against her own words. "But if your reckless behavior in any way leads to my being returned to St. Bernadette's, I'll never speak to you again! Never acknowledge you! You'll be dead to me forever. Do you understand?" Her eyes locked with

Anabette's, the strength of her own determination equal to her friend's.

"And," she added in a fierce whisper, *"I'll never forgive you."*

Anabette didn't attend matins the next morn. Nor did she appear in the dining hall to break the fast. The softer side of Brielle wanted to go to Anabette and apologize for her harsh words the night before. But another side of her remained firm in the face of the enormity of Anabette's intentions, and their possible repercussions if her friend succeeded.

But what kind of friend are you, whispered a voice, *that you ignore Anabette's needs?*

A good friend! Brielle thought with conviction, for Anabette was flighty and impulsive, even thoughtless at times. She'd caused more than her share of mischief, on occasion even drawing Brielle into her schemes. But not this time, she told herself, and ignored her conscience.

Despite her anger at her friend the next morning, Brielle found herself caught up in the hustle and bustle of a party of knights bent on beginning their journey. The sun was just rising on another cloudless April day and a brisk but gentle breeze whispered through the trees. She was given a dependable mare to ride—"A gift," Abbess Marguerite had said, "to show our love and good wishes."

"She will be a distraction for our stallions," Reynaud de St. Rémy had said, sounding to Brielle like the voice of doom.

"Oui, but she will also be faster and more biddable," Marguerite had countered. "The Turks use mares, I've heard, do they not, Sieur Reynaud?"

Brielle had been secretly delighted at the abbess's unexpected knowledge of horses and had noted with amusement how Bishop Abelard had muffled a suspicious cough behind one hand as he'd turned away, obviously unwilling to get involved in the discussion.

But she'd been even more surprised when Taillefer had blurted, *"Eh bien,* Rashid rides a—" Then abruptly cut off his sentence.

There was utter silence for a moment, before Reynaud quickly swung about and ordered his men to mount. As one of the other Templars helped Brielle onto the mare, she wondered who "Rashid" was. By the expressions on several of the nuns' faces, she surmised that others wondered as well, and an unexpected chill skittered through her at the thought of an infidel somewhere among them. . . .

But that was absurd.

Final farewells were said, and Brielle pressed back the tears that threatened. At the last minute, Abbess Marguerite gave her a small pouch of gold left by Geoffrey d'Avignon, and a fine gold chain with a tiny crucifix, "To remember us at St. Bernadette's, child," she said. "God be with you, Brielle, on your journey and your search for your father."

Brielle lightly touched the cool metal now, then took up the mare's reins and turned her to ride through the convent gate. She wondered if she would ever see Abbess Marguerite again.

At dusk, two days later, they arrived at an inn on the outskirts of Marseilles. It was then that Brielle learned just who "Rashid" was. She took her meal in her room, knowing better than to mingle in the common room below with the men. And the washerwomen.

Brielle forced down a piece of cheese that stuck in her throat at the thought. Four washerwomen rode behind the bishop's party, ostensibly to do laundry for the men. Brielle was naive, but not naive enough to reason that four women for their rather small party were unnecessary for laundry. She guessed they doubled as whores—and God knew what else—and wondered what kind of women would do such a thing . . . unless the wife or lover of a common man on crusade wished to follow him to the Holy Land, and even then could expect no special accommodations. These women wore their hair carelessly loose and uncovered when the weather permitted, the only feminine feature apparent, for they were dressed in drab but serviceable fustian, like peasants.

A knock sounded at the door. Brielle didn't even have a chance to answer before the heavy wooden panel swung open. In the wavering candlelight, Reynaud de St. Rémy stood in the doorway, tall, imposing, and forbidding. "I am come to see your injury, *demoiselle*," he told her, and strode into the room.

Brielle quickly swallowed the last bit of cheese and stood, preparing to protest . . . when she saw a small figure close the portal and step up behind the Templar. A washerwoman? she thought in consternation. The cowl fell back from her—*his*—head, to reveal a face that was anything but feminine.

Evidently there were only *three* laundresses.

Brielle froze in alarm at his dusky skin and black eyes, his high cheekbones, hawklike nose and full lips. Then she fought to recover, essaying to mask her astonishment and apprehension, for surely the man couldn't be dangerous—Saracen or nay—if he were with Reynaud. She fought back a vague revulsion as well, for a man like this had fought her father. Had possibly killed him.

The candle flames in several iron wall brackets danced in the draft from the door, casting patterns across the infidel's face, as well as that of the knight now standing immediately before her. The effect was sinister.

A new and stronger wave of fear washed over her—a feeling akin to panic, for what did she really know about these men? They could ravish her, then kill her, and blame it on some miscreant from the inn. She was at their mercy.

One hand went to clutch the tiny golden crucifix at her

breast, but Brielle refused to drop her gaze from that of Reynaud de St. Rémy Let him think what he would, but if he were up to no good, she wouldn't meet his perfidy like a whipped dog.

Reynaud watched the defiance vie with alarm in her very fine eyes. As he reached to tilt her face upward, she never wavered, even though he thought he felt the slightest trembling in her chin. Sweet Jesus! he thought. Did she think they were going to harm her? Perhaps he had been wrong to approach her with Rashid. . . .

"I thought it time you met Rashid, for he is a trusted companion."

He reached to peel the bandage away from her flesh with his left hand, his fingers infinitely tender, Brielle noted through her suspicion and the beat of her thudding heart.

"I didn't think you would be so unsettled at the sight of a Saracen once you were away from the influence of a gaggle of nuns." His amber eyes narrowed as he studied her temple. Brielle had once seen a wolf up close, before her father had been forced to kill it, and St. Rémy's eyes reminded her of that wolf's eyes—gleaming and golden. Beautiful but deadly.

"He-he's an . . . infidel," she whispered, the soft words sounding like thunder to her own ears in the otherwise quiet room.

St. Rémy's thumb lightly traced the edges of the injury, his gaze still on her temple. "The Muslims consider *us* the infidels," he murmured. "They are human beings, with families of loved ones, with feelings and thoughts in common with ours, and certain beliefs that are different. Those differences, *demoiselle,* are no excuse for slaughtering them. They love, they hate, they hurt, they bleed . . . just as we do." His voice lowered a fraction here, though not, Brielle suspected, from the heretical import of his next words as much as from the force of his conviction: "In God's scheme of things, they are our brothers."

So taken aback was Brielle, she could only utter inanely, "But—but I thought he was a washerwoman . . ."

"That was the intention in the beginning. You had enough on your mind as it was."

In spite of the fact that Brielle suspected St. Rémy was being considerate, her pride made her say, "I'm not a child, my lord Templar. Nor am I an intransigent old woman."

Rashid stepped up beside Reynaud, and Brielle tried not to stiffen.

"You would have been even more alarmed than you are now," St. Rémy told her.

Rashid looked at the healing cut the Templar had exposed. "You must remove the stitch, master," he said, "and then it needs air to heal more quickly."

"And so it does." Reynaud removed the rest of the covering. "When you address Rashid, *demoiselle,* you may call him by name. Infidel is an insult of the gravest sort—enough to make him challenge you were you a man. And he does not consider himself a laundress, although he sees to my clothing."

He threw a look over his shoulder, but Brielle couldn't make out what it meant. It could have been teasing (although she doubted it), for this Rashid drew himself up to his full height, still barely reaching St. Rémy's shoulder, and said with the barest trace of affront in perfect French, "I am no washerwoman. I care only for my master's garments."

"But he *did* commend you on the cleaning of my tunic." Reynaud looked back at her, but there was no humor in his eyes, or his voice, as far as Brielle could discern. "Sit," he bade her, and gestured toward the bed. He bent over a basin of water that stood on the small table beside the bed.

Brielle obeyed automatically, accustomed to following directions for the last five years at St. Bernadette's. Before she could even think, he was before her again with a tiny pair of scissors in one hand. The fingers of the other hand skimmed her temple area like the brush of a moth's wing, and he spoke softly to her as he cut the thread. No doubt to distract her from the pinch of pain created by the removal of the stitch. "You will note these scissors are too small to be used as a weapon, *demoiselle*," he said.

But Brielle couldn't help but think of a skilled physician as he deftly ministered to her. Or was it his awesome presence alone that kept her attention?

"Thank you, Sieur Reynaud," she said, when his hands fell away. He nodded as he handed Rashid the scissors, then ran a light finger over the healing cut. All tenderness was strangely gone.

A fist assaulted the door, startling Brielle. "Reynaud?"

"Excellent timing," Rashid commented. "A few moments earlier and you might have given the *demoiselle* another gash to go with the first."

"Oui?" Reynaud answered the query.

It was her room, she thought, paid for with her gold, yet *he* bade the person in the hall enter. . . .

It was one of the squires. "My lord, the girl—the yellow-haired mischief-maker from the convent—is here! And with her own men-at-arms!"

Four

The Venetian merchantman plowed through the translucent, blue-green waters. Its sails were bright white against the deep-blue Mediterranean sky and adorned by large scarlet crosses. A commodious vessel weighing 600 tons, the broad-bellied round ship reminded Brielle of a sturdy but unwieldy beast lumbering across the sea.

She stood at the rail and watched foam-flecked swells glide past, the breeze errantly catching briny droplets and flinging them into the air. The cold sea-spray felt good against her flushed face, for she'd just come from the hold, where Anabette lay still as death, and just as pale, in the throes of *mal de mer.*

They'd ridden out a violent storm, and Brielle felt that if they could only get her friend up on deck, the balmy breeze and warm sun would do wonders to revive her. But *he* had disagreed and told her to leave Anabette right where she was for another day. Was he mayhap punishing the headstrong girl?

She frowned at the thought, her eyes on the water, yet she still felt irritation at Anabette's brazen behavior in Marseilles. After having sought out and found John the Gaunt, her father's former sergeant at arms (evidently surmising that he would follow his lord's daughter to the Holy Land), Anabette had convinced him to allow her to go along on his trek to Marseilles. She'd struck one of her all-too-familiar bargains, she'd told Brielle, by telling him he owed her that much since she'd informed him of Brielle's leaving St. Bernadette's and her destination. And with Taillefer's interceding on her behalf with St. Rémy, everything had worked out as the bold Anabette had planned.

"And what if your father sends someone searching for you?" the Templar had asked, his expression ominous.

Anabette had waved her hand blithely. "If he does, the man will have to abduct me, for I'll refuse to go with him! I'll attend Brielle and choose my own husband!"

Taillefer had slapped his knee and laughed heartily at her answer, but Brielle had marked the reaction of both St. Rémy and Bishop Abelard. The knight's expression had remained grim, the prelate's bemused.

They could have bound and dragged her back to St. Bernadette's, but Brielle suspected the Templar had already guessed Anabette would never stay where she didn't want to be.

And the way the girl gazed at Taillefer, and he at her . . .

During one particularly devastating bout of seasickness, Anabette had begged Brielle, "Put me out of my misery! Throw me overboard, for God is punishing me tenfold!" She'd drawn up her knees beneath the light blanket and buried her face in the bedding with a groan of acute misery. A retching sound came from her, although Brielle wondered what was left in the girl's empty stomach to bring up.

"We've a special punishment reserved for runaways," St. Rémy had said from behind Brielle. He'd moved toward the bed and reached to push Anabette's damp hair back from her pale forehead.

He'd appeared as if conjured up, Brielle thought, and felt inexplicable guilt in his presence for her friend's actions. "Handing her over to pirates would be more suitable than throwing her overboard," she had told him darkly, in spite of her pity for Anabette.

Almost immediately Anabette's heaving began to ease,

surely not because of her own words to the girl, but rather
Reynaud de St. Rémy's soothing touch; and Brielle suddenly
found herself caught up in memories of those long, cool
fingers touching her own face at St. Bernadette's, and then
the inn. . . .

Even Taillefer couldn't remain in the close and gloomy
cubicle with Anabette for more than a few minutes at a time.
It was stuffy, uncomfortably warm, and stank of vomit. In
fact, many of the passengers preferred to sleep on deck, under the stars, than remain the night in the hold.

But not Reynaud de St. Rémy! He seemed impervious to
the discomforts, and often relieved Brielle for generous pe-
riods of time; and always at the time she felt herself getting
nauseous—as if he divined her needs. He would send her
above deck, stopping her halfhearted protests before she
could voice them.

Fresh spray brushed her cheek, and Brielle touched her
tongue to the corner of her mouth. The strong, salty taste
was worse than rank ale, she thought, and quickly withdrew
her tongue.

Taillefer was with Anabette now, and Brielle knew she
didn't have long before he summoned her back. Resentment
rose within her, and she lifted her face to the cloud-clotted
sky, waiting for the sun to peep through and touch her flesh.
She was missing the best part of the trip—God knew what
awaited her in the Holy Land. She loved the sea and understood from the Templar that the journey was faster and usually safer than the various routes over land.

Her eyes still closed, Brielle refused to dwell upon what
she was missing by being stuck in the hold with Anabette.

And then she felt *his* presence. He blocked the wind partially, and the warmth of his body seemed to reach out to
her.

"Why did you not become a physician?" she asked without thinking. "Or even a Hospitaller? Don't they care for the
sick?"

She realized too late that the words sounded more like an accusation than a compliment, and she opened her eyes to glance sideways at him.

But outwardly he didn't appear to take offense, for his gaze was on the horizon, and Brielle wondered if he had even heard her. The cape about his impressive shoulders billowed behind him, a royal blue ribbon of color, revealing a slash of scarlet in the play of the sea breeze.

"I'm the third son," he answered, when Brielle had finally despaired of getting a reply. " 'Twas my fate to serve the Church. While on crusade, however, my father came to so admire the Templars that he offered me what he considered to be the best of both worlds—that of knight and man of God at the same time."

He paused, and Brielle didn't quite know what to say in the face of this honest admission. But he spoke again. "Now I serve God by killing the infidel, thus assuring my salvation. There is no healing involved, but my knightly thirst for blood is satisfied."

The words were honed with self-derision, subtle but startling to Brielle. She looked up at his splendid profile, solid, unyielding, his mouth a thin line, and felt suddenly awkward. "I meant, Sieur Reynaud, that you appear to have a gift in your hands. Your touch is healing, as we've seen with Anabette. 'Tis almost magical. . . . I've felt it, too."

The look he turned on her could have turned a lesser young woman to stone. His eyes were cold, hard. " 'Tis soothing mayhap, or comforting . . . but *not* healing. The *demoiselle* Anabette would react to any man's touch, I wager. And as for you . . ." He trailed off, but the words hung in the air between them, implying that she was just like Anabette.

Her pride reared its head, and although her cheeks bloomed delicately, the manifestation of the d'Avignon temper wasn't nearly so subtle. "What of me, Sieur Reynaud? You barely know me! Do you always repay a compliment with an insult? If so, you are a poor example of *courtoisie*."

Feeling perversely gratified and at the same time appalled at her words, Brielle stood frozen to the rail, her eyes staring unseeingly out at the sea, willing away the tears that had formed in her eyes. She'd go straight to Hell before she would let this man see her weep because of something he'd said.

She felt his gaze on her face, but wouldn't turn to him. "Go you to the Holy Land to search for chivalry, *demoiselle,* or your father?" he asked quietly, then turned around when she refused to acknowledge him further, and walked away.

"Forgive me, my lady, for having so inconvenienced you."

John the Gaunt's words were low-spoken, but fervent. Brielle looked at the man her father had loved like a brother and had trusted unwaveringly. They were on deck, others sleeping around them in the balmy night air beneath thousands of stars stuck like tiny jewels to the tapestry of the midnight sky.

"I could not allow you to undertake such a dangerous journey alone," he continued urgently, "not while I can still ride a horse!" He glanced at the sleeping Anabette. "God's foot, but she is a handful! And I had no idea who she really was—that her family was wealthy and powerful—that she was the daughter of Aimery de Belvoir!"

Brielle couldn't help but smile. "The worst that can happen, John, is that her father sends a man to find her and take her back to France. We're not to blame for Anabette's reckless actions." Her smile faded. "No doubt she caused the nuns at St. Bernadette's great concern for her safety, and then guilt at having failed to prevent her leaving." She looked into his hazel eyes. "But I'm glad you're with me now. You know the Holy Land, and you were the last person with my father before the battle. If anyone can help me find him, you can." She looked thoughtful for a moment and made a moue. "Although St. Rémy thinks I'm on a fool's errand."

John nodded, his thoughts seemingly elsewhere for a few

moments. "The Templar is a wise and valiant knight, well-acquainted with the Levant, but he is not involved personally. Were he, I don't know that he would consider the situation so hopeless." He pursed his lips thoughtfully. "Has he, perchance, given you any ideas on where to begin your search, my lady?"

"Nay, but Bishop Abelard said that my father could possibly be languishing in a Damascus prison."

His silver-threaded eyebrows drew together, his eyes grew troubled as they met hers—a reaction in keeping with Reynaud de St. Rémy's. "Since Hattin?" he whispered, and slowly shook his head. "But then," he added, "where else could he be if he survived?"

"Indeed, John. You were so certain he might still be alive. Where else would he be? And if so, isn't Tyre as good a place as any to begin making inquiries?"

The man-at-arms looked unhappy, not nearly so confident that her father had survived as he had on his visit to St. Bernadette's six months earlier.

"If you didn't believe he'd survived, would you be here?"

"Aye, because of your undertaking. I've had some time to think, my lady, and—"

"Time to think, John," she said gently, one hand going to his arm, "or time to be influenced by my brother? He stands to lose everything if my father returns."

A slow, rare blush rose in his face. "I told Reginald nothing! I had been planning to leave Château d'Avignon soon, but I lingered, hoping Sieur Geoffrey would appear one day, and need my support." He turned his head to stare out at the dark sea around them. "But in my lord's absence, my loyalty is to you, not to your brother. I pledged that much to him." He glanced down at his left arm. "And 'twas only a matter of time before Reginald dismissed me—a warrior with one bad arm is of little use."

"Oh, John . . ." Brielle stepped closer, one hand coming to rest on his good arm. Her heart went out to this man who had loved and served her father. "You're still a man whole—more man than my brother could ever be." She tilted her face as she studied him. "I haven't much gold to repay you for your troubles and who knows what will become of us . . ."

"Do not insult my loyalty, child, by offering to pay for it." His voice was gruff with emotion and affront.

"Forgive me," she murmured, swallowing back her tears . . . and stiffened when she heard soft footfalls on the deck behind them.

" 'Tis only St. Rémy," he assured her softly.

She pushed away, refusing to look around. "How are things under my brother's supervision? Is he fair to the tenants? Does he—"

"He is nothing like your father."

The terse statement said enough.

"And Isabeau?"

"They have two children now. A boy and a girl." He could have been talking about a stray dog's litter for all the emotion in his voice. "Château d'Avignon is not the same as it was when your father was lord, and I was glad for a reason to leave immediately—even if that reason was . . . the Lady Anabette."

"The bishop said I could remain under his protection for no more than eight weeks." She tried not to allow the disappointment to creep into her voice.

He nodded. " 'Tis enough time to conduct a discreet search. But there is much that is different in Outremer, child, and you must be prepared for sights you would never have imagined."

"I can do anything if it will mean finding my father," she said firmly. "You can prepare me beforehand, John, for things that I—"

"I will do everything I can. But St. Rémy can prepare you better than I. Or mayhap his man . . . what is his name?"

"Taillefer."

"Nay, not the minstrel. The Arab."

"The—infidel?" she whispered, having suspected he'd meant Rashid, but hoping against hope he'd meant the minstrel from Marseilles.

"I realize 'tis a shock to you, seeing an infidel, my lady, but many races live side by side—even mingle—in the Holy Land. 'Tis complex, and one day a man can do business with you, the next he can face you in battle. If Sieur Reynaud trusts the Arab enough to keep him at his side, then you have naught to fear. A Templar's judgment is highly respected."

"I do not know about *this* particular Templar," she murmured, the breeze catching her words and amplifying them.

John frowned. "What do you mean, child?"

Brielle shook her head as he moved away from her.

"Indeed, *demoiselle,* what do you mean?" inquired Reynaud de St. Rémy from behind them.

John stiffened and swung to face the knight squarely. " 'Tis a private conversation, St. Rémy. You'll understand if I'm disturbed by your . . . eavesdropping during the lady Brielle's confidences."

"And the Lady Brielle has made a most unwise choice in confiding her private thoughts on deck with other passengers sleeping nearby."

Brielle was mortified by the thought that Reynaud de St. Rémy had overheard her words about *him* and she suddenly wanted to disappear into the sea. How dare he lurk nearby like some silent, ominous shadow?

She faced him, her chin lifted in indignation, her eyes flashing. "You are not responsible for me, *chevalier!"*

"I'm not?" he countered. "Then who, exactly, is? The bishop has Church matters on his mind and gave you into my care until we reach the Holy Land."

"Sieur Reynaud," John began, "I'm the Lady Brielle's man-at-arms, and—"

"If that's the case, John the Gaunt, then why didn't *you* take your mistress to Outremer? Why did you leave her to drag Bishop Abelard into this?" He paused then, his dark brows drawing together as he regarded Brielle. "I seem to remember the abbess mentioning your name. Weren't you the one who gave *la demoiselle* false hope and then left her to her fanciful imaginings? To hie herself off to the Holy Land in search of a phantom?"

Brielle bristled. Surely he had no right to talk to John like this—Templar knight or not. John the Gaunt was like a second father to her.

But John spoke for himself. "I have the use of only one arm, St. Rémy, and did not feel I could adequately assume responsibility for Lady Brielle. The reason I left the Holy Land—ceased fighting Saladin's hordes and making inquiries about Sieur Geoffrey—was my injury. If I couldn't carry on for Lord Geoffrey, how could I ever offer my services to my lady?"

Reynaud knew he'd gone too far, but did it really matter? What was it to him if Brielle d'Avignon was determined to get to the Holy Land on a hope no more substantial than a puff of wind? And what need was there to be so sharp? He could tell by the look on her exquisite features that she was furious with him. Of course—he'd insulted her father's sergeant at arms, after overhearing her voice very real doubts about himself.

But he was normally above taking offense at such a trivial thing. And John the Gaunt was evidently physically handicapped.

"What ails your arm?" he asked, softening his tone.

He watched John's expression grow closed, while Brielle looked from Reynaud to the man-at-arms, and back to Reynaud again, her expression turning hopeful. She'd mentioned his magical touch earlier . . . did she think him a sorcerer? A man who could perform miracles?

Reynaud wanted to laugh aloud at the irony of it, but a man's pride was involved here.

". . . bone was shattered," John the Gaunt was saying with obvious reluctance, "and it did not heal right."

Reynaud lowered his voice. "Did you see a Christian physician or an Arab?"

John dropped his gaze, and Reynaud felt rather than saw Brielle's questioning look. "Surely after spending some years in Outremer you are aware of the superiority of Arab physicians!" His softly-spoken words were almost fierce with impatience and disbelief.

"I would never go to an infidel doctor!" John said.

Reynaud merely smiled without humor, the light from a single torch nearby dancing in the wind and flickering across his features, giving them a menacing cast. "Surely you personally know a few Arabs, John the Gaunt? Mayhap have traded with or bought from Arab merchants? Why, some of them are even *Christians!*" He relaxed his tone to ease the impact of his stinging words and watched John grit his teeth, knowing the man made his living by fighting and not matching wits. But when it came to a man's arm, only a fool living in Outremer wouldn't seek out a good Arab physician. "Come below," he said.

"Are you skilled at healing?" John asked bluntly. "At resetting a bone that was skewed?" The tone of his voice left no doubt that he didn't believe the possibility for a moment.

Brielle looked up at the man-at-arms. "Please, John. Let him look at your arm. I'll come with you and—"

" 'Tis crowded enough down there as it is," Reynaud interrupted her. "And since your friend Anabette is sleeping now, I would have thought you eager to remain up here beneath the stars while you caught a few hours sleep yourself."

He watched the disappointment cross her features and felt a spurt of guilt. But there was no reason for her to be present while he examined John's arm. (There was, no doubt, little he could do anyway.) She needed her rest, now more than ever, for the climate in the Levant sapped one's energy—especially someone unaccustomed to the blistering summer heat inland from the mountains.

John the Gaunt said, "Aye, my lady. There's no need for you to come below when you can sleep up here in the fresh air."

Reynaud watched her through his lashes. *So you're both set against it,* her deep blue eyes seemed to accuse him. They were as dark as the sea around them.

"You won't be missing anything," Reynaud assured her, his tone placating and somehow insulting at the same time. He could tell she took it the wrong way, but he was tired himself, and weary of trying to say exactly the right things to a female who was foolish enough to travel to the Holy Land to search for a dead man.

"There's truly naught to be done," John said then. "Why don't you go to sleep, my lady, and I'll do the same. We're wasting Sieur Reynaud's time."

As if he would draw St. Rémy away from Brielle, John nodded to them both and swung away with a mumbled, "I'll see to the horses first."

Brielle watched him pick his way around those passengers who were sleeping on deck. "You chased him away!" she accused Reynaud softly. "I would have had you look at his arm. It pains him greatly, I know."

"Now I'm your servant, to do your bidding?" He arched an eyebrow at her. "Just what did you think could be accomplished below, Lady Brielle? I'm no sorcerer."

They stood staring at each other, the wind whispering around them, the torchlight hissing and flickering in the darkness, an occasional mumble or snore from the sleeping souls around them breaking the silence. But not the tension.

"Never mind, *chevalier.* Forgive my boldness. . . . 'Twas merely misplaced confidence." She swung back to the rail, hoping he would leave, for although she wanted nothing more than to walk away, she had nowhere beside the lower deck to go. The thought of that stuffy, confined place was enough to root her to the spot, in spite of the irritating knight standing behind her.

"Indeed, *demoiselle,* 'twas misplaced."

Damn her, he thought, as he moved toward the lower deck to look in on Anabette. How could she be so certain he could do anything for the man-at-arms when all he'd done was touch the cut on her brow and soothe Anabette with a cold cloth and comforting words? Anyone could have done that.

But he kept seeing her talking and laughing with John the Gaunt up on deck, her face alight with obvious affection for her sire's loyal man. And also a sheer love for life that went with youth and innocence. It had come to him then that Brielle d'Avignon had less reason to laugh than many well-born females—having been forced to live in a convent because of a wicked brother, and then having lost her beloved father, forced to face spending the rest of her life at St. Bernadette's.

And Reynaud understood what it was to keenly love a father. He could even understand—although he would never admit it to Brielle d'Avignon—why she was so determined to search for her sire, and why she refused to acknowledge that he was dead.

Yet she was young and resilient, he had concluded, and had not seen enough of man's follies to evince the same crushing disillusionment as he. . . .

When he reached the tiny cell where Anabette lay, he found Taillefer sleeping on the floor beside the girl's pallet. *Dieu,* but the minstrel was smitten! The air was barely breathable, but there he slept like a hound at his mistress's feet. Taillefer, who hated to step on a ship, let alone be confined to its lower deck.

He swung away and strode back toward where the animals were kept, thinking of Brielle d'Avignon and her misplaced faith. If ever there was a man who didn't deserve it, it was he, for he found it increasingly difficult not to offer his help—especially to a man who sustained an injury while fighting for what he believed was right in the Holy Land. But he was a softhearted fool.

And he had found the appeal in the very fine eyes of a certain maiden irresistible.

That was the crux of the problem, he mused as he neared the area of the hold where the horses were kept. He nodded at Humphrey of Toulouse, one of the other Templars chosen to ride in the bishop's escort; as the latter moved by him in the narrow passageway, Reynaud hoped the man wouldn't question his going to tend the animals when Humphrey had obviously just done so.

Aye, he acknowledged to himself again. If it weren't for this accursed "gift" he had, he would of a certainty have been happier in his chosen rôle in life. But no. God, in His infinite wisdom, he thought bitterly, had given him the touch that soothed and healed both Christian and infidel alike, and in doing so had turned Reynaud's life upside down. To say nothing of his philosophy, his religious beliefs, his very principles. . . .

It was also something he found very necessary—and very difficult—to keep hidden, and knew its discovery by the wrong people could easily cost him his life.

The smell of horseflesh and warm manure came to him over the underlying stink of pure, primitive fear, for no creature liked being closed up in the dark and airless hold of a ship bobbing at sea. The vessel was constantly rocking, however gently, on the best of seas. But storms reduced the horses, as well as the human passengers, to panic.

Swallowing his gorge against the stench, Reynaud moved into the makeshift pen where the horses were tied down. He moved immediately to Khamsin, taking the war horse's halter in one hand, and smoothing his other palm down the animal's long, sleek neck. Immediately, he could feel a calmness come over the stallion, and he spoke softly into its ear.

John the Gaunt was painstakingly scraping and shoveling waste, a slow and awkward task for a man with only one useful arm. The other hung stiffly, half-bent, at his left side. Reynaud remained a moment with Khamsin, then moved between the crude and crowded stalls toward the man-at-arms. "John?" he said in a voice just loud enough to be heard over the creaking ship and the neighing of the horses.

John halted his movements and looked up, surprised.

"I am not so ungracious a man as to refuse a beautiful young woman's request—or ignore a fellow crusader's needs. Although, I warn you, I am no physician."

John frowned. "My lady sent you?"

"Not exactly, but I saw her concern for you."

The older man grudgingly put aside the shovel and pushed up his tunic sleeve. Reynaud stepped closer and gently raised the arm by the elbow. He didn't watch John's expression, but rather felt the tightening of his body, which indicated the movement caused him pain; he immediately stopped and began to gently run his fingers along the arm from elbow to wrist and back.

He carefully kneaded the lax muscle beneath John's skin, feeling where the bone had not healed properly and realizing how much pain the injured arm had to be causing. "You'll never have full use of it again . . . but then you probably know that."

"Aye." The one word was weighted with resignation to a fate far from desirable.

Reynaud stilled for a few moments, his eyes still on John's exposed arm. He concentrated on taking the pain unto himself, pictured it lifting up from John's body and disappearing.

As he concentrated, John stood absolutely still; the horses were eerily quiet, even the rocking of the ship seemed to subside. Reynaud felt a deep and familiar serenity settle over him, as he did whenever the small miracle occurred, and was suddenly confident that he would be able, in some way, to help this faithful sergeant at arms of Geoffrey d'Avignon.

The irony was that it was never a sure thing. He had had only sporadic success, with which he had begun to experiment before he'd journeyed to the Holy Land. Once in Outremer, however, it seemed the beneficent power was always at his fingertips. . . .

His eyes met John's. The latter's were suddenly filled with wonder. "The pain—the pain is fading . . ." He stared down at his crippled arm as if he couldn't quite comprehend it. " 'Tis almost . . . gone."

"As far as you are concerned, it never happened."

John's chin slowly lifted and his eyes met Reynaud's once again.

"If you would express your gratitude, direct it to God. Do you understand? And don't tell a soul this happened. Who's to know that your pain didn't subside on its own?" Reynaud released his arm. "Who's to say I didn't touch your arm at the exact moment God chose to free you from the discomfort?"

Comprehension spread across John the Gaunt's face.

"You will give me your word, as one man to another?"

"I will thank God for sending you, St. Rémy," John answered softly, his face radiant. "And I will honor your request—you have my word. I will say naught of it. . . ."

Five

Taillefer helped Anabette to the deck the next day. And, as Brielle had suspected, the girl immediately began to perk up. They'd sailed southeast from Marseilles and down the coast of the Italian city-states. Now, in the open waters of the Mediterranean Sea above Africa, the weather had warmed, the water calmed—at least for the time being. It was a breathtaking day, the sky a cobalt dome, the sea like glass, and beneath the benign rays of the spring sun Anabette's pallor began to recede. Her spirits took a turn for the better too, and as Brielle watched the breeze catch and lift hanks of the girl's now dull and stringy hair, she was grateful for the improvement. So grateful that she could almost forget Anabette's deception.

" 'Twas *his* decision to make me stay in that hole," she told Brielle with soft fervor when Taillefer was out of ear-shot.

Brielle knew exactly whom she meant and felt a sudden and inexplicable urge to defend him. After all, Anabette's nausea had subsided during the night, and she certainly appeared better able to face her new surroundings today than she had yesterday. Maybe the Templar had known best . . . hadn't really refused to allow her to leave the pallet before today out of spite, as Anabette implied.

And the weather was perfect—almost as if Reynaud de St. Rémy had been able to conjure up the day.

"He's a strange one," Anabette continued with a frown, "so splendid-looking and impressive on the outside, but dark and devious within."

Brielle looked at her sharply. "Dark and devious? Because he didn't permit you to come up on deck before this morn?" She shook her head as she regarded her friend. "He allowed you to carry through your plan—persuaded Bishop Abelard to accept your presence in spite of your father's certain displeasure."

She watched Anabette draw in a deep breath of sea air. "Nay, *chère,* rather I think he allowed me to come along because of John the Gaunt. The man knew and served your father—spent time in the Holy Land fighting beside Sieur Geoffrey. He could be useful."

"But what has that to do with anything?"

Anabette gave her a knowing look. "The man-at-arms can provide further protection for you."

The idea was somehow flattering to Brielle, but she doubted if that were the case. "More, I think, to allow the *chevalier* the freedom to which he must be accustomed while John watches over me." She tossed her blowing hair over one shoulder. "He's a Templar, Anabette, with his own plans, and the bishop is to act as substitute for the Archbishop of Tyre. His Excellency cannot waste precious time helping me. 'Twas enough he permitted me to come along, so I think mayhap you're right. About John being useful where I'm concerned. . . ."

"I still say St. Rémy is withdrawn and strange—and in such a hurry to foist you off on John! And didn't you say he was dead set against your wish to accompany the bishop in the first place?"

Brielle caught sight of Rashid speaking to St. Rémy, and saw, even from a short distance, the reverence in the Arab's whole attitude toward the Templar. Taillefer went striding by them, making a passing comment to the knight, which caused him to display one of his rare smiles. Then, as the minstrel moved toward the two women at the rail, Brielle realized that Anabette was suddenly behaving almost like her old self. Her tongue was certainly not exhausted, and she seemed to be miraculously thriving out here in the open air.

Brielle couldn't help but think of Reynaud de St. Rémy's special gift and how generously he shared it. She narrowed her eyes at Anabette just as Taillefer was moving toward them, wondering how her friend, who at first was intrigued by the knight, could call him dark and devious.

Irked by the girl's lack of gratitude, Brielle acknowledged Taillefer's greeting before turning away. She wanted to speak to John the Gaunt but hadn't seen him since he'd left her last night. Instead, she saw Bishop Abelard.

"I see Anabette is feeling better," the cleric commented. " 'Tis remarkable, I think, so soon after she was ill."

Brielle's mouth curved slightly, for she liked this tall and youthful bishop with the calm demeanor and seeming wisdom of someone far older. "She was in good hands, my lord bishop."

He glanced away, his expression turning thoughtful. "As all God's children are."

Brielle was about to disagree, for he obviously was referring to God, when she was positive Reynaud de St. Rémy had performed a minor miracle. Then she remembered the Templar's denials regarding anything out of the ordinary about his healing skills. She bit her lip to prevent herself from giving the cleric her opinion . . . and possibly committing blasphemy in his eyes, in the process.

". . . you've fared well, child," he was saying with a smile. "You seem to blossom beneath the Mediterranean sun."

" 'Tis lovely except when we encounter bad weather. I've never seen the sky so blue, nor the air so fresh. I think I will love the Holy Land for its climate as well as its religious significance."

Bishop Abelard shook his head, his gaze moving up to the half-filled canvas overhead then scanning the sea about them.

"Indeed, 'tis beautiful, *mon enfant,* but this is yet spring. The Levant can be harsh, especially on the east side of the mountains, so I've heard."

Brielle frowned, and he explained. "The Levant refers to the lands bordering the Eastern shores of the Mediterranean." At her nod, he continued, "Sieur Reynaud has been telling me much about life in Outremer."

"You've never been there before?"

He shook his head as the breeze lifted the hem of his pale robes and then capriciously dropped it. "I consider myself most fortunate to be going to Tyre. I've waited a long time to make a pilgrimage to Jerusalem—although now 'tis in Muslim hands. But the Christians shall liberate it once again, and soon. 'Twill be a sight to behold."

He looked off toward the horizon, his expression calm, his eyes full of hope. He seemed lost in his thoughts for long moments.

"Know you much about Tyre?" she asked, in an attempt to draw him back.

His gaze met hers. "Nay. But Sieur Reynaud has promised to tell me all about it. And I shall hold him to his promise."

"My lord bishop . . ." she began hesitantly, "know you anything more about my father? You said he'd stayed at your monastery and—"

"And John the Gaunt, as well. I could hardly refuse such a good and loyal man permission to search for his lord, even though St. Rémy considers it futile." Then, as if he realized how hopeless the statement sounded, he quickly amended, "That, of course, is his opinion. John thinks otherwise."

"What do you think?"

He shrugged, his eyes full of sympathy as they rested on her. "I can only hope and pray John is right. I don't know much of such things as Arab dungeons. I know the infidels will hold men for ransom, but not for how long a period."

Brielle felt her spirits drop. "I don't know who would have ransomed him—surely not anyone I'm aware of in Outremer, and were word to have reached my brother, of a certainty he wouldn't have paid out his precious gold. Not even for my father." She couldn't keep the bitterness from her words, and Brielle thought that if ever she learned that Reginald had refused ransom payment for his own father, she would never again acknowledge him as her kin.

Bishop Abelard rested a hand on her shoulder. "There is always hope, child. What qualities your brother may lack are more than made up for in you. You're a brave one, and I respect you all the more for it."

Brielle's lips trembled a bit as she tried to smile with grace and gratitude. "You flatter me overmuch, Bishop Abelard. I may be a fool, as the Templar has implied, but I cannot just give up on my father after hearing what John the Gaunt had to say."

The bishop nodded and squeezed her shoulder before he dropped his hand. "Where there is no hope, there is no life, Brielle d'Avignon. Remember that." He looked about the deck. "And speaking of John, know you where he is?"

"Not for certain, Your Excellency, but I have an idea. . . . If I see him, I'll tell him you wish to speak to him."

"Merci, cher enfant," he said, and moved away, leaving Brielle standing apart from Taillefer and Anabette, who were occupied with their surroundings—and each other. Relying on her instincts alone, she made her way down the ladder to the passageway below deck. John had a keen interest in horses and would no doubt spend more time with them than anyone beside squires or servants. And he'd expressed a special admiration for the Templar's midnight steed. . . .

As much as Brielle hated to go below, her curiosity was greater than her aversion. In the shadowy passageway, she encountered Rashid, and wondered if St. Rémy were nearby. That would certainly prevent her from questioning John. The Arab paused and gave her a respectful dip of his chin before he passed by. Brielle hoped he wouldn't tell the Templar of her obvious intentions as she made her way to where the animals were kept.

The stench was almost overwhelming, although she'd thought she might become accustomed to it after dealing with Anabette. But although the smell in Anabette's tiny cell had been bad, the odor of fear, of confined beasts and their waste was enough to make her fight back a gag, especially after the bracing sea air.

She found the man-at-arms speaking softly to the Templar's stallion. He stroked the horse's nose, for it appeared agitated—as did the others: as if they knew that if the vessel sank, they would be trapped within it and dragged to their deaths.

The animal was magnificent, even in the dimness. Sieur Geoffrey had taught her something about horses, and she knew from the first moment she'd seen Khamsin in the convent yard that many a man would have willingly paid a fortune to possess so fine an animal.

". . . Khamsin," John was saying. He suddenly looked up at her.

"I—I didn't mean to startle you," she told him. "I sought you out to tell you Bishop Abelard would speak with you—and also to ask about your arm."

John stepped away from the war-horse, his expression closed. His eyes wouldn't hold hers, which she found disturbing, for John the Gaunt had always been honest and forthright. "My arm is as it should be, my lady," he said simply. "I'll escort you back on deck so I can seek out His Excellence."

But Brielle wasn't about to be put off so easily. "John," she began, one hand going to his good arm, "tell me truly what St. Rémy did for you. Tell me if he—"

"My Lady Brielle," he said in a firm voice, "I can tell you naught more than that Sieur Reynaud relieved some of the pain by massaging it. He should have been a physician, for his touch is gentle and effective." The stallion tossed his head and blew out his breath restively. "We're disturbing Khamsin here, for he doesn't know you or the sound of your voice."

He took her by the elbow and turned her away. "Why would a Templar give his stallion an infidel name?" she asked suddenly, her thoughts momentarily diverted.

John shrugged. " 'Tis an Arab name, my lady. And not all Arabs are infidels."

She nodded. "And so St. Rémy said last eve . . . although 'tis hard to believe. Rashid is Muslim, I gather?"

"He is."

"Oh, but it would make more sense if he were Christian! 'Twould explain why the Templar allows him to serve him."

"Sieur Reynaud appears to be a good judge of men." The admiration in his voice told her what she wanted to know. That respect hadn't been so obvious the night before. "Come," he said as he guided her toward the passageway. " 'Tis no place for a lady."

She glanced down at his arm as they moved along. The lanterns placed along the walls shed some light on his form. The limb appeared relaxed and hung straight down at his side, when last night it had been stiff and half-bent. She was tempted to touch it, but thought better of it.

"Brielle, child," he said in a low, urgent voice, as if he read her thoughts, "nothing out of the ordinary happened last eve."

"I don't believe that, John. Why, look at your—"

John stopped and turned her to face him, his fingers communicating an urgency. "My arm is as it's been since I left Outremer . . ."—his expression was a combination of frustration and hope—" . . . useless!"

He'd never spoken to her like this before, and Brielle recognized it as a measure of his new loyalty to Reynaud de St. Rémy. "If you have any suspicions, there isn't much I can do or say to dissuade you—I know you that well, child. But you must consider Sieur Reynaud. 'Tis best left alone— whatever blessings we believe God has or has not bestowed upon him." His voice lowered even further. "I gave him my *word!*"

And your father would have done the same, his eyes seemed to say.

Brielle remembered the scene she'd witnessed in the chapel at St. Bernadette's. An extraordinary scene between a man and his God. Chills rippled through her at the memory. Reynaud de St. Rémy obviously had enough on his mind. If he'd asked John to give his word, then Brielle wouldn't blithely disregard the Templar's wishes.

She nodded and began to move along the narrow passageway. "Indeed, John, 'twould be a poor showing of gratitude. And how thoughtless of me to press you. I'll say naught . . . to anyone."

But Brielle knew, now with more certainty than ever, that the troubled Templar had been gifted by God, whether he wished it that way or not. Could that have been the reason for his apparent spiritual struggle in the chapel at the convent? It certainly made sense—Reynaud de St. Rémy railing at God for having given him a divine healing power that would make him revered by some, hated by others. Some would be jealous, and he would be feared by those who didn't understand, therefore putting his very life at risk. . . .

The Venetian captain, Paolo, was a capable and seasoned sailor. He was a small, wiry man, with a quick wit and sharp intelligence. His dark eyes scanned the skies then the horizon ahead. "We're making good time, my lord," he told Reynaud. "If the weather holds, we should make it within a fortnight."

"Barring pirates," Reynaud added with a frown. "Especially with an unprotected merchantman."

Paolo's dark brows flattened with affront. "My ship is not unprotected. I carry expert archers—enough to hold off a good-sized pirate galley."

"There's no such thing as a *good-sized* pirate anything,

capitano," Reynaud said with irony. "The first sign of corsairs can cause real panic, and they spell death and destruction even with an escort of war galleys."

"You worry overmuch, *cavaliere,"* the captain said. "We are heavy with horses and goods, 'tis true, but not only do we have our own archers, but you and your fellow knights, as well. And we have His Excellence aboard. God will not turn a deaf ear to us."

Reynaud thought the captain a little naive—maybe it was the reason the fare had been so reasonable—but said nothing further to contradict the man's obvious beliefs. He'd been on a merchantman once when they'd been attacked by Turkish pirates. He would never forget the terror on the faces of the passengers, who no doubt had heard of the horrors perpetrated by any number of miscreants around the Mediterranean; the screams of the horses as the ship had gone down.

He glanced around at the passengers—mostly male pilgrims on their way to the Holy Land, a few women, and about a score of knights, including the bishop's party. They were in the open Mediterranean now, fair game for Levantine and Turkish pirates, Barbary corsairs . . . any number of predators who'd been scavenging the area for centuries.

But by the looks of Paolo's crewmen, many of them could have come from the ranks of corsairs and pirates themselves—with their daggers and wicked-looking cutlasses hanging menacingly from the colorful sashes about their waists. And surely if that were the case, they were as well-prepared as any to counter an attack.

Reynaud sighed inwardly. Sea predators were always a threat—so why was he suddenly so concerned? He'd recommended to the bishop that they travel over land as little as possible, even though as a knight he'd have preferred *terra firma* beneath his feet.

Mayhap it was because he'd heard that sailors considered females on board bad luck. And, although he wasn't particularly superstitious, in this instance he couldn't think of

Brielle d'Avignon and her conniving companion as anything but foul luck even in the best circumstances.

At that precise moment he caught sight of John the Gaunt assisting Brielle onto the deck. His brows met in a frown, for he didn't like what that implied. There was no reason for the young woman to have been below deck in this beautiful weather, especially now that Anabette was feeling better and on deck herself.

His first mistake had been ministering to Anabette in the first place. She'd deserved to suffer from a little seasickness after the trick she'd played on them all—including Brielle. Much as he might have wanted to, Reynaud couldn't blame Brielle d'Avignon for her friend's brazen behavior.

But now his irritation was directed at the young woman whom, he was certain, had plied John the Gaunt with any number of questions regarding the condition of his arm. He wondered how the toughened man-at-arms had handled her curiosity.

He watched Brielle as she emerged into the sun-drenched day, her golden-brown hair burnished to a shade reminding him of light filtering through the finest mead. The sapphire linen skirt she wore—one of two she'd brought from St. Bernadette's—fluttered about her ankles in the breeze, and a slim gold chain cinched her small waist. Fine kid slippers encased her feet, their thin ankle lacings emphasizing dainty ankles. He thought it a sign of Geoffrey d'Avignon's love that she was simply but well dressed. Abbess Marguerite had told him that her mother was dead, and her only brother was half a score of years older. Reginald, Brielle had named him, and not worth anything so precious as salt. Reynaud remembered the unmistakable bitterness in her voice.

He gave his head a slight shake and moved away from the captain, who was talking to another crew member. Brielle d'Avignon was creeping into his thoughts much too often. He glanced over at Taillefer and Anabette, his lips unconsciously tightening with annoyance. The minstrel was allow-

ing the other wench to occupy too much of *his* time and
thoughts as well. She was Brielle's responsibility, or so he'd
named her, unfair as it may have been. Taillefer had better
things to do than keep Anabette entertained. Like help tend
the horses below who were chained to the floor to protect
them from themselves in their distress.

What bothered him more than anything, however, was the
fact that Brielle d'Avignon had obviously been speaking to
John the Gaunt, and therefore he could only assume the
worst: that she'd questioned the man-at-arms about the condition of his arm.

He resisted the urge to roll his eyes. A bishop was no
problem—even one who'd never been to the Levant before.
But two untried girls . . .

Even without pirates, God help them all!

Brielle couldn't help but notice Reynaud de St. Rémy's
long, hose-clad legs as he walked toward them. All too
quickly, however, she saw his brow grow darker as he came
nearer, and she guessed his thoughts. Rather than suffer his
censure, she would find a way to subtly put him at ease about
her speaking to John.

"I thought to help John, my lord Templar," she said, "with
the animals."

It sounded rather pathetic, she thought, as she heard the
words emerge from her mouth. But she succeeded, at least
for the moment, in shifting the Templar's attention. As he
glanced down at the hem of her skirt, he said, "Your gown
will need the same attention as my spare tunic, I'm afraid."
He looked up to watch as enchanting color bathed her
cheeks.

"My lady was well-intentioned," John said gruffly. "She's
always been a considerate child." Then he looked sheepishly
at Brielle, obviously embarrassed at having called her a child.

But Reynaud stepped in. "Obviously, you've known the

demoiselle for most, if not all, of her life. How good of you to defend her."

He didn't look convinced, however, to Brielle. "I pity the horses, Sieur Reynaud," she said, a faint frown creasing her brow. "Surely there must be something to calm them?"

He shook his head, the breeze ruffling his chestnut hair. Brielle noticed the red-gold highlights brought out by the sun. His long lashes partly shielded his golden eyes, narrowed against the sun's glare on the water. " 'Twould only make them groggy."

"But wouldn't that be better than their fear?"

"They need to be ready for use as soon as we reach Tyre."

He was being perverse, she thought, wondering now why she'd even bothered to steer the conversation away from John's arm . . . not that she wished for any gratitude on his part for trying to put him at ease.

"Forgive me, my lord, but I'm not totally ignorant in such matters. My father kept only the best horses, and I had one of my own. I think the animals would be as useless from being in a constant state of fright for the duration of the journey as from any effects of a potion to calm them."

She watched his dark brows lift. "Indeed, *demoiselle*. And how many sea voyages have you made with horses on board?"

Brielle dropped her gaze to the deck before her, lest he see the ire that was surely burning in her eyes. In all the years at St. Bernadette's, she hadn't felt as much anger as she had since she'd met Reynaud de St. Rémy.

She felt John stiffen at her side, as well, obviously offended for her sake at the Templar's words. It seemed she could do nothing to win his favor—not that she necessarily wished to. Yet she sensed that having Reynaud de St. Rémy as an ally would be a real advantage in any situation.

That is she thought nastily, if one could put up with his sour disposition and his arrogance.

"If I sound unduly harsh," Reynaud added unexpectedly,

" 'tis merely that I am responsible for you, *demoiselle,* and I take my responsibilities seriously. I'm afraid I must ask you to stay away from the horses for the rest of the journey . . . for your own safety."

Her chin jerked up, and at the outright rebellion in her ocean-blue eyes, he felt compelled to add, "I suspect if you spend more time with Anabette, Taillefer will be freer to help John here care for the horses . . . a task for which he is well-paid."

"Perhaps 'tis for the best, my lady," John interjected here, in a placating tone. "I appreciate your efforts to be of help, but the Templar is right. 'Tis dangerous for anyone—let alone a young woman—to be around the horses until we're back on land."

As if hearing his name, Taillefer left Anabette at the rail and approached them. Before anyone could speak, however, a shout from a crewman clinging to a tiny platform high up in the masts rang out over the deck. Brielle raised her gaze, shielding her eyes against the sun with one hand, a shadow of alarm suddenly dimming the brilliance of the day.

The captain called up a question to his man, then the sailor pointed south, and let go a stream of words in his native Italian. Even if the language hadn't been so similar to French—even if the voice hadn't had the ring of panic, and even had the man not been pointing emphatically toward the southern horizon, a prickling sensation along the back of her neck would have warned Brielle. Or perhaps it was Reynaud St. Rémy's expression that caused her unease, for it wasn't fear as much as instant comprehension followed by a brief narrowing of his eyes.

His gaze followed the sailor's pointing arm, as did that of virtually everyone aboard the merchantman. There was no worry or fear distorting his chiseled profile, but rather the almost tangible mantle of determination settling over him: the set of grim purpose.

John clutched her arm as Reynaud and Taillefer strode

over to the rail. Brielle strained to see what the sailor had
observed from the rigging, but couldn't. As she moved to
follow the men, she felt Anabette's questioning gaze, but
ignored it. Now was no time to coddle the girl. Her innate
boldness would be needed to deal with any crisis that might
be in the making.

A spate of Italian broke out among some of the crew members, and Brielle saw Reynaud throw the captain a searching
look. Or was it a warning? Then Taillefer pointed to something in the distance, speaking into the Templar's ear, and
the latter nodded as his hand shielded his eyes.

The captain called once again to the sailor still aloft, and
the man answered back with one word. In that moment, Reynaud whirled from the rail and strode toward Brielle and
John. "Take your friend and go below," he said to her. *"Now.*
And don't come back on deck until I tell you. Do you understand?"

Brielle nodded and swung toward Anabette, accustomed
to taking orders from the nuns at St. Bernadette's. Those
simple commands, however, were a far cry from the commanding tone of this Templar knight. And the bleak look on
his face.

Six

"Back into the *hold?*"

Brielle saw pure disbelief pass through Anabette's eyes. And a trace of fear. " 'Tis what the Templar told me, Anabette. Now come."

Anabette balked, her eyes going briefly to Taillefer. He was, however, in deep discussion with Reynaud and the captain. She looked back at Brielle, her hand on the rail tightening visibly. "I'll never go back there! I don't care if they see Saladin himself on the horizon!"

"There's no reason for alarm, *chère*. 'Tis only a precaution," Brielle lied, wondering what happened to Anabette's bravado. Of course, the girl had been very ill. . . .

"I'm not alarmed!" Anabette insisted, her voice becoming shrill. Brielle fought the urge to cover her friend's mouth. Fortunately, the rising babble of voices around them helped cover up Anabette's near-frantic tone.

The entire atmosphere on board the ship changed suddenly, as if everyone, including the passengers, knew exactly what threat the crew believed had appeared on the southern horizon. Even a deaf and blind person would have sensed it, Brielle thought.

As if realizing how she sounded, Anabette tried to smile. "They just want to get rid of us and keep all the excitement to themselves," she declared. "Not even the horses deserve to be kept down there!" But the color that had begun to return to her cheeks was fading away even as she spoke, indicating the extent of her fear.

Brielle put an arm about her friend's thin shoulders. "Come now, Anabette," she chided, " 'tis only for a short while—the Templar said as much." She was lying again, hating the lie but feeling it was justified in that moment. She was also beginning to feel real trepidation herself, and even though one part of her was curious about what had been sighted to the south, another, more cautious, and sensible side urged her to obey St. Rémy's order.

As she half-pulled, half-led Anabette toward the hatch, she tried to get a glimpse of the sea to the south, but there were too many people in the way, and she was afraid to let go of Anabette.

Voices rose like an incoming tide to swell across the deck in a wave of panic. As if it traveled on the wind, word had already spread of the unidentified danger in the distance. Several feminine shrieks sounded as the women aboard began moving quickly toward the hatch; following the lead of some of the crew members, other men began to automatically take up positions along the freeboards. Crossbows were readied, faces grim—some surprised, others disbelieving, all displaying a growing determination in the face of uncertainty.

Brielle, however, had neither the time nor the inclination to more closely examine the reactions of those around her. "Come, 'Bette," she urged. "Here, let me help you." She used her pet name for her friend, hoping to coax some cooperation from her.

But Anabette began to struggle against her hold. "I will *not* be trapped like a drowning rat!" she insisted, her brown eyes wide with fear. "They'll come below and kill us in an instant! At least on deck we have—"

"You have *what, demoiselle?*" insisted Reynaud de St. Rémy's voice. He was suddenly before them, looking very displeased. Passengers heading for the hatch cut around him as if he were an island in a sea of panic.

"Where's Taillefer?" Anabette asked, looking around wildly.

"Taillefer is busy," he answered, "obeying orders, as you should be." He looked at Brielle. "Take her below. You'll both be safer there for now."

"Safer?" Anabette echoed, suddenly leaning heavily into Brielle. "You mean safely out of the *way.* Then when the pirates finish with you, they'll come for us . . . there'll be nowhere to hide!"

"Do you wish me to carry you?" he asked softly, pinning her with a piercing stare.

The memory of being in his arms hit Brielle unexpectedly, a potent image for all its brevity. She dismissed it and tightened her hold on Anabette. "Come, 'Bette," she said firmly, and pulled the obstinate young woman along, throwing the Templar one last look. But he was already swinging away, as if the matter was settled, and Brielle didn't know if it was due to his confidence in his own authority or his confidence in her ability to handle Anabette.

In the back of her mind, nevertheless, was the thought that Anabette was correct in her assessment of the situation . . . in fearing being trapped below. And Brielle wondered if she, too, could remain in the hold while freedom, fresh air, and action were denied them because of the threat of a corsair's arrow—if the vessel or vessels moving toward them were, indeed, marauders.

There were two brightly painted war galleys, the ships preferred by pirates and corsairs for their speed and maneuverability, moving toward them.

"Dalmatian pirates, mayhap?" Reynaud had asked Captain Paolo, thinking of the plunderers from Dalmatia, directly across the Adriatic from the Italian peninsula, who'd been preying on Venetian, Genoan, and Pisan ships. It was unfortunate enough that these maritime republics of Italy were intermittently at war among themselves. The pirates only complicated things; no one was immune to their attacks.

Reynaud had assured the captain that every one of the men in the bishop's party could accurately shoot a crossbow. Even as he said the words, however, he made note of crew members readying their own bows as they took up defensive positions.

"God help us, no matter what kind of *piratas* they should be!" Paolo replied fervently.

"I thought he said he was prepared for anything," Taillefer said from behind Reynaud. "The safety of the passengers is his responsibility—we paid him enough ducats for our passage." He held a short bow loosely in one hand—an indication of just how serious the situation was, his normally easy-going expression strained.

"I've only lost one ship to *piratas*," Paolo announced with drama, one hand raised as if he were swearing to God above.

Reynaud wondered how many more he wasn't admitting to, but that was the chance one took with any privately owned ship. And whether Captain Paolo was a liar or not, he was still a Venetian sailor—the best money could buy. He'd have been worse than a fool to sail the Mediterranean without means of protection from sea-faring marauders. An escort of war galleys would have been ideal for a fleet of merchantmen, but not financially feasible for a single vessel.

And Bishop Abelard had dismissed the idea of waiting for the more reassuring safety of a fleet.

"Do my men look ill-prepared, *signore?*" Paolo asked, his dark gaze going to the minstrel.

Reynaud followed Taillefer's narrowed eyes as the latter took in the *Madonna*'s crew members interspersed among the other men still lining up along both sides of the ship. There was no mistaking their identity—some of them looked as frightening as corsairs themselves with their sword- and dagger-weighted sashes; and Reynaud knew that legitimate captains sometimes recruited from the ranks of such men

because of their sailing skills. He'd also heard of their re-
nowned cunning and courage when face to face with an enemy.

"No, they do not, *capitano,*" Reynaud answered for Taillefer. Perhaps it was the minstrel's unexpected infatuation with
Anabette that made him seem to forget the Venetian penchant
for being overdramatic. "The only thing Taillefer here hates
more than sailing is bloodshed. It interferes most inconven-
iently with his making a living."

"And loving the ladies," Rashid added from nearby, drawing a crooked half-grin from the minstrel.

Reynaud turned and strode to the freeboard, shouldering
his way through several knights to make a place. There appeared still to be only the two vessels bearing down on the
Madonna. His mouth quirked ironically. "Only" was an inadequate word to describe the threat of a war galley. Even
one would have been cause for alarm, but two warships
would be formidable opponents for an unescorted merchantman . . . even if the attacking vessels were captained by im-
beciles.

If Reynaud de St. Rémy's faith in God and the Church
had been shaken lately, it did not apply to his confidence in
the men who formed the bishop's escort. Most of the knights
had been to the Holy Land and knew how to handle a weapon
with skill. And the Templars with him were among the best
fighting men in Outremer. Knights armed with lances and
the powerful crossbows, backed by the archers among the
Madonna's crew, would hopefully discourage the cutthroats
closing in on them from boarding.

If not, with God's help—or a little simple luck—the men
defending the *Madonna* could fend them off and send them
running. . . .

Brielle watched as Anabette lay curled upon the pallet.
Her arms were crossed over her stomach, as if she were feel-

ing nauseous again or in pain. "I didn't flee St. Bernadette's and seek out John the Gaunt only to end up like *this,*" she cried thinly. "Rather I should suffer an arrow through the heart from a Saracen!"

That comment proved too much for Brielle. "And possibly cause the death of one of the men . . . even Taillefer?" she asked in irritation, her patience with her friend at an end. "Reynaud told us to go below. Here we are, and here we stay until we're told otherwise."

Anabette raised her head, her eyes bloodshot, her cheeks tear-streaked. "How can they tell us aught if they're *dead?* And if they're overrun by corsairs, we'll go down with this hulking vessel!"

"Why would attacking pirates sink the *Madonna?*" Brielle asked in exasperation. "She's laden with valuable cargo."

"Then we'll end up being ravished. And if we live, sold into slavery—end up in some harem!" She struggled to a sitting position.

A chill moved through Brielle at the thought, and she wondered briefly where Anabette had heard such horrible tales.

She drew in a sustaining breath. "Please, Anabette," she entreated. "Let the men protect the ship. Surely we'll only be in the way of the fighting. . . ." She trailed off, sounding more like Anabette to her own ears as she spoke in a similarly negative vein.

She realized she was just as frightened as Anabette, and it was showing through her words. Yet the idea of being trapped in the hold was every bit as terrifying to her as it obviously was to her friend.

"You see?" Anabette said. "Even you admit there will be fighting—that we're going to be attacked by pirates. I say we hide ourselves somewhere on deck before they can strike us. . . ."

"How could we do that without drawing attention?" Brielle mused aloud. " 'Twould be better, mayhap, if we waited until the men were distracted by the attackers . . ."

"My master will be supremely unhappy if you disobey his orders."

Both young women's heads jerked toward the doorway of the crude cabin. Rashid loomed within its shadowy outline, his pale robes and *keffiya* making him look more like a wraith than a man.

Brielle noted the unsheathed scimitar in one hand and thought it odd to see him acting as anything but a manservant to the Templar.

"He's not *our* master," Anabette snapped, "no matter what you consider him . . . and neither are you!"

He stepped into the room. "You are even more foolish than most females," he told her, but his dark eyes went to Brielle. "It is not a matter of slavish obedience as much as intelligence. My master's task is to deliver the clergyman and yourselves to Tyre safely. Only a fool would rush unarmed into full view of an attacking enemy."

" 'Twas merely our fear and uncertainty speaking," Brielle told him, unexpectedly resenting the fact that this strange infidel was relegating them to the status of "foolish females."

As if having used up the last reserve of her energy with her sharp retort, Anabette collapsed with a sob, for the moment at least, done with arguing.

Rashid arched a brow at Brielle, as if he doubted the truth of her words.

She frowned, disliking his obvious opinion of her. "I give you my word that we will remain here until told otherwise."

The Arab studied her for a long moment, then nodded slowly. "And I will hold you to your word, *demoiselle,*" he said in perfect imitation of St. Rémy. "We do not need any distractions while dealing with corsairs." He glanced at Anabette. "And you?"

But Anabette was obviously too weak and caught up in her own misery to bother answering.

Rashid's gaze returned to Brielle. "You can give your word

for yourself, but not for her. It is hard enough to keep one's own word."

"She is my friend," Brielle said stubbornly. "I give my word for both of us."

Rashid bowed slightly in acknowledgment. "As you wish. The burden is yours."

Brielle sat beside the weeping Anabette, trying to console her, although the best thing would be for the girl to sleep. Brielle's thoughts drifted elsewhere—to the men above—in particular, Reynaud de St. Rémy. And with every shout, every thump overhead, her growing anxiety increased. Other women began to cram the narrow passageway, their voices hushed yet laced with panic. Some of them spilled into the cell where Brielle and Anabette waited, making the walls seem to close in, the air become even more stale.

"God deliver us!" one woman said in French, her arms cradling an infant.

Another, in a nun's garb, was muttering prayers under her breath, her eyes squeezed tightly shut as her fingers worked the beads of her rosary; and at that familiar and somewhat comforting sight, Brielle lowered her own head, feeling the weight of despair creep over her. To finally succeed in traveling to the Holy Land to search for her father, only to be attacked and killed by marauding corsairs. . . .

A hand on her shoulder calmed her unexpectedly. Brielle raised her eyes to meet the somber and concerned regard of Bishop Abelard, and sudden hope chased away her growing fears.

Reynaud sent John and another man to look in on the animals, in particular the horses. If their fetters didn't hold, they could easily injure themselves . . . or any man who attempted to correct the situation.

Reynaud put Humphrey of Toulouse in command of the other side of the ship. Humphrey was an excellent marksman with crossbow and lance and a typically courageous Templar. Reynaud also put half the volunteer men at his disposal and kept the other half with him. Captain Paolo's crew members were surprisingly cooperative as Reynaud gave instructions. Anyone who could shoot a bow with any accuracy was posted along either freeboard, and those who were more skilled with sword or scimitar were to keep the archers supplied with quarrels or lances until the time (if it came) that the *Madonna* was boarded and the fighting required swordplay.

Now, in tense silence, they watched the galleys maneuver around the unwieldy merchantman, obviously headed for the best position from which to ram it broadside. The quiet on the deck was ominous as the men helplessly watched the corsairs maneuver to either side of the *Madonna*.

When the attackers were within shouting distance, Captain Paolo raised his speaking horn and offered gold and goods in exchange for their lives and his ship. The men in the two galleys now on either side of the *Madonna* laughed with raucous glee at his offer.

Reynaud felt his heart sink at their outright refusal, but he really hadn't expected them to agree to anything less than completely taking over the vessel and dispatching those passengers who would be of little value on the slave market. He watched the interlopers with narrowed eyes that began to ache from the brightness of thousands of sparkling diamonds strewn over the water beneath the sun. Unbidden, Brielle d'Avignon's image rose before him, her beautiful face bloodied and a corsair standing over her. . . .

"Why are we holding back?" Taillefer asked, as he stood ready with a supply of bolts for Reynaud, and arrows for his borrowed short bow.

Once, long ago, Reynaud had witnessed the minstrel's accuracy with bow and arrow. But that was then, and things had changed. Only if Reynaud ordered him to do so would Taillefer use the weapon.

"The closer they are, the more accurate our shots—the more efficient the penetration of the bolts," Reynaud answered, knowing the minstrel was hardly ignorant on the subject. The plan was to identify and then pick off the commander of each galley, and then his officers, all who normally directed the battle from the stern castle. Eight to ten sailors controlled the tiller and the rigging, and the best men stationed themselves on a low fighting platform in the bow and a higher one in the stern castle. Those fighting men would be next.

Of course, Reynaud knew that sailors on an official war galley were not averse to donning the leather breastplate of a fallen soldier and fighting on; a soldier could take the oar of a wounded oarsman if necessary; and the oarsmen themselves were known to grab a weapon to help fill depleting ranks. Hopefully the cutthroats on board these galleys were not so organized or disciplined as a Venetian galley of state.

And yet, if any of the corsairs had numbered at one time among the Turkish infantry, the defenders would have their hands full dodging the arrows.

The men defending the *Madonna* had to carefully pick their targets and be very accurate in their shots if they were to repulse the pirate-laden galleys. Reynaud couldn't afford to be distracted by worry for Humphrey and his men, and it wasn't really necessary. But the teamwork of the two sides of the *Madonna*'s defenders was of tantamount importance, for if one side were successful in fending off the pirates and the other was having less success, there was no guarantee that a joining of forces would change the tide.

"A colorful bunch, are they not?" Taillefer said, for Reynaud's ears alone. "I wonder if they can fight as well as they can pick out their rainbow assortment of clothing."

Reynaud found himself suppressing a grin, in spite of the grimness of the situation. "Have you never seen a corsair, *troubadour?*" he asked. "They take the best from the ships they plunder after making a hefty profit selling the stolen goods. They delight in wearing their stolen finery."

"Hmmmph," Taillefer grunted. "Looks to me like they choose first, then sell the leftovers . . . although I rather fancy the leader's scarlet head piece."

Reynaud glanced along the freeboard to see how the other men's patience was holding out, for he would not give the order to fire until the attackers were almost upon them. His look returned to Taillefer, amusement flashing briefly in his eyes.

"Mais bien sûr, mon ami," the minstrel added with a straight face, "the color would emphasize the blue of my eyes."

"Indeed," Rashid said from behind them. "Especially after our friends over there have carved them from their sockets."

Taillefer glanced sideways at the Arab, then sobered. "How does the Lady Anabette fare?" he asked. "And the Lady Brielle?"

Reynaud glanced at Rashid, before turning his attention back to the galley moving in to ram the *Madonna*. But he was also listening for the Arab's answer.

"The yellow-haired female lays prostrate upon the pallet and weeps like a fountain. The other was foolish enough to take responsibility for her friend. A most unwise thing, in light of the—"

"Choose your targets!" Reynaud cut across Rashid's words as he sighted the corsairs' captain. Rashid immediately squeezed in between Reynaud and the man beside him, grabbing up an extra short bow.

"Fire!" Reynaud cried. In answer to his first, well-aimed bolt, one of the men near the corsair commander sank to his knees, then pitched forward. Before Reynaud could even span the weapon again, he noted the first volley had effectively taken out several other officers around the commander and at least two of their archers on the galley's stern castle. At the same time, however, Reynaud heard several cries of pain from those aboard the *Madonna,* attesting to the accuracy of the attackers.

"Stay low!" he ordered, for the freeboard was good protection. A man was most vulnerable when he raised his shoulders above the board to shoot.

An arrow whizzed by his ear and thunked into solid wood—no doubt the main mast, but Reynaud didn't take the time to look as he sighted the commander of the pirate galley himself with his powerful crossbow. The corsair stood out like a signal flag as the ends of his red scarf fluttered in the wind. Beneath the scarlet silk the man was fiercely mustached, his bright clothing making a brazen statement about his confidence.

Reynaud took his time, even though the prow of the galley was lunging toward them, dozens of oars lifting and dipping in terrible unison. Killing a commander and as many of his officers as possible was vital to disabling the vessel chain of command. Once that was accomplished, the others aboard the galley might decide to retreat.

And Reynaud could only pray for Humphrey and the others. . . .

He released his quarrel, and his prayers were answered as the missile ripped through the commander's chest and out the other side with the deadly force that made it so formidable a weapon. The corsair leader slumped to the deck, his blood an obscene garnet fountain spurting into the sunshine. Enemy archers were going down. But there was no time to celebrate. For all their accuracy, crossbows were slower to span or load than conventional bows, and took more strength to do so.

Reynaud thought again of the men defending the *Madonna*'s other flank. . . .

He aimed and released another bolt, for there was no time to do anything else, and felled another archer on the war galley's stern castle. As well as they seemed to be doing, however, the attacking ship didn't appear to waver in its onslaught, and Reynaud found himself silently praying.

"Brace yourselves!" he called out. "And prepare for the worst."

The jolt was tremendous.. Those below were flung about like rag dolls, pitched from narrow pallets, while others thudded against walls and bulwarks with sickening impact. Wood groaned and splintered, sea water sprayed into the cell where Brielle and Anabette were staying.

And people screamed in terror. As long as Brielle lived, she would never forget the sound.

With admirable calm, Bishop Abelard tried to reassure those immediately around them, even though he'd been stunned himself as he'd come up hard against one side of the door frame. His cassock was torn, his miter had been knocked from his head and was nowhere in sight, but his steadiness was intact.

"I'm getting out of here!" Anabette said in a low, strange voice to Brielle, as the latter picked herself up from the rough wooden floor. The girl's eyes were on the bishop as he comforted several hysterical women. "If I'm to die, 'twill not be by drowning in this hole!" In spite of her obvious weakness, she pushed herself from the pallet, pale as death. Evidently being thrown to the floor had revived her enough to speak with a hint of her old spirit.

Brielle moved to stop her, then wondered if they would have a better chance of surviving if they managed to gain the deck. If they could hide, maybe they could escape the corsairs' notice—if there were anywhere now to hide. Or mayhap they could jump into the sea.

And swim all the way to Tyre? mocked a voice.

In frustration, her hands curled into fists at her sides, and she felt self-preservation begin to overpower obedience. So what if the Templar had told them to remain below? 'Twas easy for him to give orders when *he* was up on deck and knew what was happening.

A woman seated on the floor behind her was whispering, "Help me . . . help me . . ." and Brielle automatically swung toward her. She caught Bishop Abelard's eye and he moved toward them, his eyes going to the distraught woman.

The deck above suddenly resounded with footsteps, as Brielle turned back to Anabette.

But Anabette wasn't on the pallet. . . .

Brielle pushed her way to the door and out into the passageway, calling her friend's name. Even as several men demanded the hysterical passengers stay away from the hatch, Brielle saw a flash of yellow hair. . . .

Anabette was struggling with one of the crew members at the bottom of the hatchway ladder. The man looked like a corsair himself, with his heavy moustache and bright clothing. Weapons bristled from his belt. He was handling the girl as if she were a scrap of cloth, in spite of the fact that Anabette was putting up surprising resistance.

"No!" Brielle lunged forward, clawing her way past others in the crowded, narrow passageway. "Anabette!" she called in frustration, knowing that she could barely be heard above the hysterical cries around her and the growing din overhead.

"Unhand her!" she cried, when at last she reached the ladder.

The short but burly seaman shoved Anabette away and glared at Brielle. "Are you as foolish as her?" he asked in heavily-accented French, as she heard Anabette slam against the bulwark. He brought his face close to hers. "Because those trying to board us would like nothing better than to rape and murder every woman on this ship!" Renewed thumping sounded overhead. He glanced upward with an angry frown. "Mayhap we can use you two as diversions? Or would you rather we use the two of you to bargain for the *Madonna?*"

The women behind her had quieted somewhat, but Anabette was sliding down the bulkhead, leaving a trail of blood behind her on the wall. She had a head injury, Brielle realized with horror, just as Bishop Abelard's voice reached them: "There's no need for such brute force," he said in a quiet, firm voice as he moved forward from among the others. "You've injured one of your passengers, whom you're supposed to protect . . ."

A dark-haired, dark-eyed woman in Western garb emerged from the small group, a dagger pointed straight at the crewman. She reminded Brielle vividly of someone. . . .

"Let her go up," the young woman said in heavily-accented French. Brielle recognized the accent as similar to Rashid's . . . Arabic. "Let the girl go up and we will follow. None of us wants to die down here like trapped dogs!"

Something in her eyes, in her tone, told Brielle the woman wasn't merely showing false bravado.

Bishop Abelard looked at her as if he didn't quite know whether to believe her, but took a step backward anyway. The crew member also backed away, although the look on his features was openly disdainful, and the woman motioned to Brielle. "You are her friend? Then help her." She pointed to the ladder with the dagger.

Brielle opened her mouth to protest, then caught the bishop's eye and reconsidered. She reluctantly turned toward Anabette, who seemed to have recovered enough to push away from the bulkhead and straighten. "Come, 'Bette," she said in a low, strained voice. "I'll help you . . ."

Seven

With one part of his mind, Reynaud noted that the galley on the merchantman's other side hadn't rammed them. Not yet, at least. He could only hope that Humphrey of Toulouse and his defenders had either defeated them or disabled the crew enough so that they had retreated.

He chanced a look over his shoulder. Humphrey's men were still lined up along the freeboard. . . .

The thump of grappling hooks hitting his side of the *Madonna* jerked Reynaud's attention back to his own situation. While his archers still sought to pick off as many of the marauders as possible before they could board the ship, other pirates began pulling themselves up the ropes toward the freeboard. Without corsair arrows backing them up, the men crawling up the lines would have been easy to hit, but Reynaud's men were forced to concentrate on downing the backup enemy archers.

The scent of blood lust tainted the pure sea air as the men from the merchantman aimed and shot with renewed purpose, the enemy's proximity making their task easier. At the same time, however, the clang of sword play was breaking out on the deck behind them. Reynaud knew that Taillefer would ably guard his back, and he fought to maintain his concentration. The sooner they dispatched the other cutthroats, the sooner they could turn around and take on those who were boarding.

The defending archers' success said much for both knights and the crew members, and soon Reynaud was able to swing about and unsheathe his sword. Sweat dripped into his eyes, and his palm felt damp, but he gripped his sword with new purpose and threw himself into the fray, silently thankful he and most of the others had shed their mail the first day of the voyage. For all the protection it would have offered, the armor was also heavy and tended to bake the man wearing it beneath the rays of the Mediterranean sun.

Reynaud went to Captain Paolo's rescue, for the small Venetian was embroiled with two corsairs, one much bulkier in build than he was. Paolo was holding his own, his sword flashing in the sun, as he kept the two miscreants at bay, but Reynaud didn't want to risk losing the *Madonna*'s captain. And no one from the crew seemed concerned enough to go to Paolo's aid.

"Try a *fair* fight," Reynaud said, catching the larger corsair's attention. The man gave him a nasty grin beneath his moustache and slashed his sword horizontally at Reynaud's neck, the mounded muscles in his bare upper arms gleaming in the sunlight. Reynaud ducked for his life, all thoughts of Paolo receding as he engaged the burly interloper. He straightened immediately with a lightning-fast upward arc. On its downward swing the blade descended toward the man's unprotected left side, embedding itself in his ribs.

The corsair screamed. Reynaud pulled the sword free and finished him off before his knees hit the deck. He spun about, both hands on the hilt, the weapon acting as a defensive spoke. Taillefer was dueling with another pirate, the ring of metal on metal attesting to his aggression.

In that instant, out of the corner of his eye Reynaud caught movement from across the deck. Humphrey's men were joining the skirmish, which meant they'd driven off the other galley. Relief swept over Reynaud as he engaged another silk-clad corsair; renewed energy followed hard on its heels, for the struggle was almost over. . . .

A shout from one of the men registered with him in the heat of his swordplay; Paolo appeared and drove a dagger into the huge corsair's back before the man knew he was being attacked. Reynaud spun toward the direction of the shout. The hatch had been flung open . . . a head of yellow hair suddenly came into view. For an instant his heart stuttered as he thought of Brielle; then he recognized the hair.

God's blood, that wench! he thought angrily and watched as John the Gaunt bent over the opening to help her out. She was not only endangering herself, but John as well. Reynaud glanced around. Only two corsairs remained standing—one of them already surrendering to a crusader Reynaud didn't know. The other was struggling with Rashid—whose robe was tied snugly about his thighs to prevent it from hindering him. With one swift and powerful thrust, however, Taillefer ran the corsair through from the side. It was over.

Save for the groans of the wounded and dying—and the caterwauling of Anabette as she struggled onto the deck. . . . "I would rather die up *here!*" she cried in a voice bordering on hysteria, her hair a pale tangle at the ends, and from what Reynaud could see of the back of her head, it was rust-streaked as well. "Taillefer . . . Taillefer!" she gasped, her narrowed eyes searching the deck in the bright light.

The minstrel strode forward in his now blood-spattered tunic, the sudden pallor of his face mute testament to his concern for Anabette. As she collapsed into Taillefer's arms, Reynaud watched Brielle emerge from the hatch, although with more caution. His chest tightened inexplicably at the sight, and he had the sudden urge to take her in his arms, just as the minstrel had Anabette.

But he called upon his rigid control, hiding his self-perceived weakness behind anger. Another knight stepped up to help her and, fighting his chivalrous urges, Reynaud remained where he stood and watched as the young crusader's face turned pink when he took her hand.

Brielle d'Avignon had disobeyed orders and, according to

Rashid, broken her word to the Arab. Had she been more diligent in her task, the women now emerging from the lower deck would have remained there until the crew had disposed of the bodies and scrubbed the gore from the *Madonna*'s decks.

"Do you always do the opposite of what you're told?" he asked Brielle when the young man had led her directly to him. Paolo, who was behind him, stepped forward. "How fortunate for you that you guessed the fighting was nearly over when you allowed that rash wench to come on deck." Before she could answer, he gestured around the deck. "Do you like what you see, *demoiselle?* Hacked bodies and blood-slick deck?"

" 'Twasn't my doing that Anabette left the cabin," Brielle defended herself. The fresh air was wonderfully rejuvenating and had helped brace her for the grisly scene around them.

"We're taking in water below," she told Paolo, deciding to ignore the obnoxious Templar.

"And where is Giovanni?" the captain asked with a frown. He looked at Reynaud. "He was to keep the passengers below . . . and give a full accounting of any damage."

Brielle felt a guilty warmth crawl up her cheeks. "He's trussed," she said.

Paolo's face turned crimson. "Trussed? *Dio mio!* One of my crewmen is trussed below?"

"I'm afraid so," Bishop Abelard said from behind Brielle. " 'Twas for his own . . . safety."

Captain Paolo motioned one of his crewmen toward the hatch. rapping out a sharp order in Italian.

"We aren't in danger of . . . sinking, are we?" asked Alain, a knight who'd fought with Humphrey. His face was as white as Anabette's.

Reynaud slapped him on the shoulder, and Brielle noted the easy camaraderie with which the Templar treated him. "Come now, Alain," he cajoled. "After so valiant a showing against these cutthroats, why would you worry about getting a little wet?"

"Because a knight belongs on land . . . on his horse!" grumbled Humphrey of Toulouse, looking none too happy either.

Triumph flashed in Reynaud's eyes. "You've done what many could not, *mon ami* . . . defeated a galley full of marauders before they could even board the *Madonna*. Have we not achieved something memorable, *capitano?*"

"Sí," Paolo said shortly, the look in his eyes dubious, as if he thought these Franks had gone mad.

"But I can't swim!" Alain blurted.

Rashid glanced at him sideways. "Fool," he muttered. "The sharks will make a meal of you before you can drown."

Unfortunately, Brielle caught his words . . . and so did Alain. He went slack-jawed.

"Rashid!" Reynaud said sharply, but the Arab looked unrepentant as he moved away to help throw the dead overboard. In fact, Brielle could have sworn she saw him hide a grin before he turned away.

Some crew members were already on their knees scrubbing the blood from the deck, while others were heaving corpses into the sea. "He wouldn't know of such things," Reynaud assured Alain. "He was born and raised near the Syrian desert."

"But—" Paolo began, and was immediately silenced by a look from Reynaud. Was there no man aboard the *Madonna,* crew member or otherwise, who didn't hang on Reynaud de St. Rémy's every word? Brielle wondered with acerbity.

She deliberately walked away from the scene to the side of the ship from which Humphrey and his defenders had sent the second galley fleeing. She could see it in the distance, retreating, its brightly painted sides looking dimmer now, its lone sail raised to catch the wind. Murmurs of men

and women reunited on deck came to her, but there was no
one with whom Brielle could reunite.

It came to her that she had only her father . . . if he were
still alive.

A profound loneliness moved through her, and suddenly
the sun was dimmer, the water not so deep blue, the skies
less perfect. . . .

Self-pity ill becomes you, Brielle d'Avignon. Geoffrey
d'Avignon's voice came to her on the breeze. Whenever she
had been unhappy or disappointed, her father would say those
words. *Look around you, child, and see how many things
you have to be thankful for. . . .*

She knew not how long she stood there staring out at the
scintillating sea, lost in thought. Several corpses came bobbing into view, snagging her attention. Brielle contemplated
them for a time, lifeless forms alone save for the few others
like them on a vast and endless sea. She soon averted her
gaze, suddenly feeling pity for those unshriven souls tossed
into the water like refuse.

"Save your pity, Lady Brielle. Our wounded need it more."

That voice. . . . It could make her heart race, her palms
clammy, her knees weak. It could also, she didn't doubt, coax
a child from the security of its mother's arms.

Save your pity? The words registered.

She whirled around, ready to protest his unnerving observation . . . and saw his eyes on the corpses she'd just been
watching. The denial died on her lips, for he'd read her pity
for the dead, and not herself. He truly looked like a knight
of God, his tunic still almost celestially bright, in spite of
traces of blood here and there.

"And why must you throw them all to the sharks?" she
asked him, her eyes drawn to his beautiful, too-serious
mouth. "Can you not save the wounded? Can we not tend
them?"

Reynaud leaned against the freeboard and folded his arms,
his gaze turning to the dot that was the retreating galley.

"They wanted to kill us all, for the sole purpose of taking what wasn't theirs. And if they had allowed anyone to live, those unfortunates would have been sold into slavery. Why give such monsters a chance to repeat their offenses? They're the scourge of the Mediterranean."

He canted his head as he studied the horizon. She noticed the blood, then, on the neckline of his tunic. "You're hurt," she said, with sudden concern. Why hadn't she seen it before?

" 'Tis less than nothing. Had it been a fraction deeper, I would not have been here to ask you what happened below deck."

His eyes met hers, probing, as if he could will the answer from her.

"I'm not one of your warriors, *chevalier,* to do your bidding to the letter! I made a mistake—I looked the other way when the galley hit us and gave Anabette the opportunity to steal from the cabin."

"Then why don't you admit you made a mistake? ' 'Twasn't my doing,' I believe you said."

Evidently he was determined to humiliate her. But at least they were alone. "All right. I made a mistake. Is that good enough, Sieur Reynaud?"

He watched the anger darken her magnificent eyes and wondered why he had worked to pull the admission from her. Was he punishing her for his own weakness where she was concerned? For that ensnaring smile she'd bestowed upon him in the convent refectory?

"Have you never made a mistake, *chevalier?"*

He nodded, his thoughts on that first time he'd seen her— going to that empty-headed Anabette's rescue at risk to her own life. She was loyal, he'd give her that. Too bad her loyalty extended to someone who didn't deserve it . . . someone who had jeopardized Brielle's own prospects of going to Outremer by thoughtless and selfish behavior.

"You've made more than one mistake since I've met you,

demoiselle." He was thinking of her so readily having forgiven Anabette. So willing to tend injured cutthroats. "And
any error can prove fatal."

"Then I understand that you've never made mistakes?"

*You are Christ's perfect knight. Better in every way than
I could ever be! Perfect, my son. Perfect. . . .*

Reynaud fought to dismiss his father's words from his head
and concentrated hard on the young woman before him. Her
earlier question registered then. *"Oui,* I've made more than
my share of mistakes. And it seems, by some quirk of fate,
I'm the exception to the rule. If an error can prove to be
fatal, I should have been dead long ago."

Was he toying with her? she wondered as she narrowed
her eyes at him. Or was that self-deprecation she saw in his
eyes? In the subtle change of the tone of his voice?

"You are especially loved by God, *chevalier,* else He
wouldn't have blessed you in such a manner."

Like a cloud over the sun, his expression dimmed, turning
somber, as if he were withdrawing from her. "We are, every
one of us, loved by God, *demoiselle.* That doesn't give us
the right to be careless. Ever."

She decided then and there to say nothing of the woman
who'd threatened Giovanni.

He touched her arm, his fingers sending a disturbing heat
straight through her gown sleeve to singe her flesh. Her
thoughts were suddenly ajumble, and were it not for the people about the deck, she might have given in to the sudden
weakness in her knees just to be lifted into his arms once
again.

"Will you help tend the wounded?"

She swallowed and nodded. "Tell me what to expect," she
managed, in a voice that sounded distant to her own ears.
"How many are there? Did we . . . lose anyone?"

"One crew member. The other injuries are not life-
threatening. One of the women is a mid-wife. She and the
ship's carpenter are seeing to the wounded. Rashid is helping

as well. One of the men is also a Hospitaller, skilled in caring for the sick and the injured."

"Carpenter?" she asked, grabbing at the somewhat strange idea in an effort to pull herself from the undeniable spell he seemed to cast over her.

Reynaud nodded as they approached the bow of the ship, where the wounded had been laid out. *"Oui, demoiselle,"* he told her patiently, as one would a child, "the carpenter often doubles as the ship's surgeon."

Brielle was secretly appalled at the thought, but the web of enchantment he'd been weaving around her had just been broken with his words, and she would have cut out her tongue before she would ever let him see her shock.

"And you—" she said rather breathlessly. "Your skills will be needed."

Without warning, his expression altered, as if he were throwing a protective barrier between himself and the rest of the world . . . including *her.* "Nay, I won't be needed. None of the wounds is so grave."

"But—"

"Demoiselle," he said in a flat voice, "if my help is not required, then so be it."

Brielle mentally kicked herself, for she realized that he was only protecting himself. She'd once thought how envious others could be of his gift, but now, in light of his words, she also realized that what some men did not understand, they would seek to destroy, deeming it evil.

Evidently Reynaud de St. Rémy was well aware of the danger, and would only willingly risk discovery by the wrong people when a life hung in the balance.

She said no more.

The damage from the one galley had been more frightening to the passengers than it was extensive. Repairs were made within a few hours, although now the lower deck was even less appealing than before with its new dampness and increased humidity from sea water. After the corsair attack, Brielle had found it impossible to identify the woman who helped them gain the upper deck, and after several attempts (at Reynaud's insistence), she was allowed to put the entire incident out of her mind. No one mentioned the unidentified woman again for the remainder of the voyage, although it was obvious to Brielle that Captain Paolo was uneasy about her presence aboard the *Madonna*.

"I thought the sea route was safer," Anabette said with petulance one day several weeks later as they stood on deck in the sun. She'd overcome her *mal de mer* and scalp injury and was thriving now. In fact, her bright hair shone with health beneath the sun, and she'd regained some of the weight she'd lost. But, strangely, Taillefer's attention wasn't so constant now that she was better. In fact, he'd begun to avoid her, and she was growing more and more unhappy about it.

"No journey to the Holy Land is safe, Anabette," Brielle told her. " 'Tis just that there is more danger over land—no doubt because it takes so much longer."

"Corsairs were quite enough for me. And I'm so tired of water! I want to walk on dry land so badly that I—"

Weary of Anabette's increasingly constant complaining, Brielle interrupted her. " 'Twas your choice, 'Bette. Remember, you risked much in leaving St. Bernadette's and seeking out John. And then you could have turned back at Marseilles. 'Tis hardly the time to have second thoughts."

Anabette frowned. "But Taillefer *encouraged* me! He led me to believe that . . . that he would marry me!" She turned her face to Brielle, and she looked utterly desolate. She wasn't playing a game now.

"He truly encouraged you?" Brielle asked, surprised. "Hinted of marriage?"

Anabette nodded, tears shimmering in her eyes. "I feel

like a fool, Brielle, and I . . . I think I should go back to France."

Brielle put a hand on her friend's arm. " 'Bette, did he . . . did he . . . ?" She trailed off, certain that Anabette knew what she meant.

Color splashed over Anabette's cheeks, and she gave Brielle her profile. Her chin was trembling. Brielle had never seen her truly so distressed. Had the minstrel really encouraged her to join them in Marseilles? Or had it all been a part of Anabette's overactive imagination? And, more importantly, had he had his way with her?

"You cannot go back to France until we reach Tyre, *chère*," Brielle informed her gently. "Mayhap you can hire another ship to return, or if you're willing to wait eight weeks or . . ."

"Nay!" Anabette cried softly, her hands white-knuckled on the rail. "I'll die of embarrassment if I must remain near him for eight long weeks. And in so foreign a place . . . whatever will I *do* with myself?" Her cheeks were aflame now.

Brielle bit down on her lip, a frown flitting across her forehead. She touched her friend's hand and said, "Then you must speak to Bishop Abelard. If he was willing to finance your way back in two months, he can have no objection to your returning earlier."

Anabette looked aghast. "I? Oh, Brielle, I cannot ask him such a thing! But you, mayhap—"

The old Anabette was showing, and Brielle was relieved. But she was determined that the girl face the consequences of her rash actions by speaking to the bishop herself.

There was, however, someone to whom she did wish to speak on Anabette's behalf and, as soon as prudently possible, she sought him out.

"Did you not find anything strange about the attack?" Rashid asked Captain Paolo. Reynaud, who was in the act of raising a cup of fine Damascus wine to his lips, cut him a look. Rashid would never cause alarm—would never even raise a question—if he weren't genuinely suspicious about something.

"Strange?" Paolo asked, wiping the sweat from his forehead with one brown forearm. They were in his big tiny cabin, saluting their victory over the corsairs with a draught of wine. Reynaud decided he would rather have been on deck with his drink, even though the seas had turned rough.

"Strange?" Paolo mulled this over, draining his cup and setting it down firmly on the tiny table beside the wine bottle. *"Ebbene* . . . well then, now that you bring it up, they weren't as bold as other *piratas* I've encountered." He narrowed his eyes thoughtfully. "Especially those who failed to ram us on Humphrey's side, eh?"

" 'Twas merely our exceptional skill as defenders," the knight said wryly. "Not that you don't know how to lead a fight," he added to Reynaud.

"Exactly," Rashid said. He looked at Humphrey then at the man he served. "They were too easily discouraged, I think, considering we're sailing a fully-loaded merchantman, with potential victims for the slave market and a hold full of horseflesh."

"And how could they know that?" Humphrey asked.

"No self-respecting knight would travel to the Levant without his steed," Reynaud said.

"All they had to do was notice how low the *Madonna* sits in the water," added Paolo.

"But I disagree with you, Rashid," Reynaud added. "The men who attacked our side of the *Madonna* put up a decent fight." He glanced at Humphrey, the expectation in his eyes clear.

"God's elbow!" Humphrey said, feigning offense. "Are you implying that our galley had the more cowardly crew?"

Reynaud stood, unable to straighten fully in the cell-like

room. "I think Rashid needs to get back into the fresh air
to clear his mind . . ."

Even though the conversation came to a halt as Reynaud
broke up the small gathering, he suspected he knew what
Rashid was implying, and he didn't like even thinking about
the possibility.

And he surely wasn't about to say anymore to the Arab in
the company of the others.

"Sieur Reynaud?"

Reynaud straightened from his task. He was looking over
Khamsin's shoe, for John had told him it had loosened.
When he saw Brielle, something clenched within him, deep
down. In her sapphire dress and with the scent of sea air
about her, she was a welcome diversion in the stifling,
makeshift stable.

And more than that.

He ignored his reaction, however, taking refuge in annoyance. "I asked you, did I not, *demoiselle,* to stay away from
the animals? 'Tis dangerous—they're unsettled enough as it
is and, therefore, unpredictable."

"John told me if I'm quiet and don't frighten them, I need
only avoid coming down here during rough weather."

He nodded and patted the stallion's satin-sleek neck. "Or
during a raid. Mayhap I should thank God for Anabette, else
you would have disobeyed me yet again and come down here
to soothe the horses. And put your life in jeopardy."

Her eyes narrowed slightly as she studied his features in
the dimness. It was hard to read the expression in his eyes.
"Obviously God wished it otherwise, else who would you
have to rail at for every perceived misdemeanor? And then,
of course, you would be forced to smile now and again . . .
if you didn't have Anabette and myself about to turn your
well-ordered life upside down."

Even as the words slipped out, she regretted them. She was sounding more and more like the outspoken Anabette.

He began to curry Khamsin, murmuring to the steed. It was obvious that he hadn't an answer for her—or at least one he felt comfortable giving. Or, more than likely, he didn't think her careless question deserved an answer.

She drew in a breath and began to say what she'd come to say. "Speaking of Anabette—"

"Ah," he said, looking through his lashes at her. "You didn't come here to tell me how much I must smile, after all?"

Was one corner of his mouth quivering? She couldn't be sure in the shadows. But he certainly looked less forbidding in the cramped quarters for the horses than he did on deck in the full light of day. Except, of course, when he turned the full force of his potent look upon her. "Nay, *chevalier*, only to ask you if you will speak to your minstrel."

"Taillefer?" he repeated, keeping his eyes on his work. "What has that knave done now?" He turned his penetrating gold gaze on her then, halting his brush strokes.

"He—why, he t-t-took advantage of . . ."

His brow furrowed, his eyes darkened, as he waited for her to finish. When she felt as if her face surely must be on fire, her eyes glued forever to the straw-strewn floor, he said at last, "He took advantage of *you?*"

It wasn't the question as much as the way he said it that piqued her. Piqued her enough to suddenly turn annoyed at him, for he'd unwittingly struck at her vanity. She lifted her chin in indignation, her embarrassment temporarily forgotten. "And just what do you mean by *that?*" she demanded.

He stared at her in bemusement for a moment, then realized what she'd implied . . . and what he'd said in reply. He was about to apologize—and hastily—when he realized how very entrancing she looked in her feminine outrage.

She outshone Anabette like the sun did the moon. But then, hadn't he seen as much from the first?

He allowed his gaze to return to Khamsin, fighting the inexplicable urge to tame her ire with his kiss. To tease her further and then delight in. . . .

Christ above, he was bewitched! She wasn't supposed to affect him this way. No woman was supposed to.

Nor were you supposed to despise killing the infidel.

He ignored reason's reprimand. Surely Brielle d'Avignon was closer to the truth than she realized when she'd said she had turned his world upside down. . . .

"Well?" she pressed, but in a milder tone, as if her indignation were giving way to maidenly modesty. Her eyes slid from his, her gaze alighting on Khamsin's nose.

"Forgive me if I misunderstood," he said, struggling to concentrate on her words and not *her.* "But surely you don't mean that Taillefer compromised Anabette?"

The hectic color painting her delicate cheekbones gave him her answer. As he watched her, he realized that for all the havoc she was creating with his senses, she had unknowingly managed to distract him from his problems.

"Demoiselle?" he said softly.

"Aye." It sounded like a coward's whisper to her own ears. The protracted silence was deafening, and her own reaction angered her. She bit her lower lip in an attempt to rouse her courage.

"I cannot believe that," he said suddenly. "Not that I don't believe you specifically, but that bothersome wench . . ."

Her eyes met his, unexpected amusement curving her soft mouth. "Anabette can be bothersome, can she not?" she asked, her face alight with sudden levity. "Think you she could ever drive a man to take advantage of her?"

Reynaud drank in her lightheartedness like a man just emerging from the desert. "She would, rather, drive a man to murder," he said, with a wicked grin.

Brielle laughed aloud, giddy from being in his presence while he was giving her a glimpse of his lighter side and plainly amused by his comment.

Reynaud noted the airy, tinkling sound of her laughter and was reminded of fairies in a forest . . . and enchantment. Lovely as it was, it also sounded out of place in the bowels of a round ship amidst more than a score of horses.

"But she could also lure him to compromise her with her incessant scheming," he added, in an attempt to stretch out the magic moment.

Her smile began to disappear, and Reynaud felt a disappointing sense of loss. "But why?" she asked, reminding him poignantly of her innocence.

"If she is with child, Taillefer would be obliged to wed her."

Her eyes widened, as if that possibility hadn't even occurred to her.

"But I'm inclined to suspect that she was exaggerating, my lady, in the interest of further gaining Taillefer's affection." He shook his head and resumed his currying. "I believe Taillefer doesn't want to face the fact that he's in love for the first time, and he has reacted foolishly by ignoring the object of his love. As for Anabette, you must not believe everything she tells you. Especially now that she is feeling abandoned by Taillefer."

"But—"

"I'll speak to him, though, just to make sure."

"Thank you, Sieur Reynaud." She swung away, wondering how he would know anything about love, but at a loss for further conversation with him. She was oddly reluctant to leave now. A thought struck her then, and she turned back. "What does 'Khamsin' mean?"

She felt it a silly question but had wondered about the Arabic name ever since she'd first heard it in the convent courtyard.

He looked up at her, his face cast in shadows, his mouth serious once again. " 'Tis the name for the desert wind that blows from Egypt and the Red Sea."

She nodded and said, " 'Tis a noble name," and to smooth her sudden awkwardness, she smiled shyly.

Reynaud watched her disappear, feeling suddenly very alone.

Eight

Tyre—June, 1191

A light-colored shawl over her head to protect her from the sun, Brielle shaded her eyes with one hand and surveyed the scene before her. Several Venetian war galleys and merchantmen sat in the beautiful harbor at Tyre, the water a shimmering silver-blue. The view of one of the oldest cities in the world was breathtaking, with the skyline of low-built limestone buildings and a minaret here and there poking the cerulean fabric of the sky, all set against the backdrop of the hazy-blue, misted Lebanon Mountains in the distance on the mainland beyond.

"How magnificent," Brielle said in awe.

" 'Thy borders are in the midst of the seas, thy builders have perfected their beauty . . .' " Reynaud said softly, his gaze on the noble city.

Brielle glanced at him questioningly. "Ezekiel's description of Tyre," he said, then his eyes briefly met hers. "I am the third son, educated in theology. My father wanted me to serve the Church."

His tone was flat, and Brielle realized he had just, however reluctantly, revealed a piece of the puzzle that was Reynaud de St. Rémy. Yet she deliberately forced her thoughts away from his revelation back to the island city before her.

"You'll see many Venetians in Tyre, *madonna*," Captain

Paolo had told her earlier, pride shining in his dark eyes, "for we played an important rôle in helping the crusaders conquer the city. In return for our help, we won many concessions from the Christians."

". . . like ownership of two-thirds of the property in Tyre and Ascalon," Reynaud had added, "and additional commercial quarters in other crusader-held towns, exemptions from the usual tolls and customs duties, the freedom to use their own weights and measures in all transactions—a monumental concession, I might add—and part of the annual revenues of Acre."

Brielle had been impressed, yet from what she'd seen of Paolo's crew's ability to sail the Mediterranean and fight off corsairs, she wasn't surprised.

"The Venetians dominated the seas at one time," Reynaud explained, waxing more eloquent than Brielle had ever heard him, "although now they do little for the Christian cause except to ferry pilgrims to crusader-held shrines, and occasionally transport soldiers and their equipment. Most of the Holy Land is now held by Muslims."

"Then the Venetians won undisputed control of this part of the Mediterranean for the crusaders?"

"Oui." He cast her a sidelong glance, thinking how astute she was for a young, relatively sheltered woman. He was also pleased by her interest. With a sweep of his arm that indicated the island and harbor, he continued, "Centuries ago, when Alexander the Great set out to conquer Tyre, it was an island. After several months of resistance, the city fell to Alexander when he built a causeway, allowing access from the mainland."

The *Madonna* slipped through the lane between the two towers that controlled the entrance to the harbor. "A chain can be stretched across the channel to close the entrance," he added. Brielle also noted that the harbor was protected on three sides by stone walls.

"Why all this bother?" Anabette, who was standing near them, wondered aloud.

Reynaud paused briefly before he replied, as if debating the wisdom of answering so foolish a query. "The crusaders have prepared it as a refuge in case of emergency . . . especially now."

"Look! They even have a cathedral!" Brielle exclaimed as she caught sight of the spires that seemed to reach to Heaven itself.

"Let's pray to God they don't have a convent," Anabette said with fervor.

Brielle caught Reynaud's look, and his eyes lit briefly with unexpected levity.

"The Tyre Cathedral is magnificent," he said, in answer to Brielle's observation. " 'Twas built by the crusaders."

Brielle suddenly felt extremely ignorant about the entire Eastern world, and found herself wanting to know everything about Tyre—and the land beyond. She wondered how such a beautiful and peaceful-looking place could ever be part of the bloody struggle between Christian and Saracen.

As if reading her thoughts, Rashid said, "We do not always fight, *demoiselle*. Most of the time we live in peace, side by side. One hundred years ago, your Pope decided Jerusalem belonged in Christian hands; it was only then that the Christian infidels sought to drive us from those places we'd lived since before Christianity had even come into being."

"Indeed. By the time that first crusade had reached Jerusalem to take it back from the Turks," Reynaud said, "the Egyptians had already driven them out. Muslim, Jew, and Christian were all freely allowed to live and worship there."

The word "infidel" used in conjunction with "Christian" was not lost upon Brielle, but Reynaud had spoken before she could frame an appropriate—or inappropriate—comment. "Aye," he added softly. "Even as we speak, King Philip and Richard of England have joined the two-year siege against Acre. With the addition of their hordes of over-zealous crusaders, it will be over soon."

Brielle watched the breeze ruffle his loam-dark hair and noticed the hardening of his features, the change in his voice—a sudden lack of emotion rather than the expected triumph as he gazed toward the mountains and spoke.

"If you've been gone these last few months, how could you possibly know that?" she asked in puzzlement.

"The siege is longstanding."

"But the French and English kings?" she pressed, wanting to learn everything she could about her new surroundings. "How do you know they have joined them?"

Reynaud turned the full force of his gaze upon her, but there was no amusement in his eyes now. He looked like he had the first time she'd opened her eyes and found herself in his unwilling embrace. "Word of mouth. News from the Holy Land travels like wildfire around the Mediterranean. With Philip and Richard having arrived this winter past, 'twas only a matter of time before they would have joined in the siege. Acre is the principal port on the Palestinian coast."

"And there are also the pigeons," Rashid added.

Reynaud nodded as he looked at his friend then back to the island-city before them. "We first learned of carrier pigeons—pigeons who carry written messages—from the Turks, and we have been using them in Outremer ever since."

"Birds?" Anabette said with disdain. " 'Tis a sorry way to send and receive valuable information."

Brielle watched as Taillefer's hand patted her friend's. "Don't scoff, *mon petit fleur,*" he chided lightly, tempering the words with a charming smile. "Disasters we've had, *oui,* but more often the birds have proved invaluable."

All it took, Brielle had come to realize, was a smile or kind word from Taillefer, and Anabette instantly brightened and seemed to calm her foolishly impulsive tendencies. It was obvious to Brielle that Reynaud had spoken to the minstrel. She didn't know what he'd said, but whatever it was, both her friend and Taillefer were noticeably happier, and they had been together more often for the remainder of the voyage.

It appeared, Brielle thought wryly, that Anabette had changed her mind about asking Bishop Abelard to return immediately to France. At least for now.

The crew bustled about, readying the vessel for docking. Sails were being folded, lines coiled and stored, as passengers stood to the side and reacted in uniquely different ways to arriving in one of the oldest cities in the world. Some were in visible awe, others wept openly with joy—no doubt thinking that Jesus had walked these shores. Still others—mostly crusaders who were there for the first time—cautiously held inside their reactions to their first glimpse of the Levant.

Anabette came to Brielle's side at the rail. "The men are getting ready to bring up the horses."

Interest lit Brielle's face. "Poor creatures. Sieur Reynaud seemed so certain they would be ready to ride in no time, but I wonder how they'll fare at first. 'Tis bad enough for a human being to spend weeks at sea in a bobbing ship."

Anabette shivered, then continued. "I remember well. Taillefer told me that we may be invited to stay at that Saracen's family home here in Tyre. Can you believe such a thing?"

Brielle threw her a startled look. "We? But what of an inn? And surely Bishop Abelard—"

"The good bishop will stay at some palace here, I am told." Anabette pulled a face. "We don't have to agree to it, *chère*. I would prefer an inn myself, lest we wake up and discover our throats slit."

"Don't be absurd . . . we wouldn't awaken if our throats were slit." She unthinkingly put one slender hand against that vulnerable area, then felt foolish; under normal circumstances she would have laughed outright at Anabette's comment. And hadn't Reynaud told her Christian and Muslim lived side by side much of the time? Her Christian upbringing warred with what she'd been taught about courtesy. While she had no wish to stay beneath a Muslim roof, neither did she wish to offend Rashid or his family—especially after knowing he was Reynaud de St. Rémy's friend.

From the moment Brielle could make out the figures scrambling about the docks, she was in a completely different world: a world more like a dream than anything she'd ever seen in Provence. It was hot, and everyone wore head-pieces—most often the traditional *keffiya*—and the merchants and visitors to the docks wore white or light robes. The dock workers themselves wore strange pants that reminded her of Rashid's altered robe when the *Madonna* had been attacked—full and baggy from waist to knee, and tight from knee to ankle. Women wore similar styles, but with veils over their faces. Their eyes were dramatically outlined and accented with kohl—something unheard of in France.

The docking area was full of strange sights and sounds and smells, and Brielle became quickly absorbed in her surroundings, forgetting everything else for a time, until someone took her elbow. It was Reynaud.

He guided her to the ramp, behind other debarking passengers, and so engrossed was she in the bustle around them, she barely noticed the Templar's preoccupation. Anabette chattered on behind them, and several of Bishop Abelard's comments came to Brielle, only increasing her sense of awe as she set foot on the soil of what was considered part of the Holy Land.

Perhaps her father himself had set foot in this very city.

"The prophet Isaiah praised Tyre," Bishop Abelard was telling Anabette as they descended the gentle decline of the ramp. " 'The crowning city,' he sang of it, 'whose merchants are princes, whose traffickers are the honorable of the earth.' "

While Brielle wondered if Anabette remembered Abbess Marguerite's instruction in religion, Reynaud said for her ears alone, "I wonder if the bishop knows that the infamous Jezebel was a Tyrian princess."

" 'Twould be of more interest to Anabette," she answered softly, laughter lacing her words. But the result of his warm breath tickling her ear created sensations deep within Brielle that made her feel as wicked as Jezebel.

Her thoughts, however, were quickly drawn again to the activity before her . . . scores of dusky-skinned men laboring beneath the sun, speaking in Arabic as they loaded and unloaded vessels. The tangy sea air was redolent with the earthy smells of sun-baked wood, hemp, canvas, and pitch. Spices and scented oils perfumed the air, too, as well as the scents of fresh cut cedar, pine and cypress.

A sudden thought came to her, and her steps slowed. Reynaud looked down at her questioningly.

"Khamsin," she said. "What of Khamsin? And the other horses?"

That she could think of the comfort of the animals while in the midst of completely alien surroundings took Reynaud by surprise. He watched the faint frown flit across her brow, then her gaze lift to his.

"They're being taken care of even as we speak," he said, feeling an odd little catch in the area of his heart. "Taillefer and John are overseeing their handling."

Her frown smoothed, and he thought how compassionate she was.

"Soft" is more like it, whispered a voice, *just like you.*

"But if it weren't for me, wouldn't you be doing it yourself?"

"I could do nothing less than escort Bishop Abelard," he answered truthfully. "You're not taking me away from Khamsin, if 'tis what you fear. Shall I hire a litter?" he asked, in an effort to redirect his thoughts. "Or a camel?" Once the words were out, they sounded foolish to his own ears. A young woman like Brielle d'Avignon wouldn't choose riding in a litter to walking among the new sights and sounds of Tyre.

"Litter?" she asked, looking bemused. "Is it so very far to where we're staying that I cannot walk?"

"Nay, but the sun is scorching and you're not accustomed to it yet." He reached out and pulled the silk scarf she wore on her head further forward, noting the dusting of freckles on her small, straight nose—a nose pink and peeling from exposure to the sun. "And the Lady Anabette of course," he mumbled automatically in an effort to keep his mind off the feel of her hair. It was as soft as the scarf he'd given her and insisted she wear while out on the deck of the *Madonna*.

"Anabette is hardier than she appears. And so am I, Sieur Reynaud. This land is breathtaking . . . I wouldn't miss seeing any of it! Although I would like to ride a camel before I leave here."

He was oddly pleased, once again, by her reaction, although he hadn't expected any less. He glanced back over his shoulder at the bishop and Anabette. For once the wench was quiet as she took in the sights around her with wide eyes. Bishop Abelard's dark eyes were moist with emotion.

As they stepped onto the street closest to the docks, Reynaud said, " 'Tis breathtaking, *oui,* but don't be deceived by its beauty. The hot climate, strange diseases, and the strain of constant fighting wear a man down. Crusaders don't live long here. Those who stay and wed leave widows all too soon, and their offspring are often sickly. Male children especially perish most frequently."

She turned her face to him, surprised at not only his words, but at the bitterness that edged them. "Why, I didn't think of that. I suppose 'twould wear down *any* man. Or woman. Nor did I know of such hardships for children."

He didn't like alarming her, but she had to be prepared for her stay, however brief, in the Levant. Even as he watched some of the enthusiasm leave her sea-blue eyes, he continued, "The land is filled with spies and murderers . . . you mayhap have heard of the Hashishiyun, from whose name comes the word 'assassin' and who strike terror into even the boldest heart."

He watched fear chase away the excitement in her expression and ruthlessly tamped down his softer inclinations. "A man dare not trust his own servants; he never knows when his food might be poisoned or his life ended by the thrust of a dagger."

The veil of her shadow-brown lashes lowered for a moment, as if she were trying to come to terms with what he'd said. "Surely you're trying to frighten me?" She glanced sideways at him then, and he could have sworn her lips were quivering. He'd surely done the job well, he thought with rue.

Then she met his look fully, her mouth curving into a sweet smile before she looked ahead. "Surely, *chevalier,* I can survive for eight weeks?"

He felt foolish in the wake of her lightly-put question, especially having mistaken the cause of the trembling of her mouth. But there was nothing humorous about his warning. "I certainly hope so, for I don't speak idly. And your friend . . . you must warn her against any incautious behavior. It could very well put her life in jeopardy. We're not in Provence now."

"*You* had better warn Anabette, for surely she'll not listen to me."

Reynaud sighed inwardly at the thought and, at the same time, wondered how Brielle d'Avignon had slipped under his guard so easily. She almost made him forget his unhappiness at being back in the land he'd once loved. Indeed, he was becoming one of those dying a slow death, although it was more of a spiritual thing than a physical one so far.

Or was his "guard" disintegrating like the rest of his dreams?

Man was not put on this earth to seek happiness, Reynaud, but rather a state of grace, his father's words came back to him. *Even more so should one serve the Church.* And in his efforts to win his father's admiration, to meet Gérard's lofty expectations, he'd always sought to be the best in his service of the Knights of the Poor Temple of Solomon . . . and God. He had always sought the ultimate state of grace.

Only for the last year or so had he begun to question the manner in which the Templar Rule stated that he obtain that salvation.

"Sieur Reynaud?" Bishop Abelard called from behind them.

Reynaud thought it was to the prelate's credit that he appeared perfectly at ease with Rashid accompanying him from the *Madonna.* The enchantment of the East made for strange bedfellows, it was said. But then, Reynaud mused as he turned back toward Abelard, this bishop wasn't typical of many who blindly served the Church.

And it struck him for the first time that perhaps Robert de Sablé, Templar Master, had chosen him specifically to escort Abelard to Tyre. Hadn't Robert mentioned being acquainted with the bishop? At first Reynaud had thought (and with good cause) that de Sablé had wished to get him away from the Holy Land for a while. But it was also very possible that Robert had assigned him to this particular bishop because of Abelard's apparent tolerance and even temperament. Reynaud had also guessed early on that de Sablé had assigned Humphrey as a sort of bodyguard against greedy men after the secret of his healing ability.

Reynaud had secretly put the bishop to the test, a subtle form of rebellion against the rigid discipline that was part and parcel of the Templar code. He had, from the first, introduced him to Rashid; made known the fact that he and

Rashid were as close as any two men could be—a Christian and a Muslim. And Abelard had accepted that without question. He'd passed Reynaud's little test and, in doing so, restored the smallest bit of the Templar's faith in man. Clergyman in particular.

"Forgive me, Excellence, for neglecting my duties," he apologized, realizing he'd been remiss in his attentions to the bishop when he'd been assigned to escort Abelard, who also had never been to the Holy Land and undoubtedly had many questions.

Out of courtesy, Brielle pulled her attention from the surroundings and turned back to the bishop, just as the latter waved one hand dismissively at Reynaud. "Were I you, my son, I would be more inclined to be a guide to a lovely young woman than to a stodgy cleric." He smiled beneath his miter, which had begun to slip forward down his sweat-dotted brow. Obviously undaunted, he pushed it back with the same hand he'd used to gesture to Reynaud. His face was flushed, but Reynaud guessed it was as much from excitement as from the heat.

Without looking, he knew Brielle was blushing at the bishop's words, and he felt a wave of heat—that had nothing to do with the sun—invade his features, as well. He wondered briefly if the remark were a rebuke, then dismissed it. The bishop could have no inkling of the burden Reynaud carried, or of his being sent to France to act as an escort perhaps as a manner of punishment. If the prelate did, he most certainly wouldn't seek to add to it by a comment regarding an innocent conversation.

Innocent? sneered a voice.

". . . remiss of me to neglect to inform the ladies that I've extended an invitation to them to stay at the bishop's palace." Abelard looked at Brielle, then Anabette. " 'Tis purported to be large and beautiful—the former home of the late William, Archbishop of Tyre."

"How kind, Bishop Abelard," Brielle murmured.

From the look he saw her give Anabette, Reynaud got the distinct impression that she was hoping the girl would have the good sense not to say something completely inappropriate.

"But you are hardly 'remiss' when your attention," she added, "—and that of everyone else—has been captured by our new surroundings." She gifted the bishop with that stunning smile that had so affected Reynaud in the convent refectory.

"Look!" Anabette cried, and pointed to a small pack of camels being led down the street. Reynaud resisted the urge to slap a palm over her mouth, for passersby were staring at her . . . this brazen, brassy-haired female who spoke as loudly as any man.

For the love of God, surely the wench had heard of camels?

But Bishop Abelard and Brielle d'Avignon followed Anabette's pointing finger, and both their expressions of interest intensified. In fact, Brielle's turned positively delighted after the initial surprise.

"Camels!" she breathed. "We heard about them from visitors at St. Bernadette's—surely you remember, Anabette?"

"Hummph. Ugly creatures, are they not? And Taillefer told me they are mean and unpredictable."

A shadow passed over Brielle's face, and Reynaud found himself defending the creatures, even though the minstrel had been right. "They are worth their weight in gold here in the East, and for all their faults, they are heavily depended upon by Arab peoples for their very survival."

A possible exaggeration, he acknowledged, but not so very far from the truth. Camels had always been integral to the survival of desert-dwelling Arabs. And at that moment he would have lied outright to bring the smile back to Brielle d'Avignon's face.

"A camel has many advantages over a horse," Rashid said as he looked directly at Anabette, his dark eyes registering definite disapproval. "A camel once saved the minstrel's scrawny neck, *demoiselle*. Ask him."

Bishop Abelard coughed discreetly behind one hand, while Brielle obviously attempted to keep from laughing. Reynaud could have kissed the Arab. Noting the look of fascination on the bishop's face after he had regained his composure, Reynaud asked, "Would you prefer to ride, Excellence?" Even before Abelard answered, Rashid was walking over to a man with several saddled camels. He began speaking and gesturing to the other Arab, who glanced over his shoulder at the small party standing and staring in wonder at the animals that had just passed them.

He returned shortly, leading one of the camels.

The bishop demurred at first. "Why, of course the Lady Brielle must ride," he said.

"You can both ride," Reynaud told him. "Unless you would rather have your own camel . . ." He gave the bishop a half grin, one eyebrow quirked.

Abelard raised one hand and shook his head. "Oh no, my son. 'Tisn't necessary." He looked at Brielle questioningly. "Would you mind . . . ?" He gestured toward the camel, who was in the process of kneeling.

Brielle, however, was watching in fascination as the beast dropped to its knees before them at Rashid's command in Arabic, then folded its hind legs and sank to the ground. It was one of the strangest-looking creatures she'd ever seen, its large brown eyes staring at her from beneath long, curly lashes.

"Why, it has eyelashes!" she exclaimed to no one in particular.

"To keep out the sand," Reynaud said, enjoying her pleasure in encountering the creature for the first time.

"And eyebrows," observed the bishop, similarly fascinated.

"They spit and kick," Anabette told them from the relative

safety of a few steps back. "And look at that ugly bald spot on its chest! 'Tis diseased!"

Before Reynaud could reply, Rashid gave her another frowning glance. "A natural occurrence—leathery spots such as that. But camels have been known to spit at yellow-haired human females."

Anabette hopped back another two steps.

Reynaud was ready to allow her to retreat all the way back to Marseilles, but Brielle spoke to the girl while he struggled to bite back his scathing words. "Come now, Anabette . . . How can you have even contemplated running into the path of a knight's steed, then be so squeamish about a camel? Look!" She gestured toward the activity around them. "People are riding them, and the beasts are also carrying valuable goods on their backs. Surely they can't be as bad as you would make them!"

For once Anabette looked effectively chastised, but still reluctant to approach the camel. "I'll walk with Sieur Reynaud—if he doesn't mind, that is," she added with a sidelong glance at the Templar. "I—I don't mind the heat."

Without further ado, Reynaud gave Brielle a hand up onto the camel's back, then guided the bishop into the seat behind her. Before she could collect her wits, Rashid gave the animal another command and with a rocking jolt, the two riders were on their way up . . . and up—or so it seemed to Brielle.

She bit her lip, clinging to the saddle for dear life. Once they were up, they commanded a much better view of the street before them, and Brielle suddenly felt giddy with excitement as she looked down at Reynaud and Rashid. "My lord bishop is my protection," she said, her profile to Abelard as she spoke. "Surely this animal won't be so inconsiderate as to unseat a bishop!"

" 'Tis no doubt a Muslim camel, child," Abelard quipped from behind her, "and our safety depends on my ability to quickly convert it."

They all laughed at that, and as Reynaud watched Brielle's lovely, radiant face, he felt his own expression sober, for he couldn't help but think of the fruitless and dangerous task ahead of her if she insisted on searching for Geoffrey d'Avignon. God help them all . . .

Nine

Tancred le Bref was angry.

It looked as if his trip to Masyaf was for naught. Or, worse, his overwhelming anger with the man who sat before him could cost him his life. But he'd survived until now with wits and bravado. Perhaps a bit more of the latter than the former, yet he'd never been one to back away out of fear.

He stared from beneath his heavy brow at the two guards. Both had painted faces, femininely so; their eyes were glazed, their pale, slender bodies only partially clad and gleaming with perfumed oil. He was wise enough to know, however, that no matter how incapable they appeared in their *hashish*-induced euphoria, they wouldn't hesitate to slip a dagger between his ribs should he be so foolish as to underestimate their obsessive dedication to their religion; and, therefore, their leader.

Rashid ad-Din Sinan, also known as the Old Man of the Mountain, had survived several assassination attempts before establishing himself as leader of this second colony of the *Hashishiyun* in the cliffs of Masyaf. In white robe and turban, he provided a stark contrast for his gawkily made-up young bodyguards, looking more like their kindly old father.

Their father he was not. Nor was he kind.

"Will you smoke the pipe?" Sinan asked, as a servant offered one to Tancred.

"Thank you, no." There was no telling what would become

of him if he allowed himself to be seduced by the insidious spell of *hashish*. Only the knowledge that the Old Man got along amicably with Christians had brought Tancred here personally. Sunnite Muslims were the objects of the Shi'ite *Hashishiyun's* aggression, not Christians, although the *Hashishiyun* were not averse to selling their services to the highest bidder.

They were in a man-made garden, an oasis in the barren Nosairi Mountains. The sun felt pleasantly warm beneath the cool mountain breeze, which was laced with the sweet, pungent scent of *hashish*. Tancred would normally have found the tinkling of the small fountain soothing, but he was in no mood to be soothed. He was on his guard and, in spite of his temper and his inclination to be blunt, he had to make certain that his anger didn't make him careless.

"I take it you are not happy with Ahab's efforts?"

Tancred sipped at the iced apricot sorbet, savoring the cool sweetness as it slid down his dry throat. The delicious taste distracted his angry thoughts for a time. He cleared his throat. "No . . . not if his efforts were as poor as his results. His hirelings bungled the job and retreated. St. Rémy made it to Tyre, so I am told."

Sinan nodded. "At least they didn't kill him."

Tancred sent him a fulminating look. He didn't see any humor in the remark. "I thought the *Hashishiyun* took their work seriously."

" 'Tis easier to kill a man than take him prisoner."

Tancred nodded. He had to agree with Sinan on that point, and the Old Man of the Mountain's followers were most adept at outright murder.

"And I am told that the Templar, true to his principles, would have willingly perished in the defense of the ship."

Tancred just stared at him.

"We had a . . . *friend* aboard the vessel," Sinan said smoothly, reaching for a bunch of lush, purple grapes in one of the silver bowls before him. "And we presently have a

supply ship docked in Tyre. We know St. Rémy is there to
escort the bishop of—"

"I didn't hire the *Hashishiyun* to tell me something I already knew!" Tancred snarled. One of the guards gave him
a lethargic look that was almost laughable, but Tancred knew
better than to laugh. He had to curb his tongue if he wanted
to leave the fortress of Masyaf alive.

Obviously unruffled, Sinan chewed several grapes, swallowed, then resumed speaking. "And, as I was saying, a
Frankish bishop and two young women." He paused meaningfully, holding Tancred's gaze steadily. "One of them is
purported as very striking in looks. . . ."

"Your assumption is absurd. He's the ideal Templar, if
you're hinting at some connection between the two." He
couldn't keep the bitterness from his voice.

"He is first a man, just like you."

Tancred had the grace to color. He, too, was a Templar,
although it still galled him that he'd had to buy his knighthood. And he didn't need to be reminded of his shortcom-
ings. He'd used his position only to his own advantage, as
he had done all his life. Being born a bastard, what choice
had he ever had?

The old man's eyes narrowed. "You can be as disdainful
as you like, my friend, but the *Hashishiyun* are not known
for turning on one of their own."

Of course Tancred knew exactly what he was referring to,
but the knight wasn't about to take lessons in morality from
the leader of the *Hashishiyun*. "And if one of your own goes
astray?"

Sinan shrugged and briefly stared out at the surrounding
mountains. A faint smile softened the line of his mouth. " 'Tis
rare. We give them no reason. His eyes clashed with Tancred's then. "You could possibly use the woman somehow
to capture your quarry, then you would save your silver and
not have to worry about his accidental death." He paused a

moment. "Word has it, though, that St. Rémy is not one to be toyed with."

That, of course, was true, Tancred conceded grudgingly. "I can handle St. Rémy, even if your agents cannot. Tell Ahab I want my silver back. I will accomplish my aim without outside help. 'Tis a personal grudge I bear him and I've thought better now of drawing others in to do what I can do myself."

The old man obviously knew nothing of the reason for Tancred's interest in Reynaud de St. Rémy. Very few people, he suspected, did. Or maybe Sinan did know and for his own reasons chose to say nothing. One could never be certain with the leader of the *Hashishiyun,* who was often described as omniscient.

If Tancred could discover the source of St. Rémy's power, he could use it himself. No one would refuse him anything if he could perform miracles. But if St. Rémy actually had no special gift, or if he couldn't transfer it or divulge its source, he would be put to death. Reynaud de St. Rémy had been a thorn in Tancred's side ever since he had come to the Holy Land—when Reynaud was young and eager. His family was wealthy—his father, Gérard de St. Rémy, a staunch supporter of the Templar Knights—and his bloodlines pure. Reynaud himself was energetic and idealistic. He unconsciously commanded attention and admiration—from women as well as men. He was also courageous to a fault and high in the Grand Master Templar's esteem. At least until recently, when rumors of some disagreement with the Templar Rule on St. Rémy's part spread throughout the Templar community. . . .

Before this hint of trouble, it had been rumored that St. Rémy was being considered for a higher position, possibly even Seneschal or Marshal Templar, positions that Tancred had dreamed of and worked toward. Tancred hated him with a passion, for St. Rémy was everything he was not.

And then Tancred had inadvertently witnessed Reynaud heal a man. . . .

Le Bref had wasted no time in taking advantage of his own carefully cultivated connections in the Levant in an attempt to secretly capture St. Rémy and place him at his mercy.

Tancred could only assume de Sablé didn't know of Reynaud's power (he had no idea who knew and who didn't), and therefore he wouldn't be so outraged to learn of Tancred's machinations if Reynaud de St. Rémy was in disfavor; or so le Bref reasoned.

And even if the Grand Master Templar were to be furious, why would Tancred be concerned once he possessed St. Rémy's power? If the knight had no special touch and continued to disagree with Templar strictures, his disappearance and death would be no great loss. And besides, in Tancred's bitter disappointment, he'd been planning to leave the Templar Order for months now.

If he could possess St. Rémy's powers, he could rule Outremer.

"Why don't you tell Ahab yourself?" the Old Man of the Mountain was saying. "He's in Tyre. And so is St. Rémy." He leaned forward. "As I suggested before, perhaps you can lure him into your snare. You must use your imagination, Tancred le Bref. . . ."

The bishop's palace was as surprising as the other sights in Tyre. The sheer opulence of the edifice was almost shocking, especially after the austere convent of St. Bernadette's. Beautiful marble walls and painted ceilings gave Brielle the feeling that she was in a dream world. All the rooms opened onto a splendid inner courtyard that offered shade from the merciless summer sun and a serene setting for anyone who cared to take advantage of it.

Brielle and Anabette shared a suite of rooms off the inner courtyard—a spacious bedchamber with an adjoining bath that was every bit as luxurious as the rest of the building.

"A heathen home," Anabette had called it, and Brielle had to silently concur, wondering if this palace could be any less pagan than that of Rashid's family.

The late William, Archbishop of Tyre, had lived here, she remembered. He certainly was no heathen. Bishop Abelard had told her that under William of Tyre, the archbishopric had been the most important in the Latin kingdom.

Aside from the bed, several silk-covered divans strewn with brightly-colored pillows graced the room; silk hangings colored the walls and small tables were scattered about, vessels of silver and fine glass resting upon them. The mosaic floor beckoned, and Brielle soon found herself padding barefoot over the cool, smooth tiles. She was ambivalent about the luxury of the rooms and made a mental note to ask Reynaud about the possibility of staying at an inn.

She didn't have to wait long to see him again.

She wandered into the courtyard, her curiosity and appreciation of all things beautiful overcoming her initial hesitation. It was shaded by several small trees and scented by blooming roses and jasmine. Small, meticulously trimmed shrubs surrounded the central fountain, which splashed over an arrangement of beautiful, carved stones. The pool around the fountain even contained lively-hued fish.

Brielle was enchanted and closed her eyes as she inhaled the fragrant air. When she opened them, a tall man was walking toward her. At first glance, she almost didn't recognize him. He looked Arab—although he was taller than the Arabs she'd seen thus far—from the tone of his skin, to the silk robe he wore like some Saracen prince. As he approached, she recognized him and bade her pounding heart be still. The proud bearing should have immediately labeled him as the Templar she'd first met in France, in spite of his garb. His sun-bronzed skin was a sharp contrast to his pale robe.

He passed the tinkling fountain and moved toward her, the soft material of his robe alternately molding to his long legs and then flowing away with his movements. He looked as comfortable in Arab garb as he had in a knight's chain mail.

Her surprise must have been obvious, for he said, "Don't be alarmed, *demoiselle*. Everyone here wears similar clothing—'tis cooler and more practical."

It seemed he was often telling her not to be alarmed, and she didn't like what that implied about her.

"Are you not supposed to remain in . . . Templar garb?" she asked suddenly self-conscious of her own clothing.

"As I said, everyone dresses the same. The Arabs have taught us much about this land and how to survive in it."

He must have seen the disapproval in her expression, for he added, "You may dress any way you like, Lady Brielle."

Feeling sufficiently rebuked, she was tempted to ask about her plans regarding the search for Geoffrey d'Avignon. Yet she was hesitant to stir his ire—as she knew she surely would. He'd been dead set against her coming to Outremer from the first.

She cast about in her mind for something to say. "Surely they expect you at—at your own . . ." She trailed off. Where did he live? In a monastery? A castle? Once again she acknowledged that she knew pitifully little about this land and the people who occupied it.

"Are you so eager to be rid of me?" he asked, taking her aback with his bluntness. Before she could answer, he explained, "Our numbers were decimated at Hattin; both Templars and Hospitallers are scattered here and there—only a few of our fortresses remain under our control." He stood before her, his eyes turning bleak. "We stay where we can."

Brielle turned toward the fountain, welcoming a brief but cool rush of air that moved over her. "I did not mean it as an insult, *chevalier*. I was merely curious."

He followed her to the fountain. "I am assigned to Bishop Abelard for as long as he remains here. If I'm needed to fight, I'll be summoned."

Brielle felt an unexpected spurt of happiness at the first

part of his revelation. The second part, however, made her heart turn over. The thought of Reynaud de St. Rémy engaging in battle and possibly dying was extremely disturbing.

"Now that King Philip and Richard of England are here, there will be renewed fighting," she said, struggling to hide her misgivings. "Are they not laying siege to Acre even as we speak?"

He nodded, a frown tracing its way across his forehead.

"I hope they—" She halted in mid-sentence. What was she saying? *I hope they don't call you to battle?* Her cheeks suddenly became hot. "That is, I hope they can retake all that you've lost." Surely they wouldn't expose him to death if he were so valuable in tending the wounded, she thought. If anyone of importance knew about it . . .

But that was none of her concern. Reynaud had his life to live, and she had hers.

Brielle dipped a finger in the pool, glancing down through her lashes at his sandal-clad feet. She envied him those open shoes, and she suddenly wished she could shed her clothes and frolic like a child in the fountain. Evidently, she was falling under the spell of the Holy Land.

"Is there a chapel here?" she asked out of the blue, wanting to catch these uprooted Franks in their godless practices.

"Indeed." Was that a smirk hovering about his mouth? she wondered. As if he divined her thoughts? "Or you can visit the cathedral . . . 'tis one of the most magnificent in the Levant."

Her eyes lit up at the thought, threatening to drive other concerns from her mind. Her first obligation, she reminded herself sternly, was to her father. She hadn't traveled to the Holy Land to traipse about Tyre with a handsome, if ineligible, knight.

The scent of jasmine came to her, and Brielle closed her eyes and let her head fall back, savoring the fragrance for a moment. She raised her wet hand to her exposed neck, allowing her dripping fingers to drift down that slim stem, and she was once again terribly tempted to immerse herself bodily in the cool water before them.

She didn't see Reynaud watching her unconsciously seductive movements with a suspended look in his eyes. "You can bathe if you like," he said from beside her, his gaze riveted to her uplifted face.

She opened her eyes and lowered her chin. "Yes . . . there's a bath adjoining our room. I was in such a hurry to see what the courtyard was like that I completely forgot about bathing."

"The heat sends the people to their baths often—much more often than in France. Also their health practices are better than ours, and they stress cleanliness."

Her eyes met his, and she saw something within their amber depths that caused strange stirrings deep within her. She felt entirely too warm, inside as well as out. The heat that had begun to leave her face returned with a vengeance and spread downward over her neck before it insidiously invaded her body with an intensity that made her breathless.

"Did . . . you bathe?" she asked inanely, realizing it was a very personal question. But he looked so fresh and clean, his dark hair still damp, his body smelling clean and faintly of citrus.

"Oui," he answered. " 'Tis a most pleasant experience here in the East. The Arabs have running water, you know—no lugging buckets for the city-dwellers."

"Running water?" she asked, not quite certain of his meaning.

"Rainwater is collected in cisterns, then piped in for the baths—heated beforehand—and fountains."

She was pleasantly surprised, and found herself eager to try bathing in this strange land. Surely the practice wasn't pagan. And Reynaud looked so refreshed. . . .

What of inquiring about an inn? whispered an unwelcome voice.

She ignored it and leaned one hip against the edge of the

fountain, absently trailing her hand through the water once more. Reason fought for dominance over the natural inclinations that swirled through her. She was affected in strange but wondrous ways when she was near Reynaud de St. Rémy, and now the sensations moving through her were as powerful and sensual as when they'd been together in the intimacy of the temporary stable on the *Madonna*. She strongly suspected, however, that her original purpose in coming to Outremer would be sidetracked by the distraction of the man before her—Templar or nay—if she followed her heart instead of her head. The less involved she was with him, the better—especially because she doubted whether he would help her in any way to achieve her goal. And that was definitely her loss, for Brielle knew Reynaud de St. Rémy would have been a huge asset to her had he approved of her intentions.

His opposition, however, had been obvious from the first. She deliberately dredged up memories of their discussion in Abbess Marguerite's study to stoke the anger she needed to battle her attraction to him physically and, therefore, broach the subject of Geoffrey d'Avignon.

Reynaud handed her a blood-red rose. "For my lady's hair."

She gave him a half-smile and lifted the blossom to her nose. It smelled sweet and clean and reminded her of Provence. Tears filled her eyes without warning and she lowered the flower and bowed her head to hide her emotion. It would never do to let him know she was beginning to feel homesick.

She cleared her throat in the quivering silence and lifted the rose to tuck it behind her ear. "Oooh," she said softly, as a thorn pierced her fingertip. She stood in reaction, the blossom falling to the tiled courtyard floor. She slipped the tip of her injured finger into her mouth and tasted blood. She remembered with a pang how Geoffrey d'Avignon used to kiss her scrapes and scratches when she was a child.

"Let me see," Reynaud commanded quietly, and reached to take her hand away from her mouth.

Brielle complied and let him examine her finger, the touch of his hand on hers sending a shiver up her arm and stirring an alien desire in the pit of her stomach. He smoothed the pad of his thumb over the tiny wound, a look of concentration on his face. Within moments, his eyes met hers . . . and the throbbing was gone. Her finger was mended and she felt only a slight coolness on the newly-healed flesh.

It was the *only* part of her body that felt cool in that moment . . . until she realized what he'd done. She remained very still, suddenly awestruck and unsure if she should acknowledge what had just happened. But it was obviously nothing unusual to Reynaud, for he released her hand and bent to retrieve the rose, his actions very normal, his expression noncommittal. "Unfortunately, every rose has thorns," he said, as he removed the offending thistle. "May I?" he queried in an odd voice, his hand already reaching toward her hair. It was his voice, she thought, that betrayed him.

"Oui," she whispered, frozen to the floor in anticipation.

He tucked the rose behind her ear, then gently arranged the hair around it. Even through the confusion of her turbulent thoughts, it seemed to Brielle that his fingers lingered a fraction too long as they sifted through her hair. Before she could even try and translate his behavior, he murmured, "Your hair puts the finest silk to shame."

She tilted back her head to better see his face and found herself staring at his mouth, so very close to hers, as he paused before straightening. His sweet breath brushed her face, the combined scents of citrus and male threatening to overpower her. The butterflies in her belly turned frenetic.

She couldn't answer, her tongue was paralyzed. . . .

Reynaud felt the blood rushing to his loins, his heart assaulting his rib cage like a hammer. His eyes were riveted to hers, and he felt as if he were being pulled into the aqua-marine depths of the Mediterranean. And, God help him, he couldn't seem to remove his hand from the glossy mane of her hair.

Seemingly of their own volition, silken strands the color of fresh honey wound about his fingers, trapping them, and he soon found himself caressing her scalp. He slowly, inexorably, pulled her head toward him. She didn't resist, and Reynaud cast aside his practiced discipline, his rigid control, and even the Templar Rule which forbade a knight of his stature to become involved with a woman.

More and more obviously, when he was in *this* woman's presence, his troubles faded in significance, and a peaceful calm invaded his very soul. She laughed and the sound lightened his heart; she smiled and the world was suddenly brighter.

And when they touched . . .

His lips met hers in a tentative kiss. She tasted of youth and innocence, of an unfettered soul, and Reynaud suddenly had no greater concern on his mind than immersing himself in this precious pleasure—and pleasing her in return.

His tongue gently traced the lines of her lips, and her mouth opened in innocent response, soft and lush, sweet as nectar. A new rush of desire stirred deeply within him, and he pulled her head closer, felt the edge of her teeth, the velvet-rasp of her tongue against his.

He was going wonderfully mad . . . losing himself and savoring the feeling. He just barely had the presence of mind to be thankful for the cover of the full-length robe he wore, which hid the evidence of his passion.

Passion.

The thought hit him like the bolt from a crossbow, reverberating through his mind. *Passion.*

A Templar's only passion should have been reserved for Christ.

Celibacy. Poverty. Obedience. The words ignited a spark

of reason, and Reynaud marshaled his wits and dragged his mouth away from hers. . . .

Her eyes, now a deep jade-blue with desire, grew troubled as she stared up at him in puzzlement. Her petal-soft lips were trembling from his kiss, and only a fragile filament of reason prevented him from tasting them again.

"Forgive me," he mumbled, releasing her head and turning away. He faced the fountain and drew in a deep, sustaining breath, fighting to rein in his raging emotions. "Forgive me for giving in to my baser instincts."

He turned back to her, only to see the humiliation of rejection flare in her expressive eyes. He couldn't know that she was thinking of the deep affection that had bonded her father and her mother . . . and how the late Katherine d'Avignon had told her young daughter that love between a man and woman was beautiful and sacred.

"There was nothing base about what we did," she said with utter frankness, then sank down to a stone bench nearby and stared down at the veined design in the marble. "It may have been wrong, but 'twas certainly not base."

She was embarrassed by her response to him as it was, but she was also a young woman with needs and desires; she was learning, and he was a man. That he was a Templar had become secondary in those all-too-brief moments they had kissed. He was a man first, and she a woman.

"I should know better, *demoiselle*. I took a vow of chastity, among others, and you are a maiden. I had no business taking advantage of you, Templar or not."

The righteousness in his voice irked her in the extreme. "You may rest assured that one stolen kiss can do nothing to destroy my maidenhead. Forgive yourself, *chevalier*, that you may preserve your honor."

He certainly had been no virgin when he took his precious vows, she thought shrewishly. No man—or boy—with his looks could ever have escaped the wiles of the hordes of females, from milk maid to queen, who would have risked

anything to bed him. As for poverty, another vow she knew
he'd taken, he looked anything but poor. Abbess Marguerite
had told her that the Templars were the most powerful of the
religious orders in Outremer—with vast holdings and for-
tunes in gold throughout Europe.

And now he was going to try and rationalize his behavior,
she thought; no doubt hers, as well. "You aren't perfect,
chevalier, much as you may strive to be. You are human, as
am I. I make no apologies." *Nor will I ever regret that kiss!*

"You need not. 'Twas entirely my fault."

"Aye, without a doubt . . . *Saint Reynaud.*"

Her last two words hung in the air between them, and she
looked up in time to see him flush. Was it anger or embarrassment? she wondered, and suddenly regretted naming him
a saint. He, who evidently never lost control, was obviously
struggling to regain it.

Brielle didn't know whether to be flattered by his actions,
or insulted by his apparent regret. Had it been any other man
but this proud Templar with his impossibly high standards
and expectations, perhaps she would have better been able
to show some graciousness about their indiscretion. Under
the circumstances, she had become immediately defensive
and found herself saying things she wouldn't have dared just
weeks ago.

"Why did you come here?" she asked, wishing heartily to
change the subject. "To the courtyard, I mean. Were you
looking for someone?"

For a brief space in time he was silent, and Brielle stood,
ready to retreat to her room and nurse her bruised pride.

He met her gaze and held it, the flush receding, the self-
discipline evidently back in place. "I was looking for *you,
demoiselle.* I wanted to try and talk some sense into you . . .
dissuade you from your folly."

Brielle glanced down at his hands, curled into fists at his
sides . . . the only sign of any remaining turmoil. Deliberately acting as if he alluded to their kiss, she heeded a

naughty imp prompting her to say, *"Dissuade,* Sieur Reynaud, or *persuade?"*

He frowned at her, ignoring her gibe. "Dissuade you from conducting a futile search. A search that could get you hurt or even killed . . ."

Ten

It took a moment for Brielle to realize that he wasn't talking about their kiss.

Search? Of course . . . the search for her father.

Reynaud de St. Rémy most assuredly was subject to lightning-quick mood changes, and it was this more than the actual mention of her reason for coming to the Levant that annoyed her. He was somber and sensible once again, as if they had never shared that magical moment.

"You mean you have decided, at this late date, to dissuade me from making inquiries about my father?"

He nodded. "Not the inquiries so much as an actual search. . . . Bishop Abelard has indicated that he'll allow you to remain here under his protection for a time. Why not enjoy all this—" he waved a hand to indicate the entire courtyard and the city beyond, "before you return to France? I don't mean to be insensitive, Lady Brielle, but your father cannot be alive after all this time. Why risk your life for naught?"

Brielle fought down her ire. "I didn't come all this way just to *enjoy* the scenery, Sieur Reynaud . . ."

A terrible thought struck her then: Could he be trying to persuade her to remain here in Tyre merely to be at his beck and call? For his amusement, perhaps, while he served the bishop and she remained in this place like some concubine? To serve *his* needs? After all, he seemed to be on some sort of leave of absence from his order. Maybe that meant that he could take a leave from his vows, as well. . . .

Don't you know him better than that? chided a voice. *You flatter yourself!*

Guilt sifted through her. Of course, she knew he wasn't that type of man—not with his precious honor and his determination to be a paragon of virtue!

Reynaud didn't like the accusation forming in her eyes. "You can make any inquiries from here—although you'll need funds to persuade some to divulge what they know, and then to hire others to glean what information you can."

Brielle lifted her chin and met his gaze steadily. "I didn't face a long and hazardous voyage—complete with attacking corsairs—only to make a few inquiries from the safety of a bishop's palace. You do me an injustice in suggesting I do so." She moved past him, intent on escaping his presence and implementing a course of action to learn the fate of Geoffrey d'Avignon.

From what she had so far observed, Tyre was a good-sized city—full of Christians as well as Muslims—and she was certain she didn't need this patronizing Templar knight to accomplish her goal. She could enlist advice and aid from any number of people . . . Bishop Abelard and Rashid and Taillefer and, when he returned, the bishop of Tyre himself. And there was Humphrey of Toulouse and several other Templars who had sailed for Tyre on the *Madonna*.

Why, even Captain Paolo! Hadn't he boasted of the rôle the Venetians had played in assisting the Franks in the Holy Land? There surely were Venetians the captain knew in any number of port cities. . . .

You don't speak their language, whispered a voice.

She would cross that bridge when she came to it.

Brielle unconsciously tossed her head, trying to ignore the knight standing behind her. His hand on her arm, however, brought him sharply back into focus.

He was studying her with a most intense look in his eyes—

as if he were trying to read her very thoughts . . . learn of her most secret plans.

Aye, to foil them, she thought sourly.

Giving no indication of the effect of his touch, she glared down at his hand, at the long fingers that bore a light sprinkling of dark hair above the knuckles. She couldn't tell through the sleeve of her undergown, but she knew his hands were calloused from handling weapons. She also knew how potent their touch could be for the sick and injured and how soothing to a skittish animal.

Her anger began to ebb, more from her own common sense than his mystical abilities. At least that was what she hoped, for it would have been the final irony to be unable to control her own emotions when she was with the man who could provoke her to such extremes.

"You are sounding more and more like that sharp-tongued friend of yours," he said in a clipped voice. "It ill becomes you."

She pulled her arm from his grasp and spun about to face him, burning. "At least I don't pretend to be something I'm not! A *chevalier* is never so rude to a lady!"

"I'm a Poor Knight of the Temple of Solomon, *demoiselle,* and not some lovelorn knight of Provence pining away over another's wife."

She set her teeth together, wishing she'd never met Reynaud de St. Rémy. "Will you escort me to the battle site at Hattin or nay?"

Reynaud couldn't believe his ears. She actually wanted to go to the Horns of Hattin? The very site of the slaughter of the Crusader army four years past? That place where he'd fought his first battle, and nearly lost his life . . .

"You cannot be serious!" he said, and placed a hand on each of her shoulders, ready to shake the silly notion from her head if necessary.

"Unhand me," she said softly, her eyes narrowing like a cat's. "All I need from you is a 'yes' or 'no.' "

They stood in the cool oasis of the courtyard, oblivious to the birds that sang in the trees, the melodious sounds of the fountain. Reynaud felt his hands tightening on her slender shoulders, in direct defiance of her command, and thought instead how fragile she was physically. He would never take her to the Horns of Hattin—nor would he allow anyone else to do so as long as he could lift a sword.

"Even if I consented, what could you hope to find there?" he asked, his voice frighteningly calm. "Mayhap your father's clean-picked bones?"

Her expression clouded, and he almost regretted his question. "There is nothing there now, Brielle d'Avignon. Anything of value—coins, weapons, clothing—was stripped from the bodies long ago, and any human remains were devoured by animals. Even remaining carrion has long since—" He stopped as the blood drained from her face; he feared she would faint.

But she was made of sterner stuff than that. "I thank you for your detailed description. Obviously I was mistaken in believing you could ever aid me in my search."

She pushed his hands away, turned, and stalked from the courtyard, unmindful of the rose as it slipped from her hair and fell to the tiled floor.

Reynaud watched her leave, a host of conflicting feelings tumbling through him. He bent to pick up the blossom, staring at it resting in the palm of his hand. Brielle d'Avignon had somehow become important to him—too important—and he wondered if this was one more test God was putting him through. Heaven knew he'd miserably failed the others, having discovered, once he'd come to Outremer, an unwelcome soft streak to go with his healing skills . . . he hadn't quite decided whether the "gift" was a curse or a blessing. Compassion was a good attribute for anyone . . . but in its place. But by far his worst failure was the realization that he violently disagreed with a basic premise of the Templar

Rule—the ideology of St. Bernard himself, that killing non-Christian men for Christ would reap glorious reward.

His fist clenched in reaction, crushing the rose.

And now this unexpected and unwelcome attraction to Brielle d'Avignon. . . .

In the Templar hierarchy, there was a place for *frères mariés* —married brothers. But they occupied the lower and looser ranks of brothers, made up of temporary and associate knights and sergeants. These brothers came to the Order in a married state . . . they did not wed after joining the Order. So Reynaud was breaking yet another rule, he acknowledged, by expressing forbidden feelings for a woman.

He felt as if he were being crushed between an anvil and a hammer—caught between his wishes to live up to his father's expectations and his own rebellious tendencies. He'd always worshipped his father, had wanted to please him . . . even if it meant serving the Church in some capacity. His oldest brother, William, had stood to inherit the St. Rémy holdings upon his death, and Reynaud had accepted that. The middle son, André, was to receive their mother's smaller holdings and, in the case of William's death, become the new lord.

The third son usually went into the priesthood, and his father especially had wanted him to serve God. Gérard de St. Rémy, however, also believed Reynaud could satisfy both his love of horses and sword play and his obligation to serve the Church by becoming a Templar knight.

Reynaud, of course, had been moved by his father's desire to keep him content, and had eagerly joined the Poor Knights of the Temple of Solomon in France. He had then journeyed to Outremer to fight the infidels, as his father had when he'd gone on crusade . . .

And discovered his aversion to killing other human beings for a place in Heaven.

He closed his eyes, gripped his neck with his free hand,

and let his head drop back, wiling away the all-too-familiar anguish that wracked him by day, haunted him by night.

Why *him?*

He let his head drop and opened his fingers. The rose, crumpled but intact, still nestled in the palm of his hand; it reminded him sharply of the young woman who'd entered his life weeks ago and was unwittingly adding to his already heavy burden.

He pictured her stunning blue-green eyes, the long, glossy mane of her hair, like sun shining on ripe wheat. And her determination to venture into dangerous areas to learn what had become of her father.

Brielle d'Avignon was as prickly as the rose before he'd removed its thorns, but, no matter how fragile her body had felt to him, she also had more than her share of courage.

He could only pray to God that he could resist his attraction to her for the duration of Bishop Abelard's stay . . . certainly with more success than he'd had a short while ago. And, more importantly, that her bravery would not result in harm to her . . . or cost her her life.

The familiar urge to withdraw from his worldly troubles came upon him, and slowly he felt himself giving in to it. *Coward!* He closed his eyes and silently admitted that deep inside where no one could see, he was indeed a coward. Nothing like his father . . . or even his two brothers. How disappointed Gérard de St. Rémy would be if he knew.

He struggled for a moment, roused by his conscience to fight the insidious urge rather than give in to it.

A soft, almost imperceptible rustling came from the shrubs across the way and caught his attention. His eyes snapped open and one hand went to withdraw the dagger he carried concealed in the folds of his robe.

But the man who stepped forward was no spy or assassin . . . only Rashid.

"Hiding in the bushes now, are we?" the Templar asked,

distracted for the moment from the shameful impulse to retreat.

A ruddy color invaded the Arab's cheeks. "I wasn't hiding, but my Bedouin ancestors could be stealthy when they needed to be."

Reynaud suppressed a grin, never failing to be amused by the proud Arab's flawless and formal French—and his inherent ability to lie without a qualm. "And what of your merchant family here in Tyre? Are they adept at sneaking up on unsuspecting persons as well?"

Rahsid drew himself up regally. "My family here is most successful, master, and you know as well as I that a merchant must be smooth-tongued and quick-witted."

Reynaud refrained from saying that *good at lying* would be more accurate. His mood temporarily improved by this faithful man, he asked instead, "Did you see and hear *everything?*"

"Enough." The Arab crossed his arms and looked pointedly at the rose still in Reynaud's hand. "She is like a rose, is she not? And you would seek to crush her."

Reynaud's brows drew together. "Rather save her from unnecessary heartache . . . and even from losing her life." He glanced down at the blossom. "Now she's angry—hates me, I think, because she'll not listen to reason . . . she no doubt thinks my refusal to take her to the Horns of Hattin is based on obstinacy."

"Why can you not take her there? Safe conduct can be obtained from the right people."

"That doesn't mean it isn't dangerous!" Reynaud spun away from the smaller man, running the fingers of his free hand through his dark hair in vexation. "If you suggest such a thing, you have no more sense than she does! We both know there's naught left to see. Why in God's name would she even *consider* going there?"

"To satisfy her curiosity. It may seem foolhardy to you, but not to her."

Reynaud threw the Arab a dubious look. "Think you she'll discover some grisly memento to reward her visit? Like a man's skull? Or mayhap there's even a marker proclaiming 'Geoffrey d'Avignon lies buried here'?"

Rashid shook his head, his dark eyes somber. " 'Tis nothing to make light of, master. If you would dissuade her, do it with kindness, not harsh words."

With an angry gesture, Reynaud flung the rose into the pool. "Kindness? Bah! I'm a Templar . . . not a nursemaid to coddle a child and coax her from her whimsical fancies."

Rashid studied the frustrated knight for a moment, his expression unreadable. "You are more taken with the rose than you will admit. You've lost your objectivity."

Reynaud watched the concentric rings ripple outward toward the marble pool rim, his thoughts chaotic. One thing he didn't need, he thought, was advice from Rashid on matters of the heart.

Ah, so you admit 'tis a matter of the heart, whispered a voice.

One more broken vow. . . .

It occurred to Reynaud that his friend would be pleased to see him become romantically involved with Brielle d'Avignon. And Taillefer, as well, he suspected, for both men had on occasion encouraged him to leave the Templar Order. And, he thought wryly, like a pair of circling vultures, they usually waited until one of his weaker moments to move in.

He looked up at Rashid. "I think not," he said softly. "I would refuse to take *anyone* to Hattin—unless they wished to see Galilee."

"You are fortunate she didn't ask to examine those poor wretches imprisoned in Damascus," the Arab said, then moved slowly around the fountain, his hands now crossed behind his back, his head bowed in thought. "Mayhap you should try honey instead of vinegar with our beautiful rose . . . treat her like all women like to be treated—be very agreeable as you try to distract her from her purpose."

Reynaud turned and leaned back against the fountain edge, his shrewd gaze homing in on Rashid. "Are you suggesting I break my vows?"

"That is up to you," the Arab said, as he raised his gaze to meet Reynaud's. "There are any number of ways to distract an unworldly young woman newly arrived in the Levant. Surely, if you are determined, you can do so without breaking any of your vows? You are merely attempting to keep her out of harm's way. And, after all," he added, "you are following the bishop's instructions concerning her welfare."

"Then you want me to deliberately deceive her . . . make believe I am interested in her as a woman, which would not only be breaking my vow, but would also make me a liar."

"Master, I think not a liar. If you felt no attraction to her, you wouldn't be a man whole. As for breaking your vow of celibacy, you're too noble-minded to stoop to deflowering such a maiden. And, in the unlikely event you did, surely you would be absolved if you confessed your sin to a priest."

I think not a liar . . . Was his attraction to Brielle d'Avignon so obvious? And the underlying irony of the Arab's words . . . his subtle way of mocking some of the tenets of Christianity was not lost on Reynaud. But telling him that he was only half a man if he felt nothing for Brielle d'Avignon . . . ? Yet too noble-minded to let his love rule his head?

Suddenly he grinned, half-tempted to strangle Rashid and half-tempted to sidle over to him, put their heads together, and formulate a scheme to guarantee that the lovely young Brielle wouldn't want to set foot outside the walls of Tyre.

He shrugged. "Or I could convince her that only a woman with a death wish would leave the safety of the city. Not so very far from the truth, Rashid, is it?"

The Arab returned his grin—as if they shared a secret of great import. "Or we could send the yellow-haired one to Hattin," he suggested slyly. "Any remaining bones would rise up and flee before her honed tongue."

"Don't let the minstrel hear you say that about his lady

love, or he'll spit you on a pike." They grinned in unison this time, and Reynaud suddenly felt lighter of heart.

A week passed, and Reynaud found himself enjoying the rôle he so grudgingly accepted after the scene in the court-yard. He escorted Bishop Abelard, Brielle, and Anabette to places of interest in Tyre, caught between the knowledge that most of the Templar forces were involved in the siege of Acre several miles down the coast, and his irrepressible pleasure at seeing Brielle d'Avignon every day. With Taillefer and Rashid usually accompanying them, it was like they were one big, happy family, and Reynaud found himself smiling inwardly at the thought more than once. His darker side told him he enjoyed being near Brielle d'Avignon like some moonstruck swain, but he ruthlessly ignored that cynical side.

He tried to tell himself it was Bishop Abelard's company he enjoyed so—which he did—but he knew it was more than that holding him in Tyre. True, Robert de Sablé had ordered him to remain with the bishop for as long as he was needed, but the Templar Master surely had no idea of the greater rewards of Reynaud's temporary duty.

It was true, he had to admit, that he welcomed the break from fighting and the constant strain of his nagging doubts about his life as a Templar; yet, at the same time, he won-dered if remaining with the bishop's party wouldn't make matters worse instead of better now that Brielle d'Avignon was included in Abelard's entourage. . . .

He found, as the days went by, that the other men accom-panying the bishop—his own fellow Templar's like Hum-phrey of Toulouse included—were equally taken with Brielle. It was almost comical to watch them falling over each other to be helpful and informative—even though she did nothing to encourage their attention. Her ignorance of the Holy Land, its people, and their customs was the only catalyst needed to rouse the male instincts of every one of them. Taillefer was the only one seemingly immune—and that was because he couldn't see past his nose where any female but Anabette was concerned.

John the Gaunt obviously loved her like a daughter, but even the imperturbable Rashid seemed to have fallen under her spell. Much to Reynaud's amusement, the Arab had continued to call Brielle "the rose" when she wasn't present. He began to worry that the little man, who'd lost his wife and two children to marauding Turks, would fall head over heels for a woman who could never return that love.

Or could she? Who was he to dictate who should, or could, love whom?

In spite of the fact that Rashid was a Muslim, the Arab's empathy for Brielle d'Avignon's cause might move him to take her under his wing. And not only could the man fall in love with the girl, but his sympathy conflicted with his allegiance to Reynaud, who was in direct opposition to her wishes.

How's that for jealousy, St. Rémy? taunted an unwelcome voice. *A jealousy born of your own feelings for her.*

Several days after their arrival, Reynaud received a message from Robert de Sablé, warning him that Tancred le Bref, a fellow Templar of lesser stature and disreputable behavior, had disappeared mysteriously. De Sablé assumed the knight either had been killed somewhere, or that he had gone renegade. Knowing the scheming and unscrupulous le Bref, Reynaud was inclined to believe the latter.

Although he rarely underestimated an adversary, Reynaud dismissed the warning from his mind; he had half a score of other, more important concerns than a rogue Templar who had always hated him. . . .

That same afternoon, another blight on his burgeoning contentment materialized. Two knights showed up at the bishop's palace asking for an audience with Bishop Abelard. Reynaud was with the cleric when they arrived and remained with Abelard at his request while the two Franks stated their business.

"We bring a message from my lord Aimery de Belvoir," one of them announced and handed a parchment to the bishop.

His calm expression changed to a frown as he read the words in the letter, then he slowly looked up at Reynaud, a thoughtful look on his features. . . .

"If you cannot bear to let her go, then wed the girl."

The minstrel's fingers slipped from the lute strings he'd been strumming softly, sending a discordant sound echoing across the spacious room. "I thought you were my friend," he answered with a twist of his lips. "Marriage is not for me."

Reynaud stood before the arched doorway, looking out onto the courtyard, his arms crossed over his chest. He could tell exactly how emotionally involved the minstrel was with Anabette de Belvoir by the subtle change in his voice.

Reynaud turned to face his friend, taking in the sudden tension on Taillefer's features, despite his casually draped position across a silk-covered divan. "Her dowry is substantial—you could do much worse." He cocked one eyebrow. "And 'tis time for you to start a family."

Taillefer sat up and set aside his lute. He looked askance at Reynaud. "And *you* are so wise in the ways of love."

Reynaud laughed softly. "Love and marriage have naught to do with each other. A man is supposed to love *another's* wife, isn't that what you sing about, *troubadour?*"

"I couldn't serve you then, *mon ami,* as I pledged long ago."

Reynaud rested his hands on his hips and shook his head. "You've more than repaid the debt, Taillefer. Live your own life and be content."

He knew the minstrel would object, for the hundredth time

at least, but he had never been more serious. There was no
need for Taillefer to die a slow death in Outremer just because Reynaud had become a Templar. The fair-haired
Provençal had been his faithful friend and companion now
for eight years.

"Old habits die hard," the minstrel told him, then flashed
a cocky grin.

While Bishop Abelard waited there, Reynaud stood, trying
to convince a knight-turned-minstrel to face up to his responsibilities. Taillefer had left his own wealthy family (for
reasons Reynaud could only guess) and given up his right
to inherit his father's title and estates to his younger
brother—for the relatively carefree life of a *troubadour*.

Reynaud tried a different tack. "Then the girl will go back
with her father's men. In spite of her part in this, Lord Aimery
accuses us of kidnapping her. God knows, I don't need anymore trouble now."

Taillefer stared at the floor, an uncharacteristic frown pulling his sandy brows together, and Reynaud struck while the
iron was hot. "Had you not encouraged her back at the convent—given her reason to believe your intentions were toward marriage . . ." He trailed off suggestively, disliking this
tactic, but thinking it was the only way to force the minstrel's
hand now. And surely it was the only way to get Abelard off
the proverbial hook as far as Aimery de Belvoir's men were
concerned.

"Well?" he pressed, after several lengthy moments of silence . . .

Brielle allowed the warm, scented water to relax her, allowing her frustrations to melt away for a time. The tub
was made of granite and shaped like a slipper, a perfectly-
preserved relic from long-ago days when the Phoenicians
ruled and Tyre was one of their city-kingdoms along the
eastern coast of the Mediterranean. Or so one of the ser-

vants had told her when explaining how lead pipes supplied the hot and cold water for the baths.

The same servant, a raven-haired, brown-eyed girl named Nadia, had pinned up her hair, helped her undress, and fussed over her to the point of mild embarrassment. Brielle felt like a pampered princess, not a young woman wanting desperately to find out what had become of her father after the most disastrous battle in the history of the crusades.

"Brielle?" Anabette's voice broke into her thoughts.

Brielle slowly turned her head, which had been resting against the high back of the stone tub, to regard her friend. She'd begun to smile at the girl, then felt her lips freeze at the look on Anabette's face.

Before she could speak, Anabette was on her knees beside the tub, tears welling in her eyes. "Oh, Brielle, Bishop Abelard has summoned me to his study. . . . I have a *bad* feeling about this! It must be news from my father!"

Brielle frowned and tried to concentrate on Anabette's concern. Her father . . . ?

"Why else would the bishop summon me?"

Brielle sat up, crossing her arms over her breasts. "Surely there can be other reasons?" But she suspected Anabette was right. And if Lord Aimery had so speedily tracked down his strong-willed daughter, the girl had good reason to be alarmed. Surely he'd dispatched his men the moment he'd received word of her flight from St. Bernadette's.

Anabette shook her head emphatically. "Who else would be searching for me? I know he'll command me to return to Château Belvoir with all due haste . . . take me from Taillefer to wed that old, foul-breathed toad." She rested her cheek against the tub rim and let out a soft sob.

Brielle automatically put one hand on Anabette's head in a gesture of reassurance, then realized she was dripping water over the girl's head and face.

Anabette, however, was so obviously steeped in misery that she seemed not to notice. Brielle had never seen her so distraught. *"Chère,* go wipe your face and see the bishop." Her voice was soft with compassion. "The sooner you know for certain, the better, *n'est-ce pas?"*

Eleven

"Anabette!"

A male voice, full of urgency, came to them from the bed-chamber.

Anabette raised her tear-streaked face and looked at Brielle. "Who is that?" she whispered.

Brielle, however, had no trouble recognizing that voice. She instantly sank down in the scented water, curling her body to hide what she could, praying Reynaud wouldn't have the audacity to enter their bath. " 'Tis Reynaud. Go see what he wants before he seeks you out *here!*" She practically pushed Anabette away from the tub.

With obvious reluctance, the girl rose. "The Templar wasted no time, did he?" she said bitterly. "I know he's still angry about what I did back in Marseilles, and now he'll have his revenge." She swiped away a stray tear and turned toward the door to the bedchamber they shared. "I hate him!"

"That is most unfortunate," Reynaud said from the door between the baths and the bedchamber. "Especially after my talk with Taillefer."

For a moment Brielle was speechless as a blush crept up her neck and all the way to the roots of her hair. How dare he boldly interrupt her bath?

"The minstrel wishes to speak to you in the courtyard,"

he informed Anabette brusquely before he transferred his gaze to Brielle.

He didn't have to say anything more. Anabette hurried past him, her face as bright as Brielle's.

Reynaud's gaze never wavered from Brielle as he stepped closer to the stone tub. "You will pardon my boldness, *demoiselle,* in interrupting your bath, but an urgent matter forces me to do so."

You mean you didn't want to wait even a moment longer, for then you wouldn't have been able to catch a glimpse, however brief, of the lovely Brielle disrobed. The reprimand from his conscience gave him pause, but only long enough to silently deny it.

He couldn't help but admire the slender length of her exposed neck, and the curling tendrils of ale-blond hair that caressed the lines of her delicate jaw.

"I will *not* pardon your boldness, Sieur Reynaud, for nothing but life and death could merit such an intrusion on a lady's privacy."

Sufficiently rebuked, he dipped his head in accord, but a corner of his mouth curved upward in a half-smile as he explained, " 'Tis almost such, I am certain, where Anabette and Taillefer are concerned." His smile faded then. "I would know if the Lady Anabette is in love with the minstrel . . . if you know, or at least suspect, that he is the reason she sought out John the Gaunt and followed us to Marseilles."

A frown flitted across her lovely brow, temporarily chasing away her embarrassment. "But what difference would that make now?" she asked.

"I would know if she returns his feelings, lest he curse me forever for my meddling."

At her deepened frown of bemusement, he explained, "I told him the only way to keep Anabette here was for him to make her his wife. Then her father would have no authority over her."

He watched her expression change as understanding

dawned. "Of a certainty she is in love with him," she murmured, lowering her lashes and hiding her eyes from him. "She would like nothing more than to become his wife." The color deepened in her already heated cheeks.

"I see." But he stood there, absorbing the sight of her like a wandering Bedouin would drink in the image of an oasis in the distance, fearing that it might be a mirage. He took a step forward, then another, suddenly able to see the pulse that jumped in the hollow at the base of her neck. He had the most powerful urge to place his lips there and feel the life beat of her heart.

She finally looked up at him and he stopped in his tracks, trying to gather his wits. He couldn't remember a time when his self-discipline had so totally deserted him.

"Please, Reynaud," she said softly, distress darkening her eyes. "Haven't I answered your question to your liking?"

The informal use of his given name on her lips sounded like a beckoning, and some unseen force propelled him forward again, much to his bemusement—and definitely to her chagrin. Her eyes looked huge and beautiful, but her expression was suddenly one of total vulnerability . . . that of an innocent being threatened.

With a belated burst of willpower he bade his rebellious legs to halt, taking in the beads of water that shimmered on the pearlescent skin of one shoulder. For a fleeting moment, he forgot who and where he was . . . aware only of the guileless enchantress before him.

What had she asked him?

He scoured his blank mind, desperately trying to remember . . . and suddenly, his beleaguered brain began to function again. "You've more than answered my question. I wouldn't be the cause of an even worse catastrophe because of my poor judgment in matters of . . . the heart." The last two words were a husk of sound.

Brielle felt her insides melting like butter beneath a hot sun's rays, and the heat that curled through her midsection turned to molten desire as she watched the emotions flicker across his normally imperturbable countenance. Like some desert *sheik,* he stood before her—closer than was decent— emanating a virility that made her want to touch her lips to his as intimately as they had in the courtyard only days before . . . to press her nude body up against that seductive silken robe that molded to his magnificent form with his movements. And more . . .

Time held suspended as their gazes melded, the attraction between them so potent, neither could move to break the sweet spell. . . .

Until Anabette's sudden squeal from the bedchamber cut through it like the swipe of a sword blade. Reynaud's eyes cleared as his head jerked up. He retreated toward the door, still facing Brielle as Anabette's voice came to them again: "Brielle!"

And she appeared in the doorway, her face aglow with excitement. Reynaud dragged his attention from Brielle and turned. He took one look at Anabette, who looked almost shy now, and thought, *Thank God for her interference!*

" 'Tis your doing, isn't it?" she asked him in a lowered voice. "Your talk with Taillefer? We shall name our first child after you!"

Reynaud could only nod, then withdrew without another word, Anabette's voice coming from behind him in a soft flurry of indistinguishable words.

"Are you certain Bishop Abelard will do it?" Taillefer asked when Reynaud reached the courtyard. He quickly managed to gain a look of outward composure.

"He will. I told him I'd return after the matter was settled—I was loath to leave him alone for long with de Belvoir's emissaries." He looked at Taillefer. "We'll do it as soon as they leave . . ."

But the lead knight, Armand Villiers, was furious at the

news. He was a short and stocky man, sweating profusely beneath his mail and tunic. Obviously he was unaccustomed to the heat, and he didn't know any better than to bake unnecessarily in his armor. "A *troubadour?* Bah! If the lady Anabette is wed, we have no choice but to kill any fool audacious enough to have taken her to wife!"

Reynaud narrowed his eyes at the knight. "He's more than a humble minstrel, Villiers. His antecedents are nobler than your own, I wager."

The knight was obviously insulted, but Reynaud was more concerned with what he'd revealed about Taillefer, after having vowed to keep his background secret. "And, pray tell, Templar, exactly *what* are his antecedents that make him anything more than a piddling minstrel?"

Reynaud's eyes turned icy, his voice softly menacing. "No man is 'piddling' in the eyes of God. And if you dare lay a hand on Taillefer, I'll see that 'tis the last move you ever make."

The threat quivered in the air between them.

Bishop Abelard attempted to diffuse the situation. "My son," he said to Villiers, " 'tis ungracious to press Sieur Reynaud for details he does not wish to divulge . . . and against the laws of God to threaten the life of Taillefer le Doux."

The knight with Villiers looked like he was ready to unsheathe his sword.

"I've brought an escort of six other men-at-arms to take Lady Anabette back to Provence at my Lord Aimery's behest. News of a marriage to an underling is not enough to discourage me from my mission, as the lord of Belvoir has already contracted for his daughter to wed a wealthy baron."

The cleric nodded with sympathy. "I can understand his anger, under the circumstances, my son, but what God has joined together, let no one put asunder. You may return this eve if you would like to speak to my Lady Anabette."

"But I must speak to her now!" Villiers insisted.

"You've come unannounced and uninvited. The lady is

occupied elsewhere and will not be available 'til this eve," Reynaud said bluntly, suspecting Abelard would be too kind to these overbearing knights. Also, he had no qualms about lying if it would buy time for Taillefer and Anabette. "Or you can return on the morrow if 'tis more convenient," his darker side made him add.

Villiers threw him a look that would have made a lesser man quail, then glanced with disgust at his companion before saying, "We can return this eve with the rest of the men."

It was a thinly veiled challenge.

Reynaud nodded. "You may bring as many men as you like, but only the two of you will be permitted to enter the palace—and only after you leave your weapons at the front gate. You might also keep in mind that this palace has a substantial guard, and I have my own knights close at hand."

They were wed in the chapel within an hour of Villiers's leave-taking, with Bishop Abelard presiding and Reynaud and Brielle in attendance. John the Gaunt and Humphrey of Toulouse arrived immediately after being summoned and stood sentinel at the back of the chapel.

Rashid was not present.

In spite of the problems Anabette had caused them all, Brielle wished her friend happiness and a long life. She felt the press of tears more than once during the mass, and only one time did she look over at Reynaud in an effort to collect herself. He was staring at the crucifix above the lovely, linen-draped altar, his sculptured profile to her, and an unexpected and poignant yearning blossomed within Brielle. How beautiful he was, she thought, as darkly beautiful as the archangel Michael, yet capable of compassion for others. A compassion that, combined with his healing touch, could put him in mortal danger. But she knew for a fact that he was also capable of great courage, as shown on board the *Madonna*, and surmised instinctively that he'd never refuse to share his gift with those suffering merely to ensure his own safety.

Then, as if he felt her attention on him, he swiveled his head and caught her gaze. The bishop's voice faded, and there was suddenly only Reynaud's image filling her mind, her senses—her heart.

The realization was startling enough to pull her from the brink of an inexorable madness. She turned her head sharply and tried to concentrate on the couple being joined in wedlock before them, but for the remainder of the mass, she was all too aware of Reynaud's gaze upon her.

Afterward Nadia and another young woman served them plates of lamb and rice, *hummos*—a mixture of mashed chickpeas, sesame oil, and garlic—followed by delicious melon slices, succulent oranges, juicy grapes, and an assortment of nuts from Damascus. Brielle had learned the cool, luscious drinks called sorbets were the perfect accompaniment for the modest wedding feast.

Brielle couldn't help but wonder what Aimery de Belvoir's men would have said had they returned in time to discover the celebration.

She noted the look of pride in Taillefer's eyes and the radiance on Anabette's features that made her look beautiful, and without warning she found herself envying them.

Partly in an effort to keep her thoughts away from Reynaud, partly because of her frustration with her lack of progress in learning the fate of her father, she started toward John the Gaunt, fully intending to speak to him about helping her get to Hattin.

He was speaking to Rashid, who'd joined the small gathering after the mass, and Brielle noted how strange it was, still, to see men from the West wearing Arab garb. She and Anabette were the only ones still in undergown and bliaut. Yet she felt foolish herself for stubbornly refusing to do the same, and as she greeted the two men, she suddenly envied them their airy robes.

John's smile turned into a faint frown as he observed, "You look flushed, my lady. Are you well?"

In truth, it was as much from Reynaud de St. Rémy's frequent glances (even though he was conversing with Bishop Abelard) as from the heat, but she merely nodded.

"The lady is not accustomed to our climate," Rashid said. "Nor, unfortunately, to our clothing." He studied her a moment, his head tilted consideringly, then bowed briefly and moved away. It was uncanny, she thought . . . as if he knew she wished to speak to John alone.

She put a hand on John's arm and drew him as far from the others as possible without arousing curiosity . . . she hoped.

"John, know you the way to the Horns of Hattin?"

He looked at her for a long, silent moment, his eyes turning troubled. "Aye, child. 'Tis near the town of Tiberius in the Galilee . . . but you'll find nothing there now."

She bit her lower lip. " 'Tis at least a starting point! I just want to stand on the site where the battle took place. Even if I don't find some clue or token, at least I will know where he last fought and, mayhap, perished."

She turned away, bowing her head, and hugging herself in agitation. "Oh, John, how am I ever to learn whether my father is alive or not?" Her words were low and despondent.

"If you must go to Hattin," he answered gently, "then obtain a writ guaranteeing safe passage and find a dependable escort. I would suggest, however, that you concentrate on a safe conduct to Damascus instead . . . send a small party of men to deal with the Muslim officials there." He paused. "I would be honored to accompany them."

"I would concur with John's suggestion," Reynaud said from behind them.

Brielle whirled to face him, completely surprised at not only his sudden presence, but also the fact that he'd heard their conversation. Rashid stood beside him.

Had the Arab warned him? she wondered, feeling definitely outnumbered and on the defensive. Her sudden predicament lent an uncharacteristic sharpness to her next words: "I was speaking to John, *chevalier,* and John alone. What I do with my time in Outremer is really none of your affair."

Rashid crossed his arms and regarded her with piercing dark eyes, and Brielle was suddenly certain the Arab had brought her and John to Reynaud's attention.

Reynaud, however, merely raised his eyebrows and said levelly, "Oh, but it *is* my affair, *demoiselle,* for I took on the added responsibility of your safety at the bishop's request before we even left St. Bernadette's."

"You cannot detain me. I'm not your prisoner!" Was he to become a stumbling block after she'd traveled all this way?

"I warned you back in Provence about the futility of going to Hattin—and the danger."

Brielle wanted to shake him, so great was her frustration. What was the point in having come to the Holy Land if she couldn't do as she'd planned? And, to make matters worse, she had already given up on pressing him to help her. Why, then, was he blocking her efforts to enlist John's aid?

"If I may suggest," Rashid interjected here, "why not send a few men to Damascus to make inquiries for you? You could obtain a writ of safe conduct from the emir. . . ."

Brielle looked at the Arab, feeling a flicker of hope. But the scowl Reynaud turned on Rashid was forbidding. "Even that isn't a guarantee against stragglers and robbers. And just whom would you hire to make the trek?"

"There are men who would do it for the right price," John said, and Brielle silently thanked him for his support.

Without warning, Reynaud changed his tack, his tone softening, which took her completely by surprise. "Why don't you come to Jerusalem with Bishop Abelard and myself instead?" he asked.

Brielle fought confusion. "Jerusalem?"

"Oui. His Excellency is considering making a pilgrimage

there. 'Tis simple enough to get permission for a pilgrimage—easier and safer than going to Damascus."

Jerusalem? she thought in bemusement. What was he trying to do? John was also looking at Reynaud with a puzzled frown.

As if reading her thoughts, he added, " 'Tis unthinkable to travel to the Holy Land and never see Jerusalem."

"But I didn't come to Outremer to make a pilgrimage to the Holy City! I came to find my father."

Reynaud nodded, unruffled. "And so you did. But one may be made easier by the other."

"Sieur Reynaud implies, *mon enfant*, that a pilgrimage to Jerusalem may lead to divine help in your search," said Bishop Abelard from behind them.

Brielle turned beseeching eyes to him. "And it may well be, my lord bishop, but will I have enough time to do so? My stay here is limited . . ."

"As is mine, Brielle. We must not impose on Sieur Reynaud and Sieur Humphrey for too long when they are needed elsewhere." He looked at Reynaud, then back at Brielle. "Why don't you at least give it some thought?"

"Aye," Reynaud agreed. He gestured with one hand toward the newly wedded couple, who were conversing with Sieur Humphrey. "And let's celebrate with Taillefer and Anabette while we may. Of a certainty Villiers and his men will return before the sun sets."

Armand Villiers had no intention of returning that evening, Reynaud decided, after having been summarily dismissed like some peasant begging for a morsel to eat. As the hours passed, Reynaud found the knight's failure to make a showing disturbing, for surely Aimery de Belvoir wouldn't have chosen a man who was easily discouraged to find and then bring back his daughter.

Reynaud's uneasiness would have increased tenfold had

he known that Armand Villiers was swilling excellent Bethlehem wine in the common room of one of the several inns in Tyre. Although the clientele was primarily Christian, from what Armand could discern, Muslims were present also. The latter were forbidden to drink, but appeared to be enjoying the inn's fare with as much gusto as their Christian counterparts.

"You wouldn't know by the mode of dress that we were among fellow Christians," he'd remarked upon their arrival, his sand-blond hair and western garb singling him out as a Frank. Nearly everyone save the eight man party from Château de Belvoir and a handful of Christian pilgrims scattered here and there wore robes and headdresses of some kind. "God's blood, but they look like a horde of godless Saracens!" Villiers had exclaimed in disgust.

His men looked about warily before taking up a trestle table near one wall. Armand seated himself last and motioned to a man waiting on the tables. "Is this here a Christian establishment?" he growled, ready to depart immediately if the man said no, for not only was he suspicious of anyone wearing robes, but he also found the mixture of Eastern atmosphere and the decor of the establishment disconcerting. The common room had thick, light-colored walls to keep out the heat—and even a shaded, open courtyard.

Evidently accustomed to being questioned by those new to the Levant, the man who'd been serving the customers answered in French as pure as any Armand had ever heard, "I am Raymond, and a devout Christian, *chevalier.* We came from Normandy—my late mother was Norman, too. Now my father is married to a Maronite, and they own this inn."

He was as brown as an Arab from the sun, but his blond hair and brows, his blue eyes, proclaimed him a descendant of the Vikings who'd established themselves in Normandy almost three hundred years before.

Armand absorbed all this with narrowed eyes, realizing he'd just been given an abbreviated education in the ways of many Christians who had chosen to make their home in Outremer. He was suspicious of the word "Maronite" but also felt a kinship with this fellow Norman. Pride won out over righteousness, and Armand chose not to reveal his ignorance by asking what a Maronite was.

Bayard, the knight who'd accompanied him to the bishop's palace that afternoon, leaned toward him and said, "I told you, Villiers, what to expect here. My father went to his grave telling different stories about this place." Normally a man of few words, he waxed eloquent, " 'Hostile mountains and barren deserts make up Outremer—but lush, fertile plains as well,' he said. 'Riches for the taking if you can survive hostile Saracens and a host of strange diseases.' "

"True," said the innkeeper's son. " 'Tis a land of contradictions, but it can make a man wealthy if he respects and nurtures it, or knows how to take advantage of its resources."

The man sounded like he'd told the story many times before, but Armand was a knight, with a knight's typical disdain for working the land. He wasn't interested in farming as a means of acquiring wealth, or even establishing a business in one of the port cities of the Levant. Fighting the infidels interested him; but for now he was on a mission worthy of a knight, and he wasn't about to be distracted from successfully fulfilling it.

He grunted in answer, set aside his helmet and began to unlace the mail coif that covered his head and neck. "Can you get us something to eat and a good wine, *mon ami?* We've come a long way and have a great thirst."

Raymond nodded. "As you wish."

The party from Château de Belvoir were just finishing their meal when Bayard elbowed Armand. "Look, over there. A Templar. At least *he* has enough sense not to trade his mail for a robe in the middle of a Saracen city."

"He looks to have just had a hard ride," remarked Odo, another of Armand's party.

Armand's gaze went to the knight two tables over, standing

out in a white tunic bearing a blood-red cross over his mail hauberk. The military orders of the Holy Land were well-known in Europe and highly respected.

Armand's features transformed with sudden interest. "Mayhap he's just come from the siege at Acre," he said.

"Then why is he alone?" Bayard asked.

A moment later, a man approached the Templar—a Saracen, most definitely, with his black eyes and deep olive skin. The seated Templar looked up at the interloper with visible anger, and reflexively Villiers's hand inched toward his sword hilt. . . .

"I hear you are unhappy with our efforts, Tancred le Bref," the Arab said.

Tancred's eyes widened, for Ahab al Akbaar had come upon him like a wraith from the shadows. He suppressed the urge to leap across the table and throttle the man, for he knew better than to tangle with a member of the *Hashishiyun*—especially when the Arab's bloodshot eyes revealed his recent use of *hashish*. Like his fellow *Hashishiyun*, his actions could be totally unpredictable, and he wouldn't hesitate to dispatch a victim in a public place.

"If it weren't for you, I wouldn't have been forced to ride posthaste to finish the job. For all I know, St. Rémy could already be gone from Tyre."

Tancred was hot and he was tired. He was only on his first fruited drink, craving the soothing effects of wine, yet having learned long ago that the drink did nothing but make a sweating man warmer. He hadn't even shed his mail yet.

Needless to say, his temper was like kindling that needed only a spark.

And here stood Ahab al Akbaar, the man who'd taken his silver and given him nothing in return, his arms folded within his wide sleeves, his dark eyes filled with derision.

Tancred felt curious glances coming their way. "I want

my silver, al Akbaar," he said through set teeth. "You didn't earn it."

Ignoring his demand, Ahab said, *"Inshallah.* As God wills it. . . . But the Templar is still here, and before we talk business, the least you could do is mind your manners, barbarian, and invite me to sit." He smiled fleetingly, his white teeth flashing against his skin, but without humor.

Tancred scraped back the bench with the force of his movement as he stood. Throwing caution to the wind now, he leaned on his hands toward Ahab al Akbaar and sneered, "At least this barbarian keeps a bargain when he makes one. Keep the damned silver then, infidel, but don't dare ask me to spend one more dinar on you for undeserved hospitality!"

A dark and dangerous current passed through the Arab's red-veined eyes, and an eerie chill moved over Tancred in reaction. "Don't you want to know who countermanded your orders before you die?" Ahab murmured silkily.

Before his meaning could even register, a voice said, "Come, come . . . can we not settle this over a drink?"

But it was too late. A dagger blade flashed in the low light, and Tancred felt a lance of fire pierce his throat. Clumsily, he lunged for the Arab but, elusive as quicksilver, the man disappeared as quickly as he'd come, and Tancred felt himself sinking back to the bench behind him. The knowledge that he'd been stabbed filled him with sudden fear, and he found himself fighting for breath even as he heard the gurgle of blood, felt its warm spurt on his chin and neck. With growing horror, Tancred realized he'd been mortally wounded.

The last thing he remembered was looking into the face of a man he'd never seen before—a crusader, he thought irrelevantly, fresh from France with the distinct odor of wine on his breath as he spoke harshly to another. . . .

After his initial shock, Armand Villiers quickly saw his chance to accomplish two things at once . . . get himself into the bishop's palace with the wounded man as his excuse, and then mayhap, if the Templar lived, win himself a worthy ally in this foreign land.

"Help me lift him," Villiers ordered Bayard. The knight automatically bent to lift the unconscious Templar and Odo, losing no time in clearing a pathway to the door of the inn, cried, "Stand aside!"

Bayard grunted from exertion as he took Tancred's legs and muttered, "But where'll we take him?"

"Stand aside, he said!" Armand Villiers commanded several others who moved to help. To Bayard, he said in a low voice, "The bishop's palace. We'll get in there one way or another!"

Twelve

A clamor at the front gate jerked Reynaud from a sound sleep. He leapt from the bed, grabbed his discarded robe, and slipped it on as he strode through the courtyard and down the corridor that skirted it.

As he neared the inner door of the building, two of the palace guards were already unbarring it, one calling out, "Who goes there?" as he hurried toward the outer gate, unsheathing his sword. The second man lit the way with a torch held high, its wavering flame dancing over disembodied faces on the other side of the grill.

The current archbishop of Tyre was still in Europe, drumming up more recruits to fight for Christ, so who could be causing all the commotion at this time of the night? Reynaud wondered.

"Identify yourselves!" the guard repeated.

"Armand Villiers," said a voice. "We've a badly wounded Templar here and need help!"

By now, Bishop Abelard was close behind Reynaud, and he voiced the latter's thoughts. "Think you 'tis a ruse?"

The lead guard demanded, "Didn't you know there's a hospital farther down the street, man?"

"This place was closer . . . By all that is holy, a man's *life* hangs in the balance!"

By the light of the torch, Reynaud could make out a figure being carried by two knights, one of the latter the now fa-

miliar Armand Villiers. But his concern immediately went
to the wounded man, for he was covered with blood, and
from what Reynaud could discern, pale as wax. Compassion
swelled within him, as it always did when another human
being was badly hurt. And this time it was a fellow Templar. . . .

"Bring him in," he said, without waiting for any higher
authority to admit them.

The palace guard glanced at the bishop, and he nodded.

"Where did this happen?" Reynaud asked.

"At the inn across the way," Villiers said. "An infidel attacked him with a dagger."

A chill of premonition skidded down Reynaud's spine, for
it was the method of the *Hashishiyun* to strike in such a
manner. What could this Templar have done to invoke the
wrath of the most feared religious sect in the Levant?

No one objected when five other men-at-arms followed
Villiers (who was now leading the way), Bayard, Odo, and
their grisly burden into the tiled outer courtyard.

"Take him into the bedchamber there." Bishop Abelard
pointed to the closest doorway, his own chamber for the duration of his stay. How generous of him, Reynaud thought,
when many higher-ranking clergy would never have offered
their own bed.

But the outer courtyard was as far as the rest of them were
going to get if Reynaud had anything to say about it.

The head guard, obviously in concurrence with Reynaud,
said to the remaining five, "The rest of you remain here.
We'll have food and drink brought out to you."

"Know you how many palace guards are here?" Reynaud
asked Rashid in a low voice, for like his own shadow, the
Arab had materialized behind him.

"Six, master," he said, *sotto voce.* "Then you, Taillefer,
and myself . . . a fair enough match should it come down to
that." It was as if the Arab could read his very thoughts, and
it had been that way ever since they'd first met.

Reynaud nodded. "Bring us bandages and hot water, then fetch Nadia and Leah and ask them to serve these others some refreshments. Also, tell Taillefer to stay in his room and keep Anabette out of sight."

Rashid quickly swung away and Reynaud followed the bishop and the three men into Abelard's chamber. The wounded man was laid across the bed, his blood staining the otherwise spotless bedclothes. The bishop, however, was obviously intent upon the man's welfare rather than the soiling of his bed.

"Is it mortal?" Abelard asked, looking directly at Villiers.

"I think not," the knight replied, "even though 'tis a neck wound."

The man was a poor liar, Reynaud thought, for the throat and neck area was not protected by extra flesh, and contained several important blood vessels. Any knight knew that. In fact, it wouldn't have surprised him to learn that Villiers had stabbed the Templar himself as an excuse to get into the palace. He said nothing, however, as he sat beside the fallen knight and reached for his arm to find a pulse. Even as his fingers closed over the man's wrist—as he noted the clamminess of his skin, recognition came to him.

Sweet Christ, it was Tancred le Bref! And hard on the heels of Robert de Sablé's warning.

Ignoring the certainty that had the situation been reversed, Tancred would have let him die, Reynaud concentrated on the knight's thready pulse.

"If he dies, 'twill be from blood loss," he told the bishop, then looked up at Armand Villiers.

"Be you a physician?" the latter asked, with a hint of hostility.

He was obviously still smarting from Reynaud's terse dismissal earlier that day. The silence crackled around them for a moment, and Rashid rescued the moment by appearing with the requested cloths and water. As Reynaud wet and pressed a clean square of linen over the wound, he shook his head. "A physician, nay. But I know something of healing."

"Will that be all?" Rashid asked Reynaud pointedly. It was the Arab's way of getting the others to leave the room with him so there would be no witnesses to what Reynaud would do. He protected Reynaud in situations like this with all the ferocity of a tigress and her cub.

Reynaud nodded. "Summon an Arab physician."

Bishop Abelard accepted this and gestured for Villiers and his two men to proceed out the door. Armand Villiers took the opportunity to blurt out what was really on his mind. "Very well. But since I'm here now, I would speak to Lady Anabette."

Reynaud turned back to his patient, squelching the urge to throw Villiers out on his ear, and allowed Bishop Abelard to handle the persistent knight. "If her husband has no objections at this inconvenient hour, then you may. But only in the presence of Taillefer."

The bishop ushered the men from the room, throwing one last look over his shoulder at Reynaud before he exited.

Reynaud turned back to Tancred le Bref and frowned. "So, my brother Templar," he murmured to the unconscious man, "you managed to almost lose your head this time." When he took away the cloth to get a better look at the laceration, he saw that Tancred had been very lucky, indeed. Fortunately, he'd been wearing his mail hauberk, but unfortunately, his coif had been removed, thus exposing his neck and throat to the would-be murderer's dagger.

Why had Tancred le Bref been the target of one of the *Hashishiyun?* Reynaud wondered, as he slipped one hand under the folds of his robe. He withdrew a tiny vile, unstoppered it, and applied some of its contents to Tancred's neck near the wound.

He put it away and tried to wipe his mind clean of all thought save the man beside him.

But he couldn't for long moments, to his frustration. He

kept thinking how le Bref despised him. Not quite openly; not before Templars of higher rank, or any Templars at all, for that matter. But when they were alone . . . or when no one was watching him, le Bref was capable of sending Reynaud venomous looks that usually caught the knight off guard with their unexpected intensity.

A fleeting rebellion rose in him. Why was he about to save this man's life? He would rather have saved a Muslim's life, a man, mayhap, who had reason to hate him and all Christians who sought to drive him and his brothers from their homes.

What would your father think? whispered a voice.

But Gérard de St. Rémy was nobler than he could ever hope to be. As a fighting man, as a husband and father, and even as a servant of God, Reynaud was certain, had Gérard decided to serve the Church before he'd met his beloved Katherine . . .

Gérard de St. Rémy had also told his youngest son that he must use any special talents for healing to serve God . . . to help all men who were in need. That didn't include infidels, of course (of which Reynaud had helped his share), but it certainly meant fellow Templars. What would Gérard think now if he knew that Reynaud's skill at healing had turned into something miraculous?

He shook his head. Such thoughts didn't bear considering now; and he could never be the man his father was.

But you must not disappoint him. You must keep trying . . .

It took a few more moments, moments wasted, he acknowledged. But his darker side persisted in reminding him that the man in need was only Tancred le Bref.

That unkind thought made him concentrate all the harder on wiping his mind free of everything save mending the ruptured flesh and saving a man's life, however undeserving in Reynaud's own mind. . . .

He closed his eyes and bowed his head, concentrating more deeply. He began to pray. He hoped, as he always did, that this entire incident was a dream from which he would awaken; and that if it were indeed real, the gift wouldn't be capriciously taken from him when a human life hung in the balance.

Brielle came in quietly through the adjoining bath, fearing she wouldn't be allowed in if anyone saw her, and feeling a strange need to be near Reynaud de St. Rémy. She'd been awakened from a light sleep by the sounds of men at the gate, and she'd guessed that Villiers and his men had returned.

Having successfully avoided everyone else, she now stood in the shadow of a young potted palm tree, witnessing the Templar bestow his healing touch upon the wounded man stretched across the bed . . .

She wondered if she should have dared enter unannounced to witness something meant, mayhap, only for God and his vessel, Reynaud de St. Rémy. . . .

But it was too late, she realized, as she stood transfixed. She couldn't move.

Gore blighted the man's once-white tunic, and Brielle immediately recognized it as the garb of a Templar. Reynaud's head was bowed, his eyes closed, his fingers resting lightly upon the man's chest. For an ephemeral moment, the silence, the utter stillness of the scene, transformed it into a dreamlike tableau, and Brielle felt a sense of peace and well-being penetrate her mind and body—reach into and soothe her very soul.

Then slowly, Reynaud lifted his head and opened his eyes. She couldn't make out the expression on his face, but his entire demeanor was serene; a benevolent calm blanketed the room. Reynaud heaved a sigh and seemed to slump a little, as if a great weight had been lifted from his shoulders. It was in those moments that Brielle d'Avignon realized not only did she love Reynaud de St. Rémy, whether he was an unattainable Templar knight or not, but that also she would protect him with her life, if necessary, from any who would seek to harm or destroy him out of fear or ignorance.

Those startling thoughts had barely registered when the wounded man opened his eyes, and Brielle forced her feet to move—to retreat silently and unnoticed. She had been profoundly moved, she acknowledged, but had had no right to witness what she did. Nor did she have a right to reveal her presence now and interfere with what would take place naturally in so private a matter . . .

Tancred's eyes were at first unfocused, then cleared as he recognized Reynaud. He pushed himself to his elbows and shook his head slightly. Reynaud didn't stop him, for he'd learned that with the healing came release from any pain, and often renewal.

Tancred le Bref was no doubt in better condition than before he'd been attacked.

He looked up at Reynaud and frowned fiercely. "You!" he croaked, his small, dark eyes slitted.

"None other." Reynaud canted his head consideringly as he regarded the knight. Le Bref was built like a bull and his features were thick—full lips, wide, flat nose, an overly prominent brow. It was obvious he had a potent strain of common blood running through his veins. Not that the lowest classes necessarily had a monopoly on trickery and deception, he thought with rue.

Tancred turned his attention to his surroundings. "Where am I?" he demanded. "What happened . . . why am I here?"

Reynaud stood and regarded the brother Templar who hated him. "You're at the bishop's palace. You were attacked at the inn across the way, according to the knight who brought you here."

Tancred's expression grew harsh with remembrance. "One of the *Hashishiyun*. And all because—" He halted suddenly, his expression turning closed, again reminding Reynaud of a sly peasant trying to trick his lord out of his share of food-stuffs. "And all because he wouldn't part with the silver he owed me." He motioned to his throat. "My wound . . . ?"

Reynaud sighed, staring at the newly-healed pink line on Tancred's neck. "You will live, le Bref, thanks to the mail you still wear, and your would-be killer's poor aim."

At that moment, Rashid entered the room with another Arab. The latter was bent and wizened, with flowing white beard and bright black eyes. "And thanks to Farouk's healing oil."

"Oil?" Tancred said. His hand went to his throat, and his fingers encountered the olive oil Reynaud had dabbed there moments before. It was a tried and true trick thought up by Rashid and used by Reynaud for years now. And it was easiest to put into play when they were in Tyre, where Rashid's cousin lived, a physician named Farouk, who could be counted on to play along with the ruse when asked. The man was a gifted and experienced healer and revealed nothing of what he saw or heard regarding Reynaud's miraculous gift.

Tancred looked at his fingers and rubbed them together, his frown deepening.

"An ingredient known only to certain Arab physicians," Rashid said smoothly. "Farouk had tended you, then left the room so Reynaud could pray for his Templar brother."

Tancred was almost tempted to believe them. But he knew better. St. Rémy's servant's pitiful attempts to keep his master's powers a secret were laughable. Tancred knew better— he had almost lost his life this night because of his own efforts to learn what was behind the mysterious power, and found it ironic that the one indirectly responsible for his near-fatal wound was also responsible for making him whole again.

Oil, indeed! His eyes narrowed accusingly at Reynaud while Farouk perched on the bed beside him and examined his neck. Tancred had been in the same room with St.

Rémy—the very recipient of his help—and knew no more
than before; he was in no better position to understand anything more than before Ahab had stabbed him.

Suddenly the trek from Masyaf, the strain of sparring with
Ahab, and the ensuing attempt on his life caught up with
him. Tancred's lids grew heavy. Mayhap St. Rémy had
drugged him, he thought drowsily, never realizing that he'd
lost a massive amount of blood. Well, time enough to plan
later. . . .

Reynaud put a hand on Farouk's arm. "My thanks, friend,"
he murmured, watching Tancred fall asleep as suddenly and
peacefully as a child.

Farouk looked up at him. "Allah works in wondrous ways.
He chooses us—we do not choose Him." He glanced at
Rashid. "I'll remain here for a while."

Reynaud nodded, pressed a coin into his hand, then turned
and strode from the chamber. There was another matter that
demanded his immediate attention. . . .

He entered the outer courtyard—and not a moment too
soon, he thought—in time to see Armand Villiers confronting
Taillefer. The latter was clad only in a hastily-donned tunic.
Anabette, for once looking silent and subdued, was standing
on tiptoe behind Bishop Abelard and peering over his shoulder. Maybe it was the presence of the palace guard that had
intimidated her, or the others in Villiers party, who looked
angry enough to run the guards through if they lifted one
finger to their leader.

Reynaud paused close enough to a rose bush to be unnoticed at first, and quickly took in the scene, thinking he didn't
need another crisis after his encounter with Tancred le Bref.
He always felt drained after a healing, especially if the victim's wound was severe . . . as if his own energy had been
transferred to the one he sought to heal.

He stood a moment, taking in the fragrance of roses, and

briefly savoring the cool night air after the stuffier bedchamber. He wondered briefly where Brielle was—especially with
a band of rough strangers in their midst. . . .

Taillefer, he noted, did his name proud—or, rather, the
name of the old and established family whom he'd blithely
deserted for the siren song of a troubadour's life. Reynaud
doubted if the minstrel would have cared to read his very
complimentary thought, for he was happy with his chosen
path. He stood tall and firm in his tunic and bare legs, his
guileless-blue gaze clashing with Villiers. He obviously wore
nothing underneath, and was barefooted as well. A lesser
man would have looked—to say nothing of *felt*—silly confronting a fully-armed knight thusly. Had Taillefer a sword
and mail, he'd have passed for a knight by birth. Reynaud
would have wagered anything that had the minstrel not for-
saken his birthright and pretended to abhor swordplay, he
could have easily taken Villiers one on one, then turned
around the next moment and wooed his new bride with a
sweet song to the accompaniment of his lute.

"Ah, Reynaud," he said, instead, spotting the Templar
nearby and turning his attention from Villiers as if he were
no more than a bothersome fly. "Can you help me persuade
Sieur Armand that the lady Anabette is not her sire's responsibility any longer?"

Reynaud was half-tempted to let the clever Taillefer get
himself out of this one—after all, hadn't he encouraged Anabette de Belvoir with his attentions back at St. Bernadette's?
Encouraged her enough to entice her to follow him to Marseilles?

He surely had bitten off more than he could chew this
time.

Before Reynaud could speak, however, the minstrel
stepped away from Villiers, obviously stalling for time, and
raised his palms skyward. "If not, I fear I'll have no choice
but to defend my lovely bride the only way I know how . . ."
He cast a look at several of Villiers's men through his lashes

"I'll be forced to mangle Sieur Armand with my only weapon—my lute."

In spite of everything, Reynaud fought the urge to laugh aloud. The look on Villiers's face was bad enough, but Taillefer's expression was exquisite. And then the minstrel had the audacity to slip Reynaud a wink.

"You aren't worthy of Lady Anabette!" Bayard bawled from nearby, obviously missing the humor in the situation.

"And that judgment is not for you to make," Reynaud interjected. "The lady consented to wed my friend here of her own free will." He stepped forward and turned to Villiers. "She followed our party to Marseilles—ask her!—and demanded to be taken to the Holy Land. She needed a protector and willingly entered holy wedlock with Taillefer."

"The marriage can be annulled," Villiers growled, his eyebrows lowered ominously, "having been performed without Lord Aimery's permission."

"That point is moot, my son," Abelard said. "The marriage was necessitated by the situation, and the two parties were totally agreeable."

"Indeed," said Reynaud. "Why don't you ask the Lady Anabette?"

Taillefer gave him a look of warning, but it was too late—the words were out of his mouth. Damned if the minstrel wasn't showing his protectiveness toward his wife (something heretofore reserved only for his precious lute) as any well-trained and well-mannered *chevalier* would. Ah, but what a knight he would have made. . . .

Anabette evidently found the courage to step from behind the bishop, her long yellow hair tumbled around her shoulders, standing out against her pale linen robe. Only a blind man, Reynaud thought, would have failed to take in the high color in her cheeks, the fullness of very recently kissed lips. And the residual dreaminess in her dark eyes.

She lifted her chin proudly and announced, "I consented to become Taillefer's wife, and I'm sorry you journeyed all this way for naught, Sieur Armand. Tell my father that I am my husband's responsibility now . . . we are joined for all eternity."

Reynaud thought he saw Taillefer's Adam's apple bob.

Armand's reaction was more noticeable. His fingers curled at his side, and a corresponding sneer spread across his mouth. "I will not leave Outremer until you agree to accompany me back to Château de Belvoir!"

"Here, here!" Bayard echoed, and several others took up the cry.

Surely, Reynaud thought, all of Tyre was awake by now and aware of Villiers's vow.

"Then mayhap you'd like to join the siege at Acre," Taillefer said calmly, "to pass your time while you wait, for your stay will be exceedingly lengthy."

The man nearest Reynaud reached for his sword. The Templar swiftly rapped the man-at-arms's wrist with his fist, and the latter let out a howl.

"You shouldn't even be wearing a weapon in the bishop's home," Reynaud told him, "to say nothing of that hot and heavy mail. Now, Villiers, the hour is late, and we are getting nowhere. I suggest you avoid creating a fracas in a city that is utterly foreign to you—to say nothing of the riskiness of tangling with a well-trained palace guard. Take your weary men back to the inn where you encountered Tancred le Bref—the knight whose life you saved. I assume you're staying at the same place, so I'll direct him there when he's well enough to thank you himself. I trust that is acceptable to you?"

The smile on Reynaud's face was pleasant enough, but it stopped short of his eyes. It was a firm dismissal, couched in terms that neatly alluded to any consequence of Villiers's actions should he fail to cooperate.

"We'll give you an escort to the gate," Bishop Abelard added graciously, a polite smile curving his lips. "Come . . ."

And he led the way to the other side of the courtyard where the watchman was already unlocking the grilled portals.

From the shadows, Brielle watched Rashid motion to the elderly Arab physician to follow him from the room. She'd only just returned, but regretted now that she hadn't seen the old man minister to the Templar lying upon the bishop's bed, for Reynaud had praised the skill of Arab healers.

But now, all that remained as evidence the physician had even been there was a goblet resting on the small, exquisitely-carved table beside the bed. And a vial of what appeared to be some white substance—powder, perhaps.

Wondering what more could have been done after Reynaud's work, Brielle cautiously moved into the room. She halted at the side of the bed before she realized that the man now lay beneath a light cover, his mail and clothing arranged in a neat pile in a corner, along with a basin of water. Someone, evidently, had undressed and bathed him.

But Brielle's interest was in the angry red line that stood out against his thick neck like the mark of Cain . . . a permanent reminder that someone had attempted to take his life. The blemish stood out all the more because of the chalky tone of his skin, although his cheeks were showing signs of returning color. He'd surely lost a lot of blood, she thought, with a wound to the neck.

She wondered if he was mayhap a victim of the siege of Acre—the besieged city wasn't far from Tyre she'd been told—then dismissed the idea. Even a city a few miles away would be too great a distance to transport a man with so grievous a wound. Surely they had physicians at the site.

But not a man like Reynaud de St. Rémy.

Indeed, perhaps this wounded man was a close friend of Reynaud's, in addition to being a brother Templar. Yes, that would be reason enough for someone who knew of Reynaud's skills to send the man to Tyre, no matter how risky the move.

The very idea of this man being someone close to Reynaud warmed her heart, and Brielle took a step closer to better study his face. He was as unattractive as Reynaud was beautiful, she thought, and then immediately felt ashamed of such an unkind thought. And especially about this man.

But however unkind the thought, it had the ring of truth, for there was nothing similar about the two men physically— at least as far as Brielle could determine. Even though the knight wasn't standing, she could tell he was much shorter than Reynaud and his features heavy. He was as different from Reynaud de St. Rémy as night from day, yet the man must have had some inner qualities about him to have endeared him to St. Rémy.

Aware that she might be making false assumptions, Brielle nonetheless found herself wondering what his name was and how he'd been wounded. . . .

She bowed her head and began to pray for him, the fingers of her right hand inches away from where his open, callused hand lay upon the coverlet.

Reynaud wondered with irony what else could happen before the night was over, but even though the thought was half in jest, his steps quickened as he thought of Brielle. It was strange that she hadn't appeared with all the commotion the last hour or so. Very strange indeed, for he doubted that anyone within the palace hadn't been awakened by the latest events.

Disinclined to wake her if she *were* still asleep, he knocked softly. No answer. No movement he could discern. He knocked again. No answer. He quietly pushed at the door of her room, then hesitated. Maybe it would be more appropriate to ask Anabette to look in on her. He glanced at the door of Taillefer's room. It was closed.

He pressed his lips together in frustration. He couldn't very well ask a male guard to do what *he* was reluctant to do . . .

Nadia. He could fetch Nadia if he wanted to walk over to the servants' quarters. He stifled a yawn. God's blood, it was late, and all he wanted was to make certain the wench was safely in her bed! Irritated with both himself and the situation, he peered around the edge of the partially open door. Her bed was empty. He blinked, pushed the panel open further, and still couldn't make out anything but a rumpled, unoccupied bed.

A thread of fear wound its way around his heart. Where else could she be at this hour?

Automatically, he turned and started toward the front of the palace. If that cur Villiers had somehow managed to sneak her out of the palace instead of Anabette, he'd have his head on a . . .

The wild, irrational thought was an indication of his sudden alarm. It went unfinished as he passed Bishop Abelard's room. He paused, thinking of the man within. Duty called.

And because he wasn't in a panic yet, years of rigid discipline made him open the door to the chamber and glance inside.

Brielle was standing over Tancred le Bref . . . her hair a tumbled mass of amber silk, and dainty pink toes peeped from beneath the hem of her loose undergown. And she was *smiling* at the man!

Thirteen

When Tancred opened his eyes, he was unprepared for what he beheld: a vision standing beside him. A lovely vision with bowed head, praying over him. It had to be an angel, and that meant he was in Heaven. . . .

Heaven?

That also meant he was dead.

His mind cleared instantly at the thought, and he realized that St. Rémy had let him die after all. He growled in a sudden burst of anger, and the angel's eyes flew open and looked into his. They were the color of a calm sea on a sunny day, and Tancred felt his anger ebb at the sight.

"Un ange," he whispered, and the vision smiled at him.

"I am as real as you," she said softly, her voice soothing as a lullaby.

Her words sank in. Then he wasn't dead . . . Thank God! He felt an answering smile lift the corners of his mouth. If she was a mortal woman, then the smile she wore was meant for him and only him.

Tancred felt a strange joy fill him at the implications of this . . .

"What do you here, Brielle?"

The sound of an angry male voice jarred him out of his tentative rapture.

They both looked toward the sound of that voice. Reynaud de St. Rémy stood in the open doorway, tall and ominous, filling it with his noble warrior's form, Tancred thought sourly. But he felt a spurt of satisfaction at the look on the Templar's face, for he recognized jealousy when he saw it.

As he watched St. Rémy stride into the room, he couldn't help but think that in the unfair scheme of things in life, it was just his foul luck that *this* woman belonged to the man he hated.

In that bitter thought's wake, however, flashed the memory of Rashid ad-Din Sinan's revelation: *". . . a bishop and two young women. One of them purported as very striking in looks . . ."*

But it was the Old Man of the Mountain's suggestion—that he somehow use the woman to trap St. Rémy—that suddenly stirred his blood. The woman called Brielle had visibly stiffened and turned to Reynaud.

Tancred's eyes narrowed . . .

With one slender hand going to her chest in surprise, Brielle answered Reynaud's terse query. "Why, I thought to look in on your friend, especially since there was no one else with him."

Friend? Reynaud thought in bemusement. He opened his mouth to deny that Tancred le Bref was any friend to him, then realized how small-minded that would sound. Especially regarding a brother Templar.

He forced himself to say, "That was good of you, but the burden isn't yours to assume." He deliberately used the word "burden," hoping le Bref would catch it.

But it was Brielle who frowned, obviously troubled by his attitude. "A wounded man isn't a burden—and certainty not to a maiden with naught but time on her hands," she replied tartly.

Reynaud glanced at Tancred. The sly dog had picked up on her words, his dark eyes alight with interest, obviously to see what morsels he could glean.

He should have let him die like the dog he was!

In that moment (one of his weaker), it came to the wear
knight that no matter how troubled he'd been before goin
to Provence to meet Bishop Abelard, life had still been rela
tively simple compared to what he'd been encountering sinc
he had agreed to take Brielle d'Avignon and Anabette d
Belvoir to the Holy Land.

He heaved a mental sigh, feeling like he'd just fought
long battle. The fatigue from healing the ingrate on th
bishop's bed hadn't been helped by the encounter with Ar
mand Villiers and his party. And the alarm he'd felt when h
hadn't found Brielle in her room had nearly been his undo
ing.

Now wasn't the time to reveal anything le Bref could us
to his advantage, especially with him literally holding hi
breath in anticipation. "You should be in bed," Reynaud tol
Brielle curtly. "I don't have to tell you how late the hour."

She spread her hands. "How can I sleep after—" He
words died mid-sentence.

"After all the commotion?" Reynaud finished for he
wondering why she suddenly looked uncomfortable. " 'Ti
over now. Have Nadia fix you some mulled wine."

"The disturbance was all my fault, my lady," Tancred sai
smoothly. "You must forgive my intrusion." He pushed him
self to his elbows, and Brielle bent to aid him.

Reynaud felt his fingers curl at his sides as he wrestle
with a very real desire to tear Brielle away from the conniv
ing le Bref. Instead, he merely directed his hand to the bridg
of his nose, pinching it with two fingers, his eyes closin
briefly. He needed nothing so much as a bed himself.

"Lady Brielle?" Reynaud gestured toward the open doo
giving her no way to gracefully refuse and remain with Tan
cred.

Her delicate brows drew together in a frown of genuin
concern. "Shouldn't someone be here with Sieur Tancred?"
she asked.

"Tancred is as well as you or I," he said, uncaring as to
how he could know this. "The physician said he merely
needs a good night's sleep, and he's not getting it by conversing with you. I'll see to it that the night guards take turns
looking in on him."

Brielle brightened visibly at this, much to Reynaud's annoyance. *"Bon soir,"* she bade Tancred with another smile
that made Reynaud want to wipe le Bref from her mind with
his own kiss.

Your own kiss? mocked a voice.

Tancred smiled back. *"Bon soir, demoiselle."*

She walked by Reynaud, the look of warm satisfaction on
her face that of one who's just made a new friend.

At her door, she turned to Reynaud, her eyes searching
his features. He looked exhausted. She wanted to reach out
and touch him—smooth away the lines of tension around his
eyes and mouth. Instead, she asked, "What happened in the
courtyard earlier?"

"Had you not been coddling le Bref you would have seen
for yourself." And then, because he couldn't quite help himself, he said, "Beware of le Bref. He is not what he seems."

She felt her face grow warm—not because of the sting of
his words or the time she'd spent with le Bref, but rather
because of her deception. In his present mood he would never
forgive her for spying on him, she was certain. Nor could
she blame him. And now was not the time to ask him to
explain his warning.

"Bon soir," he said pointedly, then swung away without
waiting for her answer.

"Anabette . . ." she said, as a sudden thought struck her.

"Anabette is enjoying her nuptials even as we speak," he
said over his shoulder. He turned back to her then, his expression grim. "Where exactly *were* you since Villiers and
his men brought in le Bref? Surely you weren't asleep during
all that?"

Because he was tired, because he wanted nothing more

than to go to sleep, his defenses were down, and a sudden
sneaking suspicion entered his mind. Could she have
been . . . ?

No, he told himself. But then why not just hie himself off
to join the siege at Acre, his instructions from Robert de
Sablé be damned? Surely his moment to moment existence
in the shadow of that besieged city would be infinitely less
disturbing than the events of this day. . . .

Brielle was casting about in her mind for some plausible
explanation to his question. There was only one. "I—I had
too much wine at the wedding celebration. In truth I *did*
sleep through much of the noise." Born of the first lie, another sprang from her lips.

He stared at her for a long moment, wondering finally
what it mattered where she'd been, as long as she was safe.
And he wasn't so self-inflated or so distrustful of her to really
believe she would have been intent upon observing him perform some minor miracle on the wounded le Bref.

And so what if she had? He had a strong feeling that
Brielle d'Avignon could be trusted with any secret. She
wasn't loose-tongued like Taillefer's bride.

He nodded and moved away. Now, if only he could get
Tancred le Bref out of his hair as easily as he had Armand
Villiers. . . .

"I cannot throw him out on his ear, my son," Abelard told
Reynaud the next day. "He was only just at death's door last
eve! He needs time to . . . recover!" He looked askance at
Reynaud and lowered his voice. "Doesn't he?"

They were alone in the chapel. It was mid-morn and Reynard had been leaving, the bishop passing by, when the
knight decided on the spot that the empty chapel would be
the perfect place to approach the cleric about le Bref.

"No. He's as good as he'll get. Believe me. One day longer
mayhap, for courtesy's sake, and no more."

Abelard steepled his fingers and touched them to his lips
with a thoughtful frown. "We just don't wish to do anything . . . unchristian. And he's a Templar, after all . . ."

"Not all Templars are worthy of their status." Reynaud
drove his fingers through his hair and spun toward the altar.
As he looked up at the high-set leaded glass window, the
anguish stamped on his face was stark. "In fact, it seems
more and more that men like Tancred le Bref are infiltrating
our ranks." He glanced over at the bishop, whose expression
was grave. "Know you, my lord bishop, that some maintain
the Order itself has become corrupt, excelling in pride and
avarice rather than humility and poverty?"

Abelard nodded. "I have heard that the Templars have de-
viated more and more from their original intent. Some believe 'twill be their downfall." He paused. "I've sensed from
the first, my son, that you are troubled deeply by something."
He placed a hand on Reynaud's shoulder, his look one of
sincere concern. "Could it be the corruption of the Order?"

"Aye," Reynaud admitted, staring unseeingly over Abelard's shoulder. "But, even more than that, is the belief that
an infidel's life is worth nothing if he will not accept Christ.
Indeed, killing a Muslim is a way to salvation." His eyes met
the prelate's in the silence that followed.

"Have you ever heard of the late Cistercian Abbot Isaac
of Etoile?"

"The name is vaguely familiar."

Abelard took his arm and turned him toward the front of
the chapel, their robes swirling gently with their turning motion. They could have been father and son—both tall and
slender, dark-haired. "I suspect you would agree with some
of his thoughts about the Templars," the prelate continued.
"His name is somewhat familiar because you probably heard
something about his writings at one time or another. He ve-
hemently disagreed that the Templar Order was founded for
the purpose forcing infidels to accept the faith at the point
of a sword. And he wrote also that its members wrongly

consider themselves martyrs if they are killed while unjustl
attacking pagans."

Reynaud jerked his head aside to stare at Abelard. "A Ci
tercian abbot wrote that?"

"Yes. Not even all clergy agree with some of the tene
of the Templar Order—surely you knew that?"

The knight nodded. "My father thinks they are the ide
knights—knights of Christ." He couldn't keep the bitterne
from his words.

"Every man is human. Every man makes errors, in judg
ment as well as in behavior. In beliefs. Even His Holiness .
even the men who lead the Poor Knights of the Temple (
Solomon. Even your father." He paused, then added, "R(
member, Reynaud, you bring your own dignity to any pos
tion, no matter how insignificant it is, no matter ho
elevated."

A noble philosophy, Reynaud mused, but that his fath(
would ever make a serious error was still hard to accep
Reynaud had always thought Gérard de St. Rémy the perfe(
man in every way. And if he could be like his father—or
least live up to Gérard's expectations, he might one day b
as worthy in his sire's eyes as his two older brothers—worth
of the St. Rémy name. " 'Tis generous of you to tell me (
Abbot Isaac, Father. And to listen to my rumblings of di
content. I'll bother you no more."

" 'Tis no bother, Reynaud. I am here for you wheneve
you need me."

They stopped before the altar rail and Reynaud sai
"Thank you for listening. . . . Will you take my advice r
garding le Bref?"

The bishop considered this briefly, fingering the filigree
crucifix he wore. "It will be awkward, but . . ."

"I'll take care of it, then. You have more important matter
on your mind."

Bishop Abelard looked a little dubious, then one corne
of his mouth lifted. "Like visit the *suk* today? Or mayha

ke a camel ride before the next mass?" He shook his head.
I wager, though, that you'll take care of le Bref in short
rder."

But Tancred had plans of his own. He was as eager to
ave as Reynaud was to have him go. The sooner he got his
ands on St. Rémy, the less chance of anyone else planning
ie same thing. Or worse, the less chance of some fool killing
im.

The latter thought made him wonder if mayhap Reynaud
e St. Rémy were immortal—could he heal himself if nec-
ssary?

The very idea made him giddy with excitement at the pros-
ect of possessing the ability for himself.

He was soaking away his sorrows in the bishop's bath and
njoying every moment. He'd been using the prelate's cham-
er, he'd been told. How gracious of the man, he thought
ith sarcasm. He was either an utter fool, or a saint . . .

"Sieur Tancred?" queried a feminine voice.

Tancred sat up instantly, recognizing that exquisite sound.
ll he needed to make life perfect at the moment was the
eautiful Brielle in the bath with him . . .

Lust leapt to life deep inside him.

But he knew a shy maiden wouldn't come into the baths
t his invitation, so he heaved himself from the caress of the
ater and swiftly wrapped a linen towel about his thick waist.
railing droplets across the tiled floor, Tancred strode into
ie bedchamber, surprising Brielle.

She nearly dropped the pile of garments she held in her
and as he appeared half-naked. But she remained where
he was, clutching her burden, her gaze averted. "Forgive
ie, Sieur Tancred, for intruding upon your bath," she apolo-
ized.

Conjuring up his manners, he said, "And forgive *me* for
ppearing like this, but someone, er . . . took my clothing."

He grabbed a sheet off the bed and carelessly draped
around him, his eyes on her all the while. Enchanting col·
tinged her cheeks and he felt a prurient thrill flash throug
him.

"I was the one," she confessed. She held the garmen
toward him, her eyes still not meeting his. "I laundered the
and had to wait until they dried."

As Tancred reached for the clothing, a figure silent
moved into the doorway behind Brielle. "Did you laund
his undergarments as well?"

Her startled gaze went to the door. Reynaud stood with
it, his arms crossed as he casually leaned against the jam·
He was dressed in robe and *keffiya,* as if he'd just come
from the heat outdoors. He looked more like a desert prin·
than a Templar; an angry desert prince, for although the po·
was studiedly negligent, she knew him well enough by no·
to recognize a cold anger beneath the exterior.

The flush that had begun to heat her face with Tancred
appearance heightened, but her mouth tightened with indi·
nation at the crude question. Before she could form an a·
propriate answer, however, Reynaud added, "You on·
cleaned my tunic sleeve, as I recall." He pushed away fro·
the door and moved into the room.

The unexpected sarcasm in his voice stung her, as did th·
accusation. "And you weren't injured, *chevalier,* as *I* recall
she parried in self-defense.

"We have servants to perform such tasks," he told he·
then looked at Tancred and said coldly, "Now that you ha·
your clothing back, I suggest you put it on, thank Bish·
Abelard for his hospitality, and leave. You wouldn't want ·
overstay your welcome."

Tancred frowned. "What do you mean by that? Wh·
grudge does His Excellence bear me that I'm being dismisse
like some lackey?" His tone edged on belligerent.

Reynaud's next words were more for Brielle's benef·
than le Bref's: "The last thing my lord bishop wants is ar·

of the *Hashishiyun* following you from the inn. We don't
need murderers lurking about the palace awaiting another
opportunity to kill you. I wonder that you were lounging
in the taproom of an inn in the first place, when other, more
important duties surely await your attention?" His eyes narrowed consideringly as he decided to keep de Sablé's warning to himself. "And even more, I wonder what you've done
this time, le Bref, to merit an attempt on your life?"

"Reynaud!" Brielle exclaimed softly, in obvious shock at
his treatment of a guest.

But Reynaud had succeeded in goading Tancred into
showing his darker side, as he'd intended, and felt more than
a little satisfaction when the latter snarled, "What I do is
none of your affair, St. Rémy! And this palace is run by the
Bishop of Tyre and not Abelard! Who are either of you to
tell me I must leave?"

"Bishop Abelard is temporary host here in the Bishop of
Tyre's stead," Reynaud said levelly. "But no matter who is
in charge, the policy is not to encourage thugs to continue
their murderous pursuits within a Christian establishment."
He made to turn away, then added, "Bishop Abelard kindly
summoned and then reimbursed the physician who attended
you. Will you repay him by abusing his hospitality?"

He wondered once again why he'd been so soft-hearted
as to save le Bref's life, and found it more ironic than trou-
bling that the man wouldn't have hesitated to run him
through had they been anywhere else, and had Brielle not
been present. Tancred le Bref was not known for his patience or tolerance.

But le Bref had swallowed the bait, becoming more in-
censed by the moment—it was written all over his red face.
Reynaud decided not to push too hard or, out of sheer obstinacy, the man would never leave.

Also, if he pressured le Bref, Brielle would be more inclined to take the man's side. It was only human nature.

"Sieur Tancred," Brielle said, after throwing a look of bemusement at Reynaud, "I'm certain Bishop Abelard wouldn't mind if you remained here until you feel stronger. Sieur Reynaud has been inexcusably rude."

"I suppose . . . if you're still weak, as the lady perceives," Reynaud said slowly, looking the sheet-draped Tancred up and down speculatively, "then mayhap my suggestion was a bit premature . . ."

Tancred drew himself up to his full, if unimpressive, height. "Thank you, *demoiselle*," he said to Brielle, "but I won't stay where I'm not welcome. I feel strong enough to leave right now."

Reynaud's brows raised as if in mild surprise. He looked at Brielle. "Shall we leave Sieur Tancred to dress?" He gestured toward the door, as he'd done the night before.

He could tell she was at a temporary loss for words, and he knew he was in for a dressing down because of his rudeness. But he would deal with that when the time came. He just wanted le Bref out of there.

"Good-bye, Lady Brielle," Tancred said. "Until we meet again . . ."

"Yes," she replied. "Until then . . ." Reynaud firmly took hold of her elbow, thinking it would be a cold day in Hell, if he had anything to say about it, that Brielle would meet le Bref again.

Brielle was so furious with Reynaud, she could barely speak. As he moved to guide her to her chamber, she turned on him and declared, "I'm *not* going to my room!"

She marched up to one of the guards she knew as "John" and spoke to him in a low, agitated voice. The young man discreetly glanced over her head at Reynaud, who nodded, against his better judgment. As he stood and watched Brielle lead the guard down the corridor, he knew they were leaving the palace, but was reluctant to interfere after having so angered her.

"Let her go," Rashid said softly from behind him. "She would only resent you more if you tried to stop her."

Reynaud nodded, the fact registering that she wore nothing on her head and one of her original two gowns instead of a loose robe. The sapphire blue of the garment was too deep to deflect the sun's rays, and the leather girdle cinching her waist was too confining to be comfortable in the heat. Her lower arms would be exposed to the blazing sun whenever she reached for something or lifted them. Reynaud could only hope she had enough sense—or that her escort would remind her—to stay in the shade of Tyre's buildings, or even the awnings of the *suk,* or marketplace, if she visited that area of the city.

Except, he realized, there would be no shade from any buildings now. This time of day, when the sun was directly overhead, was the worst time to go out. Perhaps, he thought bleakly, John would persuade her to return when he saw how she would suffer. . . .

But Brielle was furious—and determined to do the opposite of anything Reynaud de St. Rémy would want her to do. She reveled in her sudden freedom—with only John to tell her what and what not to do.

The young man was only a few years older than herself, she soon discovered, and was utterly enthralled by her. Her face was soon as red as his livery, and he offered his helmet for protection. They both laughed gaily at this, for the metal helm (which John soon removed) was, he told her, "enough to roast a man's head like a baked apple."

By the time Brielle realized that the heat was getting to John, it was too late for her. She was already beginning to feel drained and dizzy.

They stopped in the shade of one of the marketplace awnings and enjoyed cool, fruit drinks. This somewhat refreshed them both, but John obviously knew the folly of their excursion better than Brielle, for he suggested rather firmly that they return.

Brielle pouted prettily, determined to stay away from the bishop's palace for as long as possible. "After some good Bethlehem wine, we'll return."

Before they left the *suk* he bought her a skin of wine, warning her not to drink much (he refused to take even one sip), and also a *keffiya*. Once again they burst into laughter at the sight she made in her western garb and an Arab head-piece secured around her crown with a decorative cord.

Brielle rode most of the way back to the palace on a camel, a little tipsy and tired, and baked by the sun in spite of her masculine *keffiya*. Her comments to John became more and more absurd—and loud. She didn't notice the looks she was getting as an unveiled female. She was calling attention to herself by her brash behavior. And with a wineskin clutched in one hand . . .

The owner of the camel even cast her disapproving looks as he trailed discreetly behind them, finally dropping back far enough so that, obviously, no one would associate him with them.

As the camel rocked, so did the world . . . and Brielle's stomach. Unaccustomed to the climate, wearing improper garments, and drinking wine beneath the coruscating summer sun, she felt her stomach begin to rebel. To her mortification she lost much of her wine—and her dignity.

Lightheadedness assaulted her as they neared the palace, and Brielle clutched the saddle horn, determined to stay aloft. The wineskin slipped from her fingers as she tightened her grip on the horn, and John rescued and restoppered it. By the time they reached the palace, she lost consciousness before the camel could kneel at his master's command. Brielle slid sideways and sank into John's arms.

She slept fitfully, overheated and dehydrated. Nadia had helped her out of her clothing, but her face, hands, and lower arms were sunburned, and her head ached abominably. Even her scalp felt singed.

Once when she awoke, Nadia was there with a cup of water, and she took a swallow, then turned her head away, too exhausted to even drink.

At dinner, when she didn't appear, Reynaud asked Leah where the Lady Brielle was. Leah looked at Nadia, who paused in the act of replenishing a ewer of water. "Lady Brielle is asleep," she said, her expression suddenly concerned. "She was out in the sun too long and . . ."

Reynaud didn't hear the rest. He excused himself and strode quickly from the room, fearing the worst. And it was all his fault. He hadn't stopped her from leaving when he should have done so.

She was tangled in the bedclothes, mumbling in her sleep about the hot sun, the cool wine. He leaned over her and caught the unmistakable scent of wine on her breath. *Dieu!* he swore silently. She'd been drinking wine!

"My lord . . . I didn't see this earlier," Nadia said. He glanced over his shoulder at the servant and the wineskin she was holding. "I—I didn't realize she was so bad," she added. "I'll—"

"Get water—a pitcher of it—and a basin . . . and clean cloths. Quickly!"

He stripped off the clammy sheet and tossed it aside, fighting briefly to keep his eyes and his mind on his work. As he covered Brielle with a clean sheet, she fretted, "Father . . . is that you?"

His chest tightened, his heart doing a queer little lurch. She'd come to Outremer to find out what had happened to Geoffrey d'Avignon. Surely the man had died long ago, but Reynaud hadn't been much help or comfort to her. *You could have offered other suggestions if you didn't want her to go to Hattin,* his conscience chided him. *Or did you want her company for other reasons?* the voice continued relentlessly, making him pause in his movements.

Of course he hadn't had ulterior motives! Hadn't he had troubles enough before he'd even met Brielle d'Avignon?

Exactly. You needed a diversion—and you found one. . . .

Nadia handed him a thick mug of cool water, and Reynaud dismissed the voice from his mind. He raised Brielle up by the shoulders, shaking her gently. "Wake up, *mon coeur.* Drink and you'll feel better."

Her eyes opened, but he wasn't sure she recognized him. She drank obediently, so eagerly in fact, that he had to remove the cup from her lips. "Easy," he warned gently. "Not so fast . . ." He allowed her to drink once more, then said to Nadia, his gaze never leaving Brielle's flushed face, "Open wide the doors to the corridor and the baths . . . and get someone in here to fan her—you can help, as well."

He fleetingly considered trying to use his powers of healing, but she wasn't wounded. His touch alone could be soothing—he knew that from Anabette and her seasickness and from his experience with animals. Yet it didn't seem to be helping now.

Surely it was just his impatience, for he'd only been with her a very short time. It wasn't the thought of losing his touch that alarmed Reynaud, but rather the fact that it didn't seem to have any effect on Brielle.

He remembered then that he hadn't even attempted to use his healing touch on the cut caused by Khamsin's hoof. So how was he to even know?

She finished drinking and closed her eyes. "The sun," she said with a frown, ". . . so hot . . ." She tried to kick off the cover, but not with much strength.

"You're out of the sun now, *ma précieuse,*" he whispered against her damp hair, holding her like some precious and fragile object. She sighed, and he lay her back, thinking mayhap he'd succeeded in calming her.

He was in the middle of applying wet cloths to her face and neck when a knock on the door made him look up from his task. He thought it was Nadia, but instead John stood at the door, looking concerned and guilty at the same time. "How is she?" he asked quietly.

"Not well, thanks to your thoughtlessness," Reynaud said, looking back at Brielle. "How could you let her drink wine out in that heat?"

John shook his head, the misery in his face matching the tone of his voice. " 'Tisn't my place, Sieur Reynaud, to tell the Lady Brielle what to do. I encouraged her to drink sorbets or juices, but she insisted upon wine."

Reynaud paused in his ministrations and glared at the young man. "What use to escort her if you couldn't warn her away from wine? And the sun? Why, look at yourself! Your face is as red as a pomegranate!"

Even as he heard himself, Reynaud couldn't help the chastising words. "How long have you been in Outremér?" he demanded.

"Since Eastertide, my lord."

John was spared a further tongue-lashing—even though he was new to the Levant—by the arrival of Nadia and Leah with two large feather fans. And Bishop Abelard. Then Taillefer and Anabette trailed in.

God's blood, he thought. Brielle would be mortified to discover an audience at her door to witness her humiliation. But it would have served her right for running out to spite him . . .

And all because of Tancred le Bref!

Fourteen

When Brielle opened her eyes, it was to darkness. The deep silence of the sleeping city came to her, even through three-foot thick walls.

A small oil lamp stood sentinel on a table beside the bed, its single flame a beacon in the deeply shadowed chamber. It illuminated a ceramic pitcher and cup beside it, and a small jar of what looked like salve. Brielle reached for the cup, lifted it to her lips with a slightly unsteady hand, and relished the liquid's coolness as she drank deeply.

Her head still ached, but her stomach had settled, and the flesh on her face and arms didn't feel like it was on fire. She raised her free hand and gingerly touched her face. It still felt warm.

Of course. In a tantrum, like a spoiled child, she'd gone out into the merciless Syrian sun foolishly unprepared. And to spite Reynaud.

How could she have? she thought now, as she sat suffering in silence because of her own childish actions.

Reynaud had tended her, his touch sure and gentle. That much she knew, even if some of what happened immediately after her return was hazy.

Tears burned the backs of her eyes, then gathered, and spilled over her lower lids. It had been so long since a man had tended her hurts . . . since her father had gone to the Holy Land, five endless-seeming years ago, leaving her at

the convent of St. Bernadette's. The thought of Geoffrey
d'Avignon brought a renewed wave of tears, for she missed
him so!

Brielle set the cup back down and buried her hot face in
the bunched sheet to stifle her sobs. She knew that it was
out of the love he bore her that her father had placed her at
St. Bernadette's, and not a need to rid himself of her. But
she'd felt so alone when he'd done so, and then after the
news of the disaster at Hattin she was, indeed, alone; her
brother counted for naught.

Ever since her mother had died, her biggest fear had been
of being all alone. She'd always known that her father would
make a pilgrimage to Jerusalem, as he'd vowed to God years
ago when he'd almost lost his wife after Brielle was born.
And Geoffrey d'Avignon never broke a promise.

Now Tancred le Bref was gone—sent away by Reynaud
for some unknown reason, and she would never get to Hattin . . . would never find anyone willing to help her find
Sieur Geoffrey. Even as loyal and well-meaning as John the
Gaunt was, he couldn't do much for her by himself.

She may as well have remained at St. Bernadette's, she
thought bitterly; now she was not only entirely alone, but in
a faraway and utterly foreign land.

For one of the few times in her life, Brielle gave in to an
overwhelming hopelessness.

Reynaud quietly pushed open the door to Brielle's room.
He half expected Rashid to appear beside him and warn him
from his intentions, for the Arab slept at the foot of his bed
like a faithful hound, and missed nothing. This time, however,
he either hadn't awakened, or hadn't felt like following Reynaud to save him from his own actions.

The sounds of soft weeping came to him, and he paused
inside the doorway while his eyes adjusted to the gloom.
Everything looked the same as when he'd left—oil lamp on

the table beside a pitcher of water and a container of salve. But the sounds of feminine distress reached out to him and touched a chord of compassion deep within him. He was unused to a woman's weeping—the wailing of mourners at an occasional Muslim funeral, yes, but not this softly wrenching sound of private anguish.

Unthinkingly, he moved into the room and toward the bed, straining to make out the huddled figure that was Brielle d'Avignon. She drew in a low, shuddering gasp, as if trying to catch her breath, and Reynaud sat beside her and reached for her shoulder. *"Brielle . . ."* he murmured, the name rolling from his lips as he reveled in its rich, melodic pronunciation for the first time since he'd met her. *"Qu'as-tu, mon coeur?"*

He drew her toward him, gently, steadily, noting that she did not resist, such was the obvious depth of her misery. *"Est-ce que tu es malade?* Are you ill?" As his arms cradled her, his lips went to her hair in a reaction as natural as breathing. She fit his embrace as if God had made her for him, he thought, and then was briefly struck by such a temporal observation.

But then why shouldn't he occasionally have such thoughts? another part of his mind wondered. He was only human—a mortal man first and foremost, whether he wished it or not. And whatever his other problems, he'd felt his life begin to take on a new richness since first encountering this young woman now in his arms. And, yes, new hope . . .

He realized she was shaking her head against his chest. "I'm not . . . s-sick," she said in a muffled voice.

He stroked the length of her hair with one hand, the cool strands bringing to mind the richness of spun silk. An elusive drift of jasmine and a touch of the scented oil in the salve he'd applied to her face earlier teased his nostrils.

After long moments, during which Reynaud felt no need to separate himself from her, Brielle raised her head to look at him in the dimness. By the faint light of the oil lamp, he

could just see the puffiness around her eyes, and her cheeks
were sunburned and tear-tracked. "I . . . may as well have
d-died out there this day," she stuttered in a barely discernible
voice.

His breath caught in his lungs. "Don't ever say such a
thing," he said, appalled that she, the embodiment of youth
and life, should utter such a morbid thought. What was so
wrong that she would say such a thing? he wondered. He'd
never perceived her as being melancholy . . .

"No," he whispered again. "Don't ever say that!"

She tried to push away. It didn't take much effort, however,
to keep her close. She began to struggle in earnest then, and
he allowed her to regard him at arm's length. "I—I'm *alone*.
Don't you see? I have no one now . . ."

He held her eyes with his, suddenly wanting to deny that
she was alone. He was there—wanted to tell her he would
always be there . . .

Are you addled?

. . . wanted to tell her that he—

*You're a soldier of Christ! You have no business holding
this woman in your arms . . . wanting to say things reserved
for lovers!*

But he had needs and desires, also. And doubts. And fears.
Sweet Jesu, he had misgivings enough for both of them!

"You're not alone," he managed, holding back a flood of
assurances that sprang to his lips.

She shook her head, a faint frown between her slim, arched
eyebrows. "I was never more alone than now." Her chin
dipped, and her shoulders sagged in defeat. She drew in another audible, shuddering breath, and the glow from the lamp
caught a tear tripping down her cheek.

Something at the very core of him wrenched at this stark
admission, and it was all Reynaud could do not to press his
lips to hers in an effort to chase away her unhappiness. And
there was another reason, as well . . .

He caught the lone tear with a trembling fingertip and

212   *Linda Lang Bartell*

brought it to his own mouth to taste the salt of her sorrow. She raised tear-filled eyes to his questioningly, her long lashes dark and spiked with wetness, and so all-consuming a flood of tenderness crashed over Reynaud that the last scraps of his self-control threatened to scatter like wind-blown ashes.

He watched one callused finger lift of its own volition to trace the pure lines of her cheekbone and jaw, then glide lightly downward to linger on her delicately-shaped chin. In a belated spurt of sanity, he turned slightly to grab for the salve, like a man desperately grabbing for a handhold on a crumbling cliff.

Moving to draw her to him, and intending to treat her sunburn, he was unexpectedly clumsy in his unsteadiness. He misjudged and knocked the jar across the table. It rolled to the edge, hovered, then came to a halt . . . just out of his reach.

"Love me!" came her unexpected words, a whispered plea on the night air. He forgot the salve, and the fingers that had wiped her cheek moved to her chin and tipped her face upward to meet his kiss.

Love her? Ah, yes, but how easily he could do so—God help him! He, who had no business loving *any* woman; yet before the cresting wave of raw desire, reason shattered like the finest glass.

She melted beneath his tender assault, her mouth opening like a new spring bud to the warmth of an encouraging ray of sunlight. And Reynaud lost himself in the ambrosian delights of her mouth, lust rampaging through him like a runaway quarrel from a deadly crossbow.

He lay her back for better access, the naked length of her body beside his, with only the tangled sheet between them, setting his blood afire as he remembered the tantalizing glimpses of the ivory flesh of her legs and torso. As she twined her arms about his neck, their kiss deepened, the clash and play of their tongues a sensuous prologue to the inevitable expression of that which had brought male and female together across the distant reaches of time.

The closeness of Reynaud de St. Rémy, the feeling of being worshipped and cherished, even if it were only for this one night, was a balm to Brielle's lonely heart, her female pride. After being reft from a doting father and the life she'd known and loved, then confined to the sterile atmosphere of a convent for years, she was ripe for a closeness to someone—a bond with another human that went deeper than simple friendship.

That it should occur in this alien land, and that it should be with Reynaud de St. Rémy, didn't take away from its importance. In fact, if she could have had any man love her, she would have chosen Reynaud, in spite of his having foiled her plans to approach Tancred le Bref for help. For she loved him, in spite of everything that stood between them.

Including himself.

When his lips traveled downward from her mouth, she protested softly, unwilling to let him slip away, but a renewed rush of desire coursed along her veins when she realized that he was pulling away the sheet to look down at her body in the semi-darkness. She allowed it, not only because she wanted to be admired, *needed* to be appreciated in those moments, but also because he did it with such reverence in his expression.

The lamp limned his profile, the shock of dark hair that nudged his forehead as he removed his tunic; and for a moment that didn't last long enough, she was witness to a splendid display of male musculature that made her think of a lovingly and beautifully-sculpted statue of antiquity. Renewed desire cascaded through her body, and she reached for him with impatience.

He laughed softly, and Brielle saw the flash of white teeth against his tanned skin, even in the shadows, so striking was the contrast. "My eager lady," he teased. "How you please me."

She absorbed the words like dry parchment absorbing ink, needing to hear such praise and encouragement. "Teach me to please you in every way, she murmured, "so I'll never forget this night."

Something in the tone of her voice—a hint of finality, of tragic inevitability—caught his attention. He paused in his movements, in spite of her plea, drawing a murmur of protest from her, and looked down at her in the shadows. Her beautiful eyes were glazed with desire, but also something else he couldn't quite put a name to. In a gesture of infinite tenderness, he touched his cheek to hers, struggling to get hold of himself. The heat of her sunburned flesh reminded him that she'd just been ill, and here he was seducing her, as if she were some common . . .

His lips skimmed hers before he sat up reluctantly, guilt assailing him, but her hand on his shoulder made him turn back to her, torn between opposing urges. He opened his mouth to speak before the look in her eyes could induce him to say something they would both regret.

"Please?" she whispered, sitting up with him. "Don't leave . . ."

With a soft groan of frustration, he crushed her to him, the feel of the small bones of her back and ribs reminding him how easily he could conquer her, hurt her. Yet the feel of her breasts against him reminded him even more potently that she was a woman—an exquisite, desirable woman who wanted him. Needed him.

"I—I don't know what to do," she said into his shoulder.

He couldn't know that Brielle was thinking of the long and lonely years ahead of her once she returned to St. Bernadette's. There was no other life possible for her, unless she found her father, which seemed more and more doubtful as the days went by. She envied Anabette her seeming happiness, for she, Brielle, had nothing.

As she inhaled the male scent of him, felt his honed muscles beneath her tentative touch, Brielle determined that she would take this beautiful warrior—this very special man—and share one night with him . . . give herself totally to him in return for a precious memory to warm her on cold nights, sustain her in times of melancholy and loneliness until she breathed her last among the comforting but unfulfilling company of other lonely women.

She would expect nothing more from him—would not conspire to take him away from his Order and the life he loved. Nor would she ever expect him to marry her to spare her honor—that sacrosanct, but hollow, masculine entity that oftentimes drove men to self-destructive behavior.

She begged him silently, shamelessly, to make her his for this one night, and his lips upon hers once more filled her with triumph and joy.

He lay her back again, murmuring her name over and over again, and she realized how beautiful it sounded upon his lips, caressed by the rich register of his voice. Taking and rejoicing in his partial weight, Brielle wished fervently that he were hers forever. Silly, stupid woman. Trying to steal the very sun from the sky . . .

She ran her hands over his satin-smooth back, encountering several scars that marred the warm flesh over muscles like forged steel beneath, felt him flinch lightly when her hands touched the narrow cay of his waist.

His tongue found its way to her ear, tracing and delving by turns, sending tremors shuddering through her. She gripped his flanks, then moved her questing fingers to the firm flesh of his buttocks, heard him catch his breath as she stroked him before rising to meet the hot and turgid evidence of his desire, both eager and hesitant at the same time . . .

His mouth moved down her throat to first one breast, then the other, his tongue and teeth teasing the tender buds of her nipples without mercy until Brielle felt herself melting deep inside, like a ball of wax flung into a fire.

When he reached her lower belly, his fingers opened the cleft between her thighs, and stroked until Brielle thought she would go mad from the pressure building inside her. His fingers established a sensual rhythm, making her weep erotically for him . . . wanting something more, arching against his hand with soft moans of delight.

When he entered her, she was more than ready, except for the brief, sharp sting of her rupturing maidenhead. The pain surprised her, but it was his excruciatingly sweet movement within her that quickly absorbed her attention, refocusing all her energy on achieving that something she couldn't yet name, but knew that if it came only once in her life, it would be with Reynaud de St. Rémy . . .

He watched the changing expressions flit over her features, reveling in his power over her, yet humbled at the same time by the potency of her hold over him. As he began to thrust and withdraw from the hot, slick cavern that was the very essence of her femininity, Reynaud felt suddenly reborn. His doubts and worries fell away, like a cumbersome mantle suddenly shed, and his sexual fulfillment in these moments, and with this woman, crowded out every other concern.

If he never achieved another thing in his miserable life, his intimacy with Brielle d'Avignon would more than make up for it. The very thought increased his fervor, and when she arched into him, the liquid cocoon of her spasming around his shaft, he let himself go—bursting through any residual ties that bound him to the earthly world—spewing the rich substance of his life itself deep within her.

And wanting this glorious, exquisitely satisfying moment to last into eternity.

She fell asleep in the haven of his arms, and Reynaud couldn't bring himself to leave her until dawn began to break. He slept fitfully, alternately dozing, then waking to gaze at her peaceful countenance, new and confounding emotions drifting through him. Conflicting thoughts warred with one another, decisions were tentatively made, then discarded.

The closer morning came, the more his agitation increased.

When prudence finally won out over guilt, he left her bed. In a belated effort to spare her honor, he exited the room with the stealth he'd learned from the *Bedouin* . . . and almost tripped over Rashid, who was sleeping propped against the wall just outside the door, his chin sagging on his chest.

Reynaud sighed, knowing that out of loyalty the Arab had made it his mission to keep anyone from discovering him in Brielle's room. He nudged his friend carefully with his foot, lest he alarm the little man and cause him to whip out his dagger and spring at him with the lightning quickness that often went with a small, compact body.

As it was, Rashid came instantly awake and leapt to his feet. His right hand moved toward the knife he kept hidden within the folds of his robe, but he obviously hadn't been sleeping hard, for he recognized Reynaud and allowed a knowing grin to spread across his face.

Then, before Reynaud could speak, the smile disappeared. "I was wrong, master, to think that a priest's absolution could put all to rights. Indeed . . . now you must do the honorable thing."

For Brielle, from physical weakness came emotional strength.

Utterly satiated and content immediately afterward, she had fallen soundly asleep and didn't waken until dawn. The oil lamp was out and she was covered neatly with the light sheet.

Nothing was amiss . . . nothing, she thought with rue, except for the tenderness between her thighs, the feel of Reynaud's kisses, his caresses, that lingered in spite of the hours that had passed. She felt her warm face redden at the thought, and put her palms to her cheeks in a futile attempt to cool them. . . .

. . . And remembered the source of her burning skin; the actions that had led to Reynaud tending her, then returning sometime late in the night to love her.

She sat up, holding the cover to her breasts with one hand. Her head still hurt, but not as badly as yesterday, and she reached to drink from the cup on the table, determination building in her mind. She could regret what had happened and feel guilty. She could feel dishonored and ill-used, but she had wanted to share the ultimate intimacy with Reynaud more than anything at the time. Hadn't she wanted something, however intangible, to take back to St. Bernadette's?

And what good was her honor if she withered away in a convent cell?

She had to find some way to get to Hattin on her own. She couldn't depend on anyone but herself, she realized now. She *would* need an escort, someone who knew the way and how to deal with any hazards they might encounter.

But she wouldn't let anyone else make the decisions concerning her inquiry into her father's fate. She had been a pawn for long enough—a helpless piece of driftwood bobbing in a sea of male decisions, having been hidden away at St. Bernadette's by Sieur Geoffrey, then having suffered the agonies of awaiting the bishop's decision to allow her to accompany him to the Holy Land, only to be foiled by Reynaud de St. Rémy in her attempt to discover exactly what had become of her father.

A knock sounded at the door. Thinking it the perfunctory knock of Nadia before entering to attend her, Brielle said nothing. The portal opened and Anabette's face peered around it. *"Chère?"* she inquired tentatively.

"Oui?" Brielle answered, surprised that the girl had separated herself from her new groom for even a moment. Instantly, she regretted the unkind thought. Anabette was her friend, in spite of everything.

As she entered the room, her expression full of concern, an idea wormed its way into Brielle's mind. Her thoughts suddenly began to race, and she narrowed her gaze slightly, praying fervently that Anabette would help her. "Come in, Anabette," she invited.

If Anabette could scheme to get her way—and usually succeed—then so could she. . . .

"Will you perform the ceremony, Father?"

Bishop Abelard's eyes widened, but he managed to maintain his normal calm. "Are you certain, Reynaud?" he asked. "I hadn't expected you to take me up on my offer quite so soon, and in such a manner." His dark eyes suddenly shone with a glint of humor.

Reynaud managed a half-smile. "Why not two weddings in as many days?"

The bishop nodded, clasped his hands behind his back and looked at the floor for a moment. "Is the lady . . . in agreement?" He began to pace, as was his habit, his look thoughtful as he waited for Reynaud's answer.

"She . . . *will* be."

Abelard looked at him askance, and Reynaud felt color rising in his cheeks.

"I see."

No you don't . . . no one can understand. And he wasn't about to try to explain anything.

Abelard stopped his pacing and looked him in the eye. "I know you're disillusioned with the Order . . . but to suddenly give it up?"

"The dream was my father's," Reynaud said, putting it into words for the first time. "Mine never existed." He felt an invisible fetter tear, and the feeling it gave him was rejuvenating.

"But you've helped so many—"

"And I can continue to do so."

"Yes, but at your own peril! You'll not have the Order to protect you anymore."

"Father," Reynaud said, feeling weary of a sudden. "God will protect me. We are always in His hands, are we not?"

Bishop Abelard smiled slightly. "Who is giving counsel to whom now?" he asked, then sobered. "Of course you're right in that respect. But I would speak to the lady first. Would you object to that?"

"No. But I'm afraid she won't have much say in this. I'll be blunt. She is in much the same situation as the Lady Anabette before she married Taillefer: a woman unattached, in a foreign land, with no one to guide her or see to her welfare in a legal capacity."

Abelard raised an eyebrow. "My sponsorship is not legal?"

"Since you aren't a male relative, I would have to say no. But a husband or father would be more . . . shall we say, in keeping with the papal injunction?" He knew he had the prelate there. If he could spare Brielle the humiliation of anyone discovering what had happened last night, he would move mountains to do so. Even if his tactics smacked of blackmail. And involved a bishop of the Church.

Abelard frowned and fingered his crucifix absently. "I knew if I allowed myself to be swayed by Abbess Marguerite's reasoning along that line, it would come back to haunt me."

"I don't mean to suggest a threat, Your Excellence, but under the circumstances, 'tis best for Brielle. Talk to her if you like, but I will have to ask to be present when you do."

"Very well. By the way, how *is* she?"

"I—haven't spoken to her yet this morn"—that much was true—"but when I saw her last, she was feeling better."

"Good. Shall we go to her now, before your wedding plans go any further?"

Brielle looked up in surprise at the perfunctory knock on her door.

"Who is that?" Anabette said, a look of guilt crossing her face.

Brielle shook her head, casting a glance around the room in desperation before she answered, "Who is it?"

"Bishop Abelard."

She breathed a sigh of relief, for the last person she wanted to see right now was Reynaud. But her relief was short-lived, for as the prelate entered at her bidding, Reynaud de St. Rémy's tall form followed.

A mixture of embarrassment and anger churned up within her, and she couldn't look directly at Reynaud after the first jolt of recognition.

"Good morningtide, my daughters," Abelard said in greeting, his warm gaze quickly taking in Anabette.

"My ladies," Reynaud said quietly, his eyes on Brielle.

"My Lady Anabette," the bishop began in the ensuing silence, "might we speak to Lady Brielle for a moment in private?"

Anabette looked at Brielle in bemusement. At Brielle's nod, however, she left with obvious reluctance.

In the face of Brielle's uncharacteristic silence, Bishop Abelard suddenly looked uncertain. "Forgive our disturbing you," he began, then cleared his throat, "but it seems that Sieur Reynaud here wishes to make you his wife."

For an ephemeral eternity, Brielle's eyes locked with Reynaud's, then she felt telltale color rise in her face, and she pulled her gaze free.

"I . . . wished to know if you were in agreement, child," Bishop Abelard added.

"I am *not* in agreement, Father," she said in rising anger. How like St. Rémy to neglect to broach the subject with *her!* How like the high-handed Templar to take matters into his own hands and presume she would just go along!

His noble Templar conscience had to be squirming mightily for him to ever suggest such a thing as marriage!

"Sieur Reynaud is a Templar knight, Father. He cannot wed . . ."

So *this* is the way it's going to be, Reynaud thought. He

had dared hope that she would agree after only token resistance.

"Will you leave us to have a few words, Excellence?" he asked, a faint frown creasing his forehead.

"There is no need," Brielle said quickly, alarm spewing through her at the thought of being alone with Reynaud de St. Rémy after last night . . . and in the face of this new campaign of his. "There is absolutely no reason for any marriage! Sieur Reynaud is not free, and I am not willing. And that is that!"

"All the same," Reynaud said implacably, "I would ask the bishop for a few moments alone with you. . . ."

Fifteen

Brielle squelched the urge to grab Abelard's arm, insist he take Reynaud with him when he left (or not leave at all!), but her pride wouldn't allow her to show her sudden cowardice.

"Child?" Bishop Abelard said, watching her carefully.

"Oh . . . very well." The words rode a sigh of defeat.

"Summon me when you are ready," the prelate said to Reynaud before he left the room.

Brielle braced herself for the inevitable confrontation that must follow and, following her father's long ago advice, she took the offensive: "There is no need for you to offer marriage, *chevalier*. And why did you bring Bishop Abelard into this?"

"Brielle," he began, as he stepped toward her—he should have been warned by the light of battle that appeared in her eyes—"surely you don't think that I would—"

"I thought no such thing!" she cut across his words, afraid that he might woo her, with his soothing voice and honeyed words, over to his way of thinking. She had no intention of marrying a man who would forever regret giving up his calling because of one night of mindless bliss—no matter how precious that night would always be to her. "This is—madness!"

A sudden, insidious suspicion invaded the maelstrom of her thoughts. "You didn't *tell* him . . . ?" She endured the new wave of humiliation that struck as her words trailed off in horror, her cheeks burning beneath its onslaught.

She was quickly set to rights by Reynaud, however, as his own countenance took on the hue of indignation. "What kind of a man do you think me, Brielle? To ever reveal what happened between us?"

She swallowed visibly and plunged on: "Then please tell the bishop that you were mistaken—tell him anything you like—but you must persuade him that you've changed your mind!"

" 'Tis the honorable thing to do," he said, his expression softening and his gaze caressing her features, one by one, ". . . after what happened last night."

Honor. She was beginning to loathe the very word. Honor had taken her father away from her when she had needed him more than her dead mother had ever needed him to keep a long-forgotten promise. Now *honor* was prompting Reynaud de St. Rémy to ask for her hand in marriage. Nay, not ask, but almost demand it. *Sieur Reynaud wishes to make you his wife . . .*

To salvage his precious honor.

"Do you forget that I will return to St. Bernadette's and take my vows?" she forced herself to ask. "How can you be so insensitive as to run roughshod over my . . . plans? Throw my intentions to the winds?"

She swung away, trying to hide the tears that blurred her vision, and felt his hand on her shoulder. "I had thought to see to it that you wouldn't be alone anymore."

His words were almost her undoing, and silence gathered in the room as she bit her lip to keep from weeping. How dare he use her greatest fear against her? She shook her head, struggling desperately to get through that moment of vulnerability, grabbing wildly at any words that would save her from making a fool of herself. "Nay, *chevalier,* 'tis more likely that you seek to save face before the bishop in the wake of my refusal."

She listened to herself, and a part of her was shocked at

the caustic reply. Another part, however, hoped the words would wound his male pride enough to make him change his mind and leave.

She didn't need Reynaud de St. Rémy to fulfill her mission to the Holy Land, nor did she need him to wed her out of his ridiculous sense of honor. Did he think she couldn't live with the memory of what they'd shared? She surely had more mettle than that.

Brielle tensed as he squeezed her shoulder and exerted a gentle pressure to try to get her to face him. "I am not free to marry," she said through stiff lips. "And if I were, you can be sure I wouldn't pledge myself to a knight of Christ. I don't need to risk my salvation by luring a man of God away from His work."

"I'm not a clergyman," he said, his breath tickling the side of her neck, her ear, and sending an involuntary shiver through her.

In an effort to counteract it—and break the contact between them—she faced him again, only to find that he was studying her with a faint frown of perplexity. "Why are you dressed like an Arab?" he asked suddenly.

Hadn't he heard what she'd just said? she thought in vexation, and blurted, "Assuredly not in preparation for a wedding! Anabette and I had plans to visit the *suk* this morn, if you must know."

She watched color creep up his high cheekbones as his perplexity gave way to irritation. He obviously was unaccustomed to having his suit rejected.

"You didn't learn your lesson yesterday?" he asked.

His tone set her teeth on edge. She wasn't a child to be lectured. "I learned my lesson very well. That is the reason for the veil and shawl." She looked down at the articles still in her hand, then added, "I also planned to take an escort . . . does that satisfy you, *chevalier?*"

He'd never heard her speak so sharply. Why, he wondered, was she so upset with him when he'd offered to marry her?

"You are refusing to wed me because . . . you wish to take your vows?"

His disbelief irked her in the extreme, and as hard as it was to say the words, she somehow found the wherewithal. "I don't wish to wed you, *chevalier,* difficult as that may be for you to believe. Don't you see? I'm surely saving you from committing a grievous mistake in the name of your precious honor. Your sacrifice is quite unnecessary. Now, will you tell Bishop Abelard that there will be no marriage?"

Stung by the bitterness in her words as much as the words themselves, Reynaud felt his own anger rise, for she made him sound more like the knave than the honorable knight. "As you wish, my lady," he said formally, a part of him unexpectedly evincing a sense of loss at her refusal, in spite of the changes in his life that refusal would spare him. He'd fleetingly yet foolishly allowed himself to imagine having her at his side . . . waking up to her bright smile every morning . . . having children with her . . .

But the woman who spoke to him now surely wouldn't wear a smile in his bed—was even attempting to emasculate him with her scimitar-sharp tongue.

He allowed his expression to turn closed, his eyes mirroring the sudden chill he felt inside, then turned away from her to leave.

Brielle averted her gaze, feeling oddly hollow inside as his footsteps sounded on the tiled floor. She had to fetch Anabette and continue on with their plans, in spite of the interruption.

His low, strained voice startled her. "Have you considered the possibility of a child?" he asked from the door, and watched her chin jerk upward. Her eyes met his.

Obviously, she hadn't.

"We could have accompanied them outright," Taillefer said, as he and Reynaud left the bishop's palace shortly after

Brielle and Anabette. So far, they had established, and managed to maintain, a discreet distance behind the two women and their escort without losing sight of them. It was no easy task either, in a crowded *suk*.

Reynaud's mouth tightened as he dodged a beggar who'd popped up before him from seemingly out of nowhere. "We had . . . words. I think if Brielle knew I was following her she would run me through with my own sword," he said darkly.

"Ah," the minstrel answered, "but if you allowed her to do so, 'twould be most chivalrous . . . and I knew you could be chivalrous if you dug deep enough."

Reynaud threw Taillefer a look that would have silenced a more timid man. Then, unexpectedly, he found himself grinning, for Taillefer rarely failed to make him smile. "And how is it that you, my friend, allowed your bride to leave your bed? I'd been led to believe your stamina in that area inexhaustible."

"Indeed, but my lady wife could not refuse a request from a friend as dear to her as the Lady Brielle. 'Tis natural, I suppose, in spite of her fickle nature, for a female to have *some* loyalty to a friend in need."

The last two words sat poorly with Reynaud, and caused his grin to fade. With renewed purpose, in light of the meaning of the minstrel's comment, Reynaud focused with a frown of concentration once more on the two women they were following.

"I've lost them," he said sharply, sudden apprehension collecting in the pit of his stomach. It would have been easier by far, as Taillefer had said, to have accompanied them outright, no matter Brielle's displeasure. "Do *you* see them . . . ?"

"Have you no connections here in Tyre?" Anabette asked John for the third time.

And for the third time the guard shook his head patiently.

Brielle put her hand on her friend's arm. "We haven't even been here an hour, 'Bette. Be patient, you'll be back to your husband soon enough."

Anabette's dark eyes sought hers over the veil she wore, and Brielle detected sudden humor in them and smiled back.

"Forgive me," Anabette said with uncharacteristic humility. "We have the rest of our lives together, do we not?"

Aye, and I have the rest of my life at St. Bernadette's to look forward to, Brielle thought. Yet she was happy for her friend, and liked the changes she'd observed already in Anabette.

She adjusted the pale scarf she wore on her head and over her shoulders above a robe of the same color. Pulling the wrap down to her eyebrows in an attempt to shield the tender flesh of her face from the morning sun, she fought a renewed stirring of lightheadedness that threatened to sap her strength, her resolve. Today she observed the goings-on around them with much more interest—she wasn't distracted by her anger with Reynaud, but concerned with finding someone who could help her. Even if today's attempt was futile, Brielle was determined to get to Hattin without his help. Just because she had submitted to him in bed didn't mean she would give up on her search because he disapproved and refused to cooperate.

The outdoor market was a continually shifting pattern of color and sound. Awning-shaded stalls were set up to display exotic fruits and vegetables, grains, nuts and spices, woven baskets, colorful rugs and tapestries, pottery, and a host of other wares. It was hard to tell Muslim from Christian because of the adoption of Arab garb by the Europeans. Many Christians spoke Arabic, as well, and the babble of voices all around them contained more Italian than French, thanks to the strong presence of merchants from Venice, Pisa, and Genoa.

"The Italian merchants appear to be a quarrelsome lot," Brielle remarked to John.

"Aye. And the sailors are even worse—they're always brawling in the streets. The rivalry is intense among the Italian city-states."

Both women looked at him.

" 'Tis why we were reluctant to open the gates the other night—when Sieur Tancred was brought in. We can never be sure with those ruffians and their constant fighting."

The air was redolent with cooking food, spices, and perfume, and it was underscored by the salty tang of the sea breeze—and animals. A few donkeys could be seen here and there, but the predominant beast of burden was the camel. Camels in every shade of brown—from almost white to nearly black—carried goods and riders and were being bartered or sold. Customers haggled with sellers over prices, business was conducted in corners and shadowed doorways beyond the stalls; even slaves were being auctioned in one area.

"Oh, Brielle . . . pray come with me to see the slaves! I've never seen a slave mark—"

Brielle gave Anabette a bruising pinch through her sleeve, immediately silencing her. The startled girl frowned questioningly. "Are you *ill,* Anabette?" Brielle asked angrily. "I cannot believe that came from your mouth!"

" 'Tis no sight for a lady," John said, but Brielle was already walking away. "Let's not become separated, Lady Brielle," John cautioned. "I pray you . . ."

Brielle slowed her step, thinking of what had happened the day before when she hadn't listened to him.

"Taillefer says fair-haired, blue-eyed Frankish women—and men!—are much in demand," Anabette told Brielle. Her tone was conspiratorial, and she was obviously unperturbed by Brielle's irritation with her. "For harems . . . and other things." For once the indomitable Anabette blushed at the implications of her words. "Some slave merchants are not above abduction in a public place—they use tricks of the most devious sort."

"The *Hashishiyun* will even kill openly—look at the attempt on Tancred le Bref's life," John said soberly.

Anabette cast him a look from beneath her lashes, obviously assessing his capability to protect them against any such threats.

" 'Tis why we were told never to leave the palace without an escort," Brielle said, her eyes scanning the people around her. Her interest wasn't on possible abductors, however, but possible candidates to enlist for her own plans.

She spotted a woman who jarred her memory—a woman she thought she'd seen during her outing the day before. It was hard to tell with head covering and veil. But if it were the same woman, then Brielle had also observed her for the first time somewhere else, for her gestures were vaguely familiar. Yet try as she might, she couldn't remember where. . . .

As the Arab woman disappeared into the throngs of people, Brielle pulled her thoughts back to the problem of finding a suitable male to help her. It seemed as if every man who looked capable of championing her cause looked equally capable of less-than-noble intentions—like kidnapping Western women for the slave market. *That* thought had definitely been prompted by Anabette's comments, and Brielle tried to rationalize her way out of her newly-aroused suspicions: Nearly every man in the *suk* was dressed in Eastern garb, which, although not unusual in the Holy Land, did little to bolster her confidence in any of them. Here and there, of course, were Italian sailors, or Christian pilgrims obviously new to the Levant. But she had no use for a sailor or anyone unfamiliar with the area.

Because no one would do the job like the handsome Templar who stole your heart, whispered a voice. *Can you not picture him and only him capable enough, courageous enough, to walk into even the fires of Hell for a woman in distress?*

The voice was irksome, and although it was true, Brielle

had already determined that she would not beg Reynaud. In fact, she wouldn't even mention it to him again, for although he would have done anything for his precious Order, he obviously wouldn't grant that kind of service to her.

John put a hand on her arm, scattering her musings. "Lady Brielle?"

She followed his nod, and bade her leaping heart be still at the familiar sight of the white tunic and crimson cross of a Templar. His lack of height was an immediate giveaway that he wasn't Reynaud de St. Rémy, and the profile of his heavy-featured face confirmed his identity. He was engaged in dialogue, head bent intently, with an Arab merchant.

"Is that not le Bref?" John asked in a low voice.

"Indeed." She was barely aware of answering him, so hectic were her thoughts suddenly; then le Bref raised his head, and his gaze seemed to meet hers across the way.

She quickly noted that Anabette's attention was on an array of glittering baubles spread over the table of a stall close-by. "Stay with her," she bade John, her eyes never leaving the man across the way from her, in spite of the people between them. "I have business with Sieur Tancred."

"But Sieur Reynaud will be—" he began to object, when everything happened at once: an Arab leading a heavily-burdened camel approached too closely, and as the creature came between them for a few moments, it cut her off from John. But she was also free to go to Tancred le Bref, and in that fleeting instant, she came to her decision; and plunged through the crowd. . . .

She could tell by the narrowing of his eyes that she had taken le Bref completely by surprise. Especially when she remembered that she was dressed like an Arab woman, and according to what she had learned, an Arab woman wouldn't be so bold as to approach a man alone, and in a public place.

The merchant, whose eyes were ferret-like beneath his

filthy *keffiya,* looked even more surprised as she addressed le Bref. "Sieur Tancred?"

He studied her a moment with a frown, then his eyes widened in recognition. "Lady Brielle!" He took her offered hand. As he pressed his lips to the back of it, Brielle saw something flash in his dark eyes that was vaguely unsettling, then he was smiling broadly at her, clutching her hand for a heartbeat longer than was proper—as if, she thought fleetingly, he were afraid she would disappear like some *jinni.*

Beware of Tancred le Bref. . . .

She ignored the echo of Reynaud's warning. "I must speak to you privately," she said in a low, urgent voice, and cast an apologetic, yet what she hoped was modest, look at the merchant. The latter was still staring openly at her, and Brielle felt her skin crawl. Tancred, however, wasted no time taking her familiarly by the elbow and steering her to one side of the *suk,* toward the arches of the partially shadowed doorways of the nearby buildings.

She cast a furtive look over her shoulder, searching briefly for John and Anabette, but couldn't pick them out of the crowd, for a disturbance in that area suddenly obscured her view. And that meant that no one would know where she was.

But she couldn't worry about that now—nor the fact that John and Anabette might be somehow involved in the growing uproar behind them. . . .

The uncharacteristic movement of the spreading scuffle caught Reynaud's attention, for its momentum seemed to radiate outward, involving more and more people. "Over there!" he called to Taillefer, and plunged ahead, his heart pounding against his sternum. Every warrior's instinct told him Brielle and Anabette were involved somehow in the commotion. . . .

As they neared, it occurred to Reynaud that if someone

wanted to divert attention from an abduction, others would
be involved, and thus the spreading chaos. There was no
telling how many people were deliberately involved.

"Villiers!" Taillefer cried from behind him, and Reynaud
could feel the minstrel at his heels. A camel bawled from
somewhere, a dog nearby began barking furiously. Reynaud
prayed Taillefer was wrong: that their biggest challenge
would be getting Brielle and Anabette away from what threatened to become a riot, not tangling with Villiers and his men
in a crowded *suk*.

An awning collapsed and a table crashed to the ground,
spilling its display of melons and pomegranates to the
ground. The angry merchant shouted his frustration to anyone who cared to listen. Another awning tilted precariously
before Reynaud caught sight of Anabette, her exposed yellow
hair a beacon in the mêlée. Two men were engaging John—
one brandished a sword—and Reynaud had time only to
mouth Brielle's name before he clearly perceived Anabette's
predicament: a robed thug was trying to drag her through
the crowd, away from John and . . .

"Anabette!" Taillefer's shout was a mixture of fear and
outrage, sending a chill of premonition through Reynaud as
he literally clawed his way through the remaining bystanders
between himself and the girl, his heart silently screaming,
Brielle! Brielle! Where are you?

A tipsy Pisan sailor in vividly-hued tunic and breeches
managed to regain his balance after Reynaud's dramatic passage, and drew his cutlass in inebriated offense. But Reynaud
was already past him. As the knight rushed to Anabette's aid,
Taillefer moved in swiftly behind him to block the Pisan's
clumsy swing.

Reynaud tackled Anabette's abductor, sending the man's
headpiece flying as he was forced to relinquish his hold on
her. "Get away!" Reynaud ordered Taillefer's wife, and felt
a spurt of relief when she immediately flung herself away
from her Arab assailant as Reynard tangled with him. . . .

Arab? A flash of recognition . . . Sweet Jesu! It was no Arab, but Armand Villiers!

Other shouts went up, a woman shrieked in panic as the two men lurched sideways in a clumsy but deadly dance. Reynaud felt something slick beneath his feet and scrambled for purchase. And not a moment too soon.

Panting in Villiers's ear, Reynaud pinned his arms behind his back, then used his body as a shield, in time to see another armed miscreant materialize before them, gleaming dagger poised to strike. He let out a French battle cry, revealing he, too, was no Arab—was possibly one of Villiers's henchmen—and Reynaud opened his mouth to shout a warning to Anabette. . . .

Too late. The momentum from her backward surge threw her toward the newcomer, but it was the treacherous pomegranate pulp underfoot, crimson as fresh blood, that propelled her against the man's steel blade, impaling her through the left shoulder.

The Arab's hood fell back to reveal Villiers's man Bayard, a look of disbelief stamped across his features.

"Anabette!" Taillefer's cry was an anguished lament that hit Reynaud with the impact of a blow. The minstrel caught his wounded wife as she sank toward the ground, a look of surprise spreading across her features.

Reynaud felt helpless with Villiers imprisoned in his grasp, and was powerfully tempted to break the man's arm to disable him. Taillefer needed him . . .

The Pisan sailor launched himself at the now weaponless man who'd wounded Anabette, obviously willing to tangle with anyone in his path. In spite of the crisis, Reynaud was forced to turn his attention to the knight he held captive.

"She's dead, you fool," Villiers growled. "Now see what you've done!"

Reynaud jerked his bent arm higher up his back in reaction, barely conscious of all the brawling going on around them. He made a quick decision and shoved Villiers toward

Taillefer and the fallen Anabette. "Move," he gritted, "and no tricks or I'll cut out your black heart."

"I'll take him," said a familiar voice from behind him. "Go to Taillefer."

It was Humphrey of Toulouse, who grabbed Armand Villiers by a handful of his robe. John the Gaunt was with him and ran, sword drawn, to help young John beat off his attackers.

"We are eight now," Humphrey said, and jerked his chin to indicate several other men who were engaging what looked to be others of Villiers's men.

". . . the lady Brielle?" John the Gaunt called out as, in spite of his handicap, he admirably dispatched one of the men who'd drawn a weapon against young John. Reynaud didn't hear him. He had already relinquished his captive and was turning away.

Hunkering down beside Taillefer, he met the minstrel's anguish-filled eyes. "Can you help her?" Taillefer asked in a low, ragged voice.

The plea touched Reynaud's soul, and without answering, he reached out and touched the side of Anabette's neck. In vain he felt for the faint beat that signaled life. . . .

He closed his eyes and fought to concentrate.

Nothing. No heartbeat, no sign of life, save the warmth of her skin, the color in her cheeks.

If he could have healed her right there in the marketplace with scores of witnesses, he would have—and gladly. But there was no pulse in her neck. . . .

He closed his eyes and concentrated harder, desperately, putting all other things from his mind, including, God forgive him, Brielle d'Avignon. The more serious the injury, the harder he had to concentrate to summon enough strength and, therefore, more of his own physical resources, often leaving him exhausted. He awaited the divine flow of energy that would gather and then spill through him like liquid lightning. . . .

But to no avail.

Despair washed over him. He was not God. He could not reverse a death. Not even for Taillefer.

Emotion welled up within him so suddenly and so powerfully he thought he would faint. The sounds and movement around them faded into insignificance; helplessness added to his immense emotional burden as he faced the fact that he could not help his beloved friend. Why, he thought in angry frustration, had he been permitted to save the life of the scurrilous Tancred le Bref, but not that of Anabette? It made no sense to him, and Reynaud de St. Rémy preferred reasons and explanations for everything in life . . . not the random and mystifying course of events he'd been encountering ever since he'd come to the Levant.

He didn't have to utter a word. Taillefer read his expression. " 'Tis too late," the minstrel murmured, his eyes wet with emotion. Reynaud put a hand on his shoulder and watched as his friend hugged his bride's body to his own.

In spite of his concern for Brielle, Reynaud couldn't move.

Young John of the palace guard came up to them, his tunic bloodied. "Where's the Lady Brielle?" he asked in alarm, his breathing heavy, his face pale as wax. Then he saw the unmoving Anabette, her blood staining the robe she wore, the ends of her long blond hair tinged with the crimson juice that seemed to flow in every direction beneath her. Baubles were strewn about like a child's discarded toys.

He looked as if he were going to weep. "She saw Tancred le Bref across the way . . ."—he gestured vaguely to a place across the street.

Reynaud stood and looked toward where he indicated.

". . . and then we were separated."

"How could you be separated?" Reynaud snapped in disbelief.

Emotion glistened in John's eyes, and a tear ran down the young guard's cheek. " 'Twas only for a moment—but a camel came between us—"

A camel? Reynaud couldn't believe what he was hearing.
"It happened so fast . . ."

"Villiers here no doubt set it up," Humphrey said with
derision from behind him. "Took advantage of the confusion
and—"

"You killed her!" Armand spat from his bloodied mouth
at Reynaud. He looked at Taillefer still holding Anabette.
"You had to interfere when you had no right! Her father—"

"She was my *wife."* Taillefer's toneless statement cut across
the knight's accusatory words. "Joined to me by a Bishop of
the Church before witnesses." His misery-muddied blue eyes
met Villiers's. *"You* are the criminal here, man, not Reynaud."
He stood then, lifting Anabette's body in his arms, and looked
at Reynaud. "You must *find* the Lady Brielle," he said grimly.
"And I will be right beside you."

Reynaud nodded. "Let me help you with Anabette. . . ."

The minstrel shook his head. "I can manage, and you cannot waste precious moments."

"Then I insist that John here accompany you. You can
both rejoin us . . . later." He tore his eyes away from Taillefer
and his lifeless bride. "Was le Bref dressed like a Templar?"
he asked John the guard.

"Aye. And bareheaded."

"The fool," John the Gaunt murmured. "But he'll stand
out. Mayhap 'twill help us find them . . ."

Shrugging off the vague feeling of alarm, Brielle leaned
against the wall within the doorway where Tancred had led
her, to catch her breath . . . and marshal her wits. After all,
what did she really know about Tancred le Bref except that
he was a Templar?

Without so much as a hint of apology for the way he'd
literally dragged her into the lee of the building, le Bref asked
with the suggestion of a leer, "Is this private enough?"

Brielle's ingrained courtesy prevailed, despite his behavior.

"Forgive me for not inquiring about your health." She gave him an uncertain smile. "How are you?"

He was silent for a long moment, as if he didn't quite know what to say, and Brielle allowed a faint frown to cloud her brow as she lifted her head slightly to study him.

He is not what he seems. . . .

Reynaud's words tiptoed through her mind. Then, with a shake of his bare head, Tancred smiled broadly once more and answered, "I'm hale and hearty, my lady, and even more so now that I've met you again."

Even though they were in very close quarters, and virtually unnoticed by those with business in the *suk,* in the wake of the disappearance of le Bref's leer and his genuine-seeming pleasure at seeing her, Brielle threw aside her misgivings, drew in a breath, and put her request to him. . . .

Sixteen

"If you want me to help you, you must not go back to your companions . . . nor the bishop's palace."

Brielle stared at Tancred le Bref as if he'd gone mad. Perhaps he had, he mused . . . mad with joy at her having literally dropped into his hands like a ripe apricot, and thus greatly simplifying matters.

"You must disappear from Tyre, or St. Rémy will do everything in his power to prevent you from leaving. Don't you see?"

He watched doubt flicker in her eyes, pucker her brow briefly. "But he cannot do such a thing!" she protested, with genuine indignation.

"He cannot?" Tancred shook his head, as if dealing with an obtuse child. "Think! He is responsible for you, is he not? Just as he's responsible for Bishop Abelard. He'll never take you to Hattin, or allow you to go with anyone else, either." He moved his face toward hers until they were virtually nose to nose; he tried to ignore the scent of jasmine about her and the lust suddenly swelling within him. "And if you haven't noticed, there's no love lost between us. He threw me into the street the day after I was brought to the palace seriously wounded. Have you forgotten?"

"But after he saved your—" She quieted abruptly, her cheeks pinkening.

"Aye? What was that?" Tancred pressed, suspecting she *knew.*

"His quick thinking no doubt kept you alive until the physician came."

He dismissed her words with an impatient gesture. "Think you he would allow you to go *anywhere* with me, no matter how short the distance, no matter how safe?" He gripped her arm. "Don't be a fool. If you go back—if you breathe a word of this to him, he'll lock you in a barred cell before he'll let you leave his custody!" *And ruin my chances of luring him into my hands!* he thought silently.

She looked uncertain, obviously struggling with his logic. He had to strike while the iron was hot—work on her uncertainty before she decided against him.

He gambled on a bluff. "I've been summoned to join the siege at Acre before a fortnight is out. I have enough time to take you to Hattin, then return you safely to Tyre before I join the Christian army. The Lion Hearted has just arrived outside Acre and is calling for every spare man . . ." he added. It was the truth—at least the part about King Richard of England's arrival, and he hoped the news might impress her, sway her.

He had another pressing reason for leaving Tyre as soon as possible: the *Hashishiyun,* for there would no doubt be other attempts on his life.

"I have your word as a Templar?" she asked.

He wasn't quite certain what he was to give his word on, but at that moment he would have sold his very soul. *"Oui!* Er . . . my lady." He remembered belatedly to address her by her title—he didn't need to add to her suspicions by treating her disrespectfully. "Anything you say, just make up your mind, for we haven't much time . . ."

Southwest Syria

Sheik Tarik el Mezrab read carefully the message his sister Sahara had sent by carrier pigeon.

Sahara, he thought fondly, was named after the moon for her golden eyes. And she was as intelligent and educated as any man, for his father, noble-blooded ruler of his *Bedouin* tribe, had insisted all his children receive a wide education; that included reading and writing, speaking several languages, knowing the histories of ancient Syria, and the desert and its legends.

Tarik loved his rebellious sister very much, for she was so like him that they could often read each other's thoughts. It was no wonder she was different from the other women of the tribe, for she had been educated like a man.

The tall young *sheik* raised his head and stared toward the setting sun as it bloodied the evening sky. As friend to his late father, Rashid ad-Din Sinan, the Old Man of the Mountain, had warned him. And now his own sister. But was he really that concerned about Reynaud de St. Rémy? He knew Sahara was, but what had the first St. Rémy done but caused shame and humiliation?

And what did his son do for you?

Indeed, Tarik thought grudgingly. The son had saved his life . . . and at risk to his own. But what of the death of his own father? Half his caravan slaughtered on the way to Damascus by a party of Christian infidels?

You cannot hold one man responsible for the actions of others, nor necessarily blame him for the perfidy of his own kind. . . . His father's words came back to him—Abdul, the proud, fierce protector of his own, but also the wise and patient leader of his people.

Tarik took a deep breath of the cool evening air, catching the familiar scent of the herds . . . of baked sand and dissipating heat. The breeze lifted the edges of his *keffiya*, then capriciously retreated to allow the cloth to settle softly about his broad shoulders. He knew he should return to the tent, now a dark silhouette against the sapphire dusk sky. But it was his favorite time of the day—the night's inevitable, if temporary, triumph over the glare and heat of the day-spawned sun. He kicked at a lonely clump of desert grass with a sandaled foot, turning back to his musings.

Tarik knew St. Rémy had dangerous enemies. He also knew why. All the more reason, he supposed, to warn him—to give him advice that he probably wouldn't heed. But at least Tarik could make the attempt. And it would help ease his conscience, satisfy his sense of justice, even though he still harbored resentment toward the first St. Rémy. Even though Reynaud de St. Rémy was counted among the most feared and hated of all crusaders: a Templar knight.

As he made his plans, one part of him wanted to know more about this St. Rémy who was only a few years older than himself. In fact, as he lay upon his pallet that night in the quiet of the camel-hair tent, he had to fight the growing curiosity that kept him awake long after the rest of his family was asleep.

"I cannot help Anabette now," Taillefer told Reynaud, "but I can help you search for Lady Brielle. I'll take my wife back to the palace, and then meet up with you and the others."

Reynaud couldn't argue with that. And so it was that Humphrey and the other men, later to be joined by Taillefer, began to search Tyre.

Reynaud was the closest he'd ever been to panic. Where could she be? he thought for the hundredth time. Tancred le Bref had also disappeared, it seemed, as mysteriously as Brielle, and Reynaud's mood darkened with every passing hour. Surely she had been snatched by Tancred for, as much as Reynaud disliked the man, Armand Villiers had sworn to him that Brielle had not been a part of the knight's plan to abduct his lord's daughter. The knight's fury had calmed considerably in the face of the unexpected death of Anabette, and he had taken his men and left the palace, faced with the unpleasant task of explaining to Lord Aimery the events of the past weeks.

Yet Reynaud couldn't even pick Brielle out of the crowd now because, like Anabette, she'd been wearing a robe and shawl. At first glance, therefore, she would look like a hundred other women from any direction.

His gaze slowly quartered the *suk* as he stood like an island in the middle of a sea of people. He was searching for a bareheaded man in Templar garb. Both would single out le Bref immediately, for there were few Templars in Tyre during the great siege of Acre, and not many would be foolhardy enough—or carelessly arrogant—to venture into the hot sun with nothing on their heads.

"Master?"

Rashid broke into his thoughts. He looked fiercely at his friend. "How can I wed the wench if I cannot *find* her?"

His halfhearted attempt at levity obviously didn't fool the Arab. "Surely they were seen by someone," Rashid said. He moved away into the crowd and Reynaud let him go, knowing he had his own sources of information, for those of his family who'd left the nomadic life now lived here as merchants.

Reynaud briefly watched him go, then turned his thoughts back to Tancred le Bref. It didn't help matters to know that the renegade was also being sought out by the *Hashishiyun* . . . targeted for death. Evidently he was so supremely arrogant that he didn't fear even the blade of an assassin, or he would have left Tyre with all speed. Now Brielle was in jeopardy from those murderous fanatics by virtue of the fact that she was with le Bref.

But Reynaud wasn't one to panic, or give up easily, and because Brielle d'Avignon was missing, almost certainly in the hands of a man who had no conscience or scruples, he would do anything within his power to find her, no matter how impossible a task it seemed.

Power. He wished he could read minds, see through wooden stalls and awnings, stone walls. Why couldn't he have helped Anabette? And why, now, could he not use his "gift" to find Brielle?

*And why did you let her slip away from you this morn?
Before she could have even thought about seeking out le
Bref?* taunted his sense of honor.

Frustration pushed him purposefully through the teeming
suk and into the streets of Tyre, his every sense attuned to
any scrap of conversation he might overhear, any movement
around him that could signal the presence of Brielle or le
Bref—no small task.

She saw Tancred le Bref across the way . . . John's words
came back to him.

There could have been only one reason she had sought
out le Bref. Petty as the thought was, Reynaud acknowledged
that le Bref possessed few attributes—physical or otherwise.
A woman like Brielle d'Avignon wouldn't have looked at
him twice . . . unless she were desperate—desperate because
the man to whom she'd appealed for help had refused her
dismissively.

And to make matters worse, she had thought le Bref was
Reynaud's friend—a brother Templar.

He grimaced at the irony of it.

His height gave him a slight advantage, for most of the
people around him were of smaller stature; he also understood and spoke Arabic. Yet, as he moved through the
throngs, being bumped and jostled much of the time, he
failed to spot either Brielle or le Bref.

"Do you seek a blue-eyed Frankish woman?" a voice
asked in Arabic in his ear.

He jerked his head aside to see the speaker. It was a
heavily-veiled woman with, from what he could discern,
the usual dark hair. Yet her eyes were tawny, and she was
taller than most Arab women. She had also brazenly
flaunted protocol by approaching Reynaud on her own.

She stood waiting for his answer, her eyes never leaving
his. Once again, as in the Syrian desert months ago, the color
and shape of those eyes struck a chord of memory within
Reynaud. Surely, he thought, the heat was affecting him.

"Who are you?" he asked bluntly.

"A . . . friend. The woman you seek is with another Templar."

Now how did she know Reynaud himself was a Templar? he wondered.

". . . one foolish enough to think he could hide such a woman, although she went willingly enough."

"Know you where he took her?"

She shrugged, her gaze dropping finally. "I do not know for sure, but he is with a man named Sâlih al Barrak—a *Bedouin* from a tribe of cutthroats. He sometimes masquerades as a merchant. And if the Templar is with al Barrak, you can be sure they will not remain in Tyre. . . ."

She retreated a step, making to turn away. "Can you tell me aught else?" he asked, restraining the hand that would have reached out to stay her.

"I've told you everything I know," she answered, and melted into the crowd.

Indeed, he thought, it was just short of miraculous that the woman had appeared and revealed what she knew . . . that is, *if* she were telling the truth. If Brielle was with le Bref, Reynaud guessed that the rogue Templar might take her to Tiberius and the Horns of Hattin—definitely away from Tyre, like the stranger had said.

He drew in a sustaining breath and tried to chase away the alarm that threatened to cloud his thinking. He grabbed the back of his neck and threw his head back to the kiss of the hot sun, felt the grind of tension down his neck and across his shoulders. . . .

If he could believe the woman, Tiberius and Hattin would be the logical places to look. And if le Bref and Brielle had made plans while under the same roof, le Bref would have had some time to formulate a plan and gather enough men for a caravan to travel southeast for the two days' or so ride from Tyre. Mayhap even this Sâlih al Barrak would provide the men for the journey.

"Master?" The sound of Rashid's voice was like a cool breeze through the hot turmoil of his thoughts. "They were seen together not long ago, but disappeared. A *Bedouin* named al Barrak was with them."

Reynaud nodded and quickly relayed what the strange woman had told him. "Surely he'll have agreed to take her to Tiberius. Yet they cannot have left the city so soon—not in this heat."

"A few hours' search might find them before they can leave," Rashid replied, "but I wouldn't be so sure le Bref will do as she asks. He may agree to anything to win her trust, but *he* is not to be trusted."

Reynaud nodded. Tancred le Bref would use Brielle for his own purposes, his own pleasure. At the very thought of the renegade's possible behavior, a slow-building, icy fury began to grow within him. If le Bref so much as touched her, he would gladly kill him—and in a way that would cause him unspeakable suffering. *That* was one of the things he'd learned while living in Outremer.

Spoken like a true Christian . . . an elite Templar knight, said his conscience. *Murder a Christian and you'd go straight to Hell.*

He mentally shrugged off the warning. It would be worth the risk, he decided, to spare the woman he loved and kill his nemesis to avenge her honor.

"We'll post a man to keep watch at the city gates." His voice took on an undertone of grim determination. "We'll find them, my friend, if we have to turn Tyre upside down. But we'll find them—make no mistake about that."

Rashid nodded. *"Inshallah,"* he murmured. "If God wills. . . ."

But as darkness fell, they hadn't found them, and they were forced to return to the palace to meet with the others.

At Bishop Abelard's insistence, they were to gather in the dining hall to eat a full repast.

"First, I would like to pay my respects to Anabette," Reynaud had said to Abelard. The others followed him quietly to the chapel, for they were the men who'd accompanied Reynaud to Provence and then back to the Levant. They all were friends of Taillefer's and had celebrated his marriage to Anabette.

The minstrel had gone straight to the chapel, where Anabette had been laid out, and was kneeling beside her body when Reynaud entered. He watched as Bishop Abelard spoke quietly to Taillefer, then announced in a low voice that Taillefer had decided since everyone who knew Anabette was present, it seemed the best time for the funeral mass. The next morn they would be searching again—possibly even leaving Tyre.

Reynaud moved up to the kneeling Taillefer and put a hand on his shoulder. Indeed, he thought, as they prayed for the girl's soul, everyone whom Anabette had known in Outremer was present except her friend, Brielle. God forgive him— *Taillefer* forgive him!—he was hard put to concentrate on the mass when Brielle was in the hands of Tancred le Bref.

He whispered an extra prayer, a fervent plea to God that he wouldn't be attending such a mass for the woman who'd come to mean so much to him . . .

We are between Tyre and Tiberius. Your life for hers. Tell no one and come alone or she will die.

Reynaud stared at the message. No salutation, no signature, no names. But there was no need. He knew it was for him. He knew who had sent it. He knew whose life hung in the balance.

Robert de Sablé's warning came back to him, and he thought he knew why.

He'd been warned of the danger to his life if he insisted

on using his "gift," for there was almost no way to hide it. But that the threat would come from one of the men in his own Order had never occurred to him.

Be realistic . . . the Order is full of men capable of such treachery. Why are you surprised?

Reynaud looked up at the servant who stood waiting. "Bring in the messenger."

"I cannot, Sieur Reynaud," the man said, a pained look on his face. "He is gone."

Reynaud's fingers crushed the parchment as he fisted his hand. Damn!

"What is it?" Humphrey asked him.

Taillefer roused himself from contemplating his wine and looked at him expectantly, faint purple smudges beneath his eyes. Although they'd been awake for hours—it was closer to dawn than to midnight—Reynaud knew it wasn't lack of sleep that had put those circles there.

He felt the unassuagable ache of remorse once again, in spite of his own reaction to this newest development. "I must leave," he said simply, firmly, ". . . alone."

He could feel all eyes on him then. Rashid paused in re-filling the ewer of wine to Reynaud's left—he could see him out of the corner of his eye—and acknowledged this would be anything but easy.

He avoided the Arab's steady gaze and looked directly at Humphrey of Toulouse. "There is something I must do—"

"The Lady Brielle," Taillefer said.

Reynaud didn't answer. He looked down at the crumpled parchment on the table, wishing he could crush Tancred le Bref as easily. Sweet Jesu, why had he ever saved the man's life?

"The message is from le Bref?" Humphrey asked him.

Reynaud stood and stepped over the bench. "Aye. And I must go alone to secure her release, or he'll kill her."

Taillefer stood and faced him, his features coming to life

with anger. He slammed one fist on the table. "Nay, Reynaud! You cannot walk into such a—"

"I *must!*" Reynaud cut across his words fiercely. "Her *life* hangs in the balance!"

"But there is no guarantee he'll keep his word," Humphrey objected. "And then he'll have you both . . . to do with as he wishes!"

Reynaud's lips tightened, his features turned bleak. "If any of you truly call me 'friend,' you will *not* follow me!" He looked at Rashid and tried to ignore the stubborn look of insult he wore—as if Reynaud were offending him with his command. His hopes slipped. . . .

His gaze moved to Taillefer, who was still standing facing him. "Give me your oath, minstrel, lest the good bishop is forced to say a funeral mass for Brielle d'Avignon, as well."

" 'Tis certain death."

"Perhaps, but 'tis my decision to go." He felt Rashid's hand on his arm and shook it off in growing frustration. "You of all people should understand, minstrel," he added softly. "Wouldn't you have given your life to save the woman you loved?"

Anguish darkened Taillefer's eyes in answer.

"Then you—all of you—will abide by my wishes." He looked around . . . at Bishop Abelard, who wore a troubled frown, a solemn John the Gaunt, Gregoire and Bouchard, at Humphrey, his stern look tempered by bemusement. Obviously, his fellow Templar knew nothing of his intentions toward Brielle.

But he wasn't about to explain further now. "I will wed her," he said simply to the group at large.

"Not if you're dead!" Taillefer said with bitter irony.

"Keep Rashid here, minstrel. I need you both to see to her well-being in case—"

"An admission that you know you won't return," Rashid said with an outward disdain that didn't fool Reynaud for a moment.

"Not necessarily. But whatever the outcome, 'tis *my* choice to make." Growing ire tracked across his brow. "You leave me little choice, my so-called friend," he told Taillefer, then gave Rashid a forbidding look. "If either of you—*any* of you—follow me, you'd better stay out of range of my crossbow. *Do you understand?"*

She was lying face down, her arms and head hanging over one side—a beast of burden of some kind . . . no doubt a camel or donkey—her legs and trussed feet over the other side. And they were moving—a rolling motion that reminded her of the *Madonna* on restless seas. Something besides the oppressive heat was crushing her, adding to her extreme discomfort, pressing her down against the spine of the creature beneath her.

She could barely breathe. Panic took hold of her, and she tried to lift her head for air, but although whatever she was buried beneath was soft, it was also frighteningly heavy, and Brielle couldn't budge more than a fraction. She gasped in a frantic bid for air, and began to gag on the wadded cloth in her mouth. Pain lanced through her cranium with the movement.

Easy . . . easy! she told herself. She didn't want to die. Not yet, and not this way. Not bound like a Christmas goose, with the stench of camel in her nostrils, the blood pounding in her head and adding to the pain already seething there.

She tried to remember how she'd come to this sorry state, when someone shouted a command in Arabic, and the animal beneath her lurched forward with renewed vigor. Another wave of hurt crashed through her skull and she felt her gorge rise with the movement. Between the gag and her ignominious position, she feared she would choke on her own vomit. She groaned softly, offering up a silent prayer for swift deliverance.

The marketplace. She remembered the *suk,* and Anabette

and John with her. And . . . Tancred le Bref. She'd glimpsed
him briefly, had sought to approach him, but could remember
nothing beyond that. They had obviously become separated
when she'd started toward him. . . .

But she had no idea how much time had passed since then.
How long had she been a captive?

Without warning the animal beneath her came to a bone-
jarring halt. She felt the load above her shifting . . . sliding . . . gone. Then someone took hold of her by the waist
and hauled her from her precarious perch. As her feet hit the
ground, the numbness in her legs registered, and her knees
buckled from the impact of meeting the earth. Needles of
pain shot through her joints. Her ersatz deliverer, however,
jerked her back up by exerting pull on her robe. The world
spun crazily, and lightheadedness threatened to make her
faint. Weak and dizzy, Brielle was forced to lean into the
man beside her.

The gag was pulled roughly from her mouth, replaced by
a huge, clammy hand. "Don't utter a sound, *demoiselle,* else
I replace the gag and you ride the rest of the way slung over
this camel. *Comprenez-vous?"*

She couldn't make him out, for not only was the morning
sun behind him casting his features in shadow, but her eyes
were unaccustomed to the sudden brightness and slitted nar-
rowly in reaction. But she recognized the voice. . . .

Tancred le Bref? she thought in bewilderment. The very
one she would have turned to for help?

Beware le Bref. He is not what he seems.

But she had ignored Reynaud's warning. . . .

Le Bref seemed to be staring at her, and she struggled to
adjust to the bright light of the open plain. Then the meaning
of his words registered. *The rest of the way?*

"Where?" she croaked, her mouth as dry as the sand beneath her feet. "Where . . . ? Where are you—taking me?"

"Just far enough to lure St. Rémy from Tyre." He thrust

a skin of water into her hands. "Drink, or you'll be of no use to me."

She drank out of thirst, not obedience, and her mind began to function more clearly. Trying not to be obvious, she took in a blurred image of the small caravan of which they were a part. There appeared to be only Arabs accompanying them, and she noted le Bref had exchanged his Templar's garb for a robe and *keffiya*.

It appeared to be an ordinary caravan of Arabs.

"Why?" she asked him, reluctantly returning the water skin. "Why would you seek to *lure* Reynaud anywhere? Surely if you wish to speak to him, you need only—"

"I want to learn his secret," he said in a low voice. "He'll never admit it, let alone share it with anyone. There is no other way than to take him by force."

Exactly what did he know? she wondered with a sinking feeling. She doubted Reynaud would have revealed his rôle in le Bref's recovery. Yet surely the man knew enough to make him think Reynaud would admit he possessed a miraculous gift.

She decided on the spot that she wouldn't allow Tancred le Bref to learn anything from her. She met his piercing stare, attempting to ignore her aching head and roiling stomach, the sting of the sun on her sensitive flesh. Feigning ignorance, she said, "I—I don't understand."

His dark eyes narrowed shrewdly. "I think you do. I think you know exactly who saved my life that night Villiers and his men brought me in."

"The—the physician, of course . . ."

He grabbed her arm and gave her a shake. "Ignorance ill becomes you, wench," he growled, a far cry from the man she'd first met at the bishop's palace. "I think you know exactly who was responsible."

The way she was feeling physically, it wasn't difficult to appear confused and bewildered. She shook her head, then was sorry she had. "I don't know what you mean." She closed her eyes against the pain, wishing heartily for a comfortable bed in a cool place. And Tancred le Bref gone.

He released her arm and grabbed her chin in a grip that made her fight to keep from wincing. "You're lying, and 'twill gain you nothing. Whether you admit knowledge of St. Rémy's power or nay, you'll do exactly as I tell you, else you'll die."

One of the other men came up to him—was it the Arab to whom he'd been speaking in the *suk?* It was hard to say. The man boldly stared at her as he had in the marketplace, and she was relieved when he bent his head to speak in a low voice to le Bref.

Tancred nodded, and the Arab moved away. "If you can keep your mouth shut, you can ride upright. If any riders approach, you must say nothing—remain as unobtrusive as possible."

"And if I do not cooperate?" she said, her eyes flashing briefly with rebellion.

"I'll kill you."

His words made her blood run cold.

"And should you have a change of heart, remember . . . St. Rémy is mine either way. 'Tis your choice to live or die."

His words echoed coldly within her. What manner of man was Tancred le Bref that he would seek to abduct—and possibly kill—the very one who'd saved his life? He was no credit to the Templar Order, but rather a blight upon the human race. Surely he had no conscience, no soul, and she'd thrown herself right into his arms.

If she was to die, so be it; but if she could think of any way to prevent Reynaud from stumbling into le Bref's hands, she would also do it . . . and, if necessary, give up her life in the process.

For examined in this new and evil light, her stubborn insistence upon discovering the fate of her father paled in significance when compared to Reynaud de St. Rémy losing his life. And all because of her. . . .

Seventeen

When the sun turned into a fiery disk descending the western sky, they made camp.

They had stopped only once, briefly, to rest the animals and eat a dry, hasty meal. Brielle was so physically and mentally drained she couldn't see straight. Her head throbbed, and between the heat and her frantic efforts to conceive a way to prevent Reynaud from walking into a death trap, she was perilously close to the end of her resources. She felt empty of energy and ideas . . . and hope.

They were in the foothills of the Lebanon Mountains, surrounded by bone-dry hills dotted with scrub. Not only was the terrain more rugged and bleak, but the air was also dryer than along the coast, and seemed to leach the moisture from the body.

It was also the perfect place to hide and then surprise Reynaud.

Le Bref steered Brielle into a newly-erected tent and forced her to sit on the earthen floor.

"What—what are you doing?" she asked.

In the dimness she could barely make out his features to read his expression, and she concentrated on the tone of his voice as he answered, "We'll spend the night here."

"And then?"

He shrugged. "We wait for St. Rémy, of course."

The blood-red cross over his chest seemed to waver before

her eyes against the whiteness of his mantle, reminding her poignantly of Reynaud the first time she'd seen him. "But how do you know he'll follow us? He has no idea that we are together and—"

"Why do you ask so many questions?" he growled, cutting her off. "Think you I haven't a brain? Just because I'm not as pretty as St. Rémy doesn't mean I'm an imbecile!"

"I—I didn't mean to imply that," she amended, thinking the last thing she needed now was to insult him. But he'd inadvertently revealed a weakness . . .

Her words seemed to mollify him, and he said, "I sent a messenger telling St. Rémy all he needs to know. We wait here for him, and if you make the least sound, I'll send in Sâlih's men, one by one, to quiet you in any way they see fit."

Her eyes widened at this, and she couldn't prevent an expression of distaste from spreading across her features. She hoped he couldn't see it in the gloom of the tent and tried to quickly clear it. "If you think he'll fling himself into an obvious trap for me, you're mistaken. I mean nothing to him."

He scowled at her. "As I said, wench, I'm not stupid! He's the epitome of a Templar—at least in the eyes of some. He would sacrifice his life for anyone in distress, if it came down to that." He bent to bind her ankles, crushing her fledgling hope for escape. "You may not know it, but our noble knight is in love—I saw the way he looked at you." He sent her a look that made her cheeks grow hot, and suddenly his hands were beneath her robe, sliding up her calves. The roughness of his palms frightened her, for it reminded her that he was a hardened warrior—strong and capable of hurting her. And worse. "He'll come. . . ."

She stiffened, afraid of angering him, yet outraged that he would dare be so bold. When his hands reached her knee, she cried, "Enough!" as she dug in her heels and scooted backwards. Her effort didn't get her very far, but something in her voice must have given him pause, for his hands fell away.

"I am not stupid either, le Bref," she challenged him, in a voice unsteady with anger and underlying fear. "And I tell you Reynaud will not come . . . and if he does, 'twill be for naught, for he has no 'secret' to reveal!"

She threw all the disdain she could manage into the last few words and was rewarded by the heel of his hand catching the side of her jaw, sending her head snapping backward. Pinpoints of light shot through her head, which was still aching, and an involuntary moan escaped her lips. She tasted blood.

"You're *lying*," he charged, "and for naught. I will have him and learn the source of his power, whether you agree or nay!"

"But you—you agreed to take me to Tiberius!" she charged through the sudden pain. "I thought you were a man of your word!" Even as she said the words, however, she acknowledged that it would be to Reynaud's advantage if he had to follow them a greater distance, for it would gain him time. And mayhap she could come up with a way to foil this outrageous plan of le Bref's.

Sweet Mary, how could she ever have thought this man a friend of Reynaud de St. Rémy?

He thrust a water skin between her bound hands and dropped a piece of the round, thin bread into her lap. A hunk of what looked like goat cheese followed, and Brielle crinkled her nose in distaste at the smell, in spite of the fact that she knew she had to eat. The fetid odor acted to clear her ringing head a little, and when he had gone, instead of eating she drank from the water skin and set about trying to free herself.

She ignored the fact that there was nowhere to go even if she succeeded in unfastening her bonds and escaping unnoticed from the tent. It was either free herself or remain utterly useless in trying to help Reynaud.

But a nagging suspicion kept dogging her: Why had le Bref failed to tie her more securely? Was he hoping she would escape? Darkness was falling, and if she could get away under its cloak before he returned . . .

She doubled her efforts to loosen the knot at her ankles, thinking darkly that he was just a fool. A fool to think he could leave her alone in a tent and, although her wrists were tied, able to bend forward and use her fingers to untie her ankles. Able to maneuver around, even if more like a caterpillar than a human being.

A complete fool to think that such a gift as Reynaud's could ever be bestowed upon any man except by God. Only a fool would think to learn the secret of healing the sick and wounded from someone who possessed the power but could not explain it.

They sat cross-legged on soft pillows in the tent of *Sheik* Tarik el Mezrab. It was mid-morning, but the tent shielded them from the hot sun, the open flaps allowing a breeze to meander through the camel-hair structure. A young Arab girl, with eyes downcast, refilled their cups with delicious sorbet, then left. A brass pot of Arabic coffee sat before them, also, and a platter of nuts and fresh dates.

"I am grateful to Allah that I found you so quickly, *sheik*," Rashid told Tarik el Mezrab. "Le Bref has snatched Brielle d'Avignon from under our noses."

"The woman St. Rémy brought from France?"

"Yes," Rashid answered. "The one he will wed; but now le Bref has sent a message to Reynaud, luring him out of Tyre to rescue her."

"That same jackal hired one of the *Hashishiyun* to kidnap St. Rémy on his return from France," Tarik said in a low voice. "But the attempt failed and Sinan sent me a warning. I offered the agent twice as much for the easier task of killing le Bref instead."

"He'll kill Reynaud out of pure jealousy," Taillefer predicted, "unless we can get to him in time."

"You are his friend?" Tarik asked.

Taillefer raised his gaze to meet the *Bedouin*'s, pain dulling his blue eyes. "He is like my brother. I would give my life for him in a heartbeat."

"You are a warrior then?"

Taillefer's gaze lowered and there followed a singing silence. A score of fragmented thoughts ran helter-skelter through his mind—not the least of which was the fact that years ago he'd decided that he wasn't destined to be a knight, for he was nothing like the other men in his family—nor did he wish to be. He hadn't wanted to live up to their example, which he had often considered questionable at best, or their expectations for him. More than likely, he admitted to himself now, because he'd been afraid that he wasn't capable of so great a challenge. And, also, because he had not considered their behavior as knights as admirable as many had. He had discovered long ago that he could not take pleasure in killing for its own sake.

And because of his cowardice, his refusal to take responsibility for his actions, Anabette was dead.

His eyes met el Mezrab's. He opened his mouth to deny the painful fact that he was no warrior, but that for Reynaud's sake he would become anything he had to be. . . .

Rashid spoke before he could utter a sound: "Le Bref will not kill Reynaud until he tells him the source of his strength," he said, neatly avoiding Tarik's question. "And Reynaud can only say that Allah gives him his power. The evil one may be angry, but he won't kill Reynaud. For a while, at least."

Taillefer's dour thoughts were unexpectedly diverted by the sudden realization that something about Tarik el Mezrab was familiar. And there was the scar on his forehead. . . .

The minstrel's expression turned quizzical. "How do you know Rashid? And Reynaud?"

Tarik looked at Rashid, then back at Taillefer. "Rashid's

entire family were *Bedouin* at one time. I knew them well.
Those who now live in Tyre keep us . . . informed." He took
another deep puff from the flexible hose of the hookah, or
water pipe, and blew out the smoke. "As for St. Rémy . . .
well, I've only met him once, briefly. You were with him.
You said that you knew many Christians who had no brains."

In spite of everything, the minstrel's sense of humor as-
serted itself, and a ghost of a smile curved his mouth. He
found himself liking this *Bedouin sheik*—a man of warm
hospitality and great personal charm. That he spoke French,
and very well, was no surprise, for many a *Bedouin sheik*
was desert-cultured and learned. "Indeed . . . I spoke the
truth." He narrowed his eyes for a moment as he studied el
Mezrab. *"Sheik* Tarik . . . you must forgive me if I do not
remember you."

"Taillefer has just lost his wife," Rashid said quietly, coming once again to the minstrel's rescue. "Yesterday, in the
suk . . . when le Bref abducted the Lady Brielle."

Taillefer was tempted to ask what that had to do with his
memory, but held his silence, for at times he felt as if he'd
been moving in a dream world since Anabette's senseless
death. And now this.

Tarik nodded. "My condolences. You are truly St. Rémy's
friend if you interrupt your grieving to search for him."

"He is my brother," the minstrel repeated simply, and
caught a flash of some unnamed emotion in el Mezrab's eyes
before his lashes lowered.

Tarik studied the design at the base of the water pipe he'd
been smoking. "Not so long ago your friend saved my life—
in the face of disapproval from his companions, and danger
to his party and himself. You were with him, as was Rashid."

Taillefer allowed himself to openly study the pink scar that
stood out against the *sheik's* forehead, then meandered upward beneath his *keffiya*. He remembered then that Reynaud
had stopped to minister to a fallen Saracen on the way to
Provence. "You?"

Tarik nodded, and Taillefer thought back to the encounter that seemed centuries ago, but was in fact only months. He looked at Rashid, perplexed. "And you said nothing at the time?"

Rashid shrugged. "It would have served no purpose to reveal our friendship," he answered. "And as I remember," he added with irony, "the others were hostile toward our host here—Bouchard wanted to dispatch him right there."

Taillefer nodded at the memory. "I remember my comment now," he said to Tarik, "and I'm glad to see you hale and hearty, *Sheik*. Rashid speaks highly of you." He looked down at his crossed legs for a moment, thinking they'd spent enough time on pleasantries. "You will pardon me, I hope, if I say that we have no time to waste. Reynaud might be tangling with le Bref and al Barrak even as we speak . . ."

"Al Barrak?"

"Aye. Sâlih al Barrak. Do you know him?"

"He is *Bedouin*—his tribe a blight on our people. They are cruel to even their own—take pleasure in raiding those of their own tribe—and are totally without conscience. They are our sworn enemies, and I would as soon kill one of them as look at him."

"Then all the more reason to go to Reynaud's aid," Rashid said.

"Yes," agreed Tarik. He made to stand.

"Wait!" Taillefer held out a hand. " 'Tisn't that simple. We cannot just ride out of here after him—he ordered us not to follow him. 'Twas part of le Bref's demand, else he would kill Lady Brielle."

Tarik frowned. "Al Barrak's idea, I have no doubt. But what can St. Rémy do to you if you follow him? There is no other way."

"He can kill us," Rashid said with rue. "He threatened to use his crossbow."

Tarik's dark brows lifted. "He must love this woman. Even

so, I suspect he is a man of such principles that he could never kill you."

"Perhaps not," Taillefer said, "but he could seek to stop us. And in spite of his skill with a crossbow, his quarrel aimed to wound could miss its mark and kill."

The *sheik* stood, and Taillefer noted how tall he was for an Arab.

"Why don't you both dress as *Mezrabi Bedouin,* and accompany my men and me? Surely St. Rémy doesn't know us or our tribe?"

The idea appealed to Taillefer. Perhaps they could succeed, and without risking Reynaud's wrath . . . until their little deception didn't matter. "And why not? That might work." He looked at Rashid.

The Arab nodded. *"Bedouin* wisdom, *Sheik,"* he said to el Mezrab, a hint of levity shining in his dark eyes.

As they made ready, Taillefer found himself more and more distracted by his thoughts about their host. It troubled him more than a little, for he needed to hone his self-discipline—physical and mental. It was time to concentrate on what lay ahead of them—and his friend Reynaud. And he assuredly had to gather his wits about him, for he was allowing his distraction over the unfortunate events of the day before to cause him to imagine things . . . like the fact that beneath his short beard and mustache, *Sheik* Tarik el Mezrab looked amazingly like Reynaud de St. Rémy—even down to his height. And some of his mannerisms . . .

How could anything that unlikely be so?

He could only follow what he considered the easiest yet most direct route to Tiberius. Even though it wasn't likely le Bref and his party were traveling very fast (not if he wanted Reynaud to catch up with them), he still had to consider Khamsin. The stallion needed periodic rest, and even if Reynaud were forced to run the magnificent animal into the ground in order to achieve his objective, the horse was his only mode of transportation.

He rode light, carrying two skins of water in one side of the woven wool saddlebag, and his crossbow protruding from the other, stopping only now and then for brief rests and water. He avoided several villages, a party of horsemen, and two small caravans as they appeared in the distance, for the last thing he needed was to be accosted and detained by hostile Arabs. He also silently thanked God for the varied terrain, which helped shield him from human eyes when necessary.

On the other hand, however, he acknowledged that the hills and the scattered clumps of trees would also make him fair game for an ambush by le Bref. Yet he hadn't much choice, for it didn't matter whether le Bref was alone or with a score of others . . . whether he took Reynaud by surprise or whether Reynaud rode deliberately into his hands. What mattered was getting him to release Brielle. . . .

He had plenty of time to think . . . too much time, in fact. He found himself fighting to hold at arm's length his bleakest thoughts and concentrating on ways to outsmart le Bref.

He's ruthless and deceitful. What's to prevent him from refusing to let her go once you're in his hands?

True, but then there was the slim chance that he, Reynaud, could surprise le Bref and snatch Brielle from under his nose. Mayhap he could even spirit her away, although one exhausted stallion couldn't be counted on to carry two riders to safety. Or perhaps he could bribe some villager to hide them. . . .

The thought of hiding from a man like Tancred le Bref was abhorrent to everything he stood for and believed in. But he wasn't foolish enough to think he could successfully take on eight men.

He'd been following a group of tracks from Tyre that took almost exactly the route he would have chosen to get to the Galilee and Tiberius. Now he dismounted and studied them.

Although he couldn't say for certain that they belonged to le Bref, his instincts were shouting at him to follow them. From what he could tell, there were eight riders—two apparently on horses, the rest on dependable camels—which was also an indication the caravan wasn't in any particular hurry to get to Tiberius.

Of course not. He is probably placating Brielle by appearing to be taking her to Tiberius, when in truth he wants you to ride into his arms.

Reynaud glanced up at the sky. The sun was westering, and the tracks continued on into the foothills of the Lebanon Mountains. Perfect cover for a trap, he thought, but they would stop for the night to rest. And if he could somehow sneak up on their camp under the cover of darkness . . .

They couldn't be too far ahead, if these tracks belonged to them. And if they didn't, well, they still pointed toward the Galilee and Tiberius; he wouldn't be going much out of his way and wasting time.

He offered Khamsin water in his cupped hand, then stretched the stiffness from his body and remounted. First and foremost was the need to avoid any men le Bref might have watching for his approach.

Brielle, Brielle! his heart cried in silent anguish as he urged the great stallion forward. *Where are you, my love? Where are you . . . ?*

By the time darkness descended fully, Brielle had fallen into an exhausted asleep, frustrated by her unsuccessful efforts to free her hands. Le Bref had tied her wrists in such a way that made it seemingly impossible to free them herself, and she doubted she could get very far with her hands still bound.

She'd thought to rest—and not for the first time that night—before attempting once again to free herself and crawl from the back of the tent. But her ordeal had finally caught up with her, and she'd soon slipped into slumber.

When she awoke, she had no idea whether she'd slept moments or hours. She suspected it might be hours, for it was deathly still outside. The bonds were secure as ever, and she decided to flee as she was. Granted, it would be awkward, but at least she could move away from the camp.

She refused to think beyond that, telling herself she would deal with one obstacle at a time.

As she crawled from beneath the tent on her stomach, expecting to hear a harsh voice shatter the silence as she was discovered, or even take a punishing blow as she was caught and be hauled to her feet by one of le Bref's henchmen, no one stopped her.

The blackness of the night—the absence of a moon as far as she could discern from her prone position, told her it was near dawn. How much time she'd wasted sleeping! But she couldn't worry about that now.

She tasted grit and fought to keep from coughing as she pressed forward, inch by inch, resenting the tangle of her robe about her legs. When she was clear of the tent, she paused, straining to see in the darkness, listening carefully for any sound that might indicate someone nearby.

The sound of an interrupted snore came to her from the front of the tent. She froze, her heart leaping to her throat, then easing back into place as she realized it was only the guard, who'd obviously fallen asleep. With her cheek to the ground, she was tempted to weep with relief, but she couldn't afford the luxury.

If there were others stationed nearby, she couldn't see or hear them, and it would be only by sheerest luck that she didn't stumble into one of them, only to arouse le Bref's anger and be taken captive again.

Worse, even if she managed to get away from the camp, she had no idea where she was. She doubted if she could even appeal for help from any Arab villagers or travelers she might encounter. She spoke no Arabic, and she was obviously a Frankish Christian—hated enemy of many Muslims. What were her chances of even being allowed to try to communicate, let alone survive?

She felt small and insignificant and helpless.

Taillefer says fair-haired, blue-eyed Frankish women are much in demand . . . For harems . . . and other things. . . .

Anabette's words floated through her mind. Why had she thrown herself into Tancred le Bref's clutches? It was bad enough she had determined to seek out help in the *suk* in finding her father, and she had marched right out of the haven of the bishop's palace to spite Reynaud after his offer of marriage.

In light of her present predicament, and the possibility of Reynaud's death at le Bref's hands, the manner in which the knight had approached (or not approached) her regarding marriage before speaking to Bishop Abelard was a petty thing at best.

She'd behaved worse than Anabette, and the very thought of her foolish pride and consequent actions made her grit her teeth and pull herself along determinedly in the dark. She encountered no one, but that didn't mean there weren't others lying in wait for Reynaud around the perimeter of the camp.

And why had le Bref tied her hands before her so that she could free her ankles? Try as she might to ignore it, the question remained in the back of her mind.

When she believed she was far enough away from the tents to walk upright, she scrambled to a crouch. The camp was already out of sight, behind a low ridge that she could barely make out. That was good, but she had no idea in which direction she was moving without the sun to guide her. All she knew was they had been traveling southeast during the day, which meant she should be heading northwest. Wherever *that* was . . .

The hem of her robe caught on a clump of low bushes,

and Brielle's heartbeat quickened in alarm as she pictured one of le Bref's men grabbing her garment. But it wasn't. She yanked it free and plunged awkwardly onward, hunching her shoulders forward slightly, as if that would make her less visible. She wasn't accustomed to sandals, and the dirt that caught between her soles and the leather was uncomfortable. The stones, however, were downright painful and slowed her progress.

She decided that if she could travel far enough away by dawn, she could seek a place to hide from le Bref and his men until night fell again. Provided she could find food and water.

She trod on a fist-sized stone and her knee buckled in reaction to the bruising pain. As she reeled sideways, an arm snaked out and caught her about the waist. She opened her mouth to scream, sure that she'd been caught by one of le Bref's men. A hand over her mouth stifled her cry. She felt the hardness of chain mail at her back and thought it was le Bref himself. . . .

"Brielle . . ." murmured a voice in her ear—a voice that made her name sound like a melody. "Don't be afraid, *mon coeur*—'tis Reynaud."

Reynaud?

"Are you hurt?" A blade smoothly severed the rope at her wrists.

She shook her head, and his hand came away from her lips. "Reynaud!" she exclaimed softly as she spun to face him, relief and joy surging through her. One hand touched his face tentatively, for she feared he was only a mirage conjured up by her own fevered imaginings. "Oh, Reynaud, they're watching for you . . . waiting for you. You mustn't let them catch you—"

"Shhhhh," he whispered, his breath tickling her ear. "Can you walk?"

"Oui."

As his arms went around her, she looked up into his eyes.

They were barely visible, but she thought she caught a flash of gold.

"Brielle . . ."

She raised her face to his in response and met his lips. It was a brief but urgent kiss, at once desperate and loving, fierce and sweet. She reveled in his secure embrace, savored the feel of his solid warrior's form against hers . . . And decided that she would like nothing better than to spend the rest of her life with this man, despite what she had told him in her bedchamber.

He quickly broke away and reached to take her hand. "Where's his camp?" he asked.

She turned her head and pointed toward the onyx silhouette of the ridge. "Over there—behind that ridge."

He studied the ridge for a moment, then scanned the immediate area around them. "Do you know if you were followed?"

She shook her head, trying to stem her joy at having him safely beside her and focus her thoughts on getting away. "But there's a chance I could have been, for I think le Bref *wanted* me to try and escape."

He frowned, glanced about again. "Come. We've no time to spare." He turned to lead her away.

She limped along behind him, biting her lip to keep from groaning softly at the tenderness in the bruised arch of her foot. It wasn't so bad that she couldn't keep up with him, and she didn't want him to take the time to tend it. Every minute they had was precious.

"Khamsin is tethered not too far away," he told her in a low voice. "We must get to him. You can ride him to safety and when daylight comes, hopefully we'll be far enough away—"

The bawl of a camel came to them suddenly, along with the sound of padded hoofbeats, shattering the silence. Reynaud came to an abrupt halt, his hand squeezing hers. His other went to his sword hilt as he searched the blackness around them to find the source of the sound.

The large form of a camel was loping toward them from one side. The sight galvanized Reynaud into action, and he swung to the left, his strides lengthening to a dead run. Brielle fought to keep up with him, ignoring her foot and the tiny voice that said she was holding him back.

Another camel came pacing toward them from behind, and a cry in Arabic rent the air.

"St. Rémy!" another voice shouted as a third animal—this time a horse—joined the other two and closed in on them now from three sides. The very sound of le Bref's cry made Brielle want to scream in frustration, for her worst fears were realized. Now Tancred le Bref and his treacherous Arab co-horts would herd them back to the tents like sheep for the slaughter.

As Reynaud slowed his steps, obviously foiled, she threw a look over her shoulder—toward the direction from which she'd come. The only avenue that wasn't blocked was back toward the camp.

"Stand behind me," Reynaud commanded her, and pushed her protectively into place at his back.

"You cannot hope to fend them off," she cried softly. "They are too many—they'll kill you!" Even as she spoke the words, Brielle knew they wouldn't kill Reynaud, but she suspected that out of sheer nastiness—and to prove a point— le Bref might actually wound him, thus forcing him to demonstrate his healing ability. But her fear was that he wouldn't be able to use it on himself . . .

"Come now, St. Rémy," le Bref taunted as he slowed his horse to a walk and approached them. " 'Tis useless to fight—you're outnumbered eight to one—and you wouldn't wish to see the lady wounded now, would you now?"

Eighteen

Le Bref's words sent chips of ice scraping down his spine. Considering what the renegade surely knew by now, it wasn't an idle threat.

"You've sunk to new depths, le Bref, to even contemplate such a thing." Although he fought to keep his voice calm, Reynaud had a powerful urge to leap at the man and kill him.

"Throw down your sword and dagger, St. Rémy, and move slowly toward me."

"Do as he says," Brielle whispered.

With deliberately irritating slowness he reached for his sword, then stilled mid-motion, his mind racing. If he challenged le Bref here and now, would the man fight? Would it cause enough diversion to allow Brielle to possibly break away and get to Khamsin?

Probably not, but it was worth a try, for his biggest fear was that Brielle would come to harm if he were taken captive. Le Bref was just evil enough to hurt Brielle physically to force Reynaud to heal her. . . .

"I said *drop* it," le Bref snarled.

He could feel the tension in Brielle's body against his. *"Do it!"* she pleaded.

But Reynaud knew le Bref wouldn't kill him—at least not yet. "Khamsin is a little way past le Bref . . . over yon rise and behind a copse of low trees," he murmured over his shoulder. "When I tell you, *run*. Don't look back—don't heed any voice but mine. Do you understand?"

"But—"

"Just do as I say! The sun is rising . . . follow it toward the coast and—"

Two camels moved closer, their riders menacing forms in the gloom. Le Bref shouted, "Throw down the sword, or she dies!"

"You said my life for hers," Reynaud called out. "What of that, *brother Templar?"*

"I'm no brother of *yours* . . . and I've had my fill of Templar strictures."

"Then you'll have to take us by force," Reynaud said, and prepared to defend the woman behind him to the death.

A missile whizzed through the air from somewhere nearby, and instinctively Reynaud spun about to shield her. Too late. Brielle cried out softly and slumped against him. He caught her in his arms and tried to quickly assess the damage: a dagger to the right shoulder.

Lowering her carefully to the earth, he murmured assurances to her, but she was beyond his influence . . . she had already fainted. As he lay her gently upon the ground, fury whipped through him with all the power of a storm churning up the sea. He straightened and whirled toward le Bref, his features pale and turned to marble, his golden eyes molten with outrage.

"May you rot in Hell," he spat at le Bref, flinging his sword to the earth. The loathing in his voice tangibly hung in the air.

He turned back to Brielle and dropped to his knees beside her, fighting to clear his mind of everything but what he must do. As he searched for the strength to perform the very miracle that he would have denied was within his power to the rogue knight behind him, the sun began to limn the horizon to the east and delicate fingers of light spilled across the land. It touched her face like a benediction, and Reynaud felt inexplicably calmed.

Two lances pointed down at him from either side as the riders closed in and brought their camels to a halt. Le Bref's horse plodded toward Reynaud and the wounded Brielle.

"Now you'll show me exactly what you can do—and how you do it," Tancred ordered as he slid from his mount.

When he came into Reynaud's line of vision, the knight looked up and told him unequivocally, "I'll do no such thing before the others. Tell them to leave us, quickly, or you'll learn naught from me."

"You're bluffing. She means too much to you for you to let her die."

Reynaud fought to rid his mind of all thought save Brielle—and the fact that he had to get le Bref alone. "I can heal her before an army if I must," he said in a low, contemptuous voice, "but you'll never discover how if I don't choose to *tell* you! Make them leave!"

He closed his eyes and bowed his head, summoning his powers of concentration, and chased away his anger. Placing his hands gently over Brielle's free-bleeding wound, he silently prayed, *You granted me the power to heal the one who caused this hurt. Please let me rectify the evil before you take back this gift. I beseech You to grant me the power only one more time. . . .*

He'd long suspected that he would maintain this mystic ability for a limited time only, since it hadn't developed fully until he had come to the Holy Land, and he thought how cruel it would be for God to deny him now.

But the familiar benevolence flowed through him like the most soothing balm, filling him with peace and tranquility, even as it brought every particle of his being to vibrant life, and Reynaud felt its power move through his fingertips to Brielle's injury.

Moments passed, serene and unhurried, as his divine strength worked its wonders. He felt his own energy begin to drain away, but it was a sure sign that the healing process was taking place.

He felt rather than saw the dagger slip from the wound as if pushed by invisible fingers. It dropped to the earth.

When he opened his eyes, the bleeding had stopped; her lashes fluttered, then lifted, her stunning blue-green eyes alert and lucid. "Reynaud!" she said softly and smiled radiantly at him.

"Oui, mon coeur," he murmured with infinite sweetness, one hand on her shoulder.

She moved to sit up. "Why am I—?"

He shook his head. "Lie still for a few moments," he said softly, emotion glistening in his eyes.

"That won't be necessary," le Bref said.

Reynaud looked up at him, his sense of peace shattered, his expression turning hard and cold. For a few moments, he'd forgotten all about him and the others.

"I know from experience," Tancred elaborated as he stood before them, fists on his hips, "that the wench feels like she can do anything."

"But evidently you know naught of gratitude," Brielle said darkly, causing him to scowl at her. It was in that moment that Reynaud noticed the ugly bruise along her jaw. He struggled briefly against the urge to rise up and spring at le Bref . . .

He directed his gaze to the distance to clear his head of the temporary madness that often accompanied outrage and noted the others had gone. Probably not far, he reasoned, but nonetheless Tancred was alone for the moment.

"Now, St. Rémy," the rogue knight demanded, "tell me how you did this."

Reynaud slowly straightened and offered his hand to Brielle. When he first faced le Bref, he said, "Let her go first. My life for hers, remember?" He hated the thought of her going off alone, but her fate at the hands of Tancred le Bref and his minions would be infinitely worse. At least with

Khamsin, she could get away from the camp faster, and possibly be able to attract attention . . . and help.

"She stays here!" Le Bref went for his sword, and Reynaud threw himself at his own, which lay only a few feet away.

But he'd forgotten the physical weakness a healing sometimes caused him, something he'd heretofore considered a small price to pay when compared to what he'd been able to accomplish. Until now.

He was now ill-served by his sluggish reflexes, the desertion of his natural agility. Landing within a hair's breadth of the weapon, he made a desperate grab for it. His fingers found the hilt, but le Bref had already planted one shoe on the blade. Had Reynaud been stronger, he could have jerked the weapon from beneath Tancred's foot, but he may as well have tried to pull Excalibur from its block of stone.

Why *now?* he thought in frustration.

Le Bref laughed aloud, an ugly, taunting sound. "Look at your mighty Templar now," he said to Brielle. "He cannot even retrieve his sword!"

But Reynaud wasn't beaten yet. In the moment Tancred looked at Brielle, he managed to slip his dagger from his belt with his other hand. He slashed at le Bref's unprotected ankle just above his leather shoe and was rewarded with a scream of pain as the renegade staggered backward out of the dagger's reach. His sword suddenly free, Reynaud gripped the hilt and lurched to his feet.

He felt his face redden, not from exertion, but humiliation. His movements were those of an untrained clod before Brielle, and he had never wanted her to see him like *this*. . . .

"I'll *kill* you for that dirty trick," Tancred howled at Reynaud, and flung himself toward the knight, a grimace of pain stretched across his features.

"Don't!" Brielle cried. "His secret will die with him!"

Reynaud cast a glance her way before he deflected le Bref's wild thrust. *"Run!"* he commanded her. Twisting awkwardly aside, he fought to recover in time to counter le Bref's next move. His sword felt like it had doubled in weight, yet his seething anger began to work in his favor.

As a result of Reynaud's knife thrust, le Bref was hobbling, barely able to do much himself, and Reynaud sought to take advantage of it. He lunged at his opponent, and le Bref couldn't jump out of the way quickly enough. The blade kissed his ribs, blood blossomed over the side of his tunic. He stumbled sideways. *"Sâlih!"* he roared.

Reynaud lunged again, knowing he had to dispatch le Bref before the others could intercede. Wincing, Tancred managed to clumsily dodge the blow.

The muffled sound of padded camel hooves came to Reynaud, and he knew al Barrak and his men hadn't gone far. Now they were coming to le Bref's rescue.

"Reynaud!" Brielle cried from off to the side. "The others!"

Sweet Jesu, he thought in utter frustration, and glanced over at her. She hadn't listened to him—she was still standing nearby. And now it was too late. . . .

With two hands on the hilt, Tancred made a horizontal swipe at him, but it wasn't quick enough to be effective. The whoosh of air was his only reward as Reynaud ducked. He wondered if le Bref were just trying to tire him.

As he straightened and jumped backward, a camel came pounding toward him, its rider's raised scimitar reflecting the gold of the rising sun. It arced through the morning air. . . .

"Don't kill him!" roared le Bref.

Reynaud lifted his sword in defense, but the camel swerved away just before it reached him . . . swerved away and went toward Brielle. Le Bref was lunging at him again and he was forced to turn his attention away from the rider bearing down on Brielle and counter the swing.

The latter he did with ease, feeling some of his strength returning, but a feminine cry of distress made him jerk his head aside just in time to see the mounted Arab swoop Brielle up onto the saddle before him. He continued on toward the man.

He faced le Bref, who was staring down at his hemorrhaging ankle, his face drawn and white.

"Tell him to bring her back, le Bref," Reynaud ordered him tersely, "or you'll die where you stand!"

Tancred looked up at Reynaud, a sneer smeared across his mouth. "Not while I have a sword in my hand! You're finished, anyway, St. Rémy . . . look!"

Another rider was coming straight at him, and a dull pounding of the earth behind him heralded a third closing in. All seemed lost as Tancred made to strike again . . .

A sudden scream rent the air, a camel bawled, and Brielle's cry came to him. Reynaud retreated a few steps and looked over toward the ridge. The Arab rider was pitched from the saddle, pulling Brielle with him. The frightened camel bawled and went charging off.

The second rider cried out, and Reynaud watched as he, too, lurched sideways and toppled to the earth like a rag doll. The bolt from a crossbow protruded from his back.

Reynaud didn't know who was interceding for him, but if he didn't take care of le Bref, he wouldn't live to find out . . .

He faced le Bref again and met his sword blade in mid-air with a terrible clang and an even worse jolt to his body as he absorbed the shock of the blow. From somewhere he heard other riders, but could only direct his returning strength and skill toward disarming le Bref. He felt his reflexes returning, as well, and responded to his opponent's next attack with an offensive thrust that forced the renegade to hop clumsily backwards.

Three more riders came galloping over the ridge. Sweet Jesu, he thought in frustration, how could he go to Brielle while he was engaging le Bref?

Suddenly, with an unnaturally loud exhalation of air, Tancred came hurtling toward him, drunkenly, aimlessly. Reynaud took advantage and thrust his sword directly at his opponent's midsection . . . and impaled him.

With a dazed expression transforming his features, le Bref crumpled to the ground. Blood dribbled from his mouth, his sword dropped from a hand suddenly gone limp. And Reynaud saw, then, the bolt protruding from between his shoulder blades.

Another cry came to him, and he saw one of the riders who was just approaching tumble from his mount.

He glanced toward the east. The morning sun was almost blinding, and silhouetted against its coruscating brilliance was a party of Arab riders. . . .

He quickly wiped the sword clean of blood on le Bref's tunic, sheathed it, then swung toward Brielle. As he did so two more miscreants who were just coming over the ridge wheeled their mounts about and raced back toward the camp.

Brielle had fought free of the heavy body of her abductor, and was already getting to her feet. Her robe was bloodied yet a second time, her face smeared with dirt, her hair loose and tangled. But she threw herself into Reynaud's arms with all the power of a small battering ram.

"Reynaud!" she cried softly, leaning her head into his shoulder and clinging to him with desperate strength.

He buried his face in her hair and sought to still his thundering heart. "Are you hurt?"

She shook her head, then looked up at him with a worried frown. "Are you?"

"Nay. Just my pride."

Her look turned quizzical, but before he could speak again, hoofbeats shook the ground behind them, and they turned toward the sound. "Our saviors . . . I think," he said wryly. He studied the group approaching them from the east with eyes narrowed against the increasing brightness of the sky, but could make out nothing familiar with the sun behind them. "I hope they're allies," he said with a trace of irony, "rather than enemies."

"How could they be enemies if they came to our aid?"

"They shouldn't be . . . unless they decide, once they meet us, that they've saved the wrong people." He looked down into her anxious face. " 'Tis unlikely, though."

"Who could they be?" Brielle asked, her fingers gripping his arm tightly.

"*Bedouin*—desert wanderers. There are many such tribes scattered throughout the East." He brushed back her hair with his free hand and smiled at her reassuringly. Then he turned his attention to the approaching party, his free hand resting lightly on his sword hilt.

All but two rode horses instead of camels, and they were armed with menacing-looking lances. Their tall leader carried himself regally—obviously the *sheik*. He rode directly toward Reynaud on a sleek white camel, while others in the party spread out over the area—some going toward le Bref's camp. Two men rode immediately behind the leader—one as tall and commanding as the *sheik* himself, the other small-statured.

Reynaud felt Brielle tense beside him, and he said *sotto voce,* "They come in peace, I think. Don't be afraid."

The leader called out a greeting in Arabic. Reynaud answered and watched the Arab separate himself from the others and approach him alone. When he was near enough to speak without shouting, the stranger dismounted and stood before them, an impressive figure against the golden tapestry of the eastern sky.

"Many thanks, friend, for saving our lives," Reynaud said.

The man looked at Brielle, then turned his tawny gaze back to Reynaud. Once again, as in the Syrian desert, and the marketplace in Tyre, Reynaud was struck by those amber eyes. And something more elusive. . . .

"I am no friend to any Templar," the Arab said, his eyes boring into Reynaud, "although I have reason to make you the exception."

Reynaud's brows drew together as he puzzled over the

Bedouin's words, then answered, "Whatever you may think, I am not your enemy. And I thank you all the same."

"*Hamdillah!* Praise be to God we could be of help, Templar, for 'twas His will that I be led to you. The debt is now paid. I am *Sheik* Tarik el Mezrab."

Reynaud didn't know what he meant by his words concerning a debt, but he let it go for the moment. "And I am Reynaud de St. Rémy, *Sheik.* This is the Lady Brielle d'Avignon, who was taken against her will from Tyre by Tancred le Bref—" he canted his head slightly to indicate le Bref's body lying upon the ground. "The outlaw from whom you saved me."

A rising wind played with the hem of the Arab's robe, teased the ends of his *keffiya.* "A renegade Templar? Interesting . . . but no doubt you would have prevailed without our help, St. Rémy. At least against le Bref, if not the others. My men have gone to rout any stragglers."

Reynaud dragged his gaze from the thin, newly-healed scar marring el Mezrab's high forehead and looked over at the ridge behind which the last of le Bref's cohorts had disappeared. He wondered at an Arab *sheik* using a crossbow—and so expertly—when he knew they preferred the lighter and more easily managed short bow. His eyes met Brielle's then, and he saw the question in hers. "Aye. You may tell him," he told her quietly.

Brielle drew a deep breath and said to Tarik, "And I thank you, as well, my lord *Sheik,* for coming to my rescue."

Tarik studied her silently for a moment. "As I said, Allah led us to you, but in truth, I did not save either of you."

Reynaud's eyes narrowed slightly.

"Another was responsible for the use of the Frankish weapon. He is the one who deserves your thanks." Tarik gestured with one hand, and the two men who were closest to him walked their horses forward.

Reynaud's gaze moved immediately to the two approaching *Bedouin,* and the same breeze now played with the ends of their headpieces. He caught a glimpse of fair hair on the taller of the two . . . and a familiar horse.

Suspicion tugged at him. Then, as he eyed the smaller Arab, the suspicion turned to recognition. How in God's name . . . ?

Another was responsible for the use of the Frankish weapon.

Of course. Taillefer could shoot a crossbow with enviable skill—if he chose to do so. Surely the minstrel had been shocked to his senses by Anabette's death for him to pick up a knight's weapon and use it in so serious a situation. Or was it the blood of a line of great knights in his family that was asserting itself and finally bringing his devil-may-care tendencies, his irresponsible attitudes, to heel?

The two men halted beside Tarik el Mezrab and the taller one removed his head covering. Despite the walnut stain that darkened his face, there was no mistaking his identity.

"Taillefer!" Brielle gasped softly, echoing Reynaud's thoughts.

The minstrel gave her a ghost of his old grin and bowed slightly. "Your servant, my lady."

"In spite of your grief," Reynaud said softly, "you came . . ."

"I cannot help her now, Reynaud," he said, his expression quickly sobering as his eyes held Reynaud's. "And I would not be much of a friend if I used her death as an excuse not to go to your aid."

Reynaud looked at Brielle, who had been listening to every word. Now her expression turned stunned. "Lady Anabette was killed in the *suk* yesterday," he explained in a low voice, wishing he could shield her from the revelation for a while longer . . . at least until they were alone. " 'Twas an accident, Brielle. . . ."

As if reading Reynaud's thoughts, Taillefer quickly stepped in. "Is it safe to assume you won't make good your threat now that we are here?"

He shifted his attention back to the minstrel. "Obviously you are the one to be feared with a crossbow in your hands—although you deserve to be drawn and quartered, knave, for going against my orders." The tone of his voice softened the words.

"We are your friends, master," Rashid spoke up as he dismounted, "and not lesser-ranked Templars to take orders from you."

Taken aback by the Arab's uncharacteristically admonitory words, Reynaud held his tongue in the wake of the sober expression Rashid wore. He could only attribute it to the Arab's relief at having found him in time.

"I'm glad you're here," Reynaud said with emotion. "Both of you . . ."

"You could not ask for better friends," el Mezrab told him. Just then several mounted *Bedouin* appeared at the top of the ridge and caught the *sheik's* attention. "It appears the others got away," he observed, and strode toward the body of the miscreant who'd tried to ride away with Brielle. He nudged the body with one foot, and as it rolled slightly then settled onto its back, he said, "This is Ibrahim al Barrak, Sâlih's closest and most vicious ally." He looked over at Taillefer. "You've done all *Bedouin* a great service, Frank."

Reynaud was watching him with a strange look in his eyes. Where had he seen him before? Surely he must have encountered him somewhere . . . else why would el Mezrab mention the payment of a debt? And, perhaps more importantly, why was he so drawn to this man?

"Even with his beard and mustache, he could be your brother," Brielle told Reynaud, squeezing his arm.

He looked down at her, her words striking him like an unexpected blow. And also triggering a memory: the sight of eyes so like his own, on a wounded stranger in the Syrian desert. . . .

He looked back at Tarik el Mezrab, who was now moving

toward le Bref's body. As if he read the Templar's thoughts, the *sheik* glanced over at him and their gazes locked . . .

Suddenly Reynaud remembered. The Arab he'd tended on the way to France . . .

"Would you have us bury him?" Tarik asked him.

At the thought of le Bref's treachery, especially after Reynaud had saved his miserable life, revulsion rose in him in a suffocating wave. "Leave him for the jackals," he said in an expressionless voice.

One of Tarik's returning men told him, "The others have escaped with their tails between their legs, *Sheik*. The fallen are also of al Barrak's tribe. Only one is yet alive."

"Dispatch him," Tarik said.

The man moved off to do his *sheik's* bidding.

"Our camp is two hours from here, and I would be honored if you would allow us to extend our hospitality. Surely you need rest and sustenance before your journey back to Tyre—especially the lady."

"The honor is ours," Reynaud said, and watched as this prince of the desert held out his arm to Brielle with all the dignity of a European emperor. There was much that Reynaud wanted to know about him. . . .

"Will you ride with me?" el Mezrab invited her.

She glanced questioningly at Reynaud, but it was Rashid who told her, "You could not be safer anywhere else under the laws of *Bedouin* hospitality."

Brielle nodded shyly. "Thank you, *Sheik*." Outwardly, she seemed to have recovered from the revelation, Reynaud thought. "I would be honored."

As they moved off, he felt the remotest prick of jealousy at the sight of the striking *sheik* walking off with the woman he loved. . . .

He dismissed the thought from his mind and turned to Taillefer.

"Jealous, are you?" the minstrel asked him with an unholy gleam in his eye. "And well you should be, for he's taken your bride-to-be. Even if he already has a wife or two, Islamic law allows him four."

Reynaud didn't know whether to cuff him or embrace him. He did the latter. "Thank you, *mon cher ami,* for what you did. If only I could have been as helpful to you in your time of need."

He watched the levity fade from Taillefer's eyes. " 'Tis over and done with. You did what you could."

Reynaud turned to Rashid.

"He was determined to go after you, you know," Taillefer added, "with or without me, threat or no threat."

Reynaud hugged the Arab fiercely, then held him away and was rewarded with a blush beneath the smaller man's burnished skin. "My thanks to you, as well, my faithful Rashid. What would I do without you?"

"No doubt by now you would have had le Bref skewering his own men, one by one, after convincing him that with enough practice, he too could heal. When every last one was writhing on the ground in agony, you would have found a way to escape."

Reynaud found himself laughing softly. "And so I might have."

"It wouldn't have been difficult to fool le Bref," Taillefer added. "He never was very bright."

"They await us," Rashid observed, glancing over at the *sheik* and his men.

Reynaud swung away and gave a short, piercing whistle. He waited a moment, then repeated it. "What made you go to el Mezrab?" he asked, turning back to Rashid.

"His father was friend to my father—*Bedouin* brothers. The family friendship goes back a long way. I knew he would help me."

There was more Reynaud wanted to ask him, but the sound of Khamsin's hoofbeats came to him then, and with relief he watched the great stallion come into view, the morning sun outlining his magnificent form, burnishing his glossy coat.

Reynaud was exhausted, as was Brielle. The warm, generous hospitality for which many *Bedouin sheiks* were known couldn't have been more appealing to him at that moment.

He greeted the stallion softly, wondering how Brielle would deal with Anabette's death with two hours to ruminate between here and el Mezrab's camp. She would blame herself, he knew her well enough to predict, and he wondered how the burden of guilt—rightly assumed or not—would affect her.

She should have been riding with him, in the haven of his embrace, with his love surrounding her and—he hoped—deflecting at least some of the pain.

But he hadn't had a chance to tell her that he loved her. Demanding her hand in marriage was one thing . . . declaring his love was another. Now she was riding in the arms of a stranger.

And whose fault is that? demanded a voice. *You should have told her when you accepted her love the other night—even when you spoke to her the next morn. . . .*

Plagued by questions he still had for Rashid, the nebulous and inexplicable bond he felt with Tarik el Mezrab, and his concern about Brielle's reaction to the news of Anabette's death, he mounted Khamsin and followed Taillefer and Rashid toward the waiting party.

Nineteen

Brielle didn't know that it was an honor to be directly under the *sheik's* protection. Nor could she know that Tarik el Mezrab suspected he could discover more about Reynaud de St. Rémy by getting to know the woman for whom the Templar would have sacrificed his life. . . .

The ride seemed endless to Brielle, in spite of the fact that she was securely within the firm and competent embrace of an actual *Bedouin sheik.* He was no savage, as she had imagined a desert nomad might be—in fact he was cultured in his own way and came across as a learned man. Had she not been nagged by the shadow of Anabette's death, she would have thoroughly enjoyed their rather unorthodox dialogue. She answered his questions as he spoke them into her ear and was reminded of Reynaud by the timbre of his voice— down to his laugh, by the deceptive litheness of his powerful frame. She found herself revealing bits and pieces of her reason for journeying to the Holy Land in the company of Reynaud de St. Rémy.

"You were friend to the minstrel's wife?" he had asked her at the outset.

She'd nodded, and searched for the words to describe her relationship with Anabette. They hadn't been the closest of friends, for their differences had often come between them. Yet the Anabette whose transformation had begun after her marriage to Taillefer was a young woman to whom Brielle related more easily, even for that brief time.

At one point, Tarik had offered to do what he could to discover what had happened to her father. "If you like, I can speak to the Emir of Damascus regarding your father. . . ." And she had merely thanked him and let it go for the moment.

As they neared the *Bedouin* camp, Brielle decided that Tarik had deliberately set about distracting her from the stunning news of Anabette, and was grateful, even though his conversation only postponed the inevitable.

When they finally approached the cluster of black goat-hair tents, Brielle was struck by the sight of several herds of goats and sheep. Scores of camels—fawn-colored, some almost black, others alabaster—spread out over a good portion of the summer camping area. A few horses grazed alongside the other animals, as well.

Reynaud had once told her that Rashid's family had been wealthy as *Bedouin*, for at one time they had owned almost a hundred camels. Evidently Tarik el Mezrab's family was also wealthy. They were in a valley, on the fringe, Brielle guessed, of the Lebanon Mountains. Even in this, the dry season among these foothills, the clear spring that ran beside the camp irrigated the lush foliage that grew along its banks and beyond, providing a blanket of greenery that was refreshing to the eye.

Tarik dismounted, then reached for her and set her on the ground. His hands lingered at her waist and his eyes, as gold as the sun against his dusky skin and dark beard, searched hers. She quickly realized he was concerned about her well-being rather than being rudely familiar and gave him a wavering smile along with her thanks.

Before she could catch more than a glimpse of Reynaud or speak to Taillefer to offer her profound condolences and unburden her squirming conscience, she was ushered into a large tent by several unveiled, giggling women. They chat-

tered in Arabic as they admired her fair hair, curiously
stroked her ivory flesh where it was visible, making clucking
noises over the sunburned areas of her skin. Some of them,
she noted, wore dyed henna patterns on their hands and faces.

She didn't understand a word of what they said, but managed to communicate with them through signs and facial
expressions. She was so relieved to be back among friendly
faces—and females, no less—that she tolerated their curiosity with good humor.

From somewhere water was procured for a bath, and her
blood-stained garment removed. She was bathed and pampered like a princess, her hair washed and dried, her body
rubbed with perfumed oil. She found herself dozing several
times before they were finished with her, for she'd had virtually no sleep since leaving Tyre. Empathetic looks and murmurs told her she was among understanding friends.

When, at last, she was clean and had eaten a light repast,
they allowed her to sleep for a few hours. Feeling safe and
secure in the knowledge that Reynaud was out of danger,
she did just that.

When Brielle awoke, she didn't know where she was at
first. It was dark, except for the low flame of an oil lamp.
Indistinguishable voices came to her from somewhere
nearby—a spate of soft laughter. She sat up on the low cushions that formed her bed, looked around, and remembered
she had been brought to a *Bedouin* camp by an Arab . . . the
sheik Tarik el Mezrab.

Reynaud was safe. Taillefer and Rashid had come for him.
But Anabette was dead.

She frowned at the last thought. She had to speak to Taillefer, find out exactly what happened, and apologize to him
for having persuaded Anabette to go to the *suk* with her that
morn. If she hadn't been so bent on showing Reynaud that
she could get to Hattin without his help—if she hadn't acted

so ridiculously righteous and proud, Anabette would be alive today.

But an apology was so pitifully inadequate. . . .

A woman entered the tent, letting in a chill breath of night air and interrupting her thoughts. With a smile she motioned for Brielle to stand and helped her smooth out her clean robe. She helped her don a head scarf veil, then motioned toward the opening of the tent.

She was going to see Reynaud and her heart skipped a beat at the prospect, in spite of the heavy burden on her conscience.

A male voice on the other side of the flap stopped her, and the Arab woman answered. Rashid entered, nodded at Brielle, and said something in Arabic to the woman. After glancing at Brielle, a question in her dark eyes, she left.

Why he'd come to see her now—when she thought she had been about to join him and the others in another tent— was a mystery to her. Unless he wanted to tell her about what happened in the *suk* the day before. . . .

" 'Tis good to see you again, Rashid," she said with sincerity.

He bowed slightly. "You are a most welcome sight, as well, *demoiselle*. Allah be praised you came to no harm."

"Nor Reynaud," she added, then furrowed her brow. "But what of Anabette?" Her throat tightened with emotion. "Can you tell me what happened? Reynaud said 'twas an accident, but surely I am to blame."

He nodded, his loam-brown eyes looking bottomless. "The *demoiselle* had a choice. She made it and accompanied you. As Reynaud said, it was an accident—the will of God."

"But what *happened?*"

He lowered his gaze for a moment, as if searching for the words. "Villiers and his men were disguised as Arabs and were lying in wait for the lady Anabette. As she flung herself away from his grasp, she slipped and was impaled by the dagger of one of his men behind her. She died instantly."

She closed her eyes briefly, then grabbed his arm. "But didn't Reynaud . . . ?"

"It was too late. He couldn't help her."

A sound of distress rose to her lips; unexpectedly Rashid put his hands on her shoulders and squeezed. "You *must* be strong! If you feel the need to take the blame for her death, do it later." He lowered his voice, and urgency infused his words. "Reynaud will need you this eve . . . he will need your support and your strength. I am asking you—if you care at all—to be strong for him now. Can you put aside your remorse for his sake?"

His words penetrated her guilt, the tone of his voice making her lift her gaze to his. "Where is he?" was all she could think to ask, suddenly alarmed.

"He is being entertained in el Mezrab's tent. There is nothing amiss."

"But what do you mean by—"

His hands dropped from her shoulders. "It is not my place to reveal any more. You must be willing to place your trust in me. You will be present to see and hear what happens tonight. You will know then." His eyes knifed into hers. "Can you do it? *Will* you do it?"

She lifted her chin. "I can be strong for Reynaud—whatever the situation." She drew in a deep, sustaining breath. "I can do anything I need to, you see, for I love him."

The line of his mouth softened. "As do I. But you have more influence. Remember your love for him this night." He swung toward the exit and, with a flourish, held the flap open for her. They walked out into the cool, star-studded night.

Over the babble of the mountain-fed stream, muffled sounds of revelry drifted on the breeze. When Rashid guided her into the *sheik's* tent, Brielle had to narrow her eyes against the brightness of the oil lamps. He hesitated a moment, as if to allow her to get her bearings.

The tent was large—five wooden poles supported it, and it was bisected by a colorful woven room divider. The far side must have been for the women, for the side Rashid and Brielle had entered contained (as far as Brielle could discern at first) men only. They sat upon the ground, cushioned by rugs and pillows, in the traditional *Bedouin* pose—one leg folded, the other knee drawn up to rest the arm thereupon. Some leaned indolently on cushions propped against camel saddles, and all drank from small cups of what could have been sweet tea or cardamom-flavored coffee. Most wore the traditional robes, as well, and *keffiyas* held in place by the double bands of colored cords.

She had no trouble locating Reynaud. He sat with his back to the room divider, beside Tarik, in a clean white tunic with its blazing red cross. The *sheik* was serving coffee from where he sat, and Taillefer flanked Tarik's other side; the minstrel was still wearing his own clothing, and the sight of him, looking more somber than usual, brought a pang to Brielle's heart.

The tent quieted suddenly, and all eyes went to Rashid and Brielle. Unveiled, Brielle felt suddenly self-conscious in the company of *Bedouin* men. She had been out among the Arabs often enough since coming to the Levant to have become accustomed to seeing city women veiled in public. Now, before *Sheik* Tarik and his closest men, she felt vaguely uncomfortable, even though the women who'd tended her earlier hadn't covered their faces.

Her eyes met Reynaud's, his own lighting with pleasure—and something deeper—as they held hers across the tent. That indefinable entity made her heart dive toward her midsection. He looked like a *sheik* in his own right—fitting right in with his deep tan—and in spite of his Templar's clothing.

Except, she thought, that he was the most striking man there, despite his attire. Even Tarik el Mezrab, although so unnervingly similar in looks, paled beside Reynaud in her eyes.

He said something to Tarik, his eyes briefly leaving Brielle's face. The *sheik* nodded, and Reynaud stood and made his way toward her. She broke eye contact then, in the midst of that very intimidating gathering of stern-faced men, and looked away.

Right into the eyes of another woman. A young *Bedouin* woman whom she hadn't noticed at first and who was, as far as she could tell now, the only other female present.

For a moment, she forgot all else as she stared at the girl. She was unveiled and watched Brielle with curious eyes, and when their glances met, the *Bedouin* girl lowered her lashes. She appeared to be about the same age as Brielle and strongly resembled the *sheik;* Brielle found herself wondering not only about the young woman's looks, but also why both of them had been permitted to join the men.

Perhaps it was because she herself was a guest, Brielle reasoned; but before she could wonder any further Reynaud was standing before her, looking down into her eyes, his expression warm and welcoming. He took her by the elbow and guided her back toward where he'd been sitting—to a place beside his.

She smiled at *Sheik* Tarik and dipped her chin in greeting.

"Welcome to my humble tent, *demoiselle,*" he told her, then glanced around at the entire group before he addressed Brielle again. "There are too many of my men here for you to remember their names, and especially in Arabic, so I have taken the liberty of telling them who you are, rather than introducing each man to you separately. However, my sister Sahara is here on this occasion, as well." He looked over at the young woman with whom Brielle had exchanged glances.

She followed his glance, then smiled at Sahara. "I am honored," she said. As the young woman smiled back, it came to Brielle that the *sheik's* sister reminded her of the woman she'd seen in the *suk* the morn before.

"I will translate for you," Rashid murmured from beside

her, and she was grateful for his familiar presence. At least she wasn't between two strangers.

The buzz of conversation had begun again, and Brielle was obviously the only one present who didn't understand enough Arabic to follow it. She sat quietly, taking in the serving of the food by some of the women she had met earlier, barely aware of the unintelligible conversation that flowed around her. She suddenly wished she had learned more of the language.

She also found, even though the huge trays of flat sheets of bread mounded with mutton and savory sauce gave off a mouth-watering aroma, she had little appetite. The light fare she'd eaten earlier had satisfied her needs, and she was now too nervous to do more than nibble and sip her coffee. The stunning events of the last few days seemed like some phantasmagorical dream, and Brielle felt as if she were yet to emerge from the nightmare. Her present and unlikely surroundings only added to the feeling of unreality.

"A sheep was slaughtered before the *sheik's* tent in Reynaud's honor," Rashid told her, startling her from her musings. She'd almost forgotten about him in her absorption. Even Reynaud was deep in conversation with Tarik and had hardly spoken to her; and Taillefer, sitting on the other side of the *sheik,* was beyond her reach.

She met Rashid's steady gaze and a corner of her mouth curved briefly. "I regret that I have no appetite, and I only wish I knew more of your language."

"I will translate for you if you like, *demoiselle.*"

She nodded her thanks and couldn't help but wonder if something important was yet to come. There was a sense of expectation in the air, and she noticed Sahara often watching Tarik and Reynaud, though discreetly. Tarik met his sister's questioning glance now and then and would give her a mysterious half-smile—as if they shared some secret.

Reynaud will need you this eve . . .

A touch on her arm dispersed her thoughts. "You're not

eating, *mon coeur,*" Reynaud said as he eyed the dish before her. "What is amiss?"

She looked up into his eyes and was about to deny anything was wrong, for she wanted nothing more than to wipe the slight frown from his brow—this man whom she'd refused to marry, yet who would have given his life for her.

But Tarik suddenly addressed the group in stentorian strains, grabbing the attention of everyone present. . . .

Reynaud reluctantly withdrew his attention from Brielle, wishing that she had been allowed to sleep uninterrupted. Mauve smudges of fatigue marred the delicate flesh beneath her eyes, and her lids drooped now and then, indicating her need for more sleep. Why, he wondered, had Tarik el Mezrab commanded her presence? And that of his twin sister?

He had no more time to think on it, however, as, once Tarik had commanded everyone's attention, the *sheik* lowered his voice and began to speak in slow, well-enunciated Arabic, as if to make certain even his Frankish guests understood his every word. By virtue of the lower volume of his voice, the careful, measured manner in which he was speaking, all eyes were turned to him.

"I would tell you a story about my father, *Sheik* Abdul, which has been untold for many years. . . . His love for Sabla, my mother, was born long before they were ever wed."

Reynaud could hear the low murmur of Rashid's voice translating for Brielle.

". . . most of you know, he was a man of honor and wisdom, courage in all situations and generous to a fault." Tarik glanced down at the brass coffee server before him for a moment. "If he had one fault, it was that he was perhaps too willing to forgive—or perhaps he loved too much."

Reynaud began to relax, anticipating a lengthy recitation of some of the history of the *Mezrabi Bedouin.* It was not unusual, although he was certain many had heard the story before. He looked at Brielle and caught her pure profile as she listened, eyes downcast, to Rashid. He wondered if she would be able to remain awake for the entire recitation and felt a surge of profound tenderness for her—a wish to take her into his arms and let her sleep.

". . . for years I have lived beneath the shadow of doubt and a sense of betrayal, but now I recognize the example the wise Abdul set for me in his actions long ago—for *all* his children and his people."

Murmurs of assent ran through those present, and many leaned forward in anticipation. Reynaud glanced at Rashid in the wake of the *sheik's* mention of doubt and betrayal. Perhaps he had misinterpreted the Arabic, or maybe this story *hadn't* been told before; he wondered if Rashid, being well-acquainted with Tarik's tribe, knew what the *sheik* was about to say.

His interest was piqued more than a little, and he also wondered if the mother that Tarik had mentioned were still alive and living among them.

"My father loved my mother since they were children and took no wife before her. But Sabla was young and foolish. Rebellious. And so rewarded my father for his devotion with betrayal before they were wed."

There followed a stunned silence, and Reynaud caught looks of surprise on several faces, outrage on others, as murmurs of disapproval reverberated through the tent like a gathering swarm of locusts. When Tarik spoke again, the sounds died away, and even the women's side was absolutely silent. "I tell this story not to embarrass my mother but, rather, to laud my father's strengths, and explain why I have asked you, my closest and most trusted men, to join in what could have been a private celebration had I so chosen." He bowed his head in silence for a moment.

Without warning, Reynaud felt like a powerful hand was crushing his chest . . .

When Tarik raised his head again, he looked directly at Reynaud, anguish glimmering in his tawny eyes. And anger. As if the two emotions fought a battle within him. Reynaud fought to keep his expression schooled, for suddenly his instincts—and the intensity of Tarik el Mezrab's gaze—told him he was somehow, unwittingly, involved in this.

"My mother conceived with another man," Tarik continued in a low, unsteady voice, "—a Frankish infidel." He paused, letting the full weight of his words sink in.

There was dead silence.

A host of fragmented thoughts hurtled through Reynaud's mind. One seemed to loom larger and more ominous than the rest: the uncanny resemblance between himself and Tarik. He barely felt Brielle's hand upon his arm . . . was unaware of Sahara watching him intently from across the way. A dull roar filled his ears as the possibilities of Tarik's words began to register.

"My father insisted on wedding Sabla in spite of what she had done—the shame she had brought down upon the *Mezrabi* tribe. He begged the old *sheik* that she not be punished in any way—that her conscience would punish her enough." Tarik drew a deep breath and droplets of sweat beaded his brow below his *keffiya.* He pulled his gaze from Reynaud, sweeping the small assemblage of his faithful brothers. "I have tried to emulate my father's great capacity for forgiveness, as has my sister, by inviting to my tent the progeny of the man who defiled my mother. And also—" his topaz eyes burned into Reynaud's, "because of a stranger's generosity and selflessness in the desert, months ago after a bloody skirmish. . . ."

Reynaud felt like the great tent around them had collapsed, bearing down on him with crushing force, smothering him. . . .

"In the face of our blood ties, my brother," the *sheik* continued, "I have banished my bitterness—for you, Sahara, and I share the same sire: Gérard de St. Rémy."

* * *

He wanted to deny, outright, the veracity of what he had just heard—he wanted to cry out to all the world that what had just been revealed was a blatant lie—that Gérard de St. Rémy wasn't capable of such perfidy. In fact, so overwhelming was the urge, he went rigid with the effort of holding himself in check.

But here was Tarik el Mezrab beside him, his eyes and features, like Reynaud's, resembling those of Gérard de St. Rémy. True, there were subtle differences, but further proof was staring him in the face, across the way, in the eyes of Sahara el Mezrab.

He read compassion in those golden orbs—in Tarik's expression as well, for gone was the earlier anguish and anger.

Voices buzzed around him, and he suddenly felt Brielle's hand squeezing his forearm. How could he face her now? he thought, his eyes tearing away from Tarik's but avoiding hers. When he'd acted so righteous and superior to those like Tancred le Bref! When all along, he'd carried the tainted blood of his perfidious father—the father he'd sought to emulate in every way and had striven to please for as long as he could remember.

While Gérard had been living a lie for all these years.

And then another realization burst through him: Sahara el Mezrab was the woman who had spoken to him in the *suk*.

Someone tapped his shoulder, said into his ear, "Reynaud?"

It was Taillefer, his voice weighted with concern. He, who had just lost his wife.

Reynaud met his eyes. Who better to offer comfort than Taillefer? After all, the minstrel had fled France to escape his own dark family secrets. Reynaud put a hand over his friend's and gripped it hard, loath to look at Brielle . . . or Tarik. Or anyone else among them.

He mustered a facsimile of a smile, but he knew he couldn't fool the minstrel.

" 'Tisn't the end of the world, *mon ami,"* Taillefer said in a low voice. "You must acknowledge your half-brother and sister. And keep in mind that no doubt they were once every bit as stunned and disillusioned as you are now. Live for the present, Reynaud . . . the past is dead."

Reynaud stared, trance-like, at the rug-covered floor before him once more, and Taillefer drew away.

With a monumental effort, Reynaud looked into his half-brother's face, knowing that to question such a revelation from an honorable *Bedouin sheik* would be an insult, and from some hidden reserve deep within, summoned a semblance of his normal voice. "I am not proud of my father's behavior all those years ago, nor can I amend the hurt he caused you and Sahara," he said in Arabic, choosing his words with care. "But I can truthfully say that I was honored to save your life." He hesitated and pulled in a soft, sustaining breath. "And I'm just as honored now to call you brother."

And it was true, in spite of the riot of emotion playing havoc with his heart. Reynaud suspected that if he were to have an Arab brother, he couldn't have hand-picked a better man than Tarik el Mezrab.

Even as he watched Tarik smile in reaction, he could hear Rashid translate for Brielle.

Rashid . . . That traitor! he thought darkly as Tarik drew him to his feet and embraced him. His friend could have saved Reynaud the shock of this revelation before a score of strangers—even though Reynaud understood the honor the *sheik* had bestowed upon his faithful by letting them witness the revelation firsthand. Why had Rashid never breathed a word of this?

By now, everyone had followed suit and risen to their feet. Reynaud dared to look at Brielle, and saw nothing of condemnation in her eyes. Only . . . pity. At least he interpreted it as pity. God's teeth, not from her! Not *pity!*

He felt a muscle jump in his jaw and glanced away, only to meet Rashid's look. Someone was putting a cup of something into his hand, but he couldn't tear his eyes away from the Arab who'd been his faithful friend.

Or so he'd thought.

He would have liked nothing better than a skin of good French wine to calm his tumultuous thoughts and emotions! But that was impossible in the middle of a *Bedouin* camp.

Instead, he found himself raising his cup in unison with the others in tribute to his half-brother and sister, and himself, forcing his smile to remain in place, forcing himself to concentrate on the happiness on Sahara's beautiful face—the satisfaction and pride that shaped the expressions of the men around them.

No matter how negative his reaction to his father's behavior, he acknowledged, nothing could be done about it now. He had to make the best of the immediate situation and present circumstances. His anger and hurt were to be directed at his father—not at Tarik, nor Sahara, nor even Sabla.

Someone tapped him from behind, and as Reynaud turned, the gathering immediately began to quiet. He met the almost shy but steady gaze of an older *Bedouin* woman, the myriad lines of her face attesting to a harsh life on the fringes of the desert. Her dark eyes were full of kindness . . . and something more profound. Tenderness.

"I am Sabla," she said softly in Arabic.

He took her hand between his own, looking past the ravages of time to guess she must have once been striking, but the years and the climate had taken their toll. She could just as easily have hated him, he acknowledged, for being the offspring of the man who'd sullied her reputation, but he sensed that she had loved his father at one time.

"I am honored," he murmured, and nodded his head in acknowledgment.

Her eyes misted. "You are so like him."

In the sudden quiet, Reynaud thought her words sounded

thunderous, and said a silent prayer that Sabla hadn't offended Tarik or any of the others with her declaration. She certainly didn't sound like a woman who harbored any animosity—quite the opposite. As a matter of fact, Reynaud thought he'd caught a wistfulness underlying her words and briefly making her eyes look dreamy, before she murmured, "May Allah be with you always," and turned away.

Reynaud met Tarik's direct gaze and wondered if his half-brother had ever suspected that his mother still loved the Christian infidel who had shamed her.

Twenty

Reynaud guided Khamsin along the edge of the valley in an easy canter, enjoying the touch of the chill night breeze washing over his body like a tingling current of cool water. After the stifling atmosphere of a crowded *Bedouin* tent, it was a most welcome change. He savored the purity of the wind, dragging it into his lungs slowly and deeply, and wished he could purge his mind of its burden as easily as he could soothe his heated flesh.

Out of consideration for Khamsin, he slowed and dismounted, then led the stallion to drink from the nearby stream. The mountains loomed before him, hulking, Stygian forms against the blue-black night sky; the babbling water threw back the silvery light of the half-moon like an iridescent ribbon bisecting the valley.

He thought back to the events of the evening and deliberately conjured up the feeling of Brielle in his arms as he'd carried her back to the other tent. In spite of everything, she couldn't stay awake, and he'd boldly scooped her up into his arms before anyone could say a word and strode out into the night, echoes of Tarik's "Come back, brother, before too long . . ." ringing in his ears.

One of the women had indicated where Brielle was to sleep, and he'd set her down with infinite care—as if he could hold the turmoil of his thoughts at bay while immersed in the tender task of seeing her safely to bed. He drew out every movement, for he had a terrible premonition of impending separation . . . that this would be the last intimate detail he would ever attend to for her. He didn't dare ask her to wed him again—he, the progeny of that hypocritical breaker of sacred oaths, Gérard de St. Rémy.

And the separation would be soon, no doubt by her wish as well as his. . . .

He felt the *Bedouin* woman's presence behind him, but he refused to hurry. He lingered beside Brielle, slowly drawing the coverlet over her sleeping form, committing to memory the delicate details of her features. He drew one finger down her cheek, his touch as light as the sweep of a butterfly's wing. When he neared the corner of her mouth, his hand began to tremble as raw emotions spurted through him. Dear God, how would he ever be able to leave her? After he left the Order, he couldn't go back to St. Rémy, for he didn't want to face his father, coward that he was. He knew he could never reveal what he'd learned to his mother or brothers—but he could tell Gérard de St. Rémy that he *knew* and, in the wake of that damning declaration, he would forever destroy his relationship with his father.

You could forgive him.

The words floated through his mind, a ghostly scrap of sound. Nay, he couldn't forgive Gérard—not after stumbling onto this sordid secret. If St. Rémy had admitted his sins to his wife, perhaps Reynaud could have forgiven him.

Mayhap he did. And mayhap she forgave him long ago.

Aye, and mayhap his own father didn't even *know* he'd fathered a son and daughter by an Arab woman!

He heard the woman behind him exit the tent and reached to run the pad of his thumb over Brielle's soft, full lips. Bending, then, he brushed his own against her mouth and discovered he was still trembling. He hated for the moment to be over.

Her lashes fluttered, then lifted briefly, revealing beautiful aquamarine eyes shaded with sleep . . . like shadows upon a blue-green sea. "Reynaud?" she murmured, and gave him a sleepy half-smile that took his breath away; but before he could do more than utter, *"Oui, chère,"* she began to drift off again, her alabaster lids once more concealing the jeweled orbs beneath from his searching gaze.

Then, unexpectedly, her lashes lifted and she grasped his hand. As he lifted it to his lips in a loving salute, she murmured, "Taillefer . . . Tell him—to forgive me. . . ." A crease of concern skipped across her brow and, in reaction, Reynaud pressed his mouth more firmly against the soft flesh of her hand.

"He never blamed you, my rose." Rashid's name for Brielle came to him in a flash and fell from his lips. "There is naught to forgive."

The frown eased, but not completely, as sleep overcame her once more. . . .

Khamsin raised his head and snorted, spraying Reynaud with fine water droplets. He started slightly in reaction, his musings momentarily scattering, then shook his head to clear it; he had to ponder his future, knowing that Brielle d'Avignon would never—*could* never—be a part of it. . . .

When he had returned to the *sheik's* tent, Tarik was—at long last—alone. "One night's conversation cannot make up for half a lifetime of ignorance," he had told Reynaud. "We have so much to share. . . . Surely you don't have to return to Tyre immediately?"

Reynaud looked at his brother with the beginnings of a grudging affection. Gérard de St. Rémy's sins were his own and not his children's. Tarik wasn't to blame for his father having fallen short of Reynaud's expectations. "I have obligations, brother. For one, Bishop Abelard. For another, the Lady Brielle." But even as he uttered the words, Reynaud acknowledged that Tarik's responsibilities as *sheik* surely sat upon his shoulders more heavily than his own.

"Another day or two isn't so long," Tarik told him with a

half-smile. "What if I can, ahhh . . . *persuade* the lady to agree?"

A prickle of jealousy skittered through Reynaud at the thought of Brielle with Tarik again. It was an absurd reaction, he acknowledged, yet real, nonetheless. That very jealousy made him answer without thinking. "I'll speak to her," he said quickly, then felt discomfited by his own behavior. And, strictly speaking, he thought, it wasn't really up to her at all.

"She is lovely," Tarik told him. "I can see why you would wish no man to approach her. However, I would never attempt to engage the affections of the woman my brother loved."

Sweet Jesu, was it that obvious? Reynaud thought. "Lady Brielle is free to speak to whomever she chooses."

Tarik gave him a shrewd look. "You will escort her back to France?"

Reynaud nodded, fighting the deepening bleakness of his mood.

"And you will remain there with her, then?"

Reynaud didn't answer. He couldn't. Part of him wanted to say yes, but another wanted to deny it.

"It would be the wisest course, you know."

Reynaud's chin jerked upward as his eyes met his half-brother's.

"How so?" he asked softly. "I am a Templar knight—'tis my chosen path."

"Is it?"

In the face of Tarik's question, Reynaud remained stubbornly silent. He wouldn't admit to his brother that his father had chosen the path for him. And now, he thought suddenly, he could guess why Gérard de St. Rémy had done so: atonement for his sins. By sending his youngest son to fight for Christ in the Holy Land, Gérard had perhaps attempted to make up for his own unconscionable behavior.

Reynaud unexpectedly felt like a sacrificial lamb. The reason his father had encouraged him to become a Templar and travel to the Holy Land hadn't been noble at all but, rather, a move to ease his wriggling conscience.

Tarik was staring at the colorful woven rug beneath them. When he raised his gaze again, he said, "You know your cause—the Christian cause—is hopeless . . . that Salah al-Din has unified the Muslim tribes to the point that we are strong enough to drive the Christian infidel from here. It is only a matter of time."

Reynaud nodded. Things had changed for the worse for the Christians since the Horns of Hattin—with the Christian army having been annihilated as a fighting force, and only Tyre, Tripoli, and Antioch still under Christian control. The crusaders had been steadily losing their grip on the Latin States in the East since Saladin had come along and unified the many feuding Arab factions and become sultan of Egypt and Syria in the process.

"Had your predecessors been content with the situation before the crusaders came, we would still be at peace—with Muslims respecting the Christian veneration of their holy places." He sighed heavily. "But no, your Church wanted to take our land and our sacred shrines from us."

Reynaud said nothing. There was nothing to say. He had realized long ago that Christians, Muslims, and Jews alike had lived in peace in Jerusalem before the first crusaders had come to Outremer, ravaging the land and the people in a horrific path from Flanders all the way to Jerusalem.

"Brother?"

Reynaud met Tarik's earnest gaze.

"If you return to the Levant, you will surely die."

Reynaud's eyes narrowed as Tarik's words pulled him from his thoughts. A ghostly chill passed over him. "Every man must die one day."

Tarik shook his head slowly. "I think you know what I mean. Have you forgotten so soon?" He leaned forward, his hands resting on the knees of his crossed legs, a strange intensity in his eyes. *Sotto voce,* he said, "I know from experience exactly what miracles you're capable of. But in choosing you as His instrument, Allah has also given you a terrible burden."

Reynaud knew what was coming.

"Your gift will always be coveted by others. Just like the man who lured you out of Tyre—this Tancred le Bref. And he was a brother Templar as well, easily capable of murder to acquire your secret."

Reynaud's mouth twisted with bitter irony. "I have discovered, *mon frère,* the painful truth of the matter: Templars are all too human . . . and ofttimes less than human." *And so is their philosophy,* he thought silently.

Tarik leaned back against a pile of cushions with deceptive indolence, yet Reynaud saw nothing of indolence in his eyes or his voice when he said, "You are disillusioned, yet you stay in the Order."

"I have been disillusioned before. One learns to live with it."

"You never suspected St. Rémy was capable of fathering children with another woman? After all, a Muslim is allowed more than one wife . . ."

Reynaud stood and began to pace the immediate area of the tent, his look brooding, his thoughts dark. "That is not the Christian way! My father was—still is—devoted to my mother. He is a good Christian, a learned man."

"Not the typical Frank," Tarik observed bluntly.

Reynaud nodded. Many Arabs were poets and philosophers and considered themselves vastly superior to the boorish and illiterate Frankish knight. He looked at his half-brother askance. "I concede the point, but my father was not typical. He was educated and stressed the importance of knowledge to his sons. He was good and noble-hearted and . . ."

"He was also an adulterer . . . and deserted my mother after he'd ruined her. He was not noble."

Reynaud ceased his pacing and faced Tarik, his anger close to the surface. "But there must have been a good *reason!*"

Even as he said the words, he acknowledged how desperate they sounded. How inadequate . . .

He held up one hand, feeling the anger quickly drain from him. "Forgive me," he said, a dullness flattening his words. "There can be no reason for the desertion except that he had a family back in France." His voice lowered to a husk of sound. "In that case, he committed two grievous sins—one against my mother, the second against yours." He sank to the floor again, feeling suddenly as if the dissipating anger was also robbing him of strength.

Tarik said quietly, "He insulted and wounded my family as much as he did yours—more so, because until this night, you were all blissfully ignorant. Abdul went to Jerusalem and sought St. Rémy out, but by then he had left our land."

Reynaud raised anguish-clouded eyes to his half-brother.

"And so, after I grew to manhood and heard the story from my own mother's lips, I wished nothing so much as to kill St. Rémy. But your death instead would have satisfied my need for vengeance. Had you not saved my life that day— and thus shown yourself to me as a brother rather than an enemy—I would have killed you had I ever encountered you."

And I do not blame you. The words were dredged from his heart, but he couldn't say them aloud. "How did you even know of my existence?"

"Sabla told us. My mother knew little about Gérard de St. Rémy, but she did share with us her knowledge of the existence of several sons, the youngest of whom was only two years of age."

They were navigating dangerous waters here, Reynaud realized, and not wanting to reveal anymore about his family—which could cause further hurt for both himself and Tarik in the process—he sought to change the subject.

As he started to speak, Tarik added softly, "Allah had a hand in this, brother. He had *you* encounter *me*, rather than the other way around, and put my life in your hands. The final irony. . . ."

Reynaud stared thoughtfully at his half-brother. "He works in mysterious ways, does He not? And it isn't for us to understand, necessarily. Yet. . . ." He trailed off, his thoughts awhirl.

"Will you consider remaining in France?" Tarik pressed.

"You mean *hide* in France? Hide from my obligations as a Templar? Hide from those who would learn the secret of my accursed 'gift'?" He shook his head. " 'Tis the coward's way."

"It is the wise man's way, if one stops to consider," Tarik said. "In spite of the fact that the Frankish knights are physically larger and stronger, more heavily armed, we Arabs have much contempt for them."

"I learned that long ago," Reynaud replied dryly.

"And," Tarik continued, "the Franks are immeasurably more stupid."

Reynaud fought a smile, in spite of the insult. It was somehow amusing to him to hear this proud half-brother of his—this powerful *Bedouin sheik*—disdainfully denigrate the crusaders. Perhaps, he thought, because he had learned firsthand that much of it was true.

"Your people disdain tricks, artifices, and stratagems in warfare—such as feigned retreat. Rather, you march in the heat of the day in full armor, like so many obedient sheep, in plain view, making little or no attempt to outwit the adversary. Allah gave man a brain to use—to survive and prevail against his enemies, but the Franks would rather use their brawn—and at their own peril."

Reynaud sobered and held his gaze. "Then you are telling me to use my head—to plan a strategy of self-preservation, rather than blunder back into the thick of things here in Palestine?"

Tarik nodded. "Escort your lady back to France and remain there with her. I have concluded from our conversation

his morning that she has nothing to go back to but the bleakness of a Christian cloister." He shifted his position on the
cushions and drew up one knee to rest his wrist upon, before
giving Reynaud a long, assessing look through his dark
lashes. Reynaud had the distinct impression that he was being tested in some subtle way. "Why would you ever condemn the woman who holds your heart to such a dismal fate
while you return to serve an Order whose philosophy is not
in agreement with your own beliefs?"

"Because as far as I know, she does not return my feelings.
If she fails to find her father, then, of her own volition she
wishes to return to her convent." *And although I want her
more than anything, a woman like Brielle d'Avignon deserves better than me,* he added to himself. *Surely she would
be insulted by a proposal from a self-righteous fool. . . .*

Tarik shook his head slowly and offered Reynaud more
coffee from a brass server. "If I may be frank, brother, a
woman like the Lady Brielle was made to love and be loved,
whether she realizes it or not. It would be the greatest of
sins to condemn her to the difficult and lonely life of a convent."

Reynaud's jaw tightened, and he stared unseeingly into the
middle distance. "I have no right to offer for her hand."

Tarik frowned. "No right? It seems to me that you would
be rescuing her from the dullest of lives—by loving her and
giving her children . . ."

Children? By the Rood, but that made him an even worse
villain, for he'd knowingly stolen her virtue just a few
nights before. Further proof that his lofty ideals and his
self-righteous behavior were a sham.

In truth, he was no better than his father.

Except for the fact that you offered her marriage, reminded
his conscience.

*Knowing that she would never permit me to give up my
vows because of a forced marriage!* he silently argued back.

A sudden, heavy silence penetrated Reynaud's preoccupation, making him aware that Tarik had stopped speaking and was watching him through shrewd eyes. "I wouldn't presume to tell you what to do," el Mezrab said slowly. "But as the chosen *sheik,* I am not without some . . . understanding of the nature of men. And women." He paused and ran one hand over his bearded chin, while he obviously searched for the right words. "In spite of what you think, I do not see your returning to France as hiding from your enemies, but rather taking the Lady Brielle under your permanent protection and escorting her to safety. . . ."

Reynaud had nodded obligingly, even though a spurt of jealousy surfaced for the second time since meeting Tarik el Mezrab, and he wondered what interest his half-brother had in Brielle. Or if he were trying to achieve some response from Reynaud . . . "Yet there are things about me you do not understand," he said.

"Yes, but we are also more alike than you might imagine. Our pride and honor are so very important to us. . . ."

And so the conversation had gone, round and round, with neither brother seeing eye to eye, yet learning how alike they were in many respects. . . .

But as he stood beneath the glow of the moon watching Khamsin drink, Reynaud knew he couldn't remain with his half-brother for even another day, in spite of Tarik's request that he do so. It was his duty to return Brielle safely to Tyre—and then back to France. It was approaching the eight week mark that Bishop Abelard had stipulated to her; also, Tarik had told him that he would personally make inquiries about Geoffrey d'Avignon among his contacts in Damascus. He would find nothing, Reynaud knew, for there was little chance of Sieur Geoffrey being alive.

There were a few grisly details Reynaud had spared Brielle and Abbess Marguerite when he'd spoken briefly of the aftermath of the Battle of Hattin. Saladin usually massacred any captured Templar and Hospitaller knights because of the evident hatred they had of Muslims. After his victory at Hat-

n, Saladin had vowed, "I will purify the earth of these two
npure races . . ." and ordered two hundred knights of the
rders decapitated. Although the independent knights were
nsomed, it only made sense, after all this time, that no one
ad ransomed Geoffrey d'Avignon. And if, for some reason,
e had been forgotten in a Damascus prison . . . well, no
ne survived for four years in an Arab dungeon.

As callous as he had tried to be back in Abbess Marguee-
te's study at St. Bernadette's, he hadn't been able to bring
imself to tell Brielle d'Avignon with absolute finality that
er hopes were futile.

He gathered the reins and mounted the stallion, thinking
hat had he been brutally honest and succeeded in discour-
ging her, her life wouldn't have been jeopardized by Tancred
e Bref. And, equally important, Anabette would still be alive.

When Brielle opened her eyes, a woman was sitting
earby, watching her intently. The familiarity of her striking,
em-gold eyes caught Brielle's attention, instantly wrenching
er to full wakefulness.

She sat up quickly, glancing around the unfamiliar walls
f the tent. Both end flaps had been opened, and sunlight
treamed in through the closest side. No one else was present.

"Forgive my impatience, but I wished to speak to you,"
ahara said simply and in halting French. "If you wish to
vash first, there is fresh water behind that screen." With a
od of her head she indicated a woven divider.

How long had she been waiting? Brielle wondered as she
linked the sleep from her eyes. By the warmth in the tent
nd the brightness of the sunshine, she calculated it had to
e well past dawn, yet no one had awakened her.

And Reynaud. How was Reynaud after last night?

Sahara, dressed in a traditional dark blue dress with long
leeves, worn over a lighter-colored underdress, handed her
small cup of sweetened tea, for which Brielle was grateful.

She smiled her thanks and took a sip, while Sahara studied her with shy glances.

"You look so much like your brother . . ." Brielle ventured, *"both* your brothers." She silently admired the young woman's dusky beauty. She was lithely built, and healthy blood glowed in her sun-bronzed cheeks. Most of her luxurious dark hair was covered by a shawl, and her nose, though not as high-bridged as Tarik's, indicated her Ishmaelite blood. "Except you are much comelier," Brielle added with a soft laugh.

Sahara returned her smile. "I cannot tell you how I've yearned to meet my half-brother. All those years that Tarik harbored such resentment toward our natural father, I wanted to see him—to meet him face to face."

Honor, Brielle thought sourly. *And pride.* Again, those useless masculine entities. . . .

"I suspected I would never meet Gérard de St. Rémy, but I had often dreamed of meeting my older brother, Reynaud."

"You knew of him?" Brielle asked, intrigued.

Sahara nodded.

Suddenly, something occurred to her. " 'Twas *you* on board the *Madonna,* wasn't it? You who forced that crewman to let us out!"

"It was. Tarik didn't even know I was on that ship until it was too late. But it was the most exciting and satisfying experience in my life." Her eyes glowed with excitement. "Not only did I get to see my half-brother, but to my delight I discovered that I would have thrown myself between him and any corsair to save him."

"Thank God that wasn't necessary," Brielle said with a pang of remembrance. She sipped her tea thoughtfully. "Have you spoken to Reynaud at length?"

"Only briefly. Not nearly as much as I would like, but I have not had time alone with him." She paused, smoothing the fabric of her overgown with one sun-browned hand. "I

ave wanted—for what seems like forever—to leave this
fe."

Brielle immediately grasped her meaning. *"Bedouin* life,"
he said softly.

"Yes, but Tarik forbids it—he says it is only a woman's
ancy, born of my knowledge of my Frankish blood." Her
heeks colored delicately. "But I cannot help how I feel . . .
nd especially considering who I am."

Brielle felt a stab of pity for this half-sister of Reynaud,
ut she believed that Sahara had a brighter future than she
ad herself, with her family surrounding her. Much as she
vished it, there was nothing Brielle could offer the young
voman to help her with her problem.

"At least you have family," she said. "And Tarik obviously
llows you extraordinary freedom."

"Indeed!" Sahara's eyes flashed briefly before she lowered
er gaze. "If Tarik had his way, I would have long ago been
ved to Jamal." The last word was pronounced like a curse,
nd the color in her cheeks heightened once again, only this
ime with agitation. "And Jamal would never even allow me
o leave camp!"

Brielle thought back to the striking but arrogant-looking
1an who had been sitting beside Sahara the night before.
3rielle had thought his good looks marred by his fierce ex-
ression, and his angry obsidian eyes had caught her atten-
ion, registering a dark possessiveness whenever they'd
lighted on Sahara.

"Hamdillah! Praise be to Allah I had a choice in the mat-
er, although Tarik grows impatient with me. And Jamal . . .
1e swears he will have no other."

Brielle was taken aback. "You have a choice in the mat-
er?"

Sahara nodded. "It is shameful to force a woman to marry
omeone she doesn't like." Her expression suddenly soft-
ned, and Brielle suspected the independent-minded young

woman derived a good deal of satisfaction from confiding in her, a Western woman.

"The *troubadour* . . . the golden-haired one . . ."

"Taillefer?"

Sahara smiled shyly. "He is like no other, with his fair hair, and eyes like the summer sky. . . ." She trailed off and watched for Brielle's reaction. She really hadn't thought much about the minstrel's good looks in the shadow of Reynaud's. "But he mourns his wife, does he not?" the *Bedouin* girl added.

The question struck Brielle like an unexpected blow, taking her breath away, and she felt the half-smile slide from her face. *"Oui,"* she whispered.

Sahara's eyes darkened with distress. "Forgive me," she said softly, "for offending with so bold a question."

She made to rise, her gaze lowered, but Brielle put out one hand in appeal. "Please . . . don't leave. 'Tis just that Anabette was my friend—we came here together from France, and I—well, she wouldn't have perished had I not insisted she accompany me to the *suk."*

Sahara stilled and regarded her for a long moment. Voices drifted into the tent from outside, a goat bleated from nearby. "It was Allah's will, and not yours." She looked down at Brielle's hand, still on her arm, and slowly placed her own over it.

The unexpected contact brought tears to Brielle's eyes, for Sahara's expression held compassion, reminding her poignantly how human she was—how human they *all* were, Muslim and Christian alike.

It unexpectedly reminded Brielle of Reynaud's words to her, what now seemed ages ago: *"They love, they hate, they hurt, they bleed . . . just as we do. In God's scheme of things, they are our brothers."*

She thought she was beginning to understand his anger.

Twenty-one

Despite his best intentions, Reynaud lingered with Tarik
and his people for another two days and nights. He was reminded of his brother's words regarding stratagems—suspected that Tarik was using his own, for in the end Reynaud
could offer no reason the *sheik* would accept for their leaving
immediately for Tyre.

Obviously Tarik was employing one of the stratagems to
which he had alluded earlier, with his *Bedouin* charm and
his skill at persuasion to counter every excuse Reynaud offered.

They went hunting for gazelle, *Bedouin* style—Tarik and
his closest men and Taillefer and Rashid. They rode camels
and used the sleek saluki dogs to help them find their prey.
Other times they used fierce, broad-shouldered hunting fal-
cons.

Reynaud thought Tarik the perfect host—gracious and
generous and obviously immensely enjoying his time with
his half-brother. Even Taillefer seemed lighter of heart during
the time they spent partaking of Tarik el Mezrab's warm hospitality. Rashid had told Reynaud that Brielle had spoken to
the minstrel, and both of them appeared to have established
a new understanding between them.

Brielle. . . .

When the men were in camp, Reynaud watched her openly,
unable to be discreet where she was concerned—not with

permanent separation imminent. Was it only weeks ago that he had considered her and Anabette an unwelcome burden? Or had he been fooling himself. . . ?

And to Reynaud's pleasant surprise, she appeared perfectly content to mingle with the *Mezrabi,* to help with small tasks, in spite of the women's protests—no mean feat considering her status as guest of the *Bedouin.* Maybe it was because the women liked her so much. He also noted that she and Sahara were inseparable, chattering and often laughing like children.

Was this the young woman from St. Bernadette's who'd feared the infidel? Even Rashid, at first?

But he had always hoped her character went deeper than that. . . .

It was easy, he mused now, to enjoy the summer setting— with its green grazing grounds, the easy access to water, set against the impressive backdrop of the mountains. Reynaud felt more relaxed and worry-free than he had for months—in spite of Anabette's death and his recent revelations.

Quite literally, he'd forgotten how to unwind. Except for the weeks at the bishop's palace in Tyre after he'd decided to enjoy Brielle's company, he'd been all business in his attitudes and actions while in Outremer. He'd taken his calling seriously, as was expected, but it seemed that in his efforts to live up to others' high expectations, to always take the honorable and noble path, he'd neglected to nurture that part of him that needed an outlet—a respite from duty.

Taillefer's words came to him often: *"Live for the present, Reynaud . . . the past is dead."*

And so he enjoyed himself while in his half-brother's company—and went out of his way to distract Taillefer from his sorrow, when the relationship between them had always been the other way around. He sent a message to Bishop Abelard, and was instructed to take his time, for the cleric had been called to Acre for a while—the city had been taken finally by the Crusaders and many were sorely in need of spiritual comfort.

Reynaud was thus able to spend some time with the *Mezrabi Bedouin* while, at the same time, remaining close to Brielle. It was bittersweet, for he knew he was putting off the inevitable—escorting her back to Provence and out of his life. She seemed as content as he to remain in the foothills of the Lebanon Mountains and gave no indication that she wished to leave. Perhaps, he thought, she was hoping Tarik would hear something from Damascus regarding Sieur Geoffrey d'Avignon.

She, too, he noticed, went out of her way to spend time with the minstrel, even though Taillefer was adept at putting on a glib front. Reynaud loved her all the more for her compassion toward his bereaved friend.

Rashid, of course, was content to be wherever Reynaud was—and especially among *Bedouin*, with whom the family had such strong ties.

After three days and two nights, however, Reynaud sought out Brielle, his blood pounding through his veins in anticipation and dread—his heart aching with the things he wanted to say but had no right. . . .

She sat on a great flat rock on the bank of the mountain stream, her attention wholly absorbed by her thoughts of Reynaud. The first stars were appearing in the indigo tapestry of the sky, and a full moon shone like a benevolent beacon. Against the soft, rushing sound of the water, the quiet was broken only by an occasional bleat or groan from the animals spread over the area.

Brielle let her head drop back, wanting to reach out and touch the moon—to stay here forever, for it was the most tranquil and beautiful of places. Small wonder this land was the heart of three great religions. But also a land of tremendous bloodshed and slaughter, festering hatred and blind fanaticism.

Soft footfalls came to her, and Brielle ceased her rapt contemplation of the sky to look toward the sound.

A lone man was approaching her. At first she thought him one of the *Bedouin* men, with his robe and headdress. Yet there was only one other as tall as Reynaud de St. Rémy among the *Mezrabi* . . . and Tarik el Mezrab's stride wasn't quite the same. As he closed the distance between them, Brielle could just discern, against the white of his *keffiya,* the stern and uncompromising expression that rode his chiseled features.

She had deliberately kept her distance since the revelation about Gérard de St. Rémy, being as polite and good-humored as she knew how without pushing him away by expressing undue concern. She sensed that he did not want pity, or even empathy . . . this man who set such impossibly high standards for himself.

She had tried to occupy her time by learning more about the *Bedouin* and their ways, by getting to know Sahara and Sabla, and by renewing her tenuous friendship with Rashid. And, finally, by long talks with Taillefer about Anabette— anything she could think of regarding her late friend's background before she'd run away to St. Bernadette's. And, of course, their life at the convent. Those dialogues were evidently comforting, as well as healing, to both herself and the minstrel.

She had spent little time speaking to Reynaud de St. Rémy, even as her compassion for him threatened to overwhelm her good intentions, and she found it difficult not to remember the warmth in his eyes—the tenderness in his voice only days ago. . . .

She greeted him with a welcoming smile, in spite of the fact that apprehension twisted through her like a dull-bladed sword. His coming to her suddenly could only mean one thing: He was ready to take her back to Tyre. And then France.

"You shouldn't be out here alone."

She searched his face as he stopped before her, but

couldn't be sure of anything in the deceptive half-light of
dusk. "I am not alone," she answered. "I'm among a tribe
of *Bedouin,* who are surely guarding their herds." She softened her words with a smile, realizing in the same instant
that she *hadn't* seen any of the men among the animals.

Reynaud thought her smile lit up the entire valley and felt
his resolve waver. But he gave away nothing of his thoughts.
"If you would look more closely, my lady, you would notice
few *Bedouin* are about. Custom dictates raiders steal camels
from other tribes only after sunrise—then they have an entire
day to track the culprits."

"Oh." She stared at him in the waning light, hardly aware
of what he'd said, as she found herself wondering when and
how she could in some way extend to him a subtle empathy
for the shock of Tarik's revelation. She knew for a fact, however, that any offered comfort would be flatly refused. The
closeness they had begun to share was gone—although the
hazy memory of the words *"my rose"* on his lips lingered
tantalizingly in one corner of her mind. When had he called
her that? Or had he done so at all?

"I'm glad to see you enjoying your brother's company,"
she said with all sincerity.

" 'Tis a mixed blessing, is it not?" he answered, with an
undertone of bitterness. "Such pleasure born of such perfidy."

"Whatever you may think," she answered softly, "it has
naught to do with *you.*" There. It was out, and she felt better
for having said it, even though one part of her braced for his
reaction.

He was silent for a long moment. "It has everything to do
with me. I carry his name—the reputation and honor of St.
Rémy."

The hollowness of the words stirred anew the compassion
deep within her, yet also a flicker of irritation. "You carry
the weight of your own actions, your own reputation—you
are responsible for the character of Reynaud de St. Rémy

and no one else. If you would only rid yourself of a burden that is your father's and not your own . . ."

He gave her his proud profile, a glimpse of the pride that was at the heart of the problem, she thought.

"Pray tell me, Brielle, how I am to 'rid' myself of my father's shame? And especially after I have added my own to that which already existed?"

"Your own?" she asked, wanting to reach out and touch him, this valiant Templar knight who was capable of such tenderness, yet also such rigid, self-imposed discipline. And who felt his family's failings were his own.

His jaw tightened to stone. "I am a canker upon the Order."

Her mouth almost dropped open in surprise at this stark admission and the anguish in those few words. *He* a canker? she thought in disbelief. Because, she assumed, he had broken one of his oaths and become involved with her? She couldn't imagine anything farther from the truth!

Or was there another reason?

The glow from the rising moon played about his splendid features, alternately throwing them into silvered relief and shadowed enigma. He reminded her of the man she'd first met—cold and distant—ready to retreat to some safe haven in his mind when his pain became too great.

The pain brought on by his own impossible standards . . . by his reaching for something that was beyond *any* man.

But she wouldn't allow him to retreat—to withdraw into some nebulous void where nothing could be accomplished but temporary oblivion. "If you are a blight because of me, then you need not fear anyone will ever know what happened between us that night—"

"It has naught to do with that!" he cut her off tersely. "God grant me at least *that* was genuine."

What an odd way of referring to that night. She didn't quite know how to take it. "And what of Tancred le Bref?" she demanded, her irritation turning to real anger in her uncertainty, and goading her to utter the one name she thought had the power to crash through his defenses.

"I failed Taillefer, too," he said suddenly with self-derision, ignoring her question. "My best friend . . . and I could not save his wife!"

The admission took her off guard and she was silent a moment. The magnitude of the responsibility he'd taken upon himself was staggering. Who had he been trying to please? To live up to?

The answer flashed before her: Of course. Gérard de St. Rémy.

"What happened?" she asked softly, afraid to hear the answer, but driven to know exactly what had transpired after she'd left the *suk* with le Bref. Why hadn't Reynaud been able to save Anabette's life?

He had swung away, his back to her as he stared out over the stream and toward the behemoth forms of the mountains. Just when Brielle decided he wasn't going to answer, he spoke, his voice bleak as a cold winter day. "Anabette was dead before she hit the ground. I can heal, but I cannot reverse death."

"But you are only human!" she blurted. "Or have you forgotten that in your quest to become a deity? Just because you were blessed with a divine gift doesn't mean that God didn't give you other human weaknesses! You are only a man, Reynaud, like your father before you!"

He turned back to her in surprise and, for a fraction of time, he looked as if she'd struck him. The light wind sighed over them, like the hushed breathing of the night itself. A muffled shout echoed in the distance, the bleat of a goat. Then he quickly gained control of his expression.

She struck, before he could speak, with soft derision: "Do you feel badly for Taillefer, *chevalier*, or yourself?"

Anger leapt into his eyes. "I think," he said in a low, taut voice, " 'tis time to take you back to Tyre. I wouldn't want to take advantage of Tarik's generosity, or use it as an excuse to avoid my responsibilities any longer than I already have."

Brielle flinched inwardly at his words. Hadn't he risked his life to save hers? Yet he considered her merely a responsibility . . . and after all they had shared since her first careless venture into the *suk* that fateful day.

Think, cautioned her sensible side. *You know him better than that . . .*

But did she? Mayhap his risking his life for her had been something his all-consuming sense of honor would have commanded he do for anyone.

Of course. Why else would a man still remain so bitter in the face of the discovery of something that could never be changed? Something that was no true reflection of *him.* Perhaps he even blamed her for his having had to follow her out into the wilderness, thus putting his life in such serious jeopardy that Rashid had been forced to go to Tarik el Mezrab, and Gérard de St. Rémy's sordid secret had come spilling out into the light of day.

"What of word of my father?" she asked stiffly.

"You can wait in Tyre. It shouldn't take long."

It was as if her admonitions had never been uttered. Reynaud de St. Rémy evidently had all his shields in place now, his feelings of miserable failure effectively locked up inside and under control. . . .

"I'll take you back to France," he added in a tight voice. "Abelard himself is aware the time draws near. Although he is occupied in Acre for a while, there is no need for you to stay once you've heard from Tarik."

He sounded like the old Reynaud de St. Rémy—high-handed and telling her exactly what she should and shouldn't do. This time it wasn't how hopeless her search was for word of her father, but rather that she should leave for Provence.

Her anger with him rekindled, she found herself searching for a way to get through to him—even if it meant hurting him. She sucked in a breath and said, "I have decided, *cheva-*

lier, that I want someone else beside yourself to escort me back to France."

He turned his head aside, staring into the middle distance. "That may not be possible."

"Are you saying that you are the only dependable escort in the Levant?" she asked with exaggerated disbelief, groping for some sign from him that he was not eager to leave her forever.

He faced her, his amber eyes in deep shadow beneath his brow bone. Unexpectedly, he gave her what resembled a ghost of a smile. He reached out to her and touched her cheek with one long, callused finger. "Unfortunately, as far as you are concerned, the answer may be 'yes.' "

She jerked her face aside, afraid she would relent at his very touch, in spite of her anger and deep disappointment. What about his offer of marriage? "That is absurd," she snapped. "Surely Taillefer or Sir Humphrey—"

"Sir Humphrey is with Bishop Abelard at Acre, and as for the minstrel . . ." He trailed off.

Her hands were clenched at her sides in frustration. "He is not a knight? Is that what you were going to say?" she pressed. "Should I be flattered for myself, or offended for Taillefer?"

In the light of the moon, his eyes locked with hers. "I meant no insult to Taillefer—you saw his skill with a weapon the other morn. He wants to go to Aimery de Belvoir and personally tell him what happened in Tyre."

"Then he is more a man than many I know," she said. "I shall ask him if he would consider escorting me back."

She watched him struggle inwardly, his jaw clenching slightly, as if a part of him wished to say something more. *Speak,* she begged him silently. *Isn't there more to say . . . ?*

But he appeared firmly in control now.

"Then 'tis settled?" she asked in a perverse need to appear eager to be rid of him, even though her heart was breaking. She would go back to St. Bernadette's—surely her father was dead, she thought with a sudden and uncharacteristic pessimism. And so was Anabette now. She would live out her life shut away in a convent, with her memories of one, precious night to sustain her—like the few treasured pieces of a miser's carefully-hoarded gold.

Fool . . . whispered a voice with utter contempt. *You deceived yourself. The memory will only deepen the wound until you are consumed by it.*

The scornful voice prompted her pride to stiffen her back, lift the tilt of her chin, as she stared steadily into Reynaud de St. Rémy's eyes—the eyes of the man who had only a few days earlier represented to her the epitome of knighthood in all its glory. "Then, if we are to leave in the morning, I will speak to Taillefer this very eve."

What could he say? he thought, with the acrid taste of defeat in his mouth. He had no right to dictate what she could and couldn't do—nor could he advise Taillefer. He could have no objection to her going back to France . . .

Except that no man on earth would protect her as ferociously as he.

"You will *not* return to France without my personal escort," he said through set teeth. "Do you understand, Brielle? I told you earlier that you are my responsibility. I brought you here, and I will take you home."

He watched the delicate lines of her face take on an obstinate cast as her look turned absolutely mutinous. "If I can find a suitable escort, *chevalier,* I will return to France without you. 'Tis Bishop Abelard's wish—you said so yourself—and I don't need you to do it!"

He took hold of her arm, intending to further persuade her, even though he sensed it was futile. "Nay!" he began angrily, drawn against his will into the thick of things from which he'd been tempted to retreat.

A contradictory impulse tempted her sorely. And won. "Aye! What good a coward at my side, St. Rémy?"

His fingers tightened, his face turned a shade paler, even

in the moonlight. "I have been called many things," he growled softly, "but never *that.*"

Guilt slithered through her, for he had risked all to come to her aid—hardly the actions of a coward. She took refuge by giving free rein to her ire. "But when it suits you, you turn your back to the truth. I've seen you do it in the past, and I see you doing it now. You cannot bear the thought of your father having committed so grievous a sin. Rather than assign the failing to him, you've taken the burden upon yourself. Why can you not come to terms with his weaknesses, and thus your own? Reynaud . . . Reynaud, let the world think what it will of Gérard de St. Rémy!"

"And why do *you* insist on poking your nose into my personal affairs?" His features had turned a dull red with outrage, for he had no wish to more closely examine the need to suffer for Gérard's weakness. Too much was at stake.

"Forgive me, Sieur Reynaud," she said unapologetically. "If not my method, at least my intentions were sincere." She pushed away from her perch and looked almost yearningly toward the cluster of tents, from which the scent of the last meal still drifted on the breeze. Stars poked through the fabric of the evening sky like a sprinkling of distant torches. She wanted suddenly to be away from him. She wanted to leave here—the next morning wasn't soon enough!—and then pack her things at the bishop's palace.

The sooner she was out of the Holy Land, the sooner, she hoped, she could get away from everything to do with Reynaud de St. Rémy—everything that even *reminded* her of him—and try to immerse herself in convent life. There surely had to be some cause she could take up to keep her mind occupied, her body too tired to remember his touch. . . .

She also had her own pride to contend with, and it balked at her inclination to hover near this man—like a hungry hound waiting for some morsel to be tossed from the board.

She drew in a shaky breath, then said in a tightly controlled voice, "I never thanked you for coming to my rescue after le Bref abducted me. I will forever be grateful to you, Reynaud de St. Rémy, for saving my life." *And therefore condemning me to live it out in solitude at St. Bernadette's.*

Before he could reply, she tore her gaze from his and, with chin lifted determinedly, turned and walked away.

"He can be obstinate when he wishes," Taillefer said under his breath to Brielle "Even Rashid looks sheepish."

They were mounted and ready to leave, the sun just firing the horizon, but Tarik and Reynaud were nowhere to be seen. It was odd that Rashid wasn't with his master, she thought . . . wherever that was, but even as she thought it, the Arab moved toward her.

He stopped beside her mare and put one band upon the animal's withers, as he looked up at her in the dimness. His dark eyes were more solemn than usual. "My master has gone on a short journey with Tarik. I am to wish you a good and safe return to Tyre, where you will wait for him to escort you back to France."

As far as Brielle knew, the normally sweet-natured Taillefer, even during his quiet grieving, had never been critical of Reynaud. But now she sensed in the minstrel a real irritation with his friend as he listened to Rashid's brief explanation. "No doubt hunting," he said with a frown of disapproval, "when he should be with us. 'Tis unlike him—although it seems as if he's been consumed by the sport since we got here."

"My master said you would be more than capable of guiding *la demoiseile* to Tyre, and especially while accompanied by a few of the *sheik's* men. The journey is not so far . . ."

"Are those your words or his?" Taillefer asked dryly.

Rashid's look grew closed, as if he were affronted for Reynaud, and as he stepped back, the minstrel vowed softly in French, *"Nous parlerons plus tard.* We'll speak later, my friend."

Sahara came forward. Sabla was close behind her. "My mother and I wish you to have this—" she held out an amulet of what looked like beaten silver—a charm on a slender chain, "to ward off Evil and keep you safe."

Brielle had quickly learned that the *Bedouin* were very religious, but also very superstitious. As she leaned to accept the gift from the young woman's slender brown fingers, she noted the charm was in the shape of a closed-fingered hand, something she'd seen before in the *Mezrabi* camp. It was to ward off the Evil Eye.

If only Abbess Marguerite could see her accepting this infidel token, she thought wryly. Or Bishop Abelard. But she accepted with a gracious smile, and slipped it around her neck, half-expecting it to burn right through her shawl to her skin. "Thank you—both of you."

One of Tarik's men—the leader—nudged his camel forward until he came between Brielle and Sahara. It was Jamal.

Taillefer raised a golden brow at Brielle. "Our frustrated swain is evidently as fierce a *Bedouin* warrior as he is an unrequited lover," he said for her ears alone. "That look he wears would send a miscreant running in the opposite direction even faster than the object of his adoration."

Brielle hid a smile, and got the distinct feeling that the minstrel's comment was more to amuse her than to be critical of the intense young *Bedouin*. She caught the levity in his blue eyes and hoped he could see the same reflected in her own for, in spite of the added lines about his eyes and mouth since Anabette's death, here was a glimpse of the old Taillefer—ever bent upon entertaining. And, she thought more soberly, not holding the least bit of anger or bitterness toward her for having taken Anabette to the marketplace to meet her death.

They said their farewells, and Brielle cast one final, lingering look about the valley in the growing light of dawn. With the still-shadowed mountains as a backdrop, the place seemed a pastoral shelter for the animals that grazed con-

tentedly, the giggling stream providing plenty of precious
water for every need. Cooking fires glowed here and there
among the scattered tents, and children laughed and chased
each other around the camp area, the pale forms of the grace-
ful salukis bounding at their heels and barking at their antics.

It was an idyllic setting for these nomads who led such a
harsh life for the greater part of the year, and Brielle was
glad she had met and mingled with them while they were in
their summer camp.

And glad, in spite of everything, to have been able to meet
and get to know Tarik and Sahara . . . another happy memory
to be tucked away, treasured and examined at will.

Perhaps it was better this way, she thought, as they rode
off toward the brightening east. If she could leave Tyre before
Reynaud returned, she wouldn't have to go through the anguish of seeing him and parting again. This way it was swift
and final.

She straightened in the saddle, thinking that, after all, she
should be happy. Tarik had promised to make inquiries about
her father, and soon she would be on her way home! Away
from this beautiful but harsh land and the shadow of Anabette
de Belvoir's death—and from Reynaud de St. Rémy and his
private demons.

Why then, she thought miserably, did her heart feel like
it was shriveling within her chest?

Twenty-two

Damascus

They approached the ancient city of Damascus from the west, through mud wall protected fruit orchards up to five miles deep that lined the banks of the Barada River. Reynaud knew that from the west and the north the city was difficult to penetrate because of those very orchards. Only paths and public roads were left open, and pack-animals laden with fruit traversed them now, but they were much too narrow for easy access to an army.

"You may not like what you find. . . . Are you sure you want to do this?" Tarik asked Reynaud after they'd entered the city proper.

Reynaud nodded. "I must."

"But we do not even know if the man is Geoffrey d'Avignon—and we have no way of identifying him."

"He will tell us."

"Inshallah—if Allah wills. . . . If he hasn't died since we received word."

To anyone who cared to notice, they looked like two typical *Bedouin* men going about their business in the narrow, winding streets of Damascus. Tall and lithe, they were easy to discern as brothers, although beneath their traditional *kefiyas,* one wore a beard and mustache while the other was clean-shaven; one man was sharper featured and duskie skinned, yet both had eyes as gold as a tiger's.

The sun bore down on them as they wended their way through the heart of the city, which, because of the Barada River that ran through it and had supplied it with water for thousands of years, was an oasis on an otherwise semiaric plain. But it was sweltering now in midsummer and Reynaud was glad for the protection of the full-length robe he wore He would have baked in his mail, he thought with irony, ye he would not have entered Damascus as a Templar withou wearing it, for Saladin, who hated both Templar and Hospitaller knights, used the city as a center for his opposition to the crusaders.

Some of the way was shaded by the limestone building: lining the narrow, labyrinthine streets and alleyways, but the air was growing stiflingly close as it approached midday Reynaud glimpsed the Great Mosque in the distance, bu paid scant heed to its beauty as it gleamed in the sun. His thoughts were focused on getting into the dungeon where Tarik had been advised by an anonymous messenger to his camp, languished a Christian infidel who could possibly be Sieur Geoffrey d'Avignon. The message had been brief, Tarik said, relaying only that there were no more than a handfu of Christians who had survived the four years since the Battle of Hattin . . . hostages who had never been ransomed fo: one reason or another. They had been left to languish—some no doubt, long-forgotten; still others were probably kept incarcerated as either further punishment for failing to attrac any kind of payment from the Christian community, or Arab indifference.

The longer they walked, the older and more dismal the surroundings became as they went deeper into the oldest par of Damascus, until finally Tarik stopped before a low stone building. One soldier stood sentinel at its door. The *sheir* spoke to the man in a low voice, then Reynaud heard the muffled clink of coins. The sentry disappeared inside fo what seemed an eternity, before reappearing and addressing Tarik.

"We must surrender our weapons," Tarik said to Reynaud as he reached for the scimitar at his waist. Reynaud reluctantly followed suit, removing the borrowed scimitar he also wore, and then his dagger. He felt dangerously vulnerable as he handed them to the guard, but schooled the expression on his face to reveal none of his thoughts.

Tarik motioned to him then, and Reynaud received the merest acknowledgment from the guard before the latter led the way into the dim interior. The thick stone walls kept the room welcomely cool compared to the stifling air in the street.

Another grim-looking guard, menacingly armed, met them at a door to narrow stone steps descending into pure darkness. The first man dropped the weapons on a table, then withdrew. Reynaud watched the second Arab as he lit a pitch torch, lifted it high, and entered the crude stairwell, motioning for Tarik and Reynaud to follow him.

Tarik glanced at Reynaud, a question in his eyes. Reynaud nodded and moved past him to follow the sentry into the bowels of the building. It occurred to him that had he or Tarik been bent upon mayhem, they could have shoved the sentry down the steps with a minimum of effort, and the man's weapons would have been useless. But then, he thought, the guard's obvious lack of concern only indicated that there were few prisoners down below, and those still alive were obviously not worth a ransom. . . .

A chill dampness enveloped them as they descended, and the steps began to turn slick before they'd gone very far. Once, Reynaud was forced to brace a hand against the wall as one foot slipped, and his fingers encountered a film of slime. He quickly pulled it away, concentrating on better keeping his balance in the dancing shadows along the wall.

Even though accustomed to the horrors of war, and anything but squeamish, Reynaud felt dread form a ball in the pit of his stomach at the thought of what was below. He held little hope for Geoffrey d'Avignon, and even if he were still alive, after all this time he would have been better off dead.

Tarik's presence behind him was somehow reassuring as he descended into the Arab dungeon—a place many equated with Hell. He thought it ironic that Tarik el Mezrab, the source of his shattering disappointment in his father, would also be a source of comfort now. How strange things could be sometimes. . . .

The stench assaulted his senses long before they reached the subterranean passageways beneath the building. Save for feeble-flamed wall torches set at intervals along the crudely dug main corridor, it was lightless. The close, dank atmosphere reeked of death, and from what Reynaud could see through the small, barred apertures in the first few doors, it was even blacker within the cells.

He was torn between the urge to take in a deep, sustaining breath, and a real reluctance to inhale the miasmic air. His stomach turned and he bit his lip to keep down its contents, as the guard quickly strode forward until he reached the fourth or fifth door and held up the torch to the tiny opening. He squinted into the cell for a moment, then lifted the heavy wooden bar and pulled open the panel, motioning for Reynaud and Tarik to enter.

"You don't have to do this," Reynaud muttered to his half-brother. "You can wait upstairs . . ."

His answer was a light push, propelling him toward the open door and the horrors inside. The guard handed him the torch and stepped back, one arm over his mouth and nose. "No tricks," he said in Arabic, his voice muffled by his sleeve.

Bracing for the worst, Reynaud held up the torch and stepped inside. It took a moment for his eyes to adjust, but he had no trouble identifying the choking stink of urine and excrement and disease. It slammed into him like a fist—a stench worse than the filthiest privy. He forced his eyes to quarter the small area, noting the dirt floor had been turned to muck from waste. . . .

Of course, St. Rémy. What did you expect to find in a dungeon?

Tarik nudged him forward again, and the door banged shut behind them. The bar was dropped back into place and, for a fleeting moment, Reynaud felt panic claw its way up his spine. What was to guarantee they wouldn't be locked within and consigned to a living death?

Rashid knows where you are. And a few of Tarik's men. . . .

"There," Tarik said softly, pointing to what looked like a discarded heap of rags near one corner. He took the torch from Reynaud and as the light bounced off the walls, it revealed images of blackened stone and creatures of the dark within their sinister-looking webs.

There was nothing else in the cell—not even the barest necessities like a vessel for waste, or for drinking or washing. No pallet, no table or stool, no sign of the occupant's armor or other belongings. Tarik angled the brand enough to shed more light on the tattered pile.

"Sweet Jesu," Reynaud mumbled, and forced himself to move forward, his limbs as sluggish as in a recurring nightmare. Then compassion awakened within him, for this could be Brielle's long-lost father. And even if it were not, he thought, as he willed himself to more purposeful motions, this miserable scrap of humanity deserved more than his cowardly approach.

He went slowly to his knees beside the body, refusing to wonder what filth was contaminating his robe, and put out one trembling hand to move aside the remnant of a tunic—or what had once possibly been a blanket. He exposed the prisoner's head and scrawny neck, and gently touched the latter, searching gingerly for a pulse. The cool flesh heralded death. *"Vous êtes encore avec nous, mon brave cloisé?"* he asked softly in French. "Are you still with us?"

And received only the hissing of the torch above him in answer.

He applied slightly more pressure with his fingers, praying for some sign of a heartbeat, but acknowledging that if mercy had ever been allowed admittance to this place of suffering, the prisoner would have long-ago given up his soul.

"Sieur Geoffrey? Can you hear me?" he asked.

And then he caught the faintest tick beneath his questing fingers. Whoever he was, the man was still alive. Reynaud carefully rolled him onto his back, and tightened his lips in distaste as a rat scurried away and into the corner.

"Poor soul," Tarik muttered.

The man's hair had turned pure white—what he had left of it, and his features were so gaunt they were skeletal. Tarik had been right. They would probably never find out if this man was Geoffrey d'Avignon or not, for how could a man so obviously near death gather enough breath to say a single word?

Tarik removed a small skin of water from his belt and pushed it into Reynaud's hand. Immediately the knight wet the man's lips, then with infinite care bathed his face with his fingers, praying for some reaction.

"Just as you did for me," Tarik murmured, an odd timbre to his voice.

The words echoed round and round in Reynaud's mind.

Of course. He knew what he had to do now. The man wasn't dead yet. . . .

Tarik's steel-fingered grip on his arm broke into his thoughts and stilled his movements. He had hunkered down across from Reynaud, and their eyes met, locked, in the wavering torchlight. "I know what you're thinking, and you *must not do it!*" He spoke *sotto voce,* but there was no mistaking the conviction in his voice.

Reynaud frowned. "And why is that, brother? Why should I not try to save his life? I would do anything for her—"

"But don't give up your life for *him!*"

A slow anger rose up in Reynaud. "And why is that?" he asked again, his voice barely a whisper. "No price can be set on any man's life."

"She need never know! Why risk your life—your chance at happiness with Brielle d'Avignon—by doing this? If you save him, every Arab from here to Egypt will learn of so miraculous a feat!"

Reynaud shook his head, tried to shake his arm free, for there was no time to spare. The prisoner could expire at any moment and then be totally beyond his reach. "No one has to know—"

"Everyone will know." Tarik looked down at the unconscious prisoner, then back at Reynaud. "Only an ignorant child does not know what happens to a man after four years in a dungeon. It would be nothing short of a miracle of God if this man were suddenly restored to health again, and word would spread like Greek fire!"

I—I'm alone. Don't you see? I have no one now . . .

Brielle's tearful words came to Reynaud in a rush of bittersweet memory. "But she won't be alone again—or forced to go back to St. Bernadette's . . ."

Tarik's eyes held sadness and sudden anger at the same time. "How long can he live—if 'tis even him? He's an old man now." Tarik gave Reynaud's arm a shake. "And what of you? *You* can be with her now. And always."

Reynaud nodded, quelling the spark of irritation he felt at Tarik's attempts to interfere. "Brielle," he murmured, his mind filling with scents, sounds, images of her, the lovely rose, in spite of the dismal surroundings. "I am not worthy of her . . ."

Tarik cursed softly in Arabic. "That is absurd! There is no acceptable reason—"

"B—Bri-elle. . . ."

It was so softly spoken, it sounded to Reynaud like the prisoner's dying sigh. He looked down at him in alarm. The cracked, bloodless lips appeared unmoving still. Reynaud stared hard at the gaunt features, as if he could will the man to speak. Then the latter's mouth moved almost imperceptibly. "Bri—elle . . . Bri—elle . . ." The name was barely recognizable, a tortured husk of sound, and Reynaud wondered how one so close to the end could possibly utter even one word.

The man fell silent, his eyelids never raising.

" 'Tis d'Avignon," Reynaud said, unable to believe the twist of fate.

"And your dire misfortune. If he lives, any expectations you might have had of a normal life crumbles to ashes."

Something in Tarik's voice should have warned him—for it was more than just the words . . . but he still couldn't believe Geoffrey d'Avignon was alive—couldn't take his eyes from the man whom Brielle loved so dearly, needed so much.

He knew better now than to dream of any kind of normal life with her, with the certainty of a man about to take a sword blade through the heart. Yet if he ever could do one thing for the woman he loved, it would be healing and then returning her father to her. His heart lightened ever so subtly, for if he could accomplish something so precious to her, it would be a little bit easier to let her go.

The torch suddenly dropped from Tarik's fingers, a shrinking ball of light that sizzled and flickered on the filth-mired floor. Reynaud looked at his half-brother, feeling an uncharacteristic panic at losing the precious light. "Grab it!" he growled, fighting the urge to throw himself over d'Avignon's body and rescue it himself.

He watched in dismay as the flame lowered, sputtered, then died, plunging them into stinking, Stygian blackness.

"Tarik!"

It was a plea wrung from his heart, and the next instant, he was crawling through the muck in search of the doused brand. "Guard!" he shouted, then belatedly remembered the guard wouldn't speak French. In his panic, he couldn't think of the word in Arabic, but surely the cry would bring the

sentry running. Meanwhile, he had a more pressing problem
than that . . .

Like finding the torch. "Where *is* it?" he cried out softly
to Tarik, who'd been strangely silent the past few moments.
(Was el Mezrab even *there?* Or was this a bad dream from
which Reynaud couldn't waken? Or, worse, was he just
floundering in his own frustration—and what covered the
floor? He could not hear anything over the pounding of blood
in his ears from the stir he was creating himself.)

The unwelcome and ugly taste of fear coated his mouth.
God, help me! he prayed as he groped for the torch. He
found it and realized he had no means to light it. He wanted
to scream with helplessness.

"Guard!" he cried, louder, then footsteps sounded dully
outside the cell, and another brand illuminated the barred
window in the door briefly before the sentry yanked it open
again.

The light revealed the extinguished torch on the floor—
and Tarik crouching exactly where he'd been before it had
fallen. Reynaud lunged at the implement, then stood and
held it out to the one the sentry held. It lit, flared blindingly,
and burned once again, giving off small furls of smoke to
add to the stench of the cell.

Reynaud spun around and hunkered down beside Geoffrey
d'Avignon once more.

"Don't trouble yourself. He's dead."

Tarik took the torch from Reynaud as he spoke, his voice
holding a warning, as well as a subtle note of regret. The
guard muttered something in Arabic, but Reynaud didn't
bother to translate as he put his hand to the prisoner's neck
once more, searching for a sign that he was still alive. His
fingers encountered something wet and sticky where earlier
he had found a thready pulse.

Defeat hit him like a battering ram, and he looked up at
Tarik, slowly realizing what his half-brother had done. Con-
firmation was in those eyes so like his own. Even then, the

acknowledgment was slow to come—and he didn't want to believe it. . . .

How could Tarik betray him like this?

But the proof was smeared across his fingers, glistening in the wavering torchlight, in spite of the fact that they had been stripped of their weapons.

He wanted to leap across at Tarik, but instead he tensed against the urge, clenching his fists. The last thing he needed now was to turn against his newly-discovered half-brother. To fight like an animal in a putrid prison that represented man's capacity for baseness. Wasn't his life muddled enough? Didn't he have enough problems; hadn't he experienced enough disillusionment and unhappiness to last until he drew his last breath?

Nor did he want Tarik held responsible by the keepers of the prison—if they noticed the small wound on the body.

"Take my offering," Tarik said softly, "and God's. It seems to me you deserve better from life than you've gotten. You don't have to lie . . . or jeopardize your life because you would have extended that magnanimity of yours one time too many."

The scar suddenly seemed to turn livid against el Mezrab's forehead, as if to remind Reynaud of the risk he had taken for an enemy in the desert months ago; as if to reinforce Tarik's decree.

"You may be a wise and able leader, Tarik, but you are not my *sheik*."

Tarik seemed to lean a little closer to him, as if to make certain Reynaud heard every word he was going to say . . . or that no one else would. There were just the two of them— the guard had retreated, Geoffrey d'Avignon was dead—in a vile hole that, for those few charged moments, ceased to have any significance for either brother. "Whatever you may believe, my brother, Allah did not allow you to save my life, then later deliver you into my hands, only to force me to watch you throw your own away. Nor did He help me overcome my hatred and bitterness, only to reward me by watching helplessly as the implement of that healing destroyed itself." He glanced around with a measuring look, then stood. "Whether you agree with it or not, Reynaud de St. Rémy . . . whether you approve of it or not, the deed is done. By all that is holy, let us leave this place!"

Reynaud didn't move. He looked at the remains of Geoffrey d'Avignon before him, oblivious to everything in that moment but the import of Tarik's words. The ultimate irony, of course, was that after all his doubts—his unequivocal dismissal of Brielle's hope that her father had not been killed at Hattin after all—Geoffrey d'Avignon *had* survived the battle, and then four years in a Damascus dungeon. And Reynaud had found him, still alive, and been unable to save him, thanks to his half-brother—someone he'd never even known existed until a few days ago; and all because of his father's sins.

There was nothing he could do now, yet he found, even in that maelstrom of emotion that was tearing up his mind, a part of him clinging to the thought of Brielle like a man swept overboard in a violent sea. "I would have some token to give her," he said in a low, anguished voice.

Tarik's dark brows tented beneath his *keffiya,* as he watched his brother.

"A lock of his hair, mayhap . . ." Reynaud mumbled.

In a flash, a small-bladed knife appeared from the folds of Tarik's robe, as he swiftly bent and separated a lock from the patchy white hair still remaining on the dead man's head. The same blade, he acknowledged, that had been used to dispatch Sieur Geoffrey d'Avignon.

Or what remained of him, echoed reason.

Reynaud took the lock, tucked it into the pouch inside the loose belt at his waist, then bowed his head and said a silent prayer for Brielle's father. The man's agony had finally ended.

He felt suddenly swallowed by the tangled skein of events

in which Fate had ensnared him. Perhaps it was a vengeful God. Or an uncaring one. Yet even the blasphemy of that thought failed to banish the temptation to retreat spiritually to a safer place . . . lest he go stark, raving mad.

But he couldn't find the strength to do even that. He straightened slowly and met Tarik's eyes, his own dim and distant, barely conscious of anything but the overpowering need for peaceful oblivion.

"You will tell her we were too late?" Tarik asked softly. "And then take her home to France?"

Reynaud's eyes cleared—he was forced to focus on his half-brother's words, because "her" meant the rose. Brielle. And her image suddenly appeared in his mind's eyes, clear and pure. It possessed the power to drive away his demons— if only for that sweet, all-too-fleeting moment. "I have no choice." His eyes narrowed with sudden, cold anger. "Or would you have me tell her you killed her father? That Gérard de St. Rémy's capacity for treachery lives on in you as well as in me?"

Tarik shook his head slowly, his eyes flashing briefly with obvious ire, before Reynaud added softly, "And why do you care so much?"

"She would not understand," Tarik answered the first question. "Even though he was near death."

"And I could have saved him!"

"Could you have? How can you be sure? Have you ever saved anyone so close to death?"

Reynaud dismissed the queries with an angry gesture.

"And had you kept his heart beating, what would you have had to give *her?*"

Before Reynaud could do more than open his mouth, however, Tarik continued implacably, "I'll tell you, brother . . . a shell of a man! Who knows if his mind wasn't already gone—if he could have ever in the past years uttered anything more than his daughter's name until he breathed his last?

And could you have restored his spirit? Surely that had been crushed long ago!"

Reynaud spun on his heel. "Guard!" he called in Arabic, not wanting to hear anymore. Tarik el Mezrab was only trying to justify his act of murder . . .

Rather his act of mercy, whispered a voice.

Tarik was right behind him, one hand reaching out to Reynaud's shoulder as he neared the door. "You won't tell her . . . You *cannot!*"

Reynaud jerked from Tarik's grip and strode out into the passageway. Even the dim light of the corridor seemed celestial compared to the blackness of the cell—the air more breathable. The sentry moved toward them out of the shadows, his look suspicious.

"The prisoner is dead," Tarik told him.

Outwardly the guard registered no surprise. "Everyone dies here," he said. "Eventually."

"He will need a proper burial," Tarik said, and handed him a few bezants. "See to it."

After what seemed like an endless climb, they emerged into the room upstairs and retrieved their weapons. The first guard was evidently outside, the second occupied below, as they made ready to leave.

"I ask you again, St. Rémy," Tarik said, not liking the telltale silence, the seeming withdrawal of his half-brother. If only he could jar Reynaud out of this strange indifference. "What will you tell her?"

Reynaud shot him a look askance. "You would never wish to appear the villain in her eyes, would you?" His words turned caustic. "Mayhap you even have designs on her yourself—in the best St. Rémy tradition."

Tarik's eyes slitted in affront. "And your self-pity makes my stomach turn! Such a question is beneath any blood kin of mine! But apparently marriage is more than *you* would

offer her, is it not? You will let her return to that . . . *place.*
And why? To wither away?"

Reynaud shrugged, his eyes suddenly empty, and gave his
half-brother his rock-hard profile.

Tarik had thought he'd taken away the last reason Reynaud
had to remain in the Holy Land . . . that the death of Brielle's
sire would propel him to take her in hand and return to France
for good—to escape the constant threat of capture and ex-
ploitation—and worse; to make a life with the woman he
obviously loved.

Evidently he hadn't quite succeeded. . . .

"At least have the decency to accompany her back!" Tarik
said, his voice rising. "If you do not, your sin will be greater
than my merely ending a man's *suffering!*" The last word
had lowered to a hiss.

Tarik watched as rage moved visibly through Reynaud,
tensing his body, firing his golden eyes to molten flame as
he faced his brother. *Hamdillah! Praise be to God,* Tarik
thought.

"I am not my father!" the knight raged softly, his teeth
bared. "Nor can you lay your own sins at my head!"

"Indeed," Tarik said, taking careful verbal aim. "You are
worse. You have no wife and children to blame for your desertion!"

Reynaud stared at him for a split-second, obviously
stunned.

Taking advantage of his brother's fleeting shock, Tarik
swung away just as Reynaud drew back his fist. He strode
swiftly toward the door, leaving only the empty air for Reynaud to strike with a trembling arm.

Twenty-three

September, 1191

Reynaud rode away from Richard the Lionheart's triumph over Saladin's Turks in the Battle of Arsuf, the distinct smell of gore and death still tainting his nostrils. He was unutterably weary and allowed Khamsin to pick his own way north, toward. . . . toward where?

He never wanted to see Tarik el Mezrab again. Nor any member of the Order of the Poor Knights of the Temple of Solomon. After having ridden with the other Templars in the vanguard of King Richard's army to participate in this latest slaughter, he had decided once and for all that he was finished with the Order. Finished with killing Muslims in the name of Christ. Finished with killing anyone . . . finished with healing anyone.

Never would he raise a hand again. Not to kill—not to heal.

Nor could he ride toward France, his numb mind managed to reason, for he couldn't stomach the thought of facing Gérard de St. Rémy again and keep his vow not to kill. He was that outraged at his father. Still.

And himself.

He had tried fighting with the crusader forces at Arsuf in a spate of fury-driven energy—had shed the protective rôle Robert de Sablé had temporarily assigned him as Bishop

Abelard's escort. And consequently, he had been sickened at
the carnage in which he had taken part—its aftermath a battlefield strewn with the bodies of those Turks who hadn't
successfully retreated. Fallen flags, banners of all shapes and
sizes, and countless pennants and standards littered the
ground—colorful scraps on a field of death and destruction.
Swords, metal-tipped darts, Turkish bows, and clubs bristling
with sharp teeth were scattered over the gore-drenched earth,
and easily a score of cartloads of bolts, javelins, arrows, and
other missiles could have been collected.

And the irony was that God had not seen fit to let him
die, as Reynaud had been perfectly willing to do. Wasn't it
bad enough that He had cursed Reynaud with his ability to
heal after having guided him into the Templar Order? How
could he ever reconcile that very power with the part of the
Rule that advocated the killing of infidels to attain Heaven?

As the sun climbed higher in the sky, he adjusted the tunic
over his mail . . . the tunic he'd taken from a fallen crusader
after he'd stripped and discarded his own, for he would never
again wear the symbol of the Templar Order.

Without warning, Tarik's words drifted across his memory.
Your march in the heat of the day in full armor. . . .

It was true, he thought, shifting beneath the weight of more
than 30,000 tiny rings of steel, but his training and instinct
for self-preservation (faint as it may have been lately) caused
him merely to shift uncomfortably in his saddle.

Think about something else if you won't shed it, warned
common sense. *Something pleasant . . .*

Something pleasant? Mayhap his father's dirty deed? Mayhap the murder of Geoffrey d'Avignon by another of St.
Rémy blood?

He closed his eyes against the sun, glad he had at least
shed his coif and helm for a *keffiya*. Both he and Khamsin
needed water. He had to find a stream, mayhap a friendly
village, where they could drink their share. And then he could
shed his mail and tend the shallow cut across the stallion's

neck from a Saracen scimitar; for this one service he could perform for the faithful steed.

But after that . . . ?

Go to Tyre, fool. She is there . . . waiting. You forbade her to leave for France without you. Don't you remember? Unless she tired of waiting and has long since gone.

For a moment, his spirits lifted at the very thought of Brielle. Her image flashed before him, brighter than the sun, and infinitely more precious. Yes, he could go to Tyre . . . and Brielle.

Reality came crashing in. Of course he had to go to Tyre. Hadn't he ordered her to stay there until he could escort her personally?

You'll have to tell her then that you failed to save her father. That your half-brother—whose St. Rémy blood is as red as yours—murdered him in your presence.

The demons began again, beating away at his brain, threatening to drive him mad . . .

"I've waited long enough," Brielle told Taillefer. "He cannot forbid me to leave Tyre without his escort, and then just . . . disappear!"

But she was as worried as she was angry, for there had been no word of Reynaud for a month. Even Bishop Abelard had returned from Acre with Humphrey of Toulouse and hadn't heard from the missing Templar. Tarik, however, had sent a brief and unrevealing message: *Don't look for him. He needs time, and you must be patient for he is in Allah's hands now. . . .*

"Do you think Tarik would lie about it?" she asked the minstrel, lines of worry etching her brow. "Think you Reynaud is with him and for some reason doesn't want us to know?"

"What would be the purpose of that? Because he doesn't want you to leave Tyre without him?" Taillefer asked. He shook his head, then ceased his frowning contemplation of the colorful courtyard fountain. "That isn't like Reynaud. Nor, from what little I know about Tarik, does it seem that he would lie about Reynaud's whereabouts."

Brielle stood and moved toward a fragrant rose bush, her expression still thoughtful. "But his behavior since Tarik's revelation has been . . . strange."

Taillefer was sitting on a stone bench, an arm braced on either side of him. He let his head drop back between his shoulders to contemplate the cobalt sky. "I don't think Tarik is ignorant of Reynaud's whereabouts. But, as he said, we must be patient. Reynaud will come forward when he is ready, and not before."

Brielle's back was to him, preventing her from seeing his expression as he said the words. She carefully plucked a blossom and passed it beneath her nose. The sweet fragrance filled her head, reminding her poignantly of the time in this very same courtyard when Reynaud had given her another rose. And something not quite tangible, but even more precious. . . .

Oh, where *is* he? she thought in silent anguish.

Then an insidious thought wormed its way into her mind: What if he were just testing her obedience to him? Wouldn't that be more like him?

Or mayhap he's retreated from the pain he feels after everything that has been revealed, countered her compassionate side.

That thought gave her serious pause. She had known him capable of such a thing—but Tarik surely didn't know of his half-brother's strange retreats from reality. How could his assurances be valid then? And was Reynaud capable of protecting himself in such a state? If he was with Rashid, the Arab might know what to do to help him over the worst, and could even act as his protector. But Rashid was only one man. And the Levant was filled with spies and assassins, sordid intrigue, and perfidy for hire . . . a land especially hostile to a Christian crusader, to say nothing of a Templar knight.

"And I am to just wait here for him? Why, I should just leave this wretched place—with or without him!" she said darkly. She sounded like a shrew, she acknowledged, but she would have her say! She looked back at Taillefer. "Haven't I the right to be angry? He expects me to follow his orders like some Templar underling! And since you are so certain he's unharmed, why can't we leave?"

"You have every right," the minstrel told her quietly, as their eyes met.

"But aren't you worried about him?" she asked, concern seesawing up over her anger once again. Dear God, what if he were hurt or—infinitely worse—dead? The thought was unbearable, and Brielle felt her throat close with emotion at the very idea.

He who had so selflessly helped others—with no consideration for any consequences for himself—might be in need of help himself. Even if he were unharmed physically, the fact that he hadn't returned to Tyre in and of itself was an indication that something was very wrong.

How many times had she come to that conclusion in the last weeks? And how many times had her pride told her she was a fool to worry about a man who clearly didn't want anything to do with her?

"I am *very* worried." Taillefer ran a hand through his hair in uncharacteristic agitation and stood, but he said nothing more.

She stared at him as he began pacing, thinking that it was Reynaud who normally did the worrying, while Taillefer provided the distraction and entertainment. Yet he'd shown a different side to her—to anyone who cared to notice—since Anabette's death. A more sober side, with a new interest in things that wouldn't have engaged his attention in the past. And he definitely had a latent skill with a weapon, as she'd witnessed when he'd killed Tancred le Bref.

Brielle thought back to the pirate attack on the *Madonna*. Hadn't Reynaud observed that Taillefer would rather strum a lute than use a weapon? Yet he'd shown himself to be an able warrior when the need arose. Why, then, couldn't he conduct a search for Reynaud himself?

And why couldn't you accompany him? whispered her heart. *Isn't the safety and well-being of the man you love more important than anything else?*

Of course. And once they found him, and her fears were allayed, she could leave for France knowing Reynaud was safe.

"Then we must go and find him," she said suddenly. "I fear he may be . . ."

Taillefer halted in his tracks and swung toward her as she trailed off, his blue eyes somber. ". . . in one of his withdrawals? You are aware, then, of these moods?

She nodded. "How can I love him and not have noticed?"

"That is my greatest fear for him," he told her. "And not only may he be more vulnerable to enemies, but what if he doesn't come out of it this time? What if he cannot?"

To her mortification, she was suddenly perilously close to tears before this friend of Reynaud's—this man who was still suffering from his own pain. "Please, Taillefer," she entreated. "I—I love him, you see, and it doesn't matter whether he loves me back or not. I must know that he is safe before I leave here."

Silence gathered around them before Taillefer said with unexpected bitterness, "There is no such thing as 'safe' in this land." Then his voice became more gentle. "Brielle . . . listen to me. There is no need to search for Reynaud. Forgive me for not telling you sooner, but he is . . . here."

She forgot to breathe for a moment as his words sank in. "Reynaud? Here?" she repeated, bemused.

"Oui. He is here in Tyre."

She fought to clear the confusion from her brain. "Here? But—"

"Sit," he said firmly, and guided her to the nearest stone bench. She obeyed numbly, still trying to come to terms with what he had just told her. Reynaud was here in Tyre? But how? And where, exactly? And why hadn't he come to the bishop's palace, where he belonged—where his duty lay. And where *she* had been waiting and suffering untold agonies for days and days, wondering where he was—if he was even alive . . .

"He threatened Rashid with death if the Arab revealed his whereabouts. But you deserve to be told. Especially when I know he is nearby and unharmed." He hesitated before adding, "Besides, he needs our help. All we have to do," he said with heavy irony, "is get him to accept it."

"If he's all right, then why hasn't he been here? Why can't I see him . . . speak to him?" Bemusement and anger suddenly faded. "Taillefer . . . what is amiss? What aren't you telling me? Is he well? What do you mean by 'he needs our help'?"

He sat beside her, one hand firmly over hers, as if he were afraid she would flee. "I haven't spoken to him, for fear of betraying Rashid, but I've seen him. He's dressed like a typical crusader—obviously he doesn't want to draw attention to himself. If it weren't for the stallion—"

"Khamsin?"

"Oui. I recognized the horse first—although he appears filthy and neglected."

She frowned in disbelief, for Reynaud never neglected the steed. She tried to pull her hand from beneath his to stand, but he held firm.

"Hear me out," he said softly. "Rashid approached me near the cathedral. He told me that after threatening him with death if he said aught to anyone, Reynaud dismissed him from his service."

She felt disbelief spread across her features.

"You can believe it, Brielle. Rashid wouldn't lie about this. He says Reynaud is struggling with himself. Evidently one part of him wants to fulfill his obligation, to keep his pledge to take you back to France, yet this other side of him would hide in the shadows, confused, and unwilling to come forward. Uncertain and withdrawn, evidently."

"Because of his father's sins?" she blurted in consternation. "I care not—"

"Nay, Brielle. There is more."

She quieted instantly. More? And from the way he glanced away from her eyes, as if searching for the right words . . . worse. Since she'd first met him, Taillefer had never had to grope for the right words.

"He and Tarik found your father in Damascus."

The blood began to pound in her ears. "Father?" she whispered. "Alive?"

"Non, chère," he said gently, "Sieur Geoffrey is dead." His hand tightened over hers. "He died in Reynaud's arms before he could save him."

She was quiet a long moment, stunned by the revelation. For four years her father had been alive after all . . . suffering unthinkable tortures. Why had no one sent word to Château d'Avignon? To Reginald?

But she knew the answers even as the questions were formed: Reginald would have ignored any word of his father being alive—unwilling to give up his position as lord, to say nothing of having to part with any of his gold to secure Geoffrey's release. And he would have moved heaven and earth to keep the news from reaching Brielle . . . or even John the Gaunt.

In fact, no doubt he had had the messenger—and anyone unfortunate enough to be in that poor soul's company—murdered. And if John had voiced any of his feelings to Reginald, it was a miracle he hadn't been somehow done away with before Anabette reached him last spring.

But Brielle could accept all that. Now, at least. What was worse, however, was the certainty that Reynaud blamed himself for not having made inquiries sooner. Had he not been so certain her father had been killed—had he not taken her repeated requests so lightly, Geoffrey d'Avignon might have been saved.

Knowing Reynaud as she did, Brielle acknowledged that he would have taken full blame for Geoffrey's death.

"He blames himself." It was a statement.

"I fear so."

"Then how can he keep his vow to escort me to France when he feels he is responsible for my father's death? He's torn between guilt and duty."

"And loves you deeply, desperately," Taillefer said. "From what Rashid told me, I seriously suspect that his love for you is what brought him here and is now the only thing keeping him nearby—possibly his strongest tether to reality."

"Dear God!" she whispered.

"Nor does he consider himself a Templar anymore, which not only puts his life at greater risk should anyone recognize him as St. Rémy the healer—I have long suspected that Humphrey was to serve unobtrusively as Reynaud's watchdog—but also means that officially he is relieved of his duties to both you and Bishop Abelard. I sincerely doubt, however, that he would use that as a reason to fail to make the journey with you."

"The Reynaud we know, you mean."

He nodded, then placed his hands on his knees and lowered his head to stare at the floor. In the momentary hush before he spoke again, the birdsong was sweet and briefly soothing to Brielle's agitated state of mind. Then, "I can tell you with certainty, *chère,* that at least part of the reason he does not want his presence known to you is because he cannot bear to let you go—which is what duty, even if his own personal duty—dictates. He was always his own harshest taskmaster. And, if you see him, he reasons, you'll feel free to leave Outremer. With or without him."

"We have not lost him yet?" she asked him, a tremor in her voice, even as she dared to hope.

He shook his head. "I think not . . . but Rashid gave me no assurances. He told me that Reynaud evidently took part in the latest fighting at Arsuf, near Jaffa . . . almost as if he were looking for a diversion . . . or release. Mayhap even death. And Tarik did not dare to interfere, either."

So he had been willing enough to sacrifice himself in battle, she thought in growing horror—had evinced enough guilt and remorse to push him to seek death rather than come to her in Tyre. Yet somehow he had been spared.

And now, she thought grimly, if she could prevent it, he wouldn't have another opportunity to sacrifice his body . . . or his mind.

"I must speak to him!" she declared, standing. It didn't matter anymore if he wanted to marry her or not, she acknowledged. What was her silly pride worth in the face of *this?* Nor did it matter that she would spend the rest of her life buried at St. Bernadette's. All that mattered now was getting through to Reynaud—soothing him, reassuring him . . . helping him over this seemingly insurmountable hurdle. If she hadn't gone running to Tancred le Bref in the first place, Reynaud wouldn't be in this state.

Taillefer's eyes met hers, and she watched as a spark of what could have been approval, or relief, lit his eyes, reminding her of his usual animation before his Anabette had been killed. "There is always hope, *chère Brielle,* only you must be certain you wish to take up the challenge, for any one of us could push him the wrong way. And lose him forever."

A most sobering thought. But she wondered what would happen to him if she stood by and did nothing. There was no guarantee. . . . "But the risk is surely worth it, don't you think, Taillefer?"

It took him a moment to answer. *"Oui."*

"Then I'll speak to him—somehow I'll approach him, by surprise, if I have to."

"No. I don't think that would be wise. As far as he is concerned, no one knows he's here. We don't know if he suspects Rashid is in Tyre, but the Arab would lay down his life for him, and therefore Reynaud cannot possibly believe the man would stay away—even on pain of death."

Brielle watched his lips twist with rue. "This is not the first time Reynaud issued such a dire threat," he said with an attempt at lightness. At Brielle's questioning look, he added, "He threatened Rashid and me if we followed him when he went in search of you. 'Tis merely a desperate measure, for Reynaud doesn't make a habit of killing friends."

Brielle failed to see any humor in the situation, however. "Under normal circumstances, but you just told me Reynaud is not himself. We don't know what he's capable of now." She felt torn between a powerful urge to go to him, and dread . . . a fear of what she would find. "So, what can we *do?*" she asked with growing impatience, as the minstrel stared thoughtfully across the courtyard.

When his eyes met hers, he said, "We can take our time and think of something that will work, Brielle, for another day or so shouldn't make much difference. And if 'tis of any comfort to you, Rashid's cousin Farouk—you remember the physician who briefly attended le Bref?—is an excellent doctor. Failing all else, we can take Reynaud against his will, and mayhap—if he truly needs it—he can be treated by the Arab for . . ." he trailed off, obviously searching once again for the words, ". . . disorders of the mind."

Brielle was stunned. "Only God can do such a thing!" she said softly, touching her fingers to her lips.

"Surely Reynaud told you of the advances in medicine the Arabs have made compared to the West?"

She nodded.

"Would you deny Reynaud the opportunity for help if there's the least chance he might benefit?"

"Nay. Of course not. . . ." And she let it go at that, wondering at the vastly superior knowledge of the Eastern culture compared to that of the West—and the way her own people looked down their noses at the Arabs.

But the waiting was torture for her—even the one full day they discussed and discarded plan after plan. On two occasions she went out with Taillefer to various parts of the city—desperately trying to catch a furtive glimpse of Reynaud. Only on the second of those occasions did she see him—a lone, mounted figure on a dust-streaked stallion, standing sentinel in the shadows of a building within sight of the bishop's palace.

Taillefer hired a youth to distract Reynaud from the other side of the street—any way he could without turning the knight's attention toward the palace and their departure. The young man did his job well. He surreptitiously set loose his small herd of camels directly across from Reynaud—then shouted furiously at his partner and made a great show of trying to round up the confused animals.

Brielle caught Taillefer's eye beneath his Arab garb and saw the familiar humor lurking there, before she realized she herself was close to laughter at the merchant's antics. "Were he more himself, he wouldn't be fooled by our attempts at disguise," Taillefer had said. "Or our clumsy ploys to distract him. . . ."

Almost immediately, however, she set her mind to observing what she could of Reynaud without being obvious, even though she, too, was dressed and veiled like an Arab. She couldn't see him clearly at first, and the width of the street that ran past the palace seemed no longer a blessing, for reasons of observation. Once she realized that her identity was relatively safe, she fretted because she couldn't see Reynaud as clearly as she wished.

His behavior from the shadow of the buildings, nonetheless, was distressingly revealing. . . .

The growing turmoil in the street obviously made Khamsin nervous, for the stallion pranced about uneasily, moving forward and into the bright sunlight, then retreating until Brielle could see neither man nor mount.

How strange, she thought with a frown beneath her veil.

Reynaud always entered into the thick of things when danger threatened, yet he obviously was not about to do so now, seeking rather to remain uninvolved and anonymous. Hadn't Taillefer said Reynaud had just come from Jaffa and the Battle of Arsuf?

This man wasn't the Reynaud she knew and loved. This was a stranger who remained obviously unmoved by the merchant's "plight" and the growing confusion in the street.

She moved forward, against Taillefer's earlier instructions, with growing concern and disregard for anything but Reynaud.

Then she heard Taillefer's voice saying, "God's blood! This isn't working . . . !"

Reynaud tried to control Khamsin, but the steed did not readily respond—as if his rider were a stranger. Reynaud felt the powerful equine muscles bunch beneath him, as tension shot through the agitated animal. As he struggled with the stallion, he silently cursed the careless merchant who was causing the mêlée, for the growing commotion was interrupting his view of the bishop's palace.

What does it really matter? asked a dim voice from the recesses of his mind. *Come away . . . to where 'tis safe. . . .*

"She cannot leave!" he muttered under his breath, trying to ignore it. "Not without me!"

That is the least of your troubles, insisted the voice. *After she discovers what you did, she will detest the very sound of your name! Better to turn your back to the pain, the anguish. . . .*

Nay! commanded a stern, authoritative voice. *You are Christ's perfect knight! Better in every way than I could ever be!*

Yes, Father. . . .

He felt like a man walking on ice . . . feeling it crack and give beneath him when he least expected it, altering his direction or forcing him to a halt just when he had established a course.

A loose and irate camel came rushing toward him, causing Khamsin to rear and slash out with his hooves. The potent memory of Gérard de St. Rémy's words instantly dissolved, but left Reynaud shaken enough to do the unthinkable—he sawed on the steed's reins in a desperate attempt at control, which only hurt the horse's tender mouth and caused him to rear up higher before he crashed toward the ground. A wide-eyed pedestrian tried to lunge away from the threatening hooves.

The man cried out, his *keffiya* went flying as he barely escaped the war horse . . . just as another camel bawled in protest as it went crashing by. For the fleeting space of time before the stallion could rise onto its hind legs again, Reynaud shot a look at the bishop's palace, cursing the interruption of his vigil . . .

Then he saw her—a flash of honey-gold tresses in the sunlight against the darker blue of her shawl. She was moving from the front of the palace toward the gathering people in the street, heedless of the possible danger.

She was coming right toward him.

The heat seemed to intensify, the noise faded, and part of his mind could only tell him to pull back in reaction. He couldn't let her see him, he thought in sudden panic. Not like this . . . hiding in the shadows, paralyzed by the contradictory thoughts rushing through his head.

She'll hate you! screamed a voice, *when she discovers you could have prevented her father's death!*

Droplets of sweat patterned his brow, slicked his palms. Yet as he unconsciously fought to control Khamsin, a rational part of him acknowledged Brielle d'Avignon was putting her very life in jeopardy as she moved toward him. His mouth went dry as desert sand as fear for her safety breached the newly-erected barrier of withdrawal, burst through the mechanisms of self-defense.

He touched his rowels to Khamsin's sides, and the stallion responded this time, leaping forward to cut a swathe through the shouting people scurrying out of harm's way. Khamsin side-swiped another camel with one flank, and a woman screamed in Arabic at them, but Reynaud focused on Brielle—on her eyes as they met his across the narrowing space between them. She looked like a *Bedouin* herself, wearing the dark blue gown and head covering given to her by the women of Tarik's camp, but he would have known that hair—even the briefest glimpse of it—anywhere.

Turn around—toward safety! urged one tiny part of him.

Coward! accused another voice, heavy with derision. *It's too late to worry about anything but saving her from harm! If 'tis your last act on earth, so be it . . .*

Indeed, he thought, with a burgeoning sense of fatalism as Khamsin thundered toward her, if only he could do one last thing for her during this flash of perfect lucidity, while he could perform like the skilled knight he had once been . . .

His instincts took over where his frenetic thoughts left off, and his mind began clearing before the rush of exhilaration that always accompanied imminent danger. He felt the brush of the wind against his warm face . . . the shouts of people scattering before him, two confused camels, and a furiously barking dog. Then the cacophony began to fade as he guided Khamsin toward the figure in blue.

"Reynaud!" shouted an Arab to one side of Brielle.

His eyes narrowed as he shifted his gaze to the tall, robed man. The latter tore his *keffiya* from his blond head.

Blond . . . ? Taillefer!

He didn't have time to think of how either one of them had known he was there, in Tyre, and close to the palace, for other concerns were foremost in his mind. But his beloved friend was moving toward Brielle—as if he were going to shield her from. . . .

From him?

"Out of the way, minstrel!" he shouted, suddenly angered by Taillefer's evident intentions. In the wake of that harsh command, he watched Brielle d'Avignon halt in her tracks.

Twenty-four

Brielle stood transfixed as Khamsin came pounding toward her, his rider wearing a blood-stained tunic of indiscernible color, many days' growth shadowing his lean cheeks, his expression fixed and harsh. . . .

The sun in her eyes didn't help, and she felt as if she were dreaming. A shout issued from behind her, verifying it was no dream, then an excited jumble of Arabic.

She half-turned, heard Taillefer's voice: *"Reynaud!"*

Three Arabs and a disreputable-looking sailor had pounced on the minstrel. No one seemed concerned as Taillefer struggled with his assailants, for others around them were still occupied with establishing order . . . and still others with avoiding this newest threat of a charging steed smashing through camels and pedestrians like a battering ram through parchment.

Still a fourth man materialized and came straight at her. Brielle felt the hair raise on the back of her neck, for there was something familiar about this newest attacker fast closing in on her. . . .

Then she recognized him: the merchant who'd assisted le Bref in abducting her from the *suk*.

She suddenly realized how she had grown to hate this beautiful but savage land—for there seemed to be nowhere that was safe from avenging Saracens . . . assassins who re-

fused to die . . . stifling heat and constant war—and sordid
secrets from the past.

A knife blade caught and reflected the sun as it came
streaking down at her from Sâlih al Barrak's upraised arm.
She spun about in reaction and threw herself directly at the
oncoming charger, her eyes locking with Reynaud's in a mute
appeal for help.

He leaned low as he thundered past. She reached up. . . .

Simultaneously, she felt the kiss of the honed blade tip
skimming down her side. But the pain was overshadowed by
Reynaud's left arm closing about her waist and lifting her
from her feet; and then the brief jolt of Khamsin's charge
taking Sâlih al Barrak full in the chest and knocking him
out of the way like a discarded piece of refuse.

Safely held before him, Brielle felt rather than saw Reynaud draw his great sword as he reined in Khamsin on the
fringe of the tangle of men around Taillefer. Khamsin came
to a skidding halt, his right side to the attackers, just as Reynaud swung the blade with the strength and precision gained
from years of practice. Before his fury, one assailant lost his
head with the first pass of the broadsword—so quickly he
didn't make a sound. Brielle closed her eyes against the grue-
some image, fighting to keep down the contents of her stomach.

Reynaud cried out something in Arabic, a savage sound
that made her blood chill, and she felt a second swing. The
sailor shrieked in pain, and Khamsin rose up on his hind-
quarters, lashing out with his great hooves. Brielle felt the
spatter of warm blood across her face before the miscreant
sank beneath the stallion's hooves. She bit down on her lower
lip to keep the nausea at bay.

And then she was slipping. . . . Nay, Reynaud was *pushing*
her from Khamsin's back. Mother of God, she thought in
terror, she was going to die beneath an Arab blade. And God
knew what would happen to Reynaud. . . .

But another pair of arms received her with a soft grunt

and swung her away from the mêlée. She looked into the man's dark eyes and recognized Rashid. Never had she been so glad to see him. "Help Reynaud!" she cried, and struggled to break from his grasp. He obligingly let her go and spun away toward the men struggling with Taillefer. The minstrel was putting up a heroic fight, in spite of his hampering robe—and his reputation as the sweetest-natured *troubadour* in Provence. Even John the Gaunt was helping to drive off the assailants.

Brielle stepped nearer, her eyes searching for Reynaud, her fear for both him and Taillefer threatening to launch her back into the fray. But out of the corner of her eye she caught sight of a retreating stallion and glanced in that direction just as Reynaud came to the minstrel's aid. There was no mistaking the man, no matter how he was dressed, or how he appeared physically. Sword still drawn, he shoved aside two brawling Italian sailors who were in the way, his face a mask of fury, and grabbed from behind the single Arab who was left wielding a blade at the minstrel.

"Sâlih!" the knight roared as he spun him about, and Brielle recognized the name of the man who had plotted with Tancred le Bref—the man who had attempted to spit her just as Reynaud was pulling her to safety. Reynaud raised his sword, but the surprise that spread across al Barrak's face was not the result of St. Rémy's impending blow.

The merchant staggered forward, Rashid's dagger in his back, his own weapon flashing as it spun through the air, a scintillating signal of peril to any group who would claim, exclusively for its own, this land sacred to three great religions.

His expression suddenly wary, the faithful Muslim looked at Reynaud.

"You took *my* revenge!" the knight snarled, stabbing the air with his sword in a gesture of pure frustration. "His dagger bears Brielle's blood, and you did not let me have my satisfaction!"

"Now is not the time to split hairs," Taillefer said crossly through bloodied lips. "Where in the hell have you been all this time?" He wiped a sleeve across his mouth and winced.

"Taillefer!" Brielle cried softly in concern, but he waved her away, his gaze moving quickly from her to Reynaud, sending her a silent message.

And she knew then that he was telling her to speak to Reynaud while she had the chance—before he remounted Khamsin and disappeared again like a mirage. . . .

Calm seemed suddenly to descend upon the street, and at last, after weeks of worry, Brielle found herself face to face with the man who had come to mean everything to her. Suddenly she was uncertain of what to say to him—or, rather, to this shadow of the man she once knew. The silence seemed to magnify in the wake of the violent action that had just ended, and she felt suddenly shy, awkward, for they were in a very public place; and this Reynaud was a stranger.

What had Taillefer told her? *Any one of us could push him the wrong way. . . .*

His eyes were riveted to her face, anger and anguish dulling the gold-flecked irises to a muddy hue. He was thinner, the bones of his face more prominent—making him look predatory, even beneath the full light of the sun; and the beard growth and blood-stained tunic only added to his derelict appearance.

Dear God, she thought as she fought back tears, he was a far cry from the knight who'd come to her rescue in the yard at St. Bernadette's.

But still capable of saving your life.

Aye, she thought. And that surely meant he felt some bond to her—no matter how tenuous. He had risked his life for her . . . and then for Taillefer, in spite of the fact that he had threatened Rashid.

And that meant perhaps there was a glimmer of hope for him.

"Reynaud?" she whispered so softly she was certain he couldn't have heard.

A whinny rent the air, and Khamsin plodded past two bystanders toward Reynaud's side, his awesome form gritdusted, his mane matted. And a long, reopened gash ran down the length of his splendid neck. Blood trickled down toward his withers. A woman hurried away from the scene, her eyes huge in the holes of her veil; a startled sailor lunged out of the animal's way, his jaw going slack as he stared at the steed.

The stallion's nose against Reynaud's shoulder seemed to break whatever spell had been cast over his master, and the knight took the drooping reins in one hand and cast a look around him, as if he wasn't certain where he was or how he had come to be there. He looked back at Brielle.

She took a halting step toward him, then another, until she could slowly place one hand upon his free arm, praying that he would be momentarily distracted from his own private devils and respond by showing concern for the steed's wound. "Reynaud? Come with me, won't you? We—we must tend Khamsin. He's hurt."

He frowned, and his fingers tightened visibly upon the reins. "Hurt," he mumbled, and shook his head, his eyes seeking the middle distance. "I cannot heal him," he said softly, his voice breaking.

Brielle wanted to shield him with her embrace, take his pain unto herself—but dared not, could not; she could only hope no one else had understood what he meant—no one mayhap had even heard the words.

She heard the sound of low voices from Taillefer's direction and thought she recognized Bishop Abelard's. " 'Tis all right, Reynaud," she assured the knight gently. "We can take care of it in the stable. Will you come with me?"

"The Lady Brielle has been hurt as well, Reynaud," Bishop Abelard said in a firm but not unkind voice. "You will do nothing to . . . ?"

Reynaud visibly flinched, his mouth tightening to a white line.

"Don't be absurd, my Lord Bishop," Taillefer said, in a weary but exasperated voice. "Why in God's name would he ever harm her?"

The sound of the minstrel's voice broke through to Reynaud's anger, and he answered the cleric: "I would give my life for her."

As Brielle looked into his eyes, however, the foremost thought in her mind was not her own safety, but rather the fact that God had deserted Reynaud de St. Rémy . . . and in his hour of greatest need.

Bishop Abelard gave Brielle an encouraging look over his shoulder before he directed the palace guards to see to the dead and wounded. John the Gaunt was already moving among the fallen to determine if any of them were still alive.

When the latter straightened and shook his head, Abelard asked him to guide a shaken Taillefer back to the palace. Rashid looked indecisive for a moment—as if he didn't know whether to follow his master to the stable or the bishop to the palace.

When his eyes met Brielle's, she shook her head ever so slightly in warning, and mouthed, "On pain of death."

He caught her meaning, for with obvious reluctance, the Arab turned to follow John and Taillefer.

Young John, the guard, strode ahead of Brielle as she led Reynaud to the stable on the other side of the white marble building that was the palace. John hesitated at the entrance, a question in his eyes, but Brielle gave him the merest shake of her head, and he left them at the open doors.

It was the first time, in all the weeks she had spent in Tyre, that she had been in the stable, but found the scent of animals and clean hay and leather somehow reassuring. In fact, she was reminded of another, makeshift stable aboard the *Ma-*

donna (although not nearly so sweet-smelling), where she had had her first pleasant dialogue with Reynaud regarding, of all things, Anabette and Taillefer.

It was a fastidiously clean barn, and its neat, spacious stalls housed the horses and camels belonging to the Archbishop of Tyre, his guard, and any guests at the palace. She knew Reynaud had spent much of his time here grooming Khamsin, a task he usually did not delegate to others, and from which he derived much pleasure and satisfaction.

An Arab groom emerged from the shadows, and Brielle asked him for water. He nodded and retreated.

As she looked around, Brielle thought that somehow the stable might have a more soothing effect on Reynaud than a room in the palace proper. And perhaps he would feel more comfortable washing the worst of the dirt and blood from his body before entering the palace. If, of course, he was even willing to do so.

She made no reference to his failure to heal Khamsin, for in the grand scheme of things it wasn't so important, save for how the evident loss of his "gift" affected his mental state. And she did not wish to distress him further.

"What of your injury?" he asked her suddenly, as he threw her a look over his shoulder. But from the angle of his face and the shadows around them, it was impossible to read his expression.

" 'Tis but a scratch," she answered truthfully, for she hardly felt anything beyond a dull ache across the side of her ribs. "Barely enough to draw blood, I warrant," she added quickly.

He hesitated, glancing down at the floor, as if in indecision, then he grunted softly, turned and led Khamsin to a stall. The steed's hooves thudded dully against the straw-strewn floor.

Brielle watched him, taking temporary refuge in the simple act of removing her veil and head covering. She lay them aside and took a deep breath of the warm, pungent air of the stable, welcoming the refreshing breeze that huffed through the open doors even as she searched for the words that would heal rather than hurt.

Reynaud stood mutely, a frown of concentration stamping his brow as he skimmed his fingers over the area surrounding the gash, obviously trying to soothe the animal—or heal him.

"Why don't we cleanse the wound?" Brielle asked in a low voice just as the servant returned with two pails of water.

Reynaud stopped his stroking and stared at his hand as it rested on the animal's neck. "I am as dirty as my horse," he said in a surprisingly level voice. "And a poor healer, indeed . . ." His eyes still on Khamsin, he added, "Or, rather, I am no healer at all now."

"Tend him as you are, Reynaud," she encouraged, heartened by the tone of his voice and willing her own not to betray her. "It matters not if you can heal him with your touch. He is content to have you beside him."

His eyes narrowed and he stared over the horse's back into nothingness. "Then he is not as intelligent as I had thought, for only a fool would be content in the company of a madman." He reached toward a shelf at the front of the stall, his movements tired, mechanical, and unstoppered a small jar. It appeared to be an unguent, for he began applying it to Khamsin's wound.

"A madman knows not that he is mad," she answered, longing to reach out and comfort him . . . to shelter him in the warmth and safety of her love. She had to admit, however, that she didn't know if such a gesture would serve Reynaud's needs as much as her own.

He paused in his ministrations. "If you believe so, then you are the only one." He cast her a look through his lashes. "But I knew enough to come for you, did I not?"

"Aye," she murmured. "Where have you been, Reynaud?" she asked, and took a few steps toward him. "We have been so worried. . . ." She had no wish to betray Rashid's confidence to Taillefer.

He stiffened, his look turning hard. "Stay where you are!" She stilled, then he glanced away and continued applying the salve. "He's skittish. 'Tisn't safe to approach him thusly."

She wanted to say that there was no other way to approach them, but she held her silence . . . and felt a prickle of irritation toward him. He sounded more high-handed than uncertain of himself.

Almost immediately she felt guilty for such an unkind thought.

"I just came from the battle at Arsuf," he told her, "where I reaffirmed my ability to kill the infidel as capably as any good Christian soldier." Heavy irony infused his words. "And before that I was in Damascus . . . with Tarik." He suddenly rested his head against the steed's neck. The lines of his posture indicated exhaustion—despair.

It was all Brielle could do to stay where she was, but she could not manage to prevent the next words that rose to her lips: "Did you learn aught of my father?" If she didn't ask him that very question, she realized, he might suspect she already knew.

He set the salve aside and moved slowly out of the stall, stopping halfway between them. She watched as he inhaled slowly, deeply, then raised his eyes to her face. "I—I could not save him, Brielle." His words were tortured.

It was then that she saw the gleam of a tear on his cheek.

"I would have gladly given my life for his—I know how much you loved him, needed him. But . . . I . . . couldn't." He moved woodenly toward a bale of hay, and sat, his eyes seeking hers.

"Of course you couldn't, Reynaud," she soothed him. "If you cannot heal Khamsin, you could not heal my father—"

"Nor you. I don't expect forgiveness . . . only that you don't hate me," he added, so steeped in guilt that he was barely aware she had spoken.

She knelt down before him and took one of his hands in hers. He didn't pull away, but stared at her hand over his. "I don't hate you, Reynaud! I could never hate you, don't you know that by now? And as for my father, I am truly sorry that he survived this long."

His chin jerked upward as his eyes met hers, an unspoken question in them.

"Surely he suffered terribly? Was he even himself? Or a mindless shadow of the man he once was?"

He didn't answer at first. How could he tell her she was right? That her father had no doubt long ago lost his powers of reasoning. But she had reminded him that, in truth, he might have lost his healing gift before he had ever put his hands on Geoffrey d'Avignon.

He felt the burden on his soul lighten almost imperceptibly.

That was no reason not to stop Tarik from murdering him! accused a voice.

Then another, kinder voice said, " 'Twas a killing of mercy, no matter who did the deed . . ."

"He died with your name on his lips," he murmured, wanting to grab onto the reasoning of the gentler voice within him. After years of assuming every burden of responsibility, however, he was afraid to exonerate himself.

As he watched the tears mist her eyes, he handed her the lock of Sieur Geoffrey's hair. Instead of fresh tears, she managed to summon a smile of gratitude for him. A watery but beautiful smile that was, in and of itself, a balm to his troubled mind, his heavy heart. He wanted to reach out and stroke her gleaming, amber-gold tresses, but he felt the taint went deeper than his skin, and he didn't quite have the willpower to remove his hand from beneath hers. . . .

". . . thank you for telling me that," she was saying. "And for this token—how very thoughtful of you, Reynaud. But I want you to know, also, that there is naught to forgive. You cannot take responsibility for every tragedy in the world, *mon cher.*"

She was looking at him earnestly, entreatingly, her expression as warm and affectionate as the endearment she'd uttered.

And you are twice a fool for reading more than pity into her words and actions.

Remorse sifted through him, and he felt dangerously close to letting his emotions leak out again, like an undisciplined infant. He, who had allowed Tarik el Mezrab to end Geoffrey d'Avignon's life, was actually wanting desperately to seek solace in Sieur Geoffrey's daughter's arms—to read more than mere concern into the words she so generously would have uttered to anyone in need.

The urge was almost uncontrollable and that frightened him at a time when he wasn't certain he was in absolute control of himself. He stood abruptly, jerking his hand away from Brielle's, momentarily at a loss.

Inspiration struck. He stripped off his borrowed tunic, then looked around, searching for something other than the filthy garment with which to cleanse his body with the water the servant had brought. Mayhap if he could wash everything away. . . .

Several folded cloths sat innocuously beside one of the pails, which he had failed to notice in his panic. He made toward them like a starving man toward food and snatched the topmost pad of linen; he thrust it into the cool water and pressed it against his warm face. Sweet Jesu! he thought. If only he could get hold of himself! But all he could think suddenly was how he had failed Brielle d'Avignon. How everything he touched seemed to have turned to ashes. . . .

Why, she even wore the blood of one of the men he had killed . . . dark splotches on her blue *Bedouin* gown, minute spots on her face: proof that he would drag her down with him.

God's blood, how could he *ever* be worthy of her?

He scrubbed at his skin in frustration, his tears mingling with the water from the pail, until the faint voice of rationality cautioned, *Get hold of yourself! Think! Think!*

Brielle's fingers curling around his forearm made him still his frantic motions. He turned to meet her gaze . . . and felt as if the sun were suddenly breaking through a dense bank of clouds.

With her other hand, she took the cloth he'd been using and bade him, "Sit, *mon cher.* Let me help you." He obeyed without question, allowing her to push him gently onto a bail of hay as she began speaking of ordinary things in that sweet and soothing voice of hers. "I have bathed many a guest in my father's home," she informed him, keeping her eyes on her task lest she be distracted by the magnificent breadth of his shoulders, the span of his chest—marred only by one wicked-looking battle scar.

In spite of everything—even dirt and blood and defeat—he was the most beautiful man she had ever seen, and no matter what it took, she was determined to bring him back to health in both body and mind. "But none so splendid as you." She paused, the cloth in her hand smoothing over his unshaven jaw, and smiled lovingly into his eyes. "You are so perfectly . . . *human.*"

She moved down the corded column of his neck, not realizing that her strokes were unconsciously sensual to the man sitting before her. She evinced the strongest urge to press her lips to the pulse point where his neck joined his shoulders, then gave in to the impulse and did exactly that.

The touch of her lips against his flesh, the sweet smell of jasmine in her hair beneath his chin, momentarily chased away his doubts and misgivings about himself, his father, his half-brother . . . and sent desire whorling through his loins. If he could love her once more before he took her back to France. . . .

You mean assault her honor again, only this time in a stable! You're sinking even lower, St. Rémy, than the first time, admonished his conscience. *You are truly going mad . . .*

Brielle rinsed his face and neck, then moved down his chest. She couldn't help but peek down at his narrow waist, and then the arrow of fine dark hair threading downward and disappearing into the waistband of his chausses.

She slowed her movements, mesmerized, and his hand gripped her wrist. "You know not what you do to me," he said in a hoarse whisper. "You bring out the worst in me. . . ."

She raised her gaze to his, letting all the love she had for him shine in her eyes. "I like to think I bring out the best in you, Reynaud, for I love you, and love is good. Love is cleansing. Love is healing."

He shook his head and looked away. "How can that ever be so, Brielle? I am unworthy." His voice was as bleak as a cold, rain-swept day with nary a glimmer of sunshine in sight.

"Nay! That isn't true!" She ceased her movements, and unconsciously pressed one hand against her middle. Despite her best intentions, the tears came, for she was suddenly afraid he would leave and never come back. "Please don't leave me again, Reynaud," she pleaded in little more than a whisper. "I—I *need* you! I need you to take me back to France. I need you so . . . I love you, *mon brave chevalier,* and there will be no other for me until I breathe my last." She threw her arms around his waist then, hugging him close, and sobbing quietly against his bare chest.

She desperately needed to touch him . . . to reassure herself that he was well; that he had come back to Tyre unharmed, whether for her or not. The scent of him, the feel of him, made her sob all the harder in relief. And an overwhelming feeling of love moved through her so powerfully, so deeply, that it hurt.

"You don't need *me,* Brielle. You can find any number of more worthy—"

"I don't *want* any others!" she burst out in frustration. "Reynaud! Listen to me!" she cried softly. "Forget your pride—now it only serves you ill! In my eyes, you are the worthiest man in Christendom! I don't *care* what your father did! I don't *care* that you disagree with the Templar Rule— aye, the bishop and I have spoken at length . . . nor do I care

whether you live up to anyone else's expectations!" Sh
looked up at him, her eyes shimmering with tears. "And
care not that you could not save my father! As much as
loved him, I do not blame you for that, nor could I ever."

She drew in a breath, fearing that he would try to silenc
her or, worse, get up and walk away. "I love you as yo
are . . . need you as you *are*. I care naught about anythin
but living with you and loving you for the rest of my life!"

A host of new emotions flashed through him like quick
silver—foremost was tenderness. And the need to protec
her. And the child she would bear him.

Child? Yes. Somehow he knew—by the way she had lai
her hand against her abdomen. Her words of love, in spit
of everything, and the fact that she needed him—eased hi
emotional load a little more. Once again, he felt his inde
scribable burden lessen. Brielle d'Avignon had inched th
great bolder of despair from the mouth of the darkness tha
shrouded his soul, letting in a sliver of sunlight—a sliver o
hope.

She needed him. The child would need him. All else wa
in the past and didn't matter to her, or so she said.

But could he teach himself not to let it matter to *him*
Could she help him learn to accept things as she did?

He brought one trembling hand up to her head, stroke
her silken hair more gently and lovingly than he had eve
stroked Khamsin, and asked her the question that had gnawe
at him ever since he'd discovered she was still in Tyre. "Wh
didn't you leave here, Brielle?"

His lips against her hair muffled the sound, but not s
much that she didn't understand the words. "Don't you knov
now, Reynaud?" she asked, her eyes still on his face. "I jus
told you . . ." She backed away enough to swipe an arn
across her tear-tracked face, but her voice gentled. "Let m
love you . . . heal your hurt, your heart." She reached up t
trace his jaw with one shaking finger. So very much was a
stake here, and words were so pitifully inadequate!

She wanted to hold him in her arms, absorb his pain, for her love was strong enough to restore and sustain him, if only he would give her the chance. Somehow she knew that . . . refused to believe otherwise.

His eyes delved into hers, probing, seeking . . . and wounded. So vulnerable, yet so strong, for he was everything she would ever want—just as he was, in those heart-rending moments.

"I love you, Reynaud de St. Rémy. Just as you are. In spite of all that you perceive to be your failings. Your father's failings. . . . Do you hear me, Reynaud?"

Twenty-five

"For all we know, he may have slit her throat by now!"
John the Gaunt growled.

They were in Taillefer's room . . . the minstrel resting o
the bed while Rashid tended his injuries. John, Humphre
of Toulouse, and the bishop were gathered round; John o
the palace guard stood nearby.

Taillefer's eyes narrowed briefly at John the Gaunt as h
interpreted the man's worried expression. "Reynau
wouldn't do such a thing—no matter what his state of mind!
he said with uncharacteristic irritation. He'd grown unaccus
tomed to the discomforts of a fighting man and momentaril
allowed that—and his secret concern for Reynaud—to ti
the balance of his even nature.

Hadn't John come to know Reynaud better than that? h
thought.

"He threatened to kill Rashid!" John added darkly. "An
before that, *all* of us!"

"And do any of us look dead to you?" the minstrel sho
back. He regretted ever having revealed that threat to Rashic

"Then he threatened you again, out in the street."

"Not so. He merely ordered me out of the way. And the
he saved my life."

Abelard looked at John the guard. "How was his behavio
before you left the stable?"

It was only the fifth time the cleric had asked the question

nd Taillefer wanted to tell Abelard to go see for himself.
urely they didn't believe Reynaud had gone stark, raving
ad? Hadn't he gone effectively to Brielle's rescue? Hadn't
e saved the minstrel himself from the worst of a vicious
eating? But Taillefer was also hard-pressed to ignore his
wn unvoiced concern. . . .

Young John's look turned thoughtful. "He was stern-
aced . . . said not a word, my Lord Bishop."

"I think he was—is—exhausted and, mayhap, a little con-
used," Taillefer said in his friend's defense, for there wasn't
man alive more levelheaded than Reynaud de St. Rémy . . .
xcept, of course, himself. He glanced at Humphrey of Tou-
ouse, who had been silent thus far. "Wouldn't *you* be un-
ettled if you had just gone through what he has?" In spite
f his earlier misgivings, Taillefer had seen Reynaud in ac-
ion, and had concluded that, indeed, his friend was acting
ore troubled than out of his mind.

"Surely," observed Rashid dryly, "he has earned the right
o be unsure and temporarily self-absorbed." As if to empha-
ize his words, he applied more pressure than necessary to
gash on Taillefer's arm. The minstrel winced and resisted
e urge to jerk away his arm.

Humphrey cleared his throat and pushed himself from the
all where he'd been leaning, a contemplative frown etching
is even features. He was one of the few knights Taillefer
new who refused to don Arab dress, and his snow-white
emplar tunic with its brilliant cross served to remind the
instrel of Humphrey's rôle in all this. Was the Templar feel-
ng like he had failed Reynaud by having gone off to Acre
ith Bishop Abelard rather than going after his brother
night?

". . . known St. Rémy a long time," he was saying, "but
've also seen men go mad in this land. From disease. From
he heat of the desert. Or the ever-present threat of danger
nd death, especially for Christians." He faced the bishop.
'I do not mean to override your authority here, Father, but

speaking as his brother Templar, I believe we should concer
ourselves with getting him back to France. He is especiall
vulnerable now, in light of what we know, and what we'v
just seen."

"And if he doesn't agree?" Abelard asked.

"He'll go," Taillefer said through set teeth as Rashi
moved on to dress another cut. "He'll entrust Brielle to n
one else for the journey back to France."

"Then we must form a plan," said Humphrey.

"And I say we see to the Lady Brielle's safety first!" Joh
the Gaunt insisted, his good hand fisting at his side. H
turned toward the door, his broad shoulders set, his chin rock
hard with grim determination. . . .

"Reynaud?" she repeated softly, afraid to breathe awaitin
his response.

He said nothing for several moments—an eternity t
Brielle. She sensed a real struggle taking place within hir
and watched as one emotion after another chased throug
his expression.

"Your father is dead . . ."

"Stop it!" she said sharply. "Stop punishing yourself!"

Silence hung between them again, and with each passin
moment, Brielle felt she was losing ground with him. Th
rift was widening into a chasm, and desperation seized he
again.

"If you don't want me, Reynaud, I'll have to return to S
Bernadette's with anyone who will take me. Will it make yo
happy to picture me a withered old woman cowering in m
convent and cherishing the precious memory of our one nigh
of shared love?" She shook his arms. "And a memory is *a*
I will have, *chevalier,* for if a child is born from our unior
'twill be reft from my arms and given to a stranger. Ther
are no children in convents!"

She hadn't wanted to use the possibility of their havin

onceived a child as leverage, but her growing fear was mak-
ng her impatient at a time when patience was so impor-
ant. . . .

She bit her tongue, then watched as slowly, steadily, like
dawn breaking over a cold winter desert, a clearing of the
doubt that had dimmed his eyes took place. A new light
flared behind those topaz windows to his soul and shone
with such perfect lucidity that she felt her heart creep up her
throat, cut off her breath . . .

If he didn't *want* her? Reynaud thought suddenly. Her and
his child?

He couldn't believe his ears. Sweet Christ above, how
could she ever think that? Had his faculties deserted him so
completely that he couldn't even communicate to her how
much she meant to him?

"Didn't you ever guess how much I loved you, Brielle?
How much I wanted you? Why did you think I asked you to
marry me that day?"

Her gaze slid away from his and, in spite of herself, she
evinced definite echoes of the humiliation she had suffered
that one morning. " 'Twas the honorable thing to do," she
managed to say, in spite of the heat creeping into her cheeks.
"You said so yourself. And you always do the honorable
thing."

He put a bent knuckle beneath her chin and raised it until
their eyes met. "Brielle, Brielle . . . *mon coeur, ma vie . . . !*
From the very beginning you have been the light in the dark-
ess of my doubts—the one who drew me back to Tyre and
kept me tethered to reason. Although, I have found it impossible to be reasonable where you are concerned." He brushed
his lips across hers, making her forget any lingering frag-
ments of humiliation. When, at last, he pulled away, he whispered, "Were I so honorable as you think, my rose, I wouldn't
have taken advantage of your loneliness and deflowered you
that night."

"Then show me how dishonorable you are," she whis
pered. "Here . . . right now, Reynaud."

Her eyes held a most wicked light, and the challenge wa
irresistible to Reynaud. He pushed her down onto the fra
grant hay. . . .

Taillefer and Humphrey grabbed John the Gaunt by hi
tunic in unison. "You cannot just go charging in there lik
a bull!" the minstrel admonished him in a loud whisper, hi
irritation at his having to leave his sick bed apparent to any
one who cared to notice. But he craned his neck around John
trying to peer into the barn through the open door.

" 'Tis better that you spy on your closest friend like
snake in the grass?" Rashid asked, with a lift of his dar
brows.

"I'm not spying!" Taillefer said with troubadourian indig
nation. " 'Tis just that I cannot see a thing—'tis blacker tha
Hell after this sunlight—and there are certain, er, method
which are more appropriate in a situation like this."

"And you are more adept at spying on the ladies," Rashi
supplied with a straight face, "rather than a knight who migh
catch you at your own game and beat you senseless wit
your lute."

Despite the situation, Taillefer couldn't help but feel hi
humor return. The devil! he thought, and grinned over hi
shoulder at the Arab. But when his eyes adjusted to the dim
ness of the barn, all thought of protocol fled. Here the
were—six men—about to walk in on Reynaud de St. Rém
during the first stages of what could not be interpreted a
anything but making love to Lady Brielle d'Avignon."

"Can you see her?" asked the bishop.

"Aye," whispered John the Gaunt, elbowing the minstrel'
sore ribs. "What is he *doing* to her?"

* * *

"Will you go to France with me?" Brielle whispered between honeyed kisses that left her weak and breathless.

"Indeed, my lady," he murmured, his lips brushing the sweet flesh at her temple, one cheek, the dainty lines of her jaw. "If you deem this miserable wretch worth saving . . ." he added, a trace of irony infusing his words.

Without warning, someone cleared his throat. *"Eh bien, if I hadn't thought you worth saving, mon cher Reynaud,"* Taillefer announced in a stentorian voice equal to any bishop's, "you can be sure I wouldn't have tossed my reputation to the winds by playing the expert marksman."

They both looked up at him, startled and red-faced.

"I dare you to tell me, St. Rémy, that my reputation as the best entertainer in Provence—in all Outremer, for that matter!—is in shreds for naught!"

Reynaud recognized the minstrel's behavior for the warning it was intended to be and felt an overwhelming gratitude toward his friend as he quickly sat up, pulling Brielle with him.

But Rashid was hot on the minstrel's heels. "From the sound of that silver-tongued speech, I doubt your reputation is diminished one bit," the Arab said.

John the Gaunt came pushing forward, his eyes anxiously taking in Brielle's appearance. "You are unhurt, my lady?" he asked, throwing a frowning glance at Reynaud.

Brielle nodded, not trusting her voice in those first few moments. Not only had Reynaud's friends been concerned enough about them both to come running to the stable, but the obviously huffing Taillefer and the ever-faithful (and recently threatened) Rashid were already attempting to lighten the mood and keep it that way.

"I—I was helping Reynaud clean off the worst of the grime."

"In that case," young John offered gallantly, relief clearly visible on his features, "come and use the baths in the palace. A knight shouldn't have to bathe in a stable!"

Humphrey eyed him levelly. "But a squire might, and we were all squires at one time, were we not?"

Reynaud spoke then, appreciating their attempts at casualness, for Brielle had been caught in a rather compromising position . . . even if only Taillefer had seen them. "I seem to remember, my friend, a place or two we used for bathing that made us wonder just how important a bath really was— even here in this climate."

"Indeed," agreed Taillefer, warming to the subject. "And then again, those which were quite pleasant, like the time we—"

"I don't think we need to discuss this here and now," Bishop Abelard said, saving Reynaud the need to cut off his friend. "Won't you join us at the palace?" he invited them.

Brielle threw Reynaud a questioning look, but his eyes were on her, an old and dearly familiar warmth in them. And a suddenly unholy light. "On one condition, Excellence."

Brielle tensed. So did the others.

"And what is that, my son?"

"That you pledge to clear up an important matter that still needs to be resolved."

The bishop's eyebrows drew together briefly.

"The provision of a proper escort for the Lady Brielle to France within the sennight."

Brielle looked at Reynaud, a sinking feeling suddenly weighing her down. He would take her back, but that was all . . .

"Gladly. You may have anyone you like."

Brielle fought back traitorous tears. After all, wasn't the most important thing Reynaud's recovery? Everything else paled in importance, or so she tried to tell herself as the prospect of living the rest of her days in a convent loomed darkly over her once again.

"I'll gladly accompany you, *mon ami*," offered Taillefer, "for I must return for reasons of my own. His face had lost some of its color, his earlier animation fading.

Reynaud nodded at his friend in acceptance, then said to Abelard, "And one more thing, Father?"

"Don't push it, Reynaud," Taillefer muttered, suddenly sinking down upon an overturned pail, obviously light-headed.

"There is another matter that has yet to be resolved—pushed aside in the wake of Tancred le Bref's heinous plan."

Enlightenment lit Abelard's face. "The matter of a wedding?" he asked.

Brielle's heart somersaulted within her rib cage . . .

"Oui. If the lady will have me . . . as I am," Reynaud answered, his eyes catching and holding Brielle's.

"If you're seeking more praise, St. Rémy," Taillefer grumbled, his eyes closed, his face pale, "you'll get none from me. Enough is enough."

"Indeed," Brielle added, a slow, sweet smile moving across her lips and brightening up the entire stable, or so it seemed to Reynaud. "If we told him he was as perfect as a man could be while still retaining his humanity, his head would swell to the point that Khamsin could not support his weight." Then her gaze went to the minstrel, concern chasing away her smile. "We must get Taillefer to bed," she said.

"Then you'll marry me?" Reynaud asked, the barest quaver to his voice.

Humphrey and Rashid lifted the fading minstrel beneath his arms and began to help him toward the door.

"Please accept this time, child," Abelard said. "One never knows what God has in store for us. Take the opportunity while you can."

"But . . . 'tis inconsiderate of Taillefer in light of his own recent marriage and . . . loss."

"Don't refuse him, my lady," the *troubadour* mumbled over his shoulder, "for he speaks the truth about lost chances. And a wedding is just the tonic I need right now. . . ." He stumbled, then quieted, as he was half-carried through the door.

The men filed out; Rashid lingered, looking steadily at Reynaud.

"Can you forgive me?" Reynaud asked the Arab in a low, strained voice.

"Hamdillah, master. Praise be to God that you could never kill me for my loyalty . . . nor I ever refuse to forgive you." A look of contentment transformed his features.

"I have nothing to offer you, my love," Reynaud said as he drew Brielle into his arms. "I mean . . . I have no place to take you to live, for I will not return to St. Rémy . . . ever."

She reached up and twined her arms about his neck, ignoring the pinch in her side from Sâlih al Barrak's dagger. "I have a small inheritance from my lady mother—an estate not far from Avignon. First of all, you will be lord of my heart; then lord of Beaumarais. It wouldn't matter if you were a woodcutter in a lowly hut deep within some forest. I want . . . *need* you, and naught more. Ever."

Their lips hovered a heartbeat apart, as golden eyes delved into blue-green. "You will help me learn to forgive my father. If not, at least to accept myself for who I am, and not for what Gérard expected me to be. In spite of what I am no longer able to do." His lips brushed across hers with infinite tenderness. "Will you help me?"

"Deep down you know these things for yourself, Reynaud. But now you are free to believe them."

Their mouths met in a long and fiercely hungry kiss, and before Reynaud lost himself in the sheer bliss of the intimacy, he acknowledged that he was being given the chance to start out fresh with his life and leave all his demons behind in Outremer.

And he would thank God every day He granted him for having blessed him with a second and greater miracle: Brielle d'Avignon: his rose. . . .

SPINE TINGLING ROMANCE
FROM STELLA CAMERON!

PURE DELIGHTS   (0-8217-4798-3, $5.99)

SHEER PLEASURES   (0-8217-5093-3, $5.99)

TRUE BLISS   (0-8217-5369-X, $5.99)

Available wherever paperbacks are sold, or order direct from the Publisher. Send cover price plus 50¢ per copy for mailing and handling to Penguin USA, P.O. Box 999, c/o Dept. 17109, Bergenfield, NJ 07621. Residents of New York and Tennessee must include sales tax. DO NOT SEND CASH.

ROMANCE FROM HANNAH HOWELL

MY VALIANT KNIGHT   (0-8217-5186-7, $5.50)

ONLY FOR YOU   (0-8217-4993-5, $4.99)

UNCONQUERED   (0-8217-5417-3, $5.99)

WILD ROSES   (0-8217-5677-X, $5.99)

Available wherever paperbacks are sold, or order direct from the Publisher. Send cover price plus 50¢ per copy for mailing and handling to Penguin USA, P.O. Box 999, c/o Dept. 17109, Bergenfield, NJ 07621. Residents of New York and Tennessee must include sales tax. DO NOT SEND CASH.

PASSIONATE ROMANCE
FROM BETINA KRAHN!

HIDDEN FIRES   (0-8217-4953-6, $4.99)

LOVE'S BRAZEN FIRE   (0-8217-5691-5, $5.99)

MIDNIGHT MAGIC   (0-8217-4994-3, $4.99)

PASSION'S RANSOM   (0-8217-5130-1, $5.99)

REBEL PASSION   (0-8217-5526-9, $5.99)

Available wherever paperbacks are sold, or order direct from the Publisher. Send cover price plus 50¢ per copy for mailing and handling to Penguin USA, P.O. Box 999, c/o Dept. 17109, Bergenfield, NJ 07621. Residents of New York and Tennessee must include sales tax. DO NOT SEND CASH.

SAVAGE ROMANCE
FROM CASSIE EDWARDS!

#1: SAVAGE OBSESSION   (0-8217-5554-4, $5.99)

#2: SAVAGE INNOCENCE   (0-8217-5578-1, $5.99)

#3: SAVAGE TORMENT   (0-8217-5581-1, $5.99)

#4: SAVAGE HEART   (0-8217-5635-4, $5.99)

#5: SAVAGE PARADISE   (0-8217-5637-0, $5.99)

Available wherever paperbacks are sold, or order direct from the Publisher. Send cover price plus 50¢ per copy for mailing and handling to Penguin USA, P.O. Box 999, c/o Dept. 17109, Bergenfield, NJ 07621. Residents of New York and Tennessee must include sales tax. DO NOT SEND CASH.